HOW TO CHARM A COVEN

BY TIANA WARNER

ROGUE CANNON PUBLISHING

CHAPTER 1

Landing in Shit

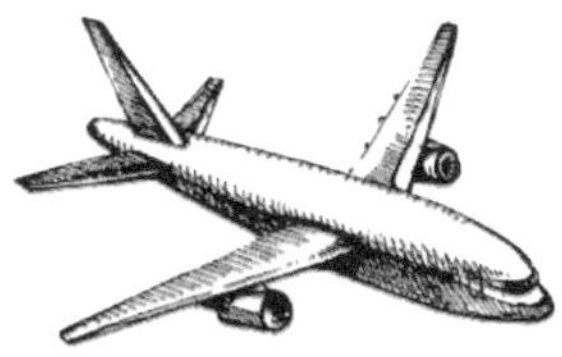

THE PROBLEM WITH SETTING magic free is that it hangs around. It stews and festers, lashing out at random times as if holding a grudge against the people who trapped it.

And maybe that's exactly what it's doing. None of us understand magic enough to know what it's thinking. If 'thinking' is even the right word.

As my plane descends through Vancouver's rainy sky, it's clear how much worse things have gotten since I fled the city. The aircraft lurches again, and my stomach relocates to somewhere near my tonsils. Turbulence doesn't usually make me anxious, but this isn't just the wind. My skin prickles like static, and there's a familiar tug inside me, leaving no doubt about what's going on: feral magic is all around us.

Crap. I sink deeper into my seat and rub my arms as if I can tame the sensation. There's no way it was this tangible when I left two and a half months ago...which means it's either gotten stronger or my ability to sense it has.

The cabin lights sputter, an ominous buzz tickling my eardrums. Nearby magic crackles through my veins like I've grabbed onto an electric fence.

Crap, crap, crap!

The magic was supposed to disperse, not linger for months. But according to the news and Natalie, anomalies have been showing up all over Vancouver, taking the form of various animals that cause traffic accidents and panicked 9-1-1 calls. For the clueless public, blame swings between invasive species as a result of climate change, a black-market animal trade, and wild conspiracy theories from aliens to lab accidents. Only witches know the reality: these are chimeras. Magic incarnate. And they're pissed off.

"I don't remember the turbulence being this bad last time," Hazel says squeakily, leaning back and gripping the arm rests. Her nostrils flare as she does some deep breathing.

No point in freaking out my bestie with the truth, so I wave my hand nonchalantly. "Spring showers. You'll get used to Vancouver's mood swings."

But as we break through the bottom of the dark clouds, I lean across her and peer out the rain-streaked window, searching for an explanation for what I'm feeling—a thunderbird flying alongside us or a leviathan thrashing in the Fraser River. Only a flock of Canada geese catches my eye. I squint at them for a long moment to make sure they're really geese and not faking it.

Seems legit... Though the one black raven among them certainly does not. My spine tingles as I look at it, like the feeling of being watched. A small cloud whips over our wing—dark, misty, almost shimmering—and we jolt again. Shadows flicker at the edge of the window, like something is hovering out of sight, ready to latch its claws into the propeller as we all sit helplessly in this metal tube in the sky.

I rub my eyes and lean back. *Stop it, Katie.* Just because chimeras ravaged Vancouver and tried to kill everyone a couple of months ago doesn't mean it's going to happen again.

Ethel meows in her kennel at my feet. I poke my fingers in to soothe her, her fluffy white fur and beige-tipped ears visible through the holes in the top as she turns in a restless circle. Not for the first time, I wonder if she can sense magic too.

"I know," I murmur. "Nearly there, sweetie."

Below us, the snow-capped mountains cradle the familiar city, from Gastown to the West End and everything in between. Even from up here, the scars left by the chimeras are visible—buildings in repair, cranes positioned throughout the city to fix the damage. The University of British Columbia campus perches on a peninsula, where I'll start May term in two weeks. I'm miraculously not behind, thanks to a feigned medical emergency and a note from Doctor Sharma permitting me to finish last term remotely, but it's going to be a heck of a lot easier to attend classes in person again.

Assuming we don't get taken out by a monster before we land.

Hazel yanks up the hood of her University of Toronto sweater, hunched against the plane's aggressive air conditioning. "I'm nervous."

I look sharply at her. Does she somehow know magic is causing this?

Then she adds, "I don't know how you did it, moving away from home."

"Oh." I blink back to reality. Right, we're here for normal things like my university classes and her new co-op job placement. "It's not so bad. I mean, it was at first, but..."

"But then you found someone worth staying for." She nudges me, grinning.

She's right. Before Natalie, I thought I was doomed to be homesick forever. Now, Vancouver is as much my home as Toronto, and I'm so ready to return to the coven's familiar underground halls—my room, the courtyard, the lounge, and all the witches I got to work with before everything went wrong. It's time to get back to business, starting with helping to rescue Natalie's dad from Sophia and Oaklyn Madsen. I'm going to make those assholes wish they'd never—

The plane drops, and Hazel and I grab each other with squeals of terror.

As my stomach recovers, I nudge her back. "You'll call this place home in no time. We'll have to find you a local boyfriend."

She grimaces. "Maybe..."

I search her face for the meaning beneath that expression, but she turns to look out the window. This has become her standard reaction when the topic of dating comes up. Either Sean broke her heart more than she admits, or there's more going on that she's not telling me.

"Try to meet someone with a safer career than Natalie's," I say lightly. "Like...a tiger trainer. Or an experimental jetpack tester."

Her laugh helps dissolve some of the tension in my shoulders.

I caved and told Hazel Natalie's a witch. It was the only thing keeping me from thinking I hallucinated everything. Anyway, when you already got in trouble with a coven, what's one more broken rule? The other details, especially anything about the Madsens, will stay a secret for Hazel's safety.

At the thought of reuniting with Natalie in a few minutes, my heart flutters wildly. *So close.* I'm going to kiss her until my lips are bruised, feel her mouth against mine, breathe in her comforting scent of something herbal and sweet...

And I'll finally tell her the three words that have been burning in my chest for seventy-eight days.

Yes, I've been counting. There's only so much intimacy you can get through video calls, especially with your parents and sisters in the next rooms. I need her to know how completely she has my heart, even if it's terrifying. Even if I risk her telling me not to fall in love at a time like this, when dangerous people are willing to do anything and kill anyone in pursuit of magic.

Last night on our video call, she'd looked at me with such tenderness that the words almost slipped out. "Natalie, I—" I'd started, before Nicky barged into my room asking to borrow my charger. It was for the best. The first time I tell Natalie I love her shouldn't be through a phone. It should be face to face, where I can see if her eyes light up or if they cloud with worry about what loving me might cost her.

Using the black screen on the seat in front of me as a mirror, I comb my fingers through my light brown locks, making sure the loose curls are sitting right. I've never put this much effort into my appearance for a travel day—smoky eyes, cherry lips, a tiny white top under an oversize jean jacket, and ripped jeans that make my legs look amazing.

"I expect you'll be out all night *catching up* with Natalie?" Hazel asks teasingly, watching me fuss.

An embarrassed little laugh escapes me. "We've got dinner plans."

And a whole lot more. We've talked about what we plan to do to each other in intimate detail. Assuming this flight doesn't end in a magical disaster, Hazel is correct.

"Well, if you need someone to watch Ethel, she can keep me company while I set up my apartment," Hazel says, poking her fingers into the kennel.

I bite my lip, my cheeks heating up. Not that I want to ditch her on our first night in Vancouver, but she gets it—and she's right about how tonight will go.

The wheels slam into the wet tarmac, and we grab each other again as the plane bounces and sways like a ship in a storm. My stomach lurches, Ethel meows, and then, miraculously, we're safely slowing down.

Thank God.

A collective sigh of relief whooshes through the cabin, and a few people clap.

The pilot's muffled voice crackles over the P.A. "Welcome to Vancouver. Local time is 3:46 PM. Apologies for that bumpy landing due to the windy conditions. We appreciate your understanding and expect to be at the gate in about ten minutes…"

Amazing that everyone else thinks it was the wind. For me, the sensation of nearby magic keeps getting stronger, like a voice in my head whispering words I can't quite understand.

Hazel and I pull out our phones and turn off airplane mode. I'll text Natalie to tell her I landed, but knowing her, she'll already be waiting for me in Arrivals.

The second my phone connects, messages come in. My heart leaps at Natalie's name—then plummets as I read her texts.

Natalie

> Katie, don't leave the baggage area.

> I'm in Arrivals.

Katie

> I feel a ton of magic nearby. Is something wrong?

Natalie

> Interesting. But no, I caught sight of Fiona. She must have followed me here.

My mouth goes dry. One of the coven's Directors secretly following her to the airport can't be a good sign. This has to be about the magic we freed.

We pissed off a lot of witches that day, but I thought Natalie's trial convinced them we had no choice if we wanted to stop the Madsens from stealing it. The coven wouldn't have pardoned her otherwise, right?

But the fury on Fiona's face still haunts me. To her, releasing magic that took a hundred years to contain was unforgivable.

After how hard I had to fight to earn a place in the coven, I would be naive to think this is over. The witches must have reconsidered exactly who's to blame. I was the one who smashed the locks on the chimeras' cages, after all.

As we taxi to our gate, I type a reply with clumsy thumbs.

Katie

What does she want? Why couldn't she wait til I'm back at C.S.A.M.M.?

Natalie

I'll try to figure that out. Just don't let her get to you before I do.

The lights suddenly feel too bright, like a spotlight is shining down on me. Fragments of the oath I swore and Natalie's warnings about breaking it come back: *trial by jury...imprisonment...*

I bounce my knee, my stomach twisting. If Fiona's here with official authority, she could detain me on the spot. And from the urgency in Natalie's texts, that's exactly what she's afraid will happen.

"You look like you might need this," Hazel says, offering me a barf bag.

I shake my head. Keeping my voice at a murmur, I force myself to say the harsh reality. "One of the, uh, higher-ups is here. Natalie seems worried about why."

Hazel's eyes widen, and she drops the barf bag. "Think it has to do with you setting free all the—" She looks around. "The *you-know-what?*"

Oh, and I told her about that, too. Just that we had to set magic free in order to keep it from some bad people. She had questions when we were driving away from shapeshifting monsters ravaging the city, okay?

"Probably," I say tightly.

She frowns. "The way Natalie is, she wouldn't have let you come back if she wasn't certain it was safe to return."

"I know, but…" A chill ripples over me. In truth, we were focused on coming up with a plan to rescue her dad, not to mention protecting me from the Madsens. We thought the coven had turned their focus back to the Madsens, too.

Hazel furrows her brow. "Is it possible the others lied to Natalie? Made her think they forgave you?"

I grimace. "Yes. They needed me to come back—easier than flying across the country to hunt me down, I guess—which meant they had to convince Natalie that they'd given up on wanting to punish me."

Hazel's face goes ashen. "You think they still want to punish you after so long?"

Time for a confession, now that we're safely on the ground. "That turbulence was you-know-what. I feel it. Which means they've been dealing with the aftermath since February, and they're *not* going to forget whose fault this is." I make a flourishing gesture at myself.

Hazel's mouth falls open.

I rub my face, frustration churning in my gut. I swore an oath to protect magic, and that's what I was doing. But Fiona thought I was a traitor for releasing the magic they'd worked to contain.

"What'll they do to me?" I ask. "What if their punishments are like…medieval?"

"Don't say that," Hazel says, her voice high. "We just have to figure out how to convince them that you did the right thing."

We. That's cute.

I reach over and pat her thigh, grateful for her loyalty, but we both know there's nothing she can do to help me get out of this.

Crap, what if she gets dragged into this and becomes collateral again? My nerves twist tighter. This is a disaster. I shouldn't be allowed near her. In fact, she should get a restraining order against me at this point for her own safety.

The seatbelt sign dings off, and people stand.

I sit frozen, my heart doing its best to escape through my throat. "How am I going to avoid her? There's only one way out of here."

"Well, the first step is to get off the plane," Hazel says logically, unbuckling her seatbelt with steady hands. "We can make a plan on our way to the luggage carousels."

"Right. Yeah." I fumble with my buckle, and a spark of inspiration strikes. "Wait—our luggage!"

Hazel shoots me an alarmed look. "Please tell me you're not suggesting what I think you're suggesting."

"Disguising myself with hats and jackets so Fiona won't recognize me?"

"Oh. I thought you were going to ask me to cram you into a suitcase and wheel you out."

I point to her enthusiastically. "Ooh, I like that better!"

The people in front of us grab their carry-ons and leave, so we stand too.

Hazel sighs. "How am I supposed to manage two sets of luggage alone? And what'll we do with all your displaced clothes?"

I shrug into my heavy backpack. "Keep thinking. We've got a few minutes to make a plan."

And probably only that long before Fiona decides my fate.

Hazel and I disembark and walk through the carpeted maze beneath fluorescent lights, everyone's rolling suitcases rumbling like thunder. Rain streams down the windows in typical West Coast fashion, blurring the familiar view of the mountains.

When we get to baggage claim, I stop in my tracks. This is the domestic terminal, which means there's no customs checkpoint—no barrier between us and the waiting area. I can see the exit from here, and so anyone watching can march right up to me.

I grab Hazel's arm and yank her behind a planter. "I don't have time to wait for my luggage. I'm a target the second I step out there."

Hazel looks around and grabs my arm right back, dropping her voice to an urgent whisper. "What if we switch clothes?"

I eye her gray University of Toronto hoodie and sweatpants. Inconspicuous. Meanwhile, I'm a beacon, and I'm sure everyone in the coven has seen me in this outfit before.

"Your choice," Hazel says, reading my internal battle.

I slump. Dammit, I wanted Natalie to see me this way. "Okay. Good idea."

We duck into the nearest bathroom and lock ourselves in neighboring stalls. Fighting my backpack and Ethel's kennel for space, I strip down, mourning my hot outfit as I toss it over the divider to Hazel. Bye, sexy cleavage.

Her sweatsuit smells like her, reminding me of when we borrowed each other's clothes in high school. Simpler times.

As we emerge from our stalls, Hazel looks pleased with her end of the deal.

I scan her up and down. "Damn, girl. You're going to get all the ladies looking like that."

She checks herself out in the mirror. "Really?"

Her tone is pretty enthusiastic for someone who is straight, but we can unpack that later. Right now, panic sets in as I check my reflection. "I'm still obviously me! Ugh, why didn't I pack my balaclava?"

That thing has gotten me through magic-related crises before, and it could do it again.

Hazel reaches out and pulls the hood up. "Hide your hair."

I tie the strings so it cinches around my face. Yup, I officially look like a weirdo for my reunion with Natalie.

"Better..." Hazel circles me like a fashion consultant who is terrible at her job. "I read a lot of spy novels as a kid, and there's more to a good disguise. You have to change your posture and the way you walk. And give me Ethel."

I hand over the kennel and hunch my shoulders. "Like this?"

"More."

I slump further down so I'm shaped like the letter S.

Hazel nods. "Perfect."

I shuffle my feet and bow my head as we return to baggage claim.

Hazel is looking around way too much, her eyes darting from person to person. "What does Fiona look like?" she whispers.

"Stop acting suspicious!" I hiss back.

"Oh, and you're telling me you don't look suspicious, Slouchy Mc-Shuffleson?"

"You told me to walk like this!"

"Just act natural! You couldn't be any more obvious about not being obvious right now."

I groan and straighten up. "This is a bad idea. Let's stuff me into a suitcase and—" The words die in my throat as magic crackles across my skin again. It's different this time—warmer, gentler, like a caress. Heat blooms deep within my chest and radiates out to the rest of me. My lips tingle, my whole body humming.

It's like I can sense her the same way I can sense the presence of magic—like my soul has a compass that points to her. Maybe it's whatever force pulled me to her in the first place. Or that sixth sense in me is growing stronger, knowing she's nearby before my other senses catch up.

I look around, and there she is.

She's standing a few strides away with one hand tucked into the pocket of her dark jeans, the other fidgeting with the top button of her black shirt. Her mane of dark hair tumbles over her left shoulder, and her eyes... God, I've missed those brown eyes.

"Natalie," I whisper, all my fears melting away.

She sees me, and though there's a flash of confusion on her face as she takes in the cinched hood around my face, it quickly dissolves into a smile. The world narrows to just her—the soft look in her eyes, the flex of her strong arms as she holds them out to wrap them around me... My body aches with the need to feel her against me after all this time apart, to breathe in her scent and taste her lips again.

I start toward her, ready to throw myself at her and give her the hug and kiss I've been dreaming of.

But before I can reach her, another figure emerges from the crowd, steps away. Fiona. She's in a shimmering red traveling cloak with her raven hair pulled into its usual bun. Her fists are clenched at her sides, and her narrowed gaze pins me in place.

Her low voice slices through the noisy airport like a blade. "Did you think we would forget what you cost us by freeing all that power, Miss Alexander?"

Natalie's expression transforms in an instant, hardening into something dangerous. Purple bleeds into her irises like spilled ink. She pivots, becoming a barrier between Fiona and me.

"Stay behind me." The words rumble from her chest.

A jolt of panic shoots through my veins, and I clench my fists. But while Natalie stands tall and confident, I can only hide behind her, powerless, wearing this borrowed sweatsuit that suddenly fits all wrong.

My nails dig into my palms. We were fools to think I could slip back into the coven as if I belong. No matter what exists between Natalie and me, the gap remains—she's a witch with an inborn place in the coven and years of service as a Guardian, and I'm just an outsider who can sense magic but never wield it. A human metal detector.

"Step aside, Natalie." Fiona's lips curl into a nasty smile that sends a chill through my bones. She raises her hands, earth magic crackling in the air. "The coven has waited long enough for this."

From the Journal of Hazel Okada

I'd like to report a bug in my life's code. On paper, everything looks perfect: I'm starting my dream co-op job at a renewable energy company next week, maintaining my grades, currently on a plane to Vancouver with my bestie...Amazing, right? Yet somehow I'm stuck in an infinite loop of emptiness. And I desperately hope this four-month escape to a new city can fix it.

Katie's fallen asleep beside me watching a rom-com, snoring with her mouth open while the characters kiss in the rain.

Ah, the passion in that kiss. What would it feel like to be so consumed by someone that you don't care about catching pneumonia? Like what Katie has with Natalie? I've seen the way her whole face changes when she talks about her...that sparkle in her eyes reserved specially for her girlfriend. Must be nice.

Meanwhile, Sean canceled our two-month anniversary date so he could get ahead on the next assignment, and I spent that night alone in my dorm reading a textbook—which, looking back, was probably more enjoyable than dinner with him would have been anyway. Ugh, what a waste of time he was.

My carefully plotted life trajectory didn't account for getting dumped by someone who chose studying over me. But I guess this time apart has helped me realize I deserve better—especially when I look at Katie's love life and see how good things could be.

If—and that's a big if—I ever date again, I want someone who is the total opposite of Sean. Someone who makes me feel special instead of treating me like a program to be debugged. Someone with an exciting side, or who at least doesn't want to spend every Saturday night optimizing code. Someone passionate and intense and unafraid to make the first move.

I still remember Katie's expression when she told me about Natalie at the Christmas market. She looked so excited and alive, even in the face of something as terrifying as curses. That's what I want: a partner who makes me feel that kind of zest. One who might introduce me to a world I never knew existed—metaphorically or literally.

Maybe that's what's missing. I've collected achievements like gold stars, but there's no fire in my life outside academia. No one who makes my heart race when they walk into the room.

Hm, nothing like having a personal crisis at 30,000 feet while a pretty flight attendant offers me pretzels.

 **PRIORITIES**

1. Get settled in my new apartment
2. Start new job
3. Do something that scares me every day
4. Think about dating someone outside my usual type

Is it weird that the last item is scarier than starting my first real software developer job?

CHAPTER 2

The Worst Welcome Home Party

I THOUGHT BECOMING A Guardian meant I finally belonged somewhere—that the coven saw me as valuable enough to welcome me in.
But as Fiona stalks toward me, it's clear how naive I was.

From the crowd behind her, two more witches emerge, both wearing floor-length black traveling cloaks with utility belts. Hayley's sharp
cheekbones and the distinctive scar running down the side of her face
make her instantly recognizable, while Neil's muscular frame and shaved
head stand out beside her. A hole seems to open in my sternum, letting
my insides plummet into the ground. The coven sent Shadows after me?
Shadows are for criminals!

Reality hits me like a punch to the gut. That's exactly what I am—I
broke the coven's strict laws, and I fled the city before I could face the
consequences. They've come to intercept me now that I'm back.

"Nobody is touching you," Natalie assures me, raising her hands. It's
not a gesture of surrender, but a promise that she's ready to use earth
magic to defend me.

My skin prickles at the charge in the air. The fluorescent airport lights flicker, casting eerie shadows across Fiona's face. Travelers glance up as they rush past with their trolleys and suitcases, and a couple of gazes linger on our standoff.

If I'm not mistaken, Fiona hesitates at the look on Natalie's face.

Stay put, Hazel, I think desperately, not daring to look back and get her dragged into this. Dammit, this is exactly what I didn't want—my carefully balanced worlds crashing together.

I step sideways to see around Natalie, my fists clenched to stop my hands from trembling. "Isn't this a bit much for a welcome home party?"

Fiona stalks closer, her heels clicking against the floor like a ticking bomb. Her voice is low, for our ears only. "Katie Alexander, you're under arrest for violating your oath to the Coven of Shadows and Alchemists for Managing Magic. Come quietly, and we won't cause a scene in front of all these people."

A chill floods my veins. Oh my God, my over-thinking anxiety brain was right for once: I'm actually under arrest.

All that time I spent living in C.S.A.M.M.—studying in the courtyard, eating in the lounge, retreating to the private suite I called home—dissolves into dust in my memory. Did it mean nothing? Am I so easily disposed of?

"I never violated my oath," I say firmly. "I risked everything to protect magic."

"You made a reckless, unauthorized decision that put our secrecy at risk, not to mention innocent lives." Something flickers in Fiona's eyes—not just anger, but something heavy and tired. "Do you have any idea how much work you caused? How much effort we've expended trying to contain what you unleashed?"

Forcing myself not to show fear, I open my arms. "You want to punish me for stopping the Madsens from getting magic? Come on, Fiona."

She narrows her eyes. "Your punishment depends on the jury. You agreed to our laws when you swore your oath, and our laws dictate we give you a trial. Don't add to the fire by resisting arrest. Hayley, Neil, let's go."

Before they can move, a swipe of Natalie's hands sends a bench skidding between us and them. Nearby people gasp and point at the possessed furniture, looking around for an explanation.

"Natalie," Fiona snarls. "Not here."

"Then back—off," she warns, her voice low and dangerous. "Or this whole building is about to get a renovation."

She forms a wall between me and the others, her body coiled and ready to strike. Dammit, I don't want her to fight her coven on my behalf—again.

Fiona's fingers curl into claws, a muscle in her jaw tensing. "Think about what side you're choosing right now."

Her words jab my stomach like a dagger, reminding me I'm no more than an outsider.

Natalie keeps her palms up. "I chose long ago."

My heart aches. How many times can I ask her to choose me over her coven before it becomes too much? I can't keep being the reason she fights with the people she's known her whole life.

The baggage carousel beeps and whirs to life behind us. I don't dare look back at Hazel.

Fiona signals, and Hayley and Neil skirt around the bench, advancing from the sides like wolves moving in for the kill. I meet their eyes, trying to find the sense of camaraderie we had a few months ago, but it's not there. They have a job to do, and I'm just another target.

"I already confessed in my trial," Natalie says, and there's no hiding the panic in her tone. "It was my doing. Katie's innocent."

"Touching." Fiona keeps her eyes locked on me. "The jury will decide for themselves how they feel about that."

My stomach twists. We should've known Natalie's trial was a mere formality, given her status. As for me? Everything I finally secured—my place in the coven, my relationship with Natalie, my chance to use my ability to help keep the world safe—could vanish with one verdict. And Natalie must know it because she refuses to step aside.

Hayley and Neil are two strides away.

"Katie, run." Natalie throws her arms wide, and a dozen luggage trolleys tear free from their owners' hands, pulling the witches' attention. Startled cries erupt as bags tumble off and the trolleys crash together like bumper cars.

"But—" I back up. If I flee, aren't I proving that I'm a criminal?

Then again, if I surrender, I'll find out what Natalie is so afraid of—and what punishment the coven's justice system has in mind for me.

"Move!" Natalie tugs my arm.

Okay, we're running.

I shed my heavy backpack, abandoning everything I have so it doesn't slow me down. We take off through the crowd, my heart hammering. Can I outrun them, or am I just delaying the inevitable?

"Parking garage. This way." Natalie stays at my side as we sprint through the airport, dodging startled travelers. Shouts and footsteps ring out behind us as Fiona and the others follow.

I tug at the strings cinching the hood around my face. It's tied so tight that I feel like a carthorse wearing blinders. I swipe it back, letting the cool air wash over my face and neck. Freaking useless disguise.

Luggage tumbles across our path as the Shadows use magic to try and block us. Natalie apparently doesn't care about subtlety, slashing the air to get as much out of the way as she can. But she's one witch against three, and we're forced to slow down as we jump and dodge obstacles.

I snatch a snow globe from a gift shop display, one with a miniature Vancouver skyline and glitter. "Natalie!"

I toss it up, and she reacts quickly, sending it rocketing behind us. There's a loud pop! and a tinkle of glass, and the pursuing footsteps falter for a precious second.

"Hate to do this, but..." Natalie spins, and there's an enormous crash that might be a snack booth.

More shouts and screams.

We keep going, racing down the escalator. A stand of tourist brochures explodes at the bottom, and I can't track who is doing what anymore.

"I'm s-sorry," I gasp between breaths. "I'm always getting you in trouble with—"

"Don't," Natalie says firmly. "This isn't your fault."

But it is. If I were a witch, if I belonged here, I wouldn't be running from my own coven. At the very least, I could fight back with more than just words and snow globes.

We bolt across the street to the parkade, tires screeching and horns honking around us.

"Sorry!" I blurt.

"This way." Natalie veers left, her fingers lacing through mine and pulling me along. We pelt down the rows of cars, passing bewildered travelers loading their luggage.

At last, I spot Natalie's black sedan peeking out. Relief surges through me as the lights flash and the doors unlock.

Wham! Something slams into my back, and the ground rushes up to meet me. My knees crack against the pavement. My hair falls forward and forms a curtain around my face, blocking my view of what's going on.

"Katie!" Natalie's voice breaks. "What the fuck, Hayley?"

"Stop running!" Hayley snaps.

A sneaker bounces beside my hand. Did I seriously just get taken down by a flying shoe?

But considering Hayley has an entire utility belt full of God-knows-what, the fact that she hit me with a shoe tells me she doesn't really want to hurt me. A tiny bubble of hope inflates in my chest. Maybe I can get out of this.

I gasp for breath, crawling toward the passenger door. We just need to get to somewhere safe.

The door flies open on its own.

"Get in," Natalie says, spinning to face our attackers.

There's a thump. A roar.

I reach the car and climb inside, wheezing, my hands and knees throbbing.

A bouquet of flowers sits on the dash—a gorgeous, colorful array of dahlias, zinnias, cosmos, roses, a pink lily... My eyes sting with tears. This should have been our reunion. I could have run to her, thrown my arms around her neck, and kissed her for a long, uninterrupted minute. Instead, I'm running for my life, once again the liability she has to protect rather than the partner who stands beside her.

Concrete dust rises, and Natalie whips open the driver's side door and dives in, coughing. "Welcome home, beautiful," she wheezes, thrusting the flowers at me. The purple in her irises fades back to brown as she holds my gaze, her eyes saying everything her voice can't.

"Thanks." At this point, I'll take whatever romance I can get. "Now go!"

She starts the car and shifts into drive—and before we've moved two feet, we lurch to a stop. Neil stands in front of us with his palms out, his face reddening as he strains to keep us from moving.

With a bang like a gunshot, the windshield cracks, a deep line snaking from bottom to top. My window shatters, and I scream as glass rains down on me. As the engine whines and dies, Neil races over and reaches in to grab my arms.

"Sorry about this," he mutters, hauling me out through the hole. I shriek as the sweater rips and tiny shards stab my skin.

"Neil, you're hurting her!" Natalie barks, her voice filling the car.

His grip falters, but it's too late to change the fact that I'm halfway out with glass crumbling beneath me. "Then stop fighting the coven's laws!" he growls.

I grit my teeth, hating that once again, I'm the damsel in distress while Natalie fights for me. How long before she resents having to constantly defend me?

Through the windshield, an SUV screeches to a halt, Hayley in the driver's seat. Fiona hops out and holds the back door open.

It's not the first time someone's tried to force me into a car since I met Natalie—Oaklyn tried last winter in a UBC parking lot, and Freddie Madsen succeeded in Fort Langley a short time later. Now, here I am up against a witch SWAT team. But unlike before, when the Shadows were on my side, Natalie is the only person fighting with me.

Sky's words from that day in Gastown rush back: "There's a place for you here, Katie. Even if Fiona and the others don't see it yet." I believed her then. I still want to believe her, but it's getting harder.

My eyes burn. I need to fix this. I need the coven to trust me again. Because if I'm going to help Natalie find her dad and the Madsens, we all have to be on the same team.

"Stop, Natalie," I rasp, the fight draining from me like the blood oozing from my sides.

I grit my teeth as Neil hauls me all the way out. Hazel's hoodie and pants are torn, but owing her a new outfit is the least of my worries. God, I hope she's still back at the luggage carousels, far away from any witches and any chance of being sucked into this.

Natalie whips open the driver's side door and jumps out. "Katie—"

"It's not worth it." I wrench out of Neil's grasp and stand on my own, breathing hard. Fleeing will just confirm what they already think of me:

that I'm an outsider and a threat to their secrecy. But if I surrender, I can make my case at my trial. "I won't keep running. I swore an oath, and I'm going to prove to you that I meant it."

And prove I deserve to be part of the coven, I think, hoping desperately that Natalie understands. I want a future where she doesn't have to keep choosing between me and her coven. Where I'm not just her girlfriend but a respected member of her community. I'm ready to fight to earn their respect, no matter what it takes.

Natalie's expression twists in anger. "You don't have to do this, Fiona."

"Frankly, we do." Fiona's voice is icy, her nostrils flaring. "You'll be detained until your trial, Katie."

"Fiona!" Natalie barks.

"It's fine," I say with as much courage as I can muster. "I'll face the consequences."

"There should be no consequences!"

"We'll hope the jury feels the same," I say. I have to believe it—it's my only way out. If the witches are going to chase me until they catch me, then I have to stop running and face them.

Natalie's chest heaves as she stands with her fists clenched, looking ready to keep blasting the others with magic.

I hold her gaze, silently begging her not to make this worse. From what I've seen, the coven has a pattern of controlling its members, and opposing their established order won't accomplish anything.

The agony in her eyes says more than words ever could. I nod. I know she would go to war for me if I asked—which is why I don't. I know what needs to be done.

"I'm coming with you," Natalie says, striding closer.

"Get in your own car," Fiona says, pointing.

Natalie growls, her fists tightening like she might punch her out. But after a pause, she makes the smart decision and steps back, her gaze locked onto me. "I'll be close behind you."

I nod. "I know."

She'll be there for me. She always is.

"Hayley," Natalie says. There's murder in her eyes as a silent exchange passes between them.

Hayley nods, dropping eye contact.

Accepting my fate, I climb into the back of the SUV—away from Natalie, away from Hazel and Ethel, and away from any hope of a normal return to Vancouver.

There has to be a way out of this, right?

As the vehicle surges forward, I twist in my seat to get one last glimpse of Natalie. Her jaw is set...but her eyes are terrified. Like she knows something about the coven's justice system that I don't—something that made her willing to fight a Director and two Shadows to keep me from this trial.

Which makes me wonder if I should have kept running, after all.

From the Journal of Hazel Okada

Three hours since literal witches chased my best friend through YVR. Three hours of sitting alone in my new Kitsilano apartment, staring at Katie's phone, waiting for Natalie to call.

Her last text: "Hazel, I hope you can read this. Katie is in custody. Are you able to bring her stuff to your apartment? I'll update when I can."

Trying not to panic, but in custody WHERE? Some witch prison? Ugh, not knowing anything about the magical world is torture.

I did what she asked, and boy, the trek here was a fucking delight. Picture this: one tiny human versus four pieces of luggage, two backpacks, four boxes of belongings, and one very unhappy cat in a carrier. The Uber driver took pity on me and helped load everything into the lobby (bless him), but I still nearly collapsed dragging it into the elevator and up to the third floor. Now, boxes and bags are piled by the door like a monument to Katie, and Ethel is gazing out the rain-streaked window as if wondering how her life led her to this moment.

Poor Katie. I have to get her out of there. But how does a regular human rescue her friend from a secret magical organization? My usual problem-solving skills are pathetically inadequate here. I can't fight witches. I can't do magic. I don't even understand what Katie's involved in, despite many nights secretly researching witchcraft after she first told me about Natalie.

I won't deny I've felt a tad jealous. I mean, come on... While I was learning about object-oriented programming and submitting job applications, Katie was being inducted into a secret coven and hunting curses. She's living in this magical world that

I can only glimpse from the outside, and even when she tells me things, I know there's much more she can't share. But after today? I'm grateful I'm a nobody to these witches. They have no reason to suspect that I know what they are, which means I can help Katie under the radar.

Thank God she has Natalie in her corner. The way Natalie literally stood between her and danger at the airport... No wonder Katie gets that gooey look whenever she texts Natalie. Or mentions her. Or even thinks about her.

Is that what's been missing from my love life? Sean was about as emotionally available as a pumpkin, and Devon thought texting "u up?" at 2 AM counted as romance. But to have someone who stands up for me... Someone strong and confident, yet gentle... Someone who can introduce me to their exciting world... Someone beautiful and soft and who smells like flowers and...

Okay, this is not the time to dissect whatever sexual crisis I'm currently having. I have to help Katie survive this mess she's landed in.

PLAN

Camp out at the Gastown steam clock until the witches show up, then force them to hand over Katie. I need a weapon.

But will the witches just manipulate anything out of my hands with magic? Or turn me into a newt? How does magic even work?

Okay, no facing off with witches. Ridiculous idea.

NEW PLAN

I have to go to the source of the issue, which is helping Katie and Natalie convince the coven she's innocent. She did the right thing by freeing magic, and she just needs to prove it.

Can I compile evidence?

HYPOTHESIS

Magic was more dangerous when the witches had it locked underground than when it's free and dispersed.

I could treat this like the corporate emissions project I did last year, except instead of mapping emissions, I'm mapping chimeras. I can make a database to track every weird animal sighting in Greater Vancouver, then analyze patterns in the magic. With enough data, I could build a case to prove Katie did the right thing!

Watch out, witches—you might have magic, but I have spreadsheets and an obsessive attention to detail. Time to face the fury of a computer nerd with a mission.

And if I happen to uncover more secrets in the process... Well, that's just a bonus. After all, Katie isn't the only one who's allowed to be curious about the secret world of witches.

Not Dancing in a Dungeon

S o I'M TOO MUCH of an outsider to be given earth magic and made a witch, but not enough of an outsider to be free from the coven's justice system. How is that fair?

The SUV rumbles through downtown Vancouver, the familiar buildings and tree-lined streets whipping past the tinted windows. My skin stings as I pick glass from my sides, and I don't bother trying to stop my blood from dripping onto the leather seats. Let them deal with the mess.

This is, again, *not* the way I wanted to return. I pictured less blood and more making out. Less "You're under arrest" and more "Now that you're back, we need your help saving the world!"

How humiliating. I made the coven sound so cool when I told Hazel about it, like it was this secret club I'd been inducted into. Now look at me.

I pick out another glass shard and grit my teeth against the pain, trying not to imagine how panicked Hazel must be.

The guilt hurts worse than anything. I didn't want to drag her into another magical debacle. Once again, I'm failing at keeping both halves of my life separate.

Hayley's eyes keep flicking to me in the rearview mirror, her demeanor softening. "We didn't want it to go down like this."

"Why did it have to go down at all?" I grumble. "I'm the reason you still have a coven to protect."

"You think you saved us?" Fiona turns around in the passenger seat to face me. "Do you have *any idea* what a mess you've caused?"

"I've been reading the news." Reports of strange animal sightings and phenomena have been hard to miss.

Fiona scoffs. "You don't know half of it. A sinkhole spawning fish in an intersection. A beetle infestation decimating a botanical garden. A camel wandering down Robson Street. These are anomalies like we've never seen."

My skin prickles as if detecting the magic she's talking about. Or maybe that's the glass shards.

Neil snorts beside me. "Makes cursed toaster ovens look like the good old days..."

Fiona shoots him a glare, and he shuts up.

"Not since the coven's inception have we been so close to being exposed," Fiona continues. "We're one goddamn unicorn sighting away from having the existence of magic blown wide open."

I'm uncomfortably aware that this is my fault. But don't they understand that letting the Madsens have free rein of all that caged magic would have been worse? This magic can control people 'right down to the neurons in someone's brain,' as Freddie explained. "We would have much bigger things to worry about if I hadn't done it," I say. "And I'll have no problem defending my actions at my trial."

"Admirable," Fiona says flatly. "But whatever reasons you had, you still broke your oath."

I scowl. I know I did the right thing, and I refuse to let them make me think otherwise. *Alexanders don't give up,* as Dad always says. "I promised to protect magic, and sometimes keeping a promise means breaking the rules. I don't regret what I did."

Fiona huffs. "A chimera injured a child last week, Miss Alexander. I suggest you dig deep and find some semblance of regret."

My gut twists. While I could argue that the Madsens would do a whole lot more harm…this doesn't make me feel good, and it certainly doesn't help my case.

We park in an alley that is nowhere near the Gastown steam clock, and my stomach lurches. Where are they taking me? This isn't the entrance I'm familiar with.

Neil and Fiona flank me like prison guards when I climb out, each grabbing an elbow as if expecting me to bolt. I look back, hoping to see Natalie's car on our tail, but only strangers walk past the alley without a glance our way. Not a single person notices three people in cloaks escorting a bloody young woman into a dark lane. Ah, the bustle of city life.

While Hayley drives off to park, the three of us march down the alley, stepping over litter and a splatter of something that looks a lot like vomit.

The familiar sensation of sinking through the earth overtakes me, and in the next breath, we're in a long brick hallway, continuing walking without breaking stride. Though we've landed on solid ground, I feel like I'm still sinking, getting further from freedom with each step.

We must be at C.S.A.M.M.—the ivy-covered brick walls are familiar, and this is still within the downtown boundaries. But this isn't the part of the subterranean complex I know. The air feels different here—cold, musty, like no one ever comes down this way.

We turn at a wooden door, which Fiona swings open to reveal a staircase descending into darkness.

Wait, another floor even deeper underground?

I stop, my feet turning to lead. "Where's Nat—"

Fiona tugs me forward by the elbow. "Keep moving."

We go down, Neil still marching behind us. The air grows colder with each step, the damp stone walls pressing in. "How long will I be down here?" I hate how my voice shakes.

"Until we set a date for your trial."

"So like...a couple days? Can I at least have my laptop? A toothbrush? Basic human rights?"

"As long as it takes."

She's being vague to scare me, which ignites a spark of anger in my chest that burns away the fear. "I helped you! When the Madsens were coming, I warned you! Without me, they'd be out there using bio magic for God-knows-what right now. Shapeshifting, mind control, murdering, amassing an army—"

"You can present your case to the jury." Her voice is a little less sharp than a moment ago. "I know you helped us. But your actions surrounding bio magic were reckless and risked everything the coven stands for. Every action has a consequence, Katie, and yours happened to be incredibly dangerous."

We reach the bottom of the stairs, and I blink in the dim light. A row of cells lines one wall, iron bars gleaming dully.

"A dungeon? Really?" I wrench my arm away from her. "How disappointingly cliché of you."

Fiona unlocks a cell and gestures for me to enter. "We haven't had the budget for renovations."

"Who else is down here?" My voice echoes strangely off the stone walls.

"You're the only guest at the moment," Fiona says.

I back up a step, bumping into Neil. The shred of bravery I summoned in the airport parking lot is leaving me. "You're keeping me in *solitary confinement*? What the fuck is wrong with you?"

She raises an eyebrow. "Would you feel better if we moved a witch serial killer into an adjacent cell to keep you company?"

I don't grace that with an answer.

My heart hammers. There's a cot, a toilet, and a thin blanket and pillow. Home sweet home.

"Trials usually happen within a few days," Neil says, casting Fiona a guilty glance, like he's afraid of being shouted at for offering me a scrap of information.

"Thank you for the actual answer," I say curtly. Forcing my feet to move, I step inside and turn around with my arms crossed. "Can Natalie visit me? Or am I limited to one carrier pigeon a day?"

Fiona regards me coolly. "That depends on whether she behaves."

The cell door clangs shut, the sound rippling down my spine like ice.

She and Neil head back up the stairs, leaving me alone in the underground chamber. As the ring of the slamming door fades, the silence presses against my ears.

I sink onto the cot, wincing as my torn clothes rub my cuts and bruises. Leaning back against the cold stone wall, I close my eyes and try to steady my breathing.

In. Out. In. Out.

I can get through this. The jury *has* to see reason at the trial.

Right?

The quiet smothers me, broken by a drip of water somewhere in the darkness and the thunder of my pulse.

It feels like a lifetime ago that I lived here among the witches.

Hoping the coven would accept me.

Thinking I was making progress.

What if they never do?

What if I'm always just the non-magical girlfriend that Natalie has to keep rescuing? She's a powerful witch with a birthright and a legacy, and somehow, I'm dating her.

My throat constricts. How long before the constant battles become too much for her? Before she realizes she can have a less complicated relationship with another witch? Someone who is already a part of her world. Someone she doesn't have to protect or explain things to.

I shake my head to dislodge these thoughts like water from my ears. Nothing productive can come from drowning in that fear right now. I have one path forward: come up with a good defense at my trial.

But a chill descends over the dungeon, and a shiver runs through me. I rub my arms, trying to stay warm. I knew the witches took the oath seriously, but I didn't think we'd come to such a firm disagreement on what upholding the oath means.

What if they find me guilty no matter what I say or do?

What if this cell is the beginning of a much longer imprisonment?

I hug my knees to my chest, wishing for Natalie. Or Hazel, or my family, or Ethel. Just *someone* to talk to who is on my side.

The dungeon is so dark that spots bloom in my vision, dancing like ghosts. My chest tightens. I close my eyes and press the heels of my hands against my eyelids, trying to pretend I'm anywhere but here.

It was easy to picture my life with Natalie before all this—both of us working for the coven while I finish my degree. Moving in together, sharing her suite. Weekends spent exploring the mountains or cozying up with books in the lounge when it rains. More missions to neutralize curses and keep the world safe. Now that all feels like a fantasy.

There's a bang, and I drop my hands to see light bathing the staircase. Footsteps thunder down. I jump to my feet, my heart in my throat.

"Katie!" Natalie's voice hits me like a gust of warm air, tingling through my limbs. Even before I see her, that inner pull tugs at my core, and a warmth spreads through me that's uniquely hers—like my body recognizes her on a deeper level than my other senses.

I scramble to meet her at the bars, our hands finding each other through the gaps. The moment our fingers intertwine, comfort rushes through me so fast I could melt into the floor. Her skin is warm, and that familiar current passes between us like she's pouring her strength into me through our connected palms. It's a ridiculous thought—I know magic doesn't work like that. But I can't help feeling like she's given me something just by touching me.

"Let me see your wounds." Her voice is urgent as she takes me in. She's out of breath, her hair is a mess, and there's a sheen of sweat on her brow—mirroring how I feel. "I can't believe they hurt you. The people I've known my whole life."

"I'm fine," I say automatically, though we both know it couldn't be further from the truth. "I mean, I guess I could use something to clean up these cuts, but—"

"I'll have Doctor Sharma come down." Natalie presses her forehead against the bars, and I lean in, wishing she could hold me.

"Can you pass through like with the steam clock?" I ask, already knowing the answer.

Sure enough, she gives her head a tiny shake. "Enchanted."

I huff. "Of course."

She squeezes my hands. "If I'd known, I—" The words catch. "I would've told you to stay in Toronto. They let me think it was safe."

"I know." I squeeze back. "Don't blame yourself. It was my choice to set bio magic free."

"*Our* choice. And I got off easy." She shuts her eyes and takes a breath. When she opens them again, she fixes me with a serious stare. "I'll have the trial moved up to tomorrow. I'm not letting you stay in here."

The pain in her voice makes my chest ache. I nod, my eyes prickling.

Our hands are locked, our foreheads separated by cold iron, her lips close enough to kiss.

"I missed you so much," I whisper, remembering all those video calls where I couldn't touch her at all. At least I have this now, even if there are bars between us.

Her thumb traces circles on the back of my hand. "This isn't how I pictured the evening going."

"What did you have in mind?" I ask. "I'll imagine it when I'm trying to fall asleep tonight."

"I had specific plans for you," she says, tracing a finger along my wrist. "Ones that involved keeping you up all night."

I bite my lip, a flutter in my belly. "Don't tease me."

"Sorry." She locks our fingers together. "I was also thinking we'd get dinner at an Italian restaurant downtown. Maybe go dancing after."

I smile. "You dance?"

She lifts a shoulder. "Sometimes."

"I look forward to seeing that once I'm out of here."

It's been so long since I saw her smile in person that I get lost in her for a second, watching her eyes crinkle and her cheeks lift. There's something so impossibly gorgeous about her that our calls couldn't capture, and it hurts how much I missed being with her.

A vision of how today should have gone flashes across my mind's eye—walking hand in hand along the Seawall, getting dinner and watching her twirl pasta around her fork, listening to her updates about what's been going on in her life. Exchanging the three words that have been on my mind.

Those words linger between us. But I sure as hell am not saying it under these shitty circumstances. It needs the right moment—one where we aren't on opposite sides of a prison cell.

Does she feel it too? This thing that's grown too big to ignore? Sometimes, like now, her lips part like she's about to say something important, but then she stops herself. Is she also waiting for the right moment, or is she afraid of what loving me might mean for her position in the coven?

"Speaking of being held captive," I whisper, breaking the silence, "any progress on finding your dad?"

She lets out a slow breath. "We think we know where he is."

"But?" I trace my index finger over the lines of her palm. The life line. The heart line.

"Now that Sophia's a witch, she's gone berserk rigging the place with curses and magic. It's like trying to navigate a minefield." Her frown deepens as she watches me trace her palm. "We could've used your help."

I pause. "Really?"

"It'd be useful to have someone who can sense magic to tell us where the danger is. It's like feeling around in the dark otherwise."

"Of course I'll help. As soon as..." I look at the bars, unsure how to finish the sentence. The outcome of the trial will dictate whether I'll actually be able to help her or not. My heart slams into my ribs as if trying to escape. The walls feel too close, the ceiling too low, the barrier too solid.

Natalie reaches through and touches my cheek. "We'll sort this out, Katie. I promise."

We stay still, her warmth seeping into me, the only thing holding me together when I feel like I could disintegrate into a thousand pieces.

The door above bangs open again, and we jump.

"Zacharias, time's up," Fiona calls.

Natalie holds both my hands in hers. "I'm not leaving."

Heels click down the stairs, and panic rises in my throat. "Go," I whisper. "You're already in trouble."

As Fiona's silhouette appears on the steps, Natalie leans in, pressing a kiss to my lips through the bars. It's awkward and partly blocked by cold metal, but the softness of her mouth against mine sends a cascade of warmth through my body. Her breath is minty, and there's a desperate pressure in her lips as she tries to convey everything she can't say. Her scent envelops me, herbal, woodsy, and the familiar comfort I need to make it through the night.

"Tomorrow," she promises.

I nod, trying not to show how scared I am. If she knew how much I wish she could stay, it'd break her. "Natalie, I need you to do a couple things for me."

"Anything." She grips the bars, her arms flexing like she's ready to rip iron from stone.

"Tell Hazel I'm okay, and see if she needs help. She's probably having a meltdown."

She nods firmly. "Promise."

I take a breath, struggling not to let my voice shake. "Second, do you think you can bring me a copy of the coven's oath and all the paperwork I signed when I was inducted?"

Her brow furrows.

"Natalie, let's go!" Fiona snaps.

"I will," Natalie says to me. She backs away slowly, like some magnetic force is holding her to me.

And then I'm alone in the bowels of C.S.A.M.M., the quiet settling in, a chill running through me. The walls seem to inch closer, constricting my chest until it's hard to breathe.

I set my jaw, refusing to panic. Time to rehearse a really fucking good argument to present at my trial. Because between Natalie, Hazel, Ethel, my family, my degree, and my whole future... I've got way too much to lose if this all goes wrong.

From the Journal of Hazel Okada

Another crisis, another day as the powerless sidekick while Katie faces a magical catastrophe. There was a time when being Katie's best friend meant I knew everything about her, but now there's this whole other side of her life that unleashes fresh hell every time I visit.

Her family chat blew up, her parents and sisters all asking whether she'd arrived yet. I pretended to be her, though the lie made me sick. Just a quick message saying everything was great and she was spending the day with me. No need for them to know that couldn't be further from the truth.

Shortly after that, Natalie called. At first, seeing her picture pop up on Katie's phone and hearing her voice gave me a small glimpse of what Katie must feel whenever she calls—like my heart jumped up my throat and into another solar system. Finally, some news.

But my heart sank right back down when she updated me. Prison. A trial tomorrow. Meanwhile, I'm here with my laptop and algorithms, trying to use logic to fight against something that defies every rational explanation.

I told Natalie about my chimera map that'll help build a case for Katie. Her response? "Hm, it's worth a try." Translation: cute that the normal human thinks she can help. But what else can I do? I can't sense magic like Katie or control it like Natalie, and I can't convince a jury of witches to see reason. Coding is my weapon, and maybe an outside perspective is what they need to solve this problem.

Ethel's curled up next to my laptop, purring away like nothing's wrong. Must be nice being a cat. Though sometimes, I swear she knows more than she lets on.

"Unusual Animal Tracks Found Near Cultus Lake"
"Exclusive: Photos of Winged Creature Captured at YVR"
"Video: Gazelle Seen at Crescent Beach"
Nearly midnight. Eyes burning from staring at headlines. Mere hours before Katie's trial. Even if I stay up all night working on this, I'll be sending Natalie an incomplete app with incomplete data, and I'll risk looking like an idiot with a half-baked plan.

But my other option is to not try at all. To give up.

What would Katie do?

 **PROJECT STATUS**

- Create interactive web map – DONE

- Log all strange animal sightings and paranormal incidents since Feb – IN PROGRESS

- Pattern analysis algorithms

CHAPTER 4

The Verdict

THE OATMEAL THAT SLID into my cell an hour ago sits like a rock in my stomach, along with the fear that I'm about to lose everything—my future with Natalie, my chance to be part of the coven, and a lot more.

I spent all night poring over the documents Natalie smuggled me—the coven's laws, my oath, every piece of information I need to build my defense—but it might not be enough. Now my eyes burn and my brain feels as brittle as a dried-up sponge.

Hayley and Neil come for me, and my heart pounds frantically as they guide me up the stairs. Natalie's scent lingers on the hoodie and joggers she gave me, which are too long and bunch around my wrists and ankles. Even the comfort of wearing her clothes can't calm me.

The sconces lighting up the brick hallway sting my eyes, and my feet are clumsy as I try to get my bearings. The scent of greenery hits my nose, but I have no idea where we are.

They escort me through the halls, taking turn after turn until we arrive at a high-ceilinged chamber that's strangely familiar. Thorny roses cloak the brick walls, their shadows writhing in the flickering torchlights.

Oh God, this is the same room where I had my induction into the coven. The furniture has been rearranged to resemble a courtroom, which does nothing for the nervous jitters rocketing through my body.

The jury sits to the left: twelve witches I mostly recognize, including Agnes with her usual high pigtails and scrunched-up face, another Director named Amir, an Alchemist named Jaques, and Sky. Relief washes over me at the sight of Natalie's sister. She's dressed more formally than I've ever seen her in a white collared shirt and slacks, her head freshly shaved, her makeup as perfect as always. When our eyes meet, she gives me the smallest nod. At least one person here is on my side.

But where's Natalie?

Nausea churns inside me. I shouldn't be surprised—the Directors definitely wouldn't allow it. Still, I'd hoped…

Hayley and Neil release my arms and melt into the jury section, leaving me exposed to everyone's stares.

A large wooden chair sits in the center of the room. My seat, I guess.

My stomach drops as I see who's behind the desk at the far end.

Of course Fiona is the judge.

"Sit," she says.

As I walk to the chair, my footsteps carrying, a hiss rises.

Whispers?

No, the roses on the walls are writhing like snakes, their thorns scraping the stone as if threatening to tear into me.

The chair scoots forward and slams into the backs of my knees, forcing me to sit. I drop into it, a surprised gasp escaping.

Snickers rise from the jury, and heat floods my cheeks. But I refuse to shrink. If they're trying to intimidate me, they're going to have to try harder.

I meet Fiona's gaze as she towers above me behind the wooden desk. A stack of papers and two empty glass vases are in front of her. She riffles the pages and clears her throat.

Her voice fills the cavernous room. "Katie Medina Alexander, you stand accused of violating your oath to the Coven of Shadows and Alchemists for Managing Magic. Specifically, you are charged with the unauthorized release of fifty-six instances of harnessed biological magic, endangering both our secrecy and public safety. You are *also* charged with the murder of Frederick Madsen, a civilian who is protected from magical harm under our laws."

The room is dead silent. Fuck, she's bringing what happened with Freddie into this?

I adjust my seat, the chair creaking. The wood feels unnaturally cold beneath me, like it's leeching my body heat.

"How do you plead?" Fiona asks.

"Not guilty," I say firmly—though my heart pounds faster hearing her put everything I did into blunt words.

"So the chimeras set themselves free?"

"I did free them, but—"

"And you broke into their cages yourself?"

"Yes, because the Madsens—"

"And you recall me and several others telling you *not* to proceed?"

I clench my fists in my lap, my gut twisting in frustration. "There wasn't time to discuss it!"

"And did you kill Freddie Madsen with a sword from one of the Alchemy rooms?"

"Yes, but—"

"There you have it," Fiona says to the jury.

"I freed the magic for everyone's benefit," I say, my voice coming out too loud. "And Freddie was—"

Fiona looks down at me over her nose. "Who told you it was for everyone's benefit? I expect you consulted a Director when you made this important decision?"

I take a breath, trying not to let her interruptions and leading questions bait me into losing my temper. "I made the decision myself."

"Well, I vividly recall asking you to stop, and instead, you sent Natalie Zacharias and several others to fight me while you kept doing what *you* deemed necessary."

I clutch the wooden seat, fighting to keep my composure. "The Madsens were about to break into the room and steal the magic, and you know it!"

Fiona leans forward, her eyes flashing dangerously. "We had it under control."

"You didn't," I snap back. "Agnes had just blurted out the location of the room, our defenses had crumbled along with the entire goddamned building, and somehow, Sophia Madsen's powers were better than several of you combined. You did *not* have it under control, and if you would put your inflated ego aside for half a second, you might actually see that!"

A deeper hush falls over the room. Fiona's expression turns stony. Agnes's scrunched face reddens until she looks like she's ready to pop.

I clench my jaw. Dammit. I need to keep my head and remember the research I did last night.

"Clause 6a of the coven's oath states that we must protect magic from those who would misuse it," I say into the tense silence. "The Madsens were moments away from stealing magic for nefarious purposes. By releasing it, I was upholding my oath."

There's a pause. The room is very still other than the shivering torchlight.

"And Clause 8b, as the Shadows know, states that the use of force against a non-witch is permitted in acts of self-defense."

In the jury, Amir leans forward with his brow furrowed. Agnes sits with her arms crossed, as sour as ever. Fiona's posture stiffens with each word.

That's right, Fiona. I'm not about to get dragged through this without a fight.

"Further," I add, my voice steadier by the second. "According to Article 17 of the coven's charter, I have the right to a full defense."

"Ah, who would you like to present as your witness?" Fiona asks in a mocking tone. "Your *girlfriend*, with whom you had a relationship that was explicitly forbidden? Or maybe Sebastian and Millie?"

At their names, the temperature in the room seems to plummet.

"Oh yes, they disappeared after they helped you," Fiona adds in a low voice. "We are searching for them, and trust me that when we find them, their role in this mess will not go unpunished."

The door bursts open, and my heart leaps as Natalie barges into the room, out of breath. She's wearing a dark gray suit, her hair pulled back in a sleek bun that accentuates her perfect jawline. She looks like my hired lawyer, and more importantly, my salvation. That familiar warmth floods through me in her presence, filling the cold void. It's like some part of me was incomplete until she walked in.

The sight of her floods me with hope—the confidence in her long strides, and the flash of reassurance as she briefly catches my eye.

"I have evidence," Natalie says, "that Katie's decision was necessary."

I straighten my spine. I have zero idea what she's talking about, but a spark of optimism ignites inside me.

Fiona opens her mouth, probably to tell Natalie off, but stays quiet as the jury looks on with interest.

Natalie pulls her phone out of her back pocket and holds it up. "A map analyzing the locations of all chimeras since the incident. If you look at the data, you'll see that anomalies in close proximity are the most severe, which means keeping chimeras trapped here was *incredibly* risky. It's safer dispersed."

I stare at her as she drags her finger over the screen. Maps, data, analysis? This sounds like something Hazel would make.

Natalie zooms in on what I assume is the map, though she's too far away for me to see it—and too far for anyone else to see it either. I resist the urge to get up and push her closer to the jury. Can't we roll a projector in here or something?

"And it *is* dispersing," Natalie explains. "The map shows a slow progression outward. In time, it will be safely out of the city and away from the Madsens. This was the safest way to stop them from getting it."

"How dare— That is not for you to decide!" Fiona snaps. "Dictating how we manage magic is beside the point of this trial."

Natalie cocks an eyebrow. "Even when this shows that Katie made the right call? You're determined to ignore the fact that we were losing our fight against the Madsens, so Madsens aside, here's proof that Katie's actions had a desirable outcome."

Agnes's scoff echoes through the chamber.

Fiona grips the desk. "All that map shows is what a mess you both made. Now, are you finished with your little presentation?"

"One last thing." Natalie clicks off her phone and crosses her arms. "I want you to consider what imprisoning Katie means. You'll be punishing someone for acting in defense of magic—someone who agreed to use her abilities to serve the coven. We need Katie to help us track down curses and feral magic...and to find my dad. And yet you're punishing the intuition that could save us."

The jury is quiet, looking between Natalie and Fiona.

Natalie dips her chin. "Thank you. I'll answer any questions you have."

Fiona glares at her for a long, tense moment. The jury whispers, heads bowed together, glances shifting my way.

Gratitude swells in my chest. If Natalie's arguments can't convince the coven that I don't deserve punishment, nothing will.

"Very well." Fiona's voice pierces the hum. "Jury, you've heard the accused and her witness. Now, let's stop wasting time. Cast your votes."

Natalie comes to stand beside me, gripping my shoulder. But with the verdict looming, even her touch isn't enough to reassure me right now.

Should I have said more? Maybe they don't fully understand how dangerous the Madsens are. I should have reminded them of how close Freddie came to killing me in that Alchemy room, and how they left a cursed plushie at my door that nearly killed Hazel. I should have shown them the threatening text I got from Oaklyn, and...

Sky lifts her hand, and a wooden token floats across the room and settles into one of the vases on Fiona's desk, where it turns green and glows like an emerald.

Agnes does the same—but her token drops into the other vase with a pointed *clack*, where it turns ruby-red.

My heart stumbles. This is how they vote, then. Tokens in jars, like this is all some game.

Hayley and Neil's chips fall into the green vase. Others go into the red one. More float through the air—green, red, red, green. I lose count.

At last, the room goes still. Every person in the jury has cast their vote.

Natalie's grip tightens over my shoulder.

Fiona's fingers dance, and the tokens rise like fireflies, where they hang suspended. She counts, her lips moving silently.

I perch forward, my pulse beating in my neck as I frantically try to count the votes. They're too far away, everything blurring together.

"Katie Medina Alexander," Fiona says, pinning me under her sharp gaze.

Natalie sucks in a breath.

My heart seems to stop.

Fiona's lips curl. "The jury hereby finds you guilty on all charges."

"No!" Natalie barks, letting go of my shoulder to step forward.

Fiona rises, her clenched jaw and imposing stance daring Natalie to keep talking.

The world tilts. *Guilty?*

The roses on the walls blur and twist, their thorns seeming to reach for me as voices warp like I'm underwater. The room gets vaster, darker, leaving me alone in a void. I grip the edge of the chair to steady myself.

The memory of swearing my oath in this room swims forward in my memory—nervously reading from a worn leather book, promising to protect magic at all costs. Well, I did, and look where it led me.

"Now." Fiona's triumphant voice cuts through the haze. "We'll convene to discuss the length of your imprisonment—"

"Fiona, this is wrong!" Natalie barks.

"Quiet!" Fiona snarls.

My head spins as they argue, the verdict knocking me off-balance. This can't be it. They never gave me a chance to reverse what I did or...

An idea sparks, and I blurt it out before I can second-guess myself. "I'll fix it."

My voice brings the room to silence. Fiona stares at me.

"Let me catch all the magic I set free," I say. "If I can return it to the coven, will you waive my prison sentence?"

Fiona laughs. "Harness bio magic? You think you can do what Trackers spend their whole lives training for? What took us a *century* to contain?"

No, my inner voice says—but I have to try. "We don't know the extent of my ability, do we?"

She studies me. The fact that she hasn't immediately shot down the idea gives me a thread of hope that I desperately cling to.

"Katie," Natalie murmurs, but I put a hand out to silence her.

"Give me a year to harness it all," I say, trying not to sound like I'm begging. "If I fail, imprison me. But at least let me try to reverse what I did."

Fiona scrutinizes me over her nose before looking at the jury.

My heart slams into my ribs. She's actually considering it.

Finally, she tilts her head. "Very well. Since you were so eager to prove yourself useful to the coven, here's your chance. But you don't get a year. You have two months. By the end of June, you will harness all fifty-six instances of bio magic you set free and return them to us. If you don't succeed: imprisonment in our cells. Jury?"

Murmurs pass over the witches, and several of them nod. Sky goes pale, her eyes huge.

Two months?

A jitter rolls through me. The whole reason Natalie and I freed it was because of how hard it would be to recapture it. Skilled witches like Natalie's dad dedicate their entire careers to the task—and I can't even do magic.

I'm delaying the inevitable—but I have a shot now. At the very least, I have a few more weeks of freedom. A few weeks with Natalie.

Fiona's eyes glint with the cold satisfaction that she's finally brought me to justice. "We're in agreement, then. Five years' imprisonment when—sorry, *if*—you fail. And if you try to flee or hide...you know we'll find you, don't you?"

I dip my chin. She's playing with me, but I won't let her see my fear.

Five. Years.

I'll be in my mid-twenties when I get out. I can't ask Natalie to wait for me that long. And what'll I tell my family and friends? They'll all move on without me while I sit in a cell during the best years of my life. My degree and career plans, my entire future, all gone.

I'd planned to introduce Natalie to my parents and sisters soon. I've lain awake at night imagining how it would go—Pearl interrogating her with no filter, Mom fussing over her. Now that'll never happen.

I have to run, to disappear into another city and change my name. If that would even work.

The jury stands, murmured conversations growing louder as everyone gets on with their day. As if they haven't shattered someone's entire future.

"N-Natalie," I stammer, unable to breathe through the panic.

This wasn't supposed to be the outcome. I never thought it would come to this when I freed those chimeras—I just did what needed to be done.

She bends down in front of me, her strong hands grounding me. "You won't face this alone, okay? I'm going to help you."

"If I'd known what breaking into that room—" I start, but she shakes her head firmly.

"You were right, Katie. Don't doubt yourself. If we'd let Sophia and Oaklyn get a hold of bio magic, they would have killed or tortured us already."

I nod. Yes, the alternative is worse, but it's hard to believe we did the right thing when a five-year prison sentence is looming over me.

"This is my fault," she says furiously. "I shouldn't have let you return to Vancouver."

"No! How were you supposed to know?" It hurts even more that she's blaming herself.

Sky rushes over, pushing through the dispersing crowd. "Nat. We need Dad."

Natalie and I turn to her, both of us struggling for breath.

"Listen." Sky puts a hand on each of our shoulders, her grip steady. "We need a Tracker's help, and Dad is one of the only witches who can catch a chimera. He's good at it. We'll find him, and he'll help us."

Natalie stares at her, her gaze slowly focusing. She nods. "Sky's right. We have a fighting chance once we find Dad, okay? Katie?" She hooks a finger under my chin and angles my face toward hers.

I want to believe her. I've faced impossible odds before, and I did what was necessary to save myself and protect magic.

I have a choice: I can give up, or I can trust Natalie and Sky, who are staying at my side. Running isn't an option—not when Sophia and Oaklyn Madsen have their dad, and not when finding him might be my only shot at freedom.

Fear coils around my throat like a boa constrictor, but I force myself to nod.

It's an infinitesimal hope, but it's going to have to be enough. After all, if there's one thing I've learned about the Zacharias family, it's that they never back down from a fight.

And honestly, neither do I.

From the Journal of Hazel Okada

Like hell am I going to let these witches ruin my best friend's life. They're not fooling me—this isn't about justice. Katie was born with this intuition that none of them have, and they resent her for it. Classic case of punishing someone for being an outlier. It's been a familiar sight since middle school, when bullies went after kids who were different. When they went after me for being smart. Fuck that.

I've been flitting around my apartment for hours, making everything perfect for Katie's arrival. Bed made up, fairy lights strung along the bedroom walls, luggage stacked neatly. Stew bubbles in her slow cooker, filling the place with a homey scent, and fluffy towels are ready in the bathroom. Natalie stopped by with flowers for Katie and to see if I needed help with anything, which made my chest ache with a familiar emptiness I've been trying to ignore.

Now, with nothing to do but wait, I'm on the couch with Ethel warming my lap, watching the street below for any sign of Natalie's car.

According to Natalie, Katie can only stay here temporarily until they figure out somewhere safer. Apparently, some people called the Madsens want to kill her—a detail she conveniently glossed over earlier. At this point, I should probably assume everyone in Vancouver is trying to murder my friend.

But I refuse to sit by helplessly. Katie has always been there for me, from midnight phone calls after a breakup to last-minute presentation help. It's my turn to step up. My chimera map wasn't enough to convince those stuck-up witches that Katie did the right thing, but that doesn't mean I can't be helpful. We'll have to come up with a plan.

There's no other option. I can't imagine life without her. Last term, while we were apart, I went through all the motions—made friends, formed a study group, even dated Sean—but there was always this Katie-shaped hole in my life. If we fail, how am I supposed to go on knowing she's locked away in some magical prison?

Sometimes I can't help thinking how much easier this would be if I were a witch too. I could fight alongside Natalie instead of sitting here with my laptop. Being a normie among witches is painfully frustrating—always on the outside, always needing things explained.

But there's nothing I can do about that.

Maybe what Katie and I both need is honesty—about magic and everything else. If she's staying here tonight, it's time to have a heart-to-heart and talk about this huge thing that's been weighing on me. I have to trust her the way she's always trusted me. To be brave and true to myself the same way she is now. Best friends tell each other everything, right?

And really, if anyone would understand what it's like to discover something about yourself that changes your world, it's her. In more ways than one.

The truth is, I figured out why I've been dreading dating again. It's not the actual dating part that makes me recoil. It's...who I would be dating. More and more, I've been imagining what it would be like to kiss plush lips, to touch a smooth face with no scratchy stubble, to run my fingers through silky hair...to press my body against soft curves...

It's so obvious when I think back over the last few years. The way I couldn't stop blushing around Meghan in high school after

I found out she was bi. My obsession with lady pirates. The way I got a little too into spin-the-bottle at the Halloween party last term. The fluttering in my gut when that pretty TA leaned over to type on my keyboard and her perfume hit my nose.

Ugh, painfully obvious, Hazel!

I want to try dating women. I want the kissing, the cuddling, and maybe more when I'm feeling brave. I want an emotional connection that goes deeper than friendship.

There. I admitted it.

My heart is racing writing that down. But when I see how happy Katie and Natalie are together and how Natalie treats her, I want that for myself.

I vowed to do things that scare me, and this is definitely scary. But it's also incredibly exciting.

It seems wrong to be thinking about this when Katie needs me. But Katie has always shown me that the scariest things are the ones most worth doing. Like pursuing a mysterious woman who might have kidnapped your cat. Or joining a coven. Or coming out to your friends.

So maybe being honest with her isn't bad timing, but exactly what we both need right now. A reminder that no matter what changes, we're still us, and we're always there for each other.

CHAPTER 5

The Impossible Task

TWO MONTHS TO CATCH all the chimeras or I lose the next five years of my life in the coven's underground cells. Ugh, this is like the world's worst Pokémon game.

My stomach revolts as Natalie drives me to Hazel's place, and I roll down the window to let the cool spring air hit my face. *Don't be sick, don't be sick. This will all work out.*

Natalie's knuckles are white on the steering wheel, the veins in her forearms bulging as she grips it too tightly. She hasn't said much since we left, but she's practically radiating anger, like standing next to a bonfire. Her jaw is clenched so hard that a muscle jumps in her cheek.

"You don't deserve this," she finally says, her voice rough. "You did the right thing, and they're too stubborn to see it."

I reach over and squeeze her thigh, my throat so tight I can't speak.

Now could be the time to tell her how I feel—to let her know exactly what she means to me before everything gets even more complicated. But what if saying the words makes this harder for both of us? What if knowing I love her makes the thought of my imprisonment even more painful for her to bear?

"This is my fault," she growls, jerking me out of my thoughts. "I should have never brought you into all this."

"Don't say that," I reply, barely audible. "Meeting you was the best thing that ever happened to me."

Natalie's scowl deepens. "Was it? Look where it's gotten you."

My eyes burn, and a lump forms in my throat. "Please don't think that way."

She shakes her head. "You don't understand. I've spent my whole life in the coven, and I know how they operate. They're setting you up to fail because you're not one of us."

The words sting more than they should. "Not one of you?"

Natalie winces. "That's not what I meant."

"Isn't it, though? I'm just the non-magical girlfriend you're not supposed to have." I pull my hand back, staring out the window as the world passes in a blur. "Be honest. Would any of this be happening if I were a witch?"

Natalie's silence is answer enough. When I look back at her, her expression is sour. "The coven has always been protective of its secrets. Outsiders are...complicated."

"Outsiders," I repeat, the word a sigh.

"I hate that they see you that way. But I can't change centuries of lawmaking overnight." She switches lanes, falling back into a moody silence.

"You didn't answer my question," I say.

She blows out a breath. "Your trial would have gone differently if you were a witch, yes." She reaches over to squeeze my hand, her fingers warm and strong. "But that doesn't mean I want it any other way."

Before I can decide whether I believe her, she adds, "There's been something on my mind lately. For weeks, and maybe longer."

She parallel parks in front of Hazel's apartment building and turns off the car.

My pulse quickens as I stare at her, wondering what she's going to say. I can't tell if it's good or bad.

She doesn't meet my eye, swallowing hard.

"Natalie, you're scaring me," I say.

"I don't want to live in C.S.A.M.M. anymore," she blurts.

The words hang between us.

My heart stops. "What? But that's... You can't..." A hundred scenarios rocket through my head at once—Natalie wanting to give up magic forever, to stop being a witch, to move out of the country.

"I still want to work there," she says quickly, maybe seeing my panic. "I'll always be a Guardian. But I want to shut work off when the day's done. I want a whole separate part of my life that isn't about being a witch. I want..." She looks down at our entwined hands. "I want to spend evenings and weekends doing normal things. Dinner parties and... I don't know, hiking? Gardening? What do normal people do?"

My eyes sting. Between the emotion of everything and my lack of sleep, I could burst into tears. This doesn't fit with the future I envisioned for us—the one where I move in with her and we spend our free time here in the lounge and courtyard. The one where I could maybe one day be a witch too.

Does she feel this way because of me? Have I impacted her life so severely that I'm making her question her identity?

"Don't..." I swallow around the lump in my throat, trying not to sound like I'm about to cry. "Don't make any decisions you can't reverse. Everything is so messed up right now, but once we clear my name..."

She shakes her head. "I've been thinking about this for a long time. I want to step back from the coven's rules and be my own person. I want this for us—and for me."

I nod, trying to understand. Given the way the coven is treating me, I get why she's disillusioned. "I feel like this is my fault," I say quietly.

"It's not. You helped me see the darkness that was already there." She tips my chin up so I meet her eyes, which are also full of tears.

Is she right? I recall what she once confessed to me: *"Being in the coven…it's like our whole identity."* I just never imagined this.

Through the window, the front door of the apartment building flies open. A dishevelled young woman bursts out with Ethel in her arms, wearing an oversize red sweater that comes to her knees, pajama pants, and fuzzy slippers.

"Hazel," I whisper.

Natalie and I break apart. We'll have to finish this conversation later.

Hazel's face crumples, and by the time I climb out of the car, tears are spilling down her cheeks.

We collide in a fierce hug. Ethel meows and purrs between us, clambering for me. For a fleeting moment, I let myself pretend everything is normal—like this is another reunion with my bestie, not the aftermath of a verdict that could destroy my future.

"I really didn't expect to return to a coven that hates me," I say into Hazel's shoulder, my throat tightening.

"They don't deserve you." She squeezes tighter. "Anyway, you've got me and Natalie on your team, and we love you."

There's a pause as the word *love* hangs in the air. Maybe I'm the only one to notice it.

Around us, the day is mockingly normal. Weak afternoon sun glints off the windows on the modest brick building, a breeze carries the scent of the ocean mixed with Kitsilano's ever-present coffee shop aromas, traffic hums in the distance, and pedestrians and cyclists pass by on their way home from work.

We break apart, and I squish Ethel against my chest, burying my face in her soft fur. "I'm so screwed. Think they'll let me do some interior decorating in my cell? A bean bag chair and some posters?"

"We'll get you out of this," Natalie says. She leans against her car, her hands in the pockets of her gray suit, wearing the same numb, solemn expression she's had since we left. Like she's still processing how quickly everything went wrong.

"Natalie's dad should be able to help," I tell Hazel. "He captures feral magic for a living." My voice is hollow and devoid of hope. Because first we need to free her dad from wherever the Madsens have him captive. If that's even possible.

Hazel nods, her eyes glossy but her jaw set. "You can do it, Katie. I've seen you trap a rabid demon kitten under a laundry hamper."

I almost crack a smile but am too tired and scared to let it form. Though her faith in me warms my chest, she doesn't understand. One kitten, no matter how possessed, is nothing compared to fifty-six chimeras. Fiona only agreed because she knew I'd fail.

I furrow my brow at the mention of my old kitten, recalling the chaotic morning that became my introduction to magic. "Natalie, didn't you say Lucy was bio magic? Why could I trap her so easily?"

I don't dare to hope... But if I have a rare magic-sensing ability, then...?

Natalie shakes her head. "She was already harnessed and had a curse placed on her. She wasn't a feral chimera."

My stomach sinks. "Ah."

Deep breaths. Don't puke.

"Hazel, your map might still come in handy," Natalie says.

"It *was* you," I say. "Hazel, that map was brilliant."

"Didn't work, though," she grumbles.

"It helps us track all the chimeras' last-known locations," Natalie says. "We can still use it to hunt them down."

Hazel flushes, and a dimple appears in one cheek. "Then I'll keep working on it."

I let out a shaky breath, overwhelmed by their support. "Thank you. Both of you."

"Get some sleep, Katie." Natalie steps forward and pulls me into a hug, her strong arms encircling me.

"Chimera-hunting tomorrow?" I ask.

She presses a kiss to my temple, her lips lingering against my skin and her soft hair tickling my face. "First, I need to make a plan with Sky for rescuing Dad. Just settle in, help Hazel get ready for her new job—"

"Settle? *Job*?" I exclaim, pulling back. The thought of doing normal things is baffling.

"There's not much you can do until we find Dad. I'll call you, okay?"

I blow out a breath. She's right. I should try to uphold the normal life I'm fighting so hard for—and I can start researching chimera sightings in the meantime.

I nod, and she pulls me in again. Her familiar earthy scent wraps around me, and I let myself melt into her. Her heartbeat pulses against me, and her breath catches ever so subtly when I press closer. The solidness of her body grounds me like nothing else can—and for this moment in her arms, I'm completely safe.

Hazel has already turned her apartment into a sanctuary. It smells like home-cooked food, her belongings are unpacked and tidy, and music streams from her laptop. Warm light pours through big windows that overlook the buildings across the street, and there's a glimpse of the ocean between them. Ethel scampers to the windowsill, apparently having found her favorite spot for birdwatching.

In the center of it all, blooming bright on the kitchen table, are the flowers from Natalie.

My throat tightens at the thought of my best friend and girlfriend working together to free me from that cell. I reach for the wall to steady myself, light-headed as the reality of my situation crashes over me again. Five years in prison. A formative era of my life, gone.

Hazel must sense my anxiety because she puts her hands on my shoulders and guides me toward the bathroom. "Hot shower and cozy PJs. I've got stew in your slow cooker and will make buttermilk biscuits while you shower."

My stomach clenches hungrily, and I moan. "You're the best."

"Figured you'd want comfort food. Now go."

I do what she says, soothed by the sound of her in the kitchen—clattering baking sheets, a beeping timer, the occasional gasp or curse as something hits the floor. The aroma of fresh baking fills the apartment, making my mouth water.

"I owe you a new sweatsuit," I say as I shuffle back out to the kitchen, running a brush through my wet hair. Steam follows me into the hallway. "We'll add it to the tab of Things Katie Owes People—right below fifty-six chimeras."

Hazel grimaces as she ladles steaming stew into ceramic bowls. "Don't worry about it."

"Come on, first thing we can do when I'm out of this mess is go shopping on Robson. It'll be fun."

A dimple appears in her cheek. "Well, I won't say no to that."

As we settle on the couch with our giant bowls and golden biscuits, Ethel purring between us, last night's imprisonment feels like it happened to someone else. Like if I focus hard enough on this normal life with my best friend, the rest will fade like a bad dream.

I take a bite, sighing as the flaky, pillowy biscuit melts on my tongue. Through the windows, the bay sparkles, and the North Shore mountains are still dusted with snow from the long winter. But even as I try to stay in the moment, that dank prison cell remains burned into my retinas.

Natalie is right. The coven's dark side must have been there all along.

I gaze at the flowers from her and let out a slow breath, trying to relax. My hands are trembling. I set my spoon into my bowl and settle deeper into the couch before Hazel notices. "Looks cute in here, by the way. How was your first day in Vancouver?"

She splutters mid-bite. "There wasn't a lot of time for tourism."

"What about getting ready for your new job? Downloading a dating app? Calling your parents?" My throat tightens, and I force a small smile. "Come on, I can't think about my own life right now or I'll completely lose it. Can we focus on you for a bit?"

She fumbles her spoon, then puts the bowl down on the coffee table to take a sip of water instead. "Dating app?" she repeats at last.

"Yeah. Can we set up your profile? I promise I'll pick flattering pictures this time. I need to feel useful at something tonight."

And I need to believe there's still a normal future ahead.

Hazel studies me as if trying to gauge whether I'm teetering on the edge of a breakdown, then nods, going to get her phone. "I swear, if you include that picture of me mid-sneeze again..."

"You still got three matches with that one."

We spend the meal choosing her nicest photos and writing a bio, until today feels like it was supposed to, the two of us in a new city at the start of summer term.

"Mention you work at a tech company," I say as we sit down with cookies and tea for dessert. "It highlights how smart you are."

"I haven't even started working there yet."

"But you will in a couple days." Which means I'll be starting classes in less than two weeks. An excited flutter comes to life in my belly at the prospect of a new term and old friends—before reality crashes back. Will I even get to finish my degree?

Hazel updates her bio, then stares at her phone for a long minute, chewing her lip.

"What's wrong?" I ask. "Dreading the onslaught of bros holding dead fish?"

She stays quiet and starts organizing everything on the coffee table, which leads me to believe there's something she's not telling me.

I grab a cookie. "Everything okay?"

"Well..." She sits back with her tea, not meeting my eye. "I'm thinking about...changing my gender preference on my profile."

I spew cookie crumbs on my lap and put the rest down before I can drop it in excitement. "Are you serious?"

Sitting between us on the couch, Ethel startles and stares at me with wide eyes.

Hazel lifts a shoulder, the color deepening in her cheeks. "Dating men hasn't exactly been great, and I see how happy you are with Natalie..." She looks down at her mug, letting her hair fall across her face as if trying to hide how much she's blushing. "I've been noticing girls a lot more lately. Like...I'm curious, I guess."

Holy crap, *this* is why she's been weird when the topic of dating comes up? I wish she'd told me sooner!

"Hazel, that's so exciting!" I scoot closer on the couch and throw an arm around her in a side-hug. "You should go on a few dates. See how you feel."

"Is it fair to go on a date with a woman though if I'm just testing the waters?"

"As long as you make yourself clear up front." I reach over and scroll back up on her profile. "Set your sexuality to curious or questioning, and let people know you're looking for casual dating."

She bites her lip, and I can see a spark of excitement in her eyes that's usually reserved for conversations about environmental activism. I'm honored she's opened up to me.

I nudge her, a real smile tugging at my cheeks for the first time in a while. "I'll set you up with a sapphic starter kit. *The L Word*, *Carol*, some nail clippers..."

She laughs and covers her face. "Oh my God."

We swipe through a few profiles, getting giggly as we analyze them. Ethel bats the phone screen and manages to like three women before we get the chance to read their bios, so I wrangle her into my arms. "Stop trying to get dates for yourself!"

She purrs and nuzzles me.

"She's got better game than both of us combined," Hazel says.

Talking about her love life feels so blissfully normal and makes the coven feel less important—like I can slip back into an ordinary existence and the problem will go away.

But at that thought, the smile fades. When my time runs out, will the Shadows come for me like they did at the airport, dragging me off to fulfill my prison sentence?

There's no escaping this. I have to at least *try* to round up the chimeras I set loose. If I succeed, I get to keep this amazing life. And if not...

Well, I can't think about that. I can only think about what needs to be done. If Fiona thinks this is going to break me, she doesn't know how stubborn I can be.

I've got some chimeras to catch. And this time, I'm going to need a lot more than a laundry hamper.

From the Journal of Hazel Okada

It's like living in a new city has finally given me the space and freedom to figure myself out. How long have I been questioning my sexuality? A year? Two years? Since puberty?

I knew Katie would react well, but some part of me was afraid of being judged for not really knowing my sexuality. Like I'm supposed to have it figured out before I go out with any women. But she's right—I'll start with casual dates.

That is, if I can find time between starting my new job and building this chimera tracking app.

Watching Katie's face light up when I came out almost made me forget about the situation for a minute. Almost. But every time I swipe through the app, guilt twists in my gut. How can I think about dating when Katie's future is at stake? Like, I matched with a gorgeous marine biology grad student named Jackie who loves hiking and has a rescue dog...but do I have the energy to message her at a time like this?

No, the pretty girls on my phone can wait a little longer. Right now, my best friend needs me, and swiping on a dating app is the last thing I should be doing.

I've got an idea—a system for tracking freaky incidents and analyzing patterns in real time.

A chimera is likely gone by the time a news article is published about it, but there are other ways to track them, like by monitoring social media. We just need to get there before the press does.

This had better work. Katie's future depends on it.

CHAPTER 6

Château Madsen

THE CARGO VAN HURTLES away from the setting sun, Sky behind the wheel treating speed limits like light suggestions. I'm wedged between Natalie and Hayley on what has to be the world's most awkward road trip. Neil and three other Shadows take up the rest of the seats. It's the same van we took to Fort Langley when the Madsens led us into a trap in the graveyard.

"We think they're keeping Dad in their vacation house near Harrison Hot Springs," Natalie says. "We've checked every location connected to them, and this one..." She glances at Sky. "The amount of magic protecting it is suspicious."

"The place has Oaklyn and Sophia written all over it," Sky says. "Roots, thorns, and enough curses to double as a haunted house."

"How can I help?" I flex my fingers beneath the enchanted fig leaf gauntlet. God, I missed punching things with this. And I've got enough pent-up anger that I'm ready to hit someone with the strength of a thousand bulls.

"We need you to identify the danger zones," Natalie says. "It's too dangerous to even walk up to the house otherwise."

I straighten up, aware that everyone's attention is on me. This is my chance to show them what I can do. "I'll find us a safe path," I vow, trying to sound confident.

In reality, the fate of this rescue mission lies in the hands of a girl who got stuck in a tree last summer while trying to save her sister's kite—but they don't need to know that.

I settle in against Natalie, drawing strength from her. She extricates her arm and pulls me closer, her body heat seeping into me. This earns a few glances and side-eyes, but come on, word about our relationship must have made it around the block by now.

In the close quarters of the van, with her arm around me and her scent enveloping me, I'm struck by how natural this feels—being with her, hurtling into danger together. Her presence is like a beacon to my senses, as if my body recognizes her on some deeper level. If we weren't surrounded by other witches, I might finally tell her what I've been holding in. The words feel so right they're almost painful to contain.

Does the way I look at her and touch her convey what I haven't been able to vocalize? She must know. And the question is whether she feels it too.

After two hours, we turn onto a dirt road, and magic hits me like walking face-first into a spider web. My breath catches. "We're close."

Natalie looks sharply at me and gives me a reassuring squeeze.

"Let's see what you got, curse-hunter," Hayley says. There's no mockery in her tone, and to my surprise, she offers a tiny hint of a smile.

A faint warm feeling spreads through my chest. Maybe not everyone is as angry with me as Fiona is.

At the end of a long driveway, Sky kills the engine. Between twilight and the looming evergreens, the colors are dark and muted. No lights shine from the waterfront cabin, but the blackness inside seems to pulse with energy. Thorny vines scale the walls, and gnarled roots rise from the earth as if trying to drag the house underground.

Sky climbs out, and the rest of us follow, the slamming doors echoing through the woods. A cold breeze sweeps through the glade, and branches hiss against each other. Beyond the cabin, lake water laps the rocky shore.

I zip up my bomber jacket and scowl, my skin prickling. "*Haunted house* is an understatement."

Pushing back my braid and taking a deep breath, I step carefully toward the front door as if I'm approaching a bear den—and a creak tickles my eardrums. Every tree and bush shifts with me, like a cat swishing its tail as it gets ready to pounce. Pine branches reach out like grasping fingers, and the lake slaps the shore more insistently.

My steps falter. "I thought witches had to actively control objects," I whisper. "Is Sophia here?"

Everyone stops.

Sky takes a vial out of her utility belt and pops the cork, the noise filling the glade. She pours a burgundy powder into her palm, raises it to her lips, and blows. The powder lifts into the wind and drifts toward the house.

"Tracking dust," Natalie explains, her voice at a murmur.

I nod. Nobody else speaks as the dust spreads across the front yard, where it glows silver for a moment before flickering and dying. Only a small patch remains suspended in the air, the last to flicker and die.

"One occupant," Sky says.

A pause. Nobody seems to be breathing.

"Let's hope it's Dad," she adds, scowling as she slides the vial back into her belt.

Natalie eyes the shifting trees, which are still moving far too much for the lack of wind. "Skilled witches can do enchantments so objects respond on their own. Another reason her abilities are concerning. She's had magic for a short time but is already more proficient than...uh, most witches, to be honest."

I adjust the gauntlet and make a fist, wondering how useful this thing will be if an entire forest attacks me. Wouldn't be the first time I got into a fight with a tree, given all the hiking misadventures with my sisters growing up. "There must be a safe way in that the Madsens use, right?"

"Or it only lets them pass," Sky says. "Like how our suites are sealed to everyone but the occupant."

Natalie moves closer, her shoulder brushing mine. "We can handle the killer plants for long enough to get by. It's the other stuff I'm worried about. You focus on finding the curses, okay?"

I nod, my heart pounding. I can feel their pull already, like hooks in my chest.

I look at each of the witches surrounding me, gathering courage. "Ready?"

They flank me, and we advance.

It's like we've hit a trip wire. Pine branches snap toward us, their sharp needles about to draw blood.

"Go!" Sky roars, and the air comes alive with a charge. Loose strands of my hair float around my face as the witches create a shield of swirling debris—leaves, rocks, sticks, dirt.

We sprint forward, my heart slamming into my ribs.

A fern snaps at my legs like a piranha. I leap around it. A pinecone whips at my face like a bullet, and I raise the gauntlet, deflecting it with a *twang!*

I'm about to hop onto the wraparound porch when instinct pulls me to a stop. Gasping, I fling out my arms to block the others. "Wait!"

"What is it?" Hayley asks.

The sensation crawls up my limbs and across my back. My fingers twitch, wanting to reach for something I can't see. "There's a curse, but it's..." I scan the porch—the floorboards, the wooden bench, the white front door...and faded brown welcome mat.

My heart stumbles. "It's the mat."

Natalie follows my gaze. "Positive?"

Something sharp stings the back of my neck, and I hiss, lifting my hand to it. Probably a pine tree with excellent aim.

"Nat! Hurry up, dumbass!" Sky grunts as she and the others continue raising shields to block the attack.

"Okay, okay!" Natalie uncorks the vial and draws out the contents. The shimmering amber substance morphs in the air before she sends it downward. It hits the mat with a wet *slap*, where it spreads like syrup.

She yanks me backward.

A hiss. A spark.

BOOM!

A crater opens in the porch, black smoke rising as the mat and the wood beneath it disintegrates to ash.

"I think that did—ow!" I flinch as something else strikes the back of my head.

"Go!" Natalie shouts.

We scramble onto the porch and stop at the crater.

"Open the door with magic," I say. "Don't touch anything."

Neil raises his hands, his face tightening with concentration. "It won't budge."

My skin prickles so fiercely in the presence of magic it's like I've rolled in stinging nettle. I grab Natalie's hand and pull her onward. "This way. Something's wrong here."

We edge along the broken porch, the crater smoldering, while branches try to punch through our shield. The lake water stirs like a storm, waves reaching for our ankles.

At the side door, Natalie lifts her palm, and it blasts open.

Sky nudges me. "Nice work, Katie."

I take one step, then freeze.

Multiple curses tug at me from different directions. I focus on the closest one—coming from near my feet. I crouch, concentrating on the pull inside me. Gumboots... Umbrella... *There.* The black doormat practically screams "grab me!", which is exactly why I don't.

"This one's also cursed," I say, pointing to the mat.

Natalie opens a second vial and slaps the amber substance onto it.

"Damn, Katie," Neil says. "You're good at this."

The praise takes me aback, and I smile awkwardly as I cover my ears.

The mat explodes, and I lead the way inside, crossing the threshold of the Madsens' vacation house.

We step into a kitchen that hasn't been updated since probably the 1970s. The tug gets stronger, my pulse throbbing in my neck. I scan every appliance, fists up, searching for more explanations for the magic rampaging around me. My spine tingles like someone is watching us.

A gust of wind passes over the house, making it creak. I shiver. Branches thrash and squeal against the windows. Beyond them, a blanket of white fog creeps closer over the black lake. My next breath comes out in a puff, the temperature plummeting.

"What's happening?" I ask, my voice wavering.

A crackling sound makes us all flinch. My gaze snaps to an ancient boombox in the corner of the living room.

"Oh no," I whisper as the static morphs into music, dropping us into Céline Dion's *It's All Coming Back to Me Now.*

Natalie whips out a vial. "Who touched something?"

Everyone else raises their hands to prove their innocence. But pain ripples up my arms, and I hiss, shaking them out as they turn red and blotchy. Bumps rise on my skin like a hundred mosquito bites. Or hives.

Crap. Looks like I'm the lucky target.

"Uh..." I say as the hives begin to itch.

All gazes turn to me, and Natalie sucks in a breath. We both check to see if I brushed against anything, but I'm only standing on linoleum.

The song escalates. Shit, is it building up to something? What's going to happen when the chorus hits?

"Can you sense what it's from?" Natalie asks urgently.

"It's... I can't tell," I say through numb lips. The itching is making it hard to think.

A scurrying sound fills me with dread.

Yes, Céline, it *is* all coming back to me.

I leap aside, diving behind the kitchen table as four rats skitter past and out the door.

"It's the house!" Sky cries. "The curse activated when you crossed the threshold."

Natalie scoffs. "Come on, a whole *house* can't be cursed."

I gasp, understanding slamming into me. "No, she's right. It's why I can't get a read on which direction it's coming from."

Sky's eyes widen in horror. "But we can't neutralize it until we get Dad out!"

"Then start looking!" I yell as the music crescendos.

Natalie cups my chin, her fingers hot against my skin as she forces me to meet her gaze. Her touch sends that familiar current through me, and I can feel her fear pulsing between us. "Katie, are you sure—"

Something smacks into my back, little claws digging through my jacket. I scream over Céline, trying to shake the animal off as Natalie lunges to help.

"Get—off!" She grabs it, and I spin to see a fat raccoon wriggling in her hands before she grunts in pain and lets go. It hits the ground and whirls around to hiss at us.

More raccoons drop from the ceiling, raining down. I throw my arms over my head and dodge their claws. The thumps of their chubby bodies hitting the linoleum are drowned beneath the music.

Natalie and I scream, leaping over and between the furious animals as they scurry past and out the open door.

Meanwhile, the Shadows have split up, their footsteps pounding through the house as they search every room.

"Katie—" Natalie starts.

I push her forward. "Go!"

"Here!" Hayley shouts. "Basement stairs!"

I race toward her voice, but the curse has other plans. My toe catches on a floorboard, sending me sprawling. Pain jolts up my arms.

"*God—damned—curses!*" I shriek, stumbling to my feet.

The cacophony drowns out my string of swear words as I limp after Hayley.

She leads the way down the steps, all of us following. I'm the only one whose foot breaks through the third step, and I cry out in pain as my leg sinks to the thigh.

Natalie and Neil grab me under the arms and haul me out like I'm a bag of flour.

"You good?" Neil asks, dusting me off.

I grit my teeth, patting my torn jeans and coming away with a bloody palm. "Keep going. The faster we find him, the faster we can neutralize this fucking thing."

I don't meet Natalie's eye, afraid she'll read my thoughts. My breathing's okay for now, but it probably won't be long until my airway starts to close.

As we descend, the song becomes muffled, and an awful stench hits my nose—urine and sweat mixed with the stale, underground scent of a basement.

Hayley tugs the light string.

Oh God.

Iron bars. Cracked cement. A cot with a crumpled blanket. A toilet in the corner. It's not unlike the cell I spent the night in, but it's a hell of a lot dirtier.

A man who can only be Natalie's dad stands in the center, staring at us. He's skeletal, his cheeks gaunt, his pale skin covered in scars and scabs, his dark hair and beard long and matted. He's wearing a dirty blue hospital gown.

The worst part is his hands—they're fully engulfed in metal casings, presumably forcing them to stay balled into fists so he can't do earth magic to get out.

My stomach churns, bile rising in my throat. Holy shit, has he been like this for several months? This is actual torture.

"Am I dead?" he grunts, the sound rough and broken.

"No. It's us, Dad." Sky's voice cracks. Her hands fly to the bars, white-knuckled and trembling. All her usual bravado, that shield she maintains that makes her seem invincible, shatters as tears spill down her cheeks. "We're getting you out."

Natalie goes rigid beside me. Her breath catches, then stops altogether. Her throat works as she tries to speak, her dark eyes fixed on her father's broken body.

I reach out and take her hand, trying to offer support in any way I can. I can't imagine what she must be feeling to see him like this. This is the man who raised her after her mother was killed by Sophia Madsen, the parent she's spent weeks searching for since we found out he'd been abducted.

"Dad," she finally whispers, barely audible.

Slowly, recognition floods his hollow face. "Nat? Sky?" His voice cracks, and he stumbles forward. "You shouldn't be here. It's danger-ous—"

"We're not leaving without you," Natalie says fiercely.

Sky opens her fists to sever the bars with magic. Sparks ricochet like angry fireflies, and she flinches. "What—no!"

"Here." Natalie lets go of my hand to try as well. Both of them sweep their palms over the bars, but it only sends more sparks flying.

The others search for a way in, scouring for weaknesses or keys.

"She's enchanted it," Sky snarls.

I push between them. "Let me."

Everyone watches as I draw back my fist, the gauntlet glinting in the dim light, and punch the lock as hard as I can.

The lock shatters like cheap plastic, my fist breaking through it.

"Dang," Neil murmurs.

"Move fast." I kick the door, which opens with a banshee-like creak.

Sky and Natalie surge into the cell, taking their father's arms.

Sky reaches for his metal-encased hand. "How do we get these off?"

My skin is so itchy that I can't stand still. I shake out my hands and shift from foot to foot, trying to ignore the sensation of being stabbed with thousands of needles. My throat feels like it's full of cotton balls—like my airway is starting to constrict.

Breathe. Hold on another minute.

I can't panic and be a liability. This is exactly what everyone in the coven expects—for me to be a weak link. But I didn't come this far to let Fiona be right.

Natalie's gaze snaps to me, catching my discomfort. Her free hand jerks toward the vials in her inner pocket. "We'll deal with his restraints in the van. Let's move."

We leave the cell, their dad supported between them. The world swims around me as I follow, tripping over my own feet.

"When was the last time the Madsens were here?" Natalie asks.

"This morning." Their dad's words rasp out between labored breaths. "Overheard them saying they were going to check out an anomaly. Bio magic. Sophia's cocky enough to think she can harness it."

Natalie's eyes meet mine, maybe thinking the same thing: we aren't sure *what* Sophia is capable of. And we need that bio magic ourselves, fifty-six times over.

We reach the top of the stairs, where Céline is still passionately reminiscing.

Abruptly, my legs give out, and my knees hit the floor with a painful crack—and a splash.

Frigid water is pooling, rushing in through the back door.

The glacier-fed lake is reaching in, trying to sweep us out of the house.

"Katie!" Natalie shouts.

"I've got her," Hayley says, hauling me up by the elbow. "Keep going."

Hayley's arm slides around me, and she hauls me to my feet. My limbs feel like overcooked noodles as the curse spreads through my body, but I push on, refusing to slow us down. We slosh through the rising water toward the exit, wheezing sounds escaping my lips as I suck in each breath. My heart is hyperactive, as if aware of the danger it's in.

Don't panic. A few more seconds.

The van swims in and out of focus. The world is on a pendulum as I try to put one foot in front of the other.

On my next inhale, no air passes through. My chest spasms.

No, no...

My knees buckle. Hands grab me.

"Hurry!" someone shouts.

Voices swim past my ears, distorted. Above it all, the song continues to ring out, mocking me with the memories of every other time a curse nearly killed me or someone I love. If I survive this, I'm never listening to a power ballad again.

The van's doors fly open. Natalie's dad stumbles as the others help him climb in.

Can't breathe.

The ground moves under me as someone pulls me in next. Natalie's face swims into view, her eyes full of panic and her forehead clammy. "Hold onto me... Don't let go..."

There's a *pop-pop-pop* of corks ejecting from three vials.

Three amber blobs wriggle and morph like slugs, hugging the house and stretching across it, growing bigger, bigger, until...

Hisss...

"Cover!" Natalie wraps her arms around me and holds me to her chest.

There's a scramble as everyone tries to get into the van in time.

The song hits one final "now," and the entire house explodes.

From the Journal of Hazel Okada

PROJECT STATUS

- Create interactive web map – DONE

- Scrape the internet and social media for strange animal sightings and paranormal incidents – DONE

- Pattern analysis algorithms – DONE

- Notification system for new weird articles and posts – IN PROGRESS

- Add moving timeline to help see patterns

- Research ley lines?? If those are real and related?

Side note: Buy bear spray for personal protection, because holy shit, a lot of magical monsters are showing up everywhere.

LOVE LIFE STATUS

- Set up dating profile – DONE

- Match with girls – DONE

- Get up the nerve to actually message girls – IN PROGRESS

- Go on a date with a girl

- Kiss a girl!

I've been struggling all day to craft the perfect first message to marine biologist Jackie. I've typed and deleted about fifteen variations of "Hey, I like your dog" and "Marine biology, eh?"

Is that too focused on her pet and career? If I say she's cute, is that too focused on looks? Is "Hey" too simple?

Ugh, this is hard. I feel like an impostor.

Honestly, I'm scared she'll be able to tell I've never dated a woman before. I'm scared she'll think I'm not "gay enough," whatever that means. All these girls seem confident in their sexuality, and I'm just...straight-looking, I guess. I tested out wearing my hair in different ways earlier, and when Katie wasn't home yet, I may have tried on some of her clothes. It all looks like I'm trying too hard.

I know, I know—be yourself. But what if "being myself" isn't good enough to get a girlfriend?

CHAPTER 7

How to Catch a Chimera

"So you blew up a lake house, rescued your girlfriend's dad, and developed a magically induced full-body rash that makes poison ivy look minor," Hazel says from the kitchen table. "All in the span of an evening."

"Yep." I plunk down on the couch to slather coconut oil over my angry red skin, which feels too tight and on fire. "They had him locked in a dark basement."

I had Natalie drop me off while she and Sky went to tend to their dad. My brain feels like it's been through a blender, tumble-dried, then put back into a blender, but sleep isn't an option when every time I close my eyes, I see those iron bars and his hollow face. Thank God Hazel's still up.

I peel off my socks and inspect my blotchy feet, which look like they've been attacked by radioactive mosquitoes. What's the proper treatment for magical inflammation anyway? Is there a WebMD for curse victims?

Hazel goggles at me, her paint-by-numbers sunflower field forgotten. "These Madsen people sound horrible. And you're still in trouble for killing one of them in self-defense?"

"Yup." The injustice hits me all over again, and I slump back.

"What will they do when they find out you blew up their house and took Natalie's dad?"

"Well, they already want to kill me, so does it matter?" I lift a shoulder as if this isn't terrifying. "Anyway, with luck, they'll think he exploded with the house."

She studies me closely as I try to relieve my inflamed arms. I don't know if it's helping, but it's all I could think of, and it's soothing after the curse attacked me. At least I'll smell like a tropical vacation while I process my trauma.

"Are you okay?" Hazel asks, searching my face.

"We succeeded," I say, willing myself to feel some sense of victory. "We freed Natalie's dad, which means soon we'll have the guidance we need to start catching chimeras."

It's hard to get Natalie's distraught face out of my head, and the pain in her voice. I can't imagine how scared and angry she must have been, knowing how close she was to losing both parents to the Madsens.

Hazel smiles sadly. "You didn't answer my question."

I open my mouth to say I'm fine. *Of course. Everything's working out.*

But the words lodge in my throat. And something in her steady gaze makes me swallow them right back down.

The cell flashes across my mind again—iron bars, putrid air, the defeat in his eyes. My stomach churns, bile rising. I dig out another glob of coconut oil and attack my arms like I can scrub away the memory.

"No," I admit, my voice strained. "I'm not okay. My parents and sisters called to ask how I'm settling in, and I almost burst into tears at the thought that I might not see them for five years while I rot in a cell. And I don't know what I'm going to tell them because it's not like I can tell the truth, and they're all going to worry, and I don't want to do that to them, and I'm going to—to really miss them—"

Fuck, I'm crying.

I swipe at my cheeks, wincing as my irritated skin protests at the contact. Hazel studies me, her expression shifting to a familiar determination. She sets down her paintbrush.

I watch her wearily as she gets up and comes closer.

She wraps her arms around me, not quite touching me because of my tender skin. "I am absolutely not letting you go to witch prison, and neither is Natalie. We've got two months to figure this out, okay?"

Ethel pads over and sniffs my ankle, either sensing my distress or debating whether to lick off the coconut oil.

Of course Hazel's prepared to help me tackle this. That's what best friends do, right? Help you move, bail you out of jail, and hunt down shapeshifting monsters?

Knowing I have her and Natalie in my corner helps, but to think we might fail anyway still makes my chest unbearably tight.

"Katie." Hazel waits until I meet her eyes before continuing. "You might have come back with battle wounds—or um, a battle rash—but you kicked ass tonight. You saved Natalie's dad, and you're ready to catch some chimeras. You can do this, okay?"

I smile a little, relaxing into her hug.

She's right. If I stop panicking about what'll happen if I fail, there's an opportunity to feel hopeful about what comes next: an actual shot at catching a chimera.

"Show me your chimera map," I say, putting the lid on the coconut oil.

"That's the spirit."

Hazel grabs her laptop and returns to sit beside me on the couch.

The map has way more pins than the last time she showed me—at least thirty are scattered everywhere between downtown and the suburbs, the majority in clusters.

"I made a sliding timeline, and watch what happens." She drags the slider from left to right, and the pins appear in succession, moving slowly outward, like a weather map showing cloud movement. "I think a lot of these clusters are the same few chimeras shapeshifting as they migrate. Like, if you look at this pin that started in the West End in February, over time you can see it move east."

I lean in, my heart beating faster. "Hazel, you're a genius."

"Just wait," she says, animated. "Based on these movements, I can use predictive analytics to guess where each one will appear next."

"Oh my God." I reach over to play with the map, dragging it around and moving the timeline slider. "So let's say we look at the most recent sighting—this one at Cambie. Going back in time…" I drag the slider backward, and more pins appear near it. "If this is the same one hanging out in the area, you're saying we can predict where it'll be next?"

"Theoretically." She tilts the laptop back toward her and opens a different window. Her fingers fly over the keyboard. I stay silent as she works, not wanting to interrupt her thought process.

"Hm. Interesting," she says at last.

"What?"

"This trail of pins moving south. I think we can predict where this chimera is headed." She points, and I drag the timeline to watch the pins appear in succession.

"So…we should keep a lookout in White Rock?" I ask.

"Yep. Seems to be moving that way at a steady rate."

My heart leaps. "I'll tell Natalie."

She gives me a reassuring smile and continues tweaking her code. "In the meantime, want to help me craft the perfect pickup line for a girl I matched with?"

I sit up straight. "Yes! Who is she?"

As she tells me about how the dating app has been going, I'm more grateful for her than ever. She's the anchor to normalcy I desperately need when I'm wedged between curses and chimeras. And she's fighting right alongside me when she could easily back away with her hands raised in surrender.

My next step is as clear as a pin on her map. Tomorrow, I'm going to return to C.S.A.M.M. and learn about chimera catching from Natalie's dad. Then, it's time to start hunting.

I spend the morning rubbing tea tree oil, baking soda, calamine lotion, and anything else I can think of all over my hives. Thankfully, by the time Natalie picks me up, my skin has calmed enough that I won't meet her dad looking like I've caught something contagious.

We enter C.S.A.M.M. through the steam clock, and the familiar brick halls feel darker, more threatening. Everyone is hushed, whispering about what happened to Troy Zacharias.

The place has been restored since the Madsens attacked in February, but something's off, like paint over a deep scratch. The fireplace, stone chimney, booths, and tables are repaired, but the ivy-covered walls and other plants aren't as lush as before. The poor willow tree is propped up with wooden supports—but it's alive, surviving against impossible odds. The bean bags, bookshelf, and board games that were once beneath it have been moved to give it space to heal.

Heads turn as we pass, familiar faces watching me but saying nothing. I ignore them. I've got enough to worry about without caring about being stared at.

The infirmary is as I remember it—sterile, white, the only part of the building not covered in plants and wood. My stomach churns as a sense memory hits me, a jolt of pain shooting through my ankle. Last time I was here, Natalie had to carry me in after Wyatt treated my leg like a tug-o-war rope.

Sky sits beside the nearest bed, her hand on her father's arm like she's afraid he'll disappear if she lets go.

I hover at the threshold. This feels too private for an outsider to intrude upon.

But Natalie's hand finds the small of my back, and she gently guides me to the bedside.

"...heard bits of conversation down there," her dad is telling Sky, his voice labored and sandpapery. "Knew they were going to invade but had no way to warn you. Just glad something worse didn't happen."

He looks better than when we rescued him, but not by much. His trimmed beard reveals how gaunt his face is, his cheekbones sharp enough to cast shadows. He's more covered in scars than I thought, jagged white lines stretching like webs over every inch of visible skin. But there's still life in his eyes after all those months, a spark of defiance that the Madsens couldn't extinguish. An IV drips into one arm while the other rests atop the blanket, curled into a loose fist.

"Hey, Dad," Natalie says, pulling up chairs for us. "How're you holding up?"

He lifts one skeletal hand and drops it with a hollow *thwap*. "Wondering if I'll ever regain the use of these things."

"You will," Sky says fiercely. "Don't say that."

His mouth forms a grim line as he meets his younger daughter's gaze.

As I sit, he turns to me, his dark brown eyes so much like Natalie's. "Nat tells me you—have an ability," he says between breaths.

I dip my chin. "We're hoping it helps us track down all the loose bio magic."

"It just might." His gaze is assessing, like he's trying to see through me to whatever makes me different. It's the same look Natalie gave me when she first realized I could sense curses.

I fight the urge to perch forward and ask him to spill everything he knows. Every second counts if I want to avoid ending up in my own cell, but the man clearly needs rest more than he needs my interrogation.

"It's been fun watching the Madsens—get twisted about catching it." He shifts with a wince. "They haven't caught a single one, and not for lack of trying."

Natalie, Sky, and I exhale in relief. More proof that setting the chimeras free was right, even if the coven doesn't see it that way.

And now you have to catch them all again, my inner voice taunts—but I tamp it down. There'll be plenty of time to be anxious about that in a minute.

"Did they want you to tell them how to harness it?" Sky asks tightly, like she's not sure if she wants the answer.

"I damn near did, hoping they'd let me out." He laughs bitterly, which turns into a coughing fit.

Sky offers him water, but he jerks his chin.

"They'd promised that before." He frowns, gazing blankly at the far wall. "But when you're at rock bottom...with nothing to gain by telling them how to end the world... Figured if I was going to die, might as well die keeping one last secret from them."

Sky swipes at her eyes and squeezes her dad's arm.

A chill slides down my spine as I think of what I once witnessed—Millie raising her bloody palms toward a chimera, symbols etched into them. The final step to embodying bio magic that the Madsens would kill for.

"Mr. Zacharias?" My voice comes out small as all eyes turn to me.

"Call me Troy," he says, those familiar dark eyes studying me.

"Troy." I lean forward, my heart pounding. "What are the chances they could find out through some other means? Are the steps recorded anywhere?"

He shakes his head, then winces at the movement. "We never write down instructions that could be so apocalyptic if leaked. It's all passed verbally...and only to those who need to know."

I nod. For once, the coven's *need-to-know* rules are working with me instead of against me. At least, I think they are. Will he share information with me?

Time to cut to the chase. Every word seems to drain more of his strength.

"Can you tell me how—"

The door swings open, and Fiona appears. "Troy. Can I borrow your daughters?"

Natalie and Sky exchange a look but don't budge.

My shoulders tense. What could she want so desperately that she would interrupt a hospital visit with their father?

Troy dips his chin.

"Come on," Fiona says sharply. "The others are waiting for a mission recap."

They rise and sweep out of the room, Natalie's hand brushing over my waist as she passes.

"We need a division to guard the elementary school in case that rhino comes back," Fiona tells Sky as they pass through the double doors. "I won't have another injured child on my watch."

Before I can process what's happening, the doors swing shut, and I'm alone with Natalie's dad.

Oh God. Do I leave? Do I make awkward conversation until Natalie returns—however long that takes?

"I hear you and Nat are an item," Troy says.

Yep, I should've run when I had the chance.

I shift in my chair, wondering if I can somehow melt into it. "Yes."

"Is it serious?"

Heat floods my face. Wow, okay. "We—we haven't had time to talk about that."

"But do you think it is?"

I wasn't planning on telling Natalie's dad before Natalie herself, but something in his direct gaze pulls the truth from me. I nod.

He studies me for a long moment, then dips his chin. "Good. Nat deserves that."

A light, tingly feeling fills me.

"She brought you here for a reason…" He closes his eyes as if gathering strength. His scarred, lined face makes him look decades older. "I suspect you need the wisdom of a Tracker."

"I do. I have to capture all fifty-six chimeras we set free."

"Ever think you shouldn't have set them free in the first place?"

"I had no choice," I say, unable to keep the defensive note out of my voice. "We were handing them to the Madsens on a platter."

Troy's chest rises and falls. He opens his eyes with a grimace of pain, his permanently curled fingers twitching. "I know. I believe you."

I study him, trying to read his sincerity. Is he on my side or Fiona's? Or is it more complicated than that?

"So how does a person go about capturing a chimera?" I ask.

The corner of his mouth lifts. "Is this a *need-to-know* thing?"

"Very much so."

The half-smile disappears, a deep frown creasing his face. "I sure as hell want you to find them before the Madsens do."

A low hum hits my ears—my phone is buzzing in my bag on the floor.

"Don't we all," I say bitterly, nudging my bag as if that'll shut my phone up. Whoever it is can wait until I'm done getting answers that could change the course of my life.

"A lotta intuition involved," Troy says. "Trusting your gut. Tapping into a sense that not everyone possesses. That's why not everyone is cut out for it." His haunted eyes lock onto mine, a silent question about what I can do.

My heart skips. Finally, someone who understands how valuable my ability is.

So why are the witches determined to cast me out? I've proven myself useful, even risked my life. It's not fair that I have to fight this hard to belong.

My phone stops buzzing, then starts up again. I nudge my bag aside and perch forward. "When I'm near magic, it's as if it's pulling me closer. It's like this...*urgency* inside me. Is that what it's like for you too?"

A crease appears between his unruly eyebrows. His fingers twitch as if remembering what it was like to do magic. "Yes. Sensing it... Feeling it... That's the first step to catching it."

"What happens after I find one?" I ask, trying to tamp down the memory of the rampaging bear that almost ate me last time I came face-to-face with a chimera.

"You'll need magical help to catch it."

The buzzing stops again.

"Same vials used for curses?" I ask.

A wry smile crosses his face. "That stuff works about as well as a tranquilizer gun."

I stare at him, wondering how well a tranquilizer gun works on a monster.

"Not at all," he adds, reading my expression. "No, you catch it by doing whatever it takes. It can turn into a real rodeo."

My phone starts up again. I focus on what Troy is telling me, imagining trying to lasso any of the creatures that terrorized Gastown in February. "But they're shapeshifters. They'd just morph the second someone throws something at them."

"Exactly." His eyes gleam. "Ever try to trap a deer only to have it transform into a wasp and buzz away? Frustrating as hell."

Well, shit.

He studies me for a long time, seeming to debate his next words.

"We have special equipment." He pauses, drawing a deep breath to gather strength. "Trackers have been perfecting nets for centuries. Subdues magic better than anything. Now, I destroyed mine when the Madsens captured me... Couldn't let 'em have it. But I've got a spare. I told Nat where it is."

"Nets?" I picture myself running around swinging one. "What, like a butterfly net?"

A gravelly laugh escapes his throat. "More like a fishing net."

"And I just throw it on the chimera?"

"You'll need earth magic to trap it. Funnel it toward you."

Earth magic. Of course. Once again, I'll be relying on Natalie and other more capable people to do the heavy lifting.

"Make it panic. Force it to change form," Troy continues. "The more it shapeshifts in a short amount of time, the weaker it gets. Keep at it until you're close enough—"

The door flies open with a bang that makes me jump.

Natalie bursts in, breathing hard. "Katie, Hazel's been trying to reach you. There's a chimera on the beach in White Rock."

I leap to my feet and look at Troy, my heart skipping. Now? Already? God, Hazel's prediction was right!

Troy must read my hesitation. "Go before you lose it," he says firmly, and there's a flash of the confident, strong Tracker he once was. "We'll talk more when you bring it back to me."

"But... We've barely scratched the surface..."

"It's enough. Get that butterfly net ready, kid."

From the Journal of Hazel Okada

I KNEW IT! Those sleepless nights coding and analyzing data paid off! Take that, Natalie "hm, it's worth a try" Zacharias. I can contribute to solving a magical problem after all.

Currently on a barstool at the window of a White Rock cafe, finishing my third coffee while I wait for Katie and Natalie. They'd better arrive before the police or animal control, or all my work and staking out for hours will have been for nothing. So far, the chimera seems harmless, running around the beach and boardwalk as a pig.

Yes, that's right. A pig. Not the griffin who tore apart the Harbour Centre or a tiger or something—just an ordinary-looking pig causing extraordinary chaos. Screams and laughter drift through the windows as it chases people who get too close.

The cafe's cleared out—as soon as word spread about a pig on the beach, everyone had to race over to see. Other than the two baristas, who seem disgruntled about being stuck here while something exciting happens, the only other person is a girl my age. She's standing feet away with a latte, checking her phone and watching the mayhem through the window. Like she's waiting too. Like maybe we're both in on the same secret.

Should I talk to her? She might know more than I do about this situation. Hell, maybe she's a witch.

Also... Okay, ulterior motive: she's smoking hot. And she looks like the complete opposite of Sean with his pressed shirts and preppy attitude.

Oh shit, she caught me staring. Quick, look busy. I'm just a normal person writing normal things while definitely not speculating about her sexuality and whether she knows about magic...

She's still looking at me. And is that...a little smile?

Help, my heart is going double-speed.

Pros of talking to her:

+ Might know something about the chimera situation

+ Could be a witch (!!!)

+ Really pretty

+ Keeps looking over and possibly checking me out?

+ I promised myself I'd do things that scare me

Cons:

- Might reject me because she's got better things to do than talk to a normie

Okay, pros win. Seriously, there's a chance they're all true—that she's not only checking me out, but she's also a witch who has insight about the chimera.

I know, I'm being hopeful. Like I'm desperate to find my version of Natalie.

But...what if? This could be my door into the magical world. Katie has held me on the outskirts, and I know she's keeping me safe, but...maybe I don't want to be on the sidelines anymore. I'm tired of being the one who stares at my phone waiting for updates while Katie and Natalie dive into danger.

This might be my chance to get swept off my feet and into the world of witches and magic.

And if this stranger isn't a witch, well, then I will have said hi to a pretty girl. Can't go wrong either way.

Screw it, I'm talking to her.

Will report back.

CHAPTER 8

Chimera Catching 101: An Introduction to Shapeshifting

As Natalie steers us down Marine Drive, pedestrians on the boardwalk crane their necks and point at something we can't see. Traffic is backed up as cars slow down to look. Dark clouds gather overhead, wind whips through the trees lining the street, and magic pulls at my blood like a tide.

I fold my arms across my queasy stomach and sink lower in the passenger seat. This would be less daunting with Sky and the other Shadows here, but Fiona made herself clear in that special brand of ice-queen disapproval she saves just for me: *"This is not a Shadow's job. You're lucky I'm letting Natalie help you."*

So I'm here with my intuition and Troy's enchanted net in the trunk, hoping for the best. Oh, and a fake Animal Control uniform to match Natalie's.

Meanwhile, Natalie's hands are steady and capable on the steering wheel, her fingers tapping a rhythm as she navigates traffic. Does she ever doubt herself? Or is insecurity not in a witch's repertoire?

She parallel parks, and we climb out into the salty sea air. Train tracks and a boardwalk separate us from the rocky shore, where seagulls, driftwood, and tangles of seaweed bob in the high tide. The town's iconic wooden pier stretches toward Washington, and trotting along the weathered planks is... Yup, that's a pig all right. Round, pink, and as bizarrely out of place as...well, as a pig at the beach. It's chasing seagulls like an excited puppy.

My skin prickles as magic hits my senses. While my eyes see 'escaped livestock,' my gut screams 'dangerous magical creature that's about to ruin everyone's day.'

"How is the coven planning to explain this when it shapeshifts?" I ask, fastening the enchanted gauntlet to my hand.

"Publicity stunt." Natalie cuffs the sleeves of her Animal Control shirt. With her toned arms filling it out and her hair in a low bun, she manages to make the fake uniform look hot. "Some influencer with zero regard for public safety trying to go viral."

"That actually works?"

"Sebastian usually volunteers for cover-ups. He'd probably do it again if..."

If we can find him. His and Millie's disappearance after the Madsens infiltrated C.S.A.M.M. hangs between us.

My phone vibrates in my pocket.

Hazel

> The uniform suits you.

> I'm in the cafe across the street.

I should've known she would hang around. I look back, but the cafe windows only reflect the traffic.

Hazel

Can I come help? I don't want to miss the fun part.

Katie

Considering this thing could transform into a giant dragon and kill us all, I'm gonna say no.

Hazel

Fiiine. Give me a signal if you change your mind.

Katie

What signal?

Hazel

I dunno. Wave your arms or do the YMCA.

Katie

Just stay there and make a getaway plan. I'm not in the mood to watch my bestie get trampled by a pig.

My stomach twists. If this goes sideways, I don't want that to be the last thing I ever said to her.

Wish me luck. Love you.

As I pocket my phone, Natalie hands me the net from the trunk. Though it's big enough to cover the pig when unraveled, it weighs nothing, like holding sunbeams. Magic seeps from the golden threads into my bloodstream, giving me a buzz like an espresso shot.

"I can't use magic freely with all these people watching, but I'll do everything I can to push the chimera toward you," she says, her fingers lingering on mine. "Make your move as soon as you're close. Don't hesitate."

I swallow hard. There's a pause, and she bends to brush her lips over mine, sending a ripple of heat through me. Her breath tickles my face, her taste sweet and intoxicating. After all these months, her kiss is still as exhilarating and seductive as forbidden magic flowing into my veins.

"I've got you, okay?" she whispers against my mouth. The words send a pleasant tingle through me, taking me back to better times—and begging the question of if I'll ever get a chance to tell her how much I love her.

But right now, we need to focus.

I dip my chin, too nervous to speak. Her fingers trace my cheek before she steps back and squares her shoulders, all business.

With her kiss still warming my lips, we set off. High tide crashes against the rocks, and shouts carry over the waves. The pig trots around at the far end of the half-kilometer pier, the size of a paperclip from here. A handful of pedestrians remain, but they speed-walk away as the pig chases them. Most people are taking videos from a safe distance.

"Won't it just transform into a bird and fly away the second it sees me with the net?" I ask, craning my neck to keep it in sight.

"Feral magic usually tries to kill its attacker if it feels threatened, so we'll have a chance to catch it when it fights us."

"Oh," I say in a small voice. "Good."

That explains why Troy is covered in scars.

Natalie stops at the pier's entrance. "Ready?"

My brain screams *nope*, but my mouth says, "Sure."

The net pulses against my palms like a second heartbeat. There's a strange hiss in the back of my mind, like someone whispering from across a quiet room.

That can't be a good sign.

"Could you imagine if this was just someone's escaped pet pig?" I say, attempting a smile. "And we're here with this net, going way overboard trying to catch it?"

Natalie laughs—and then stops as the pig turns and looks right at us.

Only a group of teenagers remain between us and the chimera, giggling and clutching each other as they try to get closer. The pig lowers its head, looking right past them and staring us down.

I take a step onto the weathered planks, which creak under my feet. The salty spray sticks to my face, and that weird hiss in my mind grows louder. The seagulls have gone quiet, like they know something supernatural is about to go down. A long shadow stretches over the planks beside the pig, though it isn't sunny, and I swear the shadow doesn't match the animal's shape.

"Little hunter, you dare to bind what was never meant for chains?" a voice hisses in the back of my mind.

What? Who said that?

I whip my head around, but nobody is there.

"Did you hear that?" I ask Natalie.

"The train?" she asks, pointing.

"No, I..." I spin to see a long freight train appear around the distant curve of the shore, its headlight cutting through the gloom. A low rumble meets my ears.

"Okay, everybody away from the beach!" Natalie's voice shifts into authoritative mode as she positions herself between me and potential witnesses. "Anyone remaining will be fined. Move back behind the tracks, now!"

She herds people away, beckoning sternly to the teenagers. Smart—the passing train will give us cover.

My heartbeat quickens. I grip the net tighter, my palms sweating and my skin prickling all over. Do we really think I can do this? Yeah, I can sense the bio magic in front of me, but so what? Just because a person can see a tornado doesn't mean they can trap it in a jar.

My phone buzzes, and I steal a glance in case it's Hazel with something important.

I found an article on how to catch a pig.

I stare blankly at the link. Okay, first of all—

I shake my head and pocket my phone, focusing.

When I look up, the pig's form ripples like disturbed water, and my heart lurches. Pink skin transforms into wrinkled gray hide. Tusks burst out like ivory daggers. A trunk unfurls, huge ears fan out, and I'm suddenly facing an elephant.

The boardwalk groans under its massive weight.

Well, this is inconvenient.

"Natalie?" I call, fidgeting with the net that's now pitifully small. "We might need a backup plan."

The elephant trumpets, the sound so out of place that my spine tingles.

"Crap," Natalie says as screams erupt.

The train rumbles closer.

Every survival instinct tells me to run, but the same pull that drew me to Lucy, to curses, to this life, roots me in place. I *have* to catch this thing.

"Keep moving!" Natalie roars at the crowd. "Off the tracks!"

People scurry away as she raises her voice. Loose rocks and driftwood gather at her feet—ammunition ready while everyone's focus is on the elephant.

The elephant's ears flare outward as it shakes its head. And I'm no wildlife expert, but I'm pretty sure this means it's about to charge.

The railway crossing bell rings. Barrier arms lower. The ground rumbles.

The elephant starts toward us, the planks groaning under each heavy step. I spin and grab Natalie's wrist, pulling her off the pier with me. We hurtle onto the brick boardwalk, its thundering strides gaining on us.

The freight train roars past, a wall of metal between us and the crowd.

Natalie seizes her chance, whirling around and raising her arms. My hair lifts from the surge of power as she launches her arsenal. Rocks and driftwood rise from the beach and encircle the elephant, bringing it to a stop on the boardwalk.

Watching her control the earth with such grace is a harsh reminder of the gulf between us. She's so utterly, incredibly extraordinary.

"Get ready with the net!" Natalie shouts.

The elephant swings its head left and right, calculating its next move.

"How? It's too small and so am I!" I shout, searching for a height advantage. The railings on the pier... The giant white rock that the city was named for... Ugh, who am I kidding? I'm not a ninja.

The swirl of stones and wood constricts around the elephant, about to slam into it. Its form ripples again, shrinking beneath the debris. Gray hide melts into spotted fur, its trunk shortens, and its body condenses into something lean and deadly.

"Oh, come on," I mutter as a cheetah crouches on the boardwalk, its tail lashing.

Beneath the train's rumble, the whispers grow louder. *"We remember the cages. We remember the fires. Turn back while you still draw breath."*

That voice again! Who's talking to me? Are the Madsens behind this?

The image of a familiar long room lined with metal bars and torches flashes across my vision like a bright light. I blink, stumbling backward, and then it's gone.

Oh God. Is the voice...?

I shake my head and raise the net, refusing to be thrown off. There will be time to decipher that later. Right now, I'm not letting this thing get away.

The cheetah bares its fangs, its haunches tensing as its purple eyes lock onto me.

Something in its eyes freezes me in place. Maybe it's the shade of purple—the same as Natalie's when she's using magic, and Lucy's when she terrorized my bedroom, and—

The cheetah launches forward like a bullet.

Adrenaline surges through me. With a battle cry that sounds braver than I feel, I throw the net. The golden threads fan out, beautiful and enchanted, gleaming like treasure—and it misses entirely, falling limp onto the damp rocks at our feet.

"Dammit!"

The cheetah twists past me fluidly, and Natalie raises a wall of rocks to funnel it back. But it shrinks into a tiny sparrow, zipping through a gap.

"This is ridiculous," I say, collecting the tangled net. "Isn't there a better way?"

"We knew it'd be impossible," Natalie grunts, raising an avalanche of rocks, sticks, shells, and debris above the bird to force it lower.

The sparrow spins and dives, so small among the flying rubble that I struggle to keep track of it.

Natalie moves her arms like a dance, creating a vortex. With her hair loose and billowing in the wind, she's a formidable sight as she works to trap the bird.

And I'm stumbling clumsily over the beach, untangling the net as I go.

Overhead, the vortex tightens into an upside-down tornado. I run underneath it with the net held in front of me, feeling like a cartoon character trying to catch everything that's falling at once. "It's still out of reach!" I stop running and thrust the net toward her. "Here. Use magic to throw it."

"If I do that," Natalie says, her voice strained with the effort, "I'm going to drop half these rocks."

I growl in frustration. "This would be easier if you'd let me have magic!"

Natalie's face goes blank with surprise, and I bite my tongue. The words slipped out before I could filter them. I know it's not up to her whether I'm allowed to be a witch, and the coven has a lot of laws, but she can't deny it'd be a game-changer. I wouldn't be stumbling around like a klutz while Natalie does all the work. I could launch the net at the chimera with magic instead of weakly throwing it.

Out of nowhere, a piece of driftwood rockets toward me and slams into my hip. I hit the ground hard, pain shooting through my wrist as I catch myself.

Before I can get up, a rock hurtles at my head, and I barely raise the gauntlet in time. The stone ricochets with a *clang!*

"Katie!" Natalie's concentration breaks, debris raining down as she rushes to my side.

"I'm fine!" I scramble to my feet, my hip screaming in protest, and look around for my attacker. My skin prickles uncomfortably, and I rub my arm. "It's coming from..."

A lithe figure stands on the boardwalk in a crimson trench coat, her hands raised as she manipulates rocks and wood with earth magic. Power radiates from her like heat waves.

My stomach drops as I recognize that white-blonde braid and nasty sneer.

Sophia Madsen has joined the party. And suddenly, catching this chimera got a lot more complicated.

From the Journal of Hazel Okada

OHMYGOD OHMYGOD.

Freaking out for two reasons.

First, I lost sight of Katie behind a train, and I am NOT confident about her chances against a magical creature. Was that an actual elephant I saw before the train whipped past, or is my brain making stuff up? The way it transformed... No wonder Katie's been so stressed about catching these things.

Second, um... I talked to that girl.

"Not interested in going closer to see what the fuss is about?" I asked.

"If I wanted to see a pig, I'd go to a petting zoo," she replied, deadpan.

Yeah, she definitely knew something. What else would explain why she was ignoring utter chaos so casually?

"Sounds like you've seen this sort of thing before," I said.

Her gaze swept over my body in a way that made heat bloom in my belly. "The things I've seen would shock you, sweetheart."

"How about I get your number and you can tell me about it over drinks?"...would have been a smooth line. Instead, I blushed and giggled awkwardly because she called me sweetheart, and I apparently have a thing for punk girls who give me sass.

Did I mention how hot she is? Muscular under an open leather jacket and ripped jeans, black hair in a shag cut, black lipstick and eyeshadow over snow-white skin, septum piercing, razor lines in her eyebrows... Yeah, this works for me. Are bad girls my type?

"Anyway, why aren't you out there?" she asked. Her little smirk told me she definitely noticed me checking her out.

I scrambled for a witty response that didn't reveal I know witches exist. "Meh, I haven't been fond of pigs since one trampled my dad at the pumpkin patch."

This...might have been a weird reply. But it's true, and it's the first thing that came to mind. And she apparently liked the weirdness because she laughed.

God, she had a nice smile. Like, stunning pearly whites, dimples, the works. I couldn't stop drinking in the contrast between her dark aesthetic and her bright, mesmerizing eyes and teeth.

She stepped closer, and I could smell her leather jacket and caramel latte as I looked up into her ice-blue eyes.

"So you're in here hiding instead of trying to get a video like everyone else?" she asked.

"Yes." I closed my journal before she could read it. "And you?"

She sipped her drink. "Yep."

"You live around here?" I asked, tapping my pen.

"Nope. You?"

"Nope."

We stared at each other. Her blackened lips curved into a little smirk, which made my heart do a somersault. And though I can't say for certain, I'm pretty sure that pause held a shit-ton of secrets—maybe the entire truth about magic and witches.

She took another step closer, her eyes penetrating deep into me until my lips tingled. "What are you writing?"

"Journaling."

"About what's going on outside?"

"About anything. What I see. Things and...people...that interest me." I was losing the ability to breathe. Looking up at her while I sat on the barstool, it was easy to imagine her leaning down and...

"You're cute," she purred.

This effectively reduced me to a puddle on the floor. She somehow turned the word into a challenge—like she was daring me to prove I was more than just cute.

Her phone beeped. She checked it and glanced out the window. "Hey, I gotta go, but we should talk more. Sounds like you've got some unresolved farm-related trauma to sort through, and I'm happy to listen."

"I guess I do," I said, gripping the table to steady myself.

She hesitated, then handed me her phone with a new contact entry open. "Tomorrow at seven?"

Ohmygod ohmygod.

With clumsy fingers, I typed in my name and number. "Yeah, sounds good," I said, trying to act casual even though my insides were practically exploding like fireworks.

She took the phone back, letting our fingers brush, which sent a zap through my whole body.

She looked at the screen and nodded, flashing a stunning smile. "Hazel. I'm Oaklyn."

And that, dear diary, is how I gave a girl my number!! I don't think I've ever been this excited about a date. Watching her strut out of the cafe, I could have floated into the ceiling.

But the feeling didn't last long. Now, staring out the window at the passing train, my chest tightens. What is Katie up against on the other side? Will she and Natalie be okay?

I can't help wondering if this stranger, Oaklyn, knows something. Maybe she's a witch, or maybe she's witch-adjacent like me. But if I'm meeting her tomorrow night, I'll have to come up with a way to ask.

CHAPTER 9

Chimera Catching 102: Not Dying

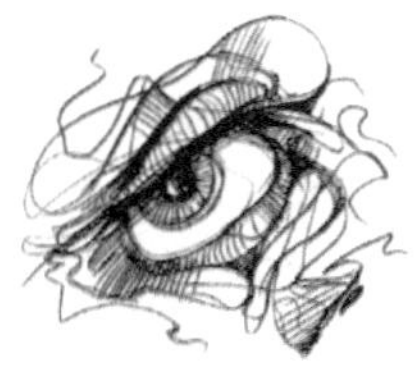

"Think Sophia's here to kill us or get the chimera?" I ask, sucking in rattling breaths, the salt air burning my lungs.

Beside me, Natalie follows my gaze to our guest, her body tensing. "Shit. Probably both."

Great. This mission just went from catch-or-jail to catch-or-die.

While Natalie tries to force the bird downward, Sophia advances along the brick boardwalk with her arms out. Her fingers curl like claws, raising a swirl of debris to match Natalie's. Her white-blonde braid whips in the wind like a snake ready to strike. She looks way too confident for someone who's been a witch for barely three months.

"Wish I'd known you planned to visit our vacation house yesterday," she shouts over the rumbling train. "We would have prepared the guest room for you."

"Keep her busy," I tell Natalie, edging toward the bird. The sensation of magic is overwhelming, slamming into me from all directions, and I fight to stay focused.

Natalie dips her chin and faces Sophia, the air crackling as she prepares to unleash her magic. "Sorry we left the place a bit messy. Nothing insurance won't cover, I'm sure."

I inch closer to the bird, which Natalie is forcing lower beneath the vortex of debris, but it's still too high. Sophia's gaze snaps to me, and then overhead, her eyes narrowed and calculating.

"A little cold for a beach day," Natalie says, pulling her attention back.

Sophia chuckles. "I've got eyes everywhere, honey. A chimera shows up, and I know within the hour."

I lift the net, but it's like trying to catch a bullet.

Natalie barks out a humorless laugh. "Eyes everywhere, huh? Too bad that hasn't helped you catch one. Must be frustrating, failing over and over."

"Failing?" Sophia sneers. With a flick of her wrist, wood splinters fire at Natalie like a swarm of arrows.

Natalie redirects one of her hands to raise a shield. But her divided attention isn't enough to protect her, and she grunts, stumbling back.

Bright red lines appear on her face. My heart lurches into my throat.

"Natalie!" I abandon the chimera and race toward her. The sight of her blood makes any other priority fade away.

"Katie, don't," she says firmly. "Remember why we're here."

I freeze, torn between what I'm supposed to do and the need to protect her. "You're hurt," I choke out.

"Go!" She wipes her eyes and smears blood across her face. "I can handle—"

Sophia sends another barrage at Natalie, who struggles to deflect it. Overhead, the cone around the bird breaks apart.

My chest constricts. Dammit, Sophia was talented with magic last time I saw her, but has she gotten even better? The ground beneath her feet cracks with each step as the earth bends to her power.

"I know the coven sent Guardians to Whistler this morning," she snarls, her eyes blazing purple. "I know where a dozen chimeras are and how they're migrating. I know Katie arrived at YVR on Tuesday at 3:46 P.M., and you, Fiona, and two Shadows were there to greet her."

My insides turn to ice. Has Sophia been watching us? Or is she paying other people to watch us?

Natalie falters, red rivers trickling down her cheeks and neck, and the bird seizes its chance to blast through a gap and away from us.

White-hot anger mixes with the fear in my gut, churning and unsettled. I want to hurt Sophia for everything she's done to Natalie—and seeing the blood streaming down her perfect face only makes it worse. My nails dig into my palms, a tremor passing through me. I step forward, torn over which direction to run.

Then, like a shimmering mirage, a cheetah takes form again, bolting away across the rocky beach.

"Don't lose it, Katie!" Natalie grits out as she barely deflects another attack. A chunk of concrete slips past her shield and slams into her shoulder, making her cry out.

The sound lances through me. But she's right—I can't let it get away.

Fighting every instinct to sprint over and defend her, I force myself to chase after the chimera. Each step away from Natalie feels wrong, like I'm tearing myself in half. My legs are slow and clumsy, but I push on, desperate not to lose it.

Both Natalie and Sophia send obstacles into the chimera's path before returning their attention to each other. Sophia's movements are chillingly casual as she sends boulders flying. The world fills with debris like we're stuck in a tornado. All that's missing is a cow.

"Leave this chimera to me, and I'll stop fighting you," Sophia growls, her long fingers stroking the air as she manipulates her surroundings.

"Aw, afraid you'll lose?" Natalie taunts, but I don't miss the hitch in her words as she deflects a chunk of concrete. Blood and sweat trickle down her face, but she can't afford to drop her hands to wipe it away.

The cheetah makes it to the water and transforms into a seal, diving through the shallow tide toward the open ocean.

My stomach drops. "No!"

I change course and sprint back to the pier, determined not to lose it.

Rocks rain down in front of the seal like meteors, slowing its pace. I can't tell if it's Natalie or Sophia doing it, but it doesn't matter—I'm the one with the net, and I'm the one who's going to catch it.

God, I *have* to catch it.

My feet pound on the wooden planks as I follow the seal's path. Rocks continue to rain down, forcing it closer.

"Yes, keep doing that!" I shout, not daring to look back and lose sight of the dark shape beneath the surface.

I slam into the railing, knocking the wind out of me, and unfurl the net—but the seal vanishes under the pier.

"Katie, hurry!" Natalie shouts, her voice strained as she holds Sophia back. The desperation in her tone cuts through me.

"I know!" My heart is beating out of my chest as my strategy dissolves into *don't miss and don't die.*

I race to the other railing and climb up, wobbling as I lean over with the net ready. The cold spray hits my face, mingling with my sweat.

Abruptly, the net jerks in my hands like it's being pulled. I tighten my grip, nearly losing my balance. "Hey!"

Back where I came from, Sophia is forcing Natalie back with a park bench—and one of her hands is extended my way.

Oh crap. She's not only here for the chimera—she wants the net.

And based on how easily she's deflecting Natalie's attacks, there's a chance she might get it. It tugs again, and I keep a tight hold, jumping off the railing before she can send me tumbling into the frigid water.

The train is coming to its end, the last car visible along the shore. We're running out of time—and I've lost sight of the chimera beneath the waves.

A chunk of wood rips up at my feet, and I hop aside to avoid the gaping hole.

"Katie, get off the pier!" Natalie shouts, her voice strained with the effort of fending off Sophia. Even in the midst of a fight, she's thinking of me first—always protecting me, always putting me before her.

My eyes prickle. Bundling the net tightly in my arms, I do what she says and break into a run.

The pier disintegrates beneath me, making me stumble as I sprint for safety.

Fuck, Sophia ruined my chance. The chimera is probably halfway across the bay.

But maybe that doesn't matter right now—not when we're being destroyed by a woman who shouldn't be this powerful. Her magic is so strong I swear I can see it, like purple mist emanating from her pores. As she sends a hunk of the pier at Natalie, knocking her off her feet, it's sickeningly clear that we might not make it out of this alive.

Sophia laughs, taking pleasure in watching Natalie cough and splutter on the rocks. My vision narrows, a haze creeping in at the edges. I've never wanted to hurt someone so badly before. If I had magic right now, I'd use every drop of it to make Sophia pay.

The ripping pier trips me as I reach the end, and I fall to my knees, pain jolting through my legs.

"You can't protect her forever, Natalie!" Sophia sings.

There's a pause—a heartbeat of absolute stillness. A ripple passes over me from head to toe as something shifts in the wind. I suck in a breath as if it's my first gulp of oxygen after my head was trapped underwater.

The air crackles like we're in a thundercloud as Natalie straightens up, her chest heaving, blood streaming from a dozen cuts. Even from here, I catch the spark of fury in her eyes—a dangerous flash of purple to match Sophia's.

I've seen Natalie angry, but there's something different now. I'm looking at a witch whose father was tortured and whose mother was killed by the woman standing before her. And now Sophia just threatened my life too.

At the look on Natalie's face and the low, rumbling quake beneath us, Sophia's sneer falters.

I get to my feet, backing away on shaky legs.

With a roar, Natalie sweeps out her arms, and the ground under Sophia ruptures. Bricks rise out of the boardwalk like a tidal wave, concrete splits and reforms into deadly spikes, and the rocky beach surges upward in a violent explosion that knocks Sophia off her feet.

Sophia lands with a shriek, flinging her hands out to catch herself.

"Not so confident now?" Natalie advances, gathering more ammunition, until even the train beside us shakes with the force of her power.

A surge of victory hits me as Sophia scrambles back on her hands, shouting in pain as the bricks roll over her. She tries to deflect, but Natalie is relentless, sending an endless torrent of brick and stone at Sophia while she's down.

"You think because you stole magic, you understand it?" Natalie's voice carries over the chaos. "Magic isn't just power—it's sacrifice. It's protection." She sends a precise attack, burying Sophia under more rubble. "It's everything you'll never understand."

Awe ripples through me—and like before, a twinge of fear as a different side of Natalie breaks through. This is the part of her I'll never fully grasp, the magic flowing through her veins that I can sense but never have. In moments like this, the gap between us feels enormous... And yet, somehow, it was my name on Sophia's lips that unleashed this storm.

Her chest heaves and sweat beads on her face as she lifts her arm for another blow—but the last train car rumbles past, giving us an audience again.

Under the gazes of at least thirty people on the other side of the railway crossing, Natalie hesitates, her arm still raised. Her face twists in frustration as the desire to stop Sophia butts up against her duty to keep magic hidden.

A car engine revs. Behind the crowd, a silver Toyota FJ Cruiser turns off the road and motors down the concrete steps toward the pier like an advertisement for a four-wheel drive vehicle. The crowd splits in a panic, shouting and grabbing each other.

My stomach drops. *Oaklyn.*

"Natalie, look out!" I scream.

The car swerves onto the pedestrian path, tires squealing as it barrels toward Natalie. She spins, but there's not enough time to raise a shield. She dives aside, rolling over the broken beach while the car misses her by inches.

I gasp, my legs weak. The image of what could have happened flashes before my eyes, and I shake it away, forcing my feet to move.

Sophia blasts free from the rubble and limps to the car. As she whips open the passenger door, the deep bark of a German Shepherd with a grudge fills the air, and I stop dead, ready to catapult myself into the nearest dumpster.

But Sophia pushes Wyatt back and climbs in. I catch a glimpse of her face—no longer sneering and confident, but pale with fear. It's the look of someone who just realized they're not the most dangerous person in the fight.

The engine revs, rocks spitting out from under the tires as Oaklyn drives away.

Natalie raises her hands.

"Don't," I say, glancing at the crowd.

She stands frozen, trembling as she watches them escape. For a moment, it looks like she might run after the car and unleash another attack—her body is as tense as a drawn bow. But then her gaze finds mine, and she softens, the purple fire in her irises dimming.

They leave us with shattered bricks, twisted metal, splintered wood, and a lot of explaining to do.

Not to mention a missing chimera.

"Fuck," I say under my breath, loosening my grip on the net. At least she didn't get it from us.

Natalie growls in frustration and strides over. "You—okay?" she asks between ragged breaths, scanning me for injuries. The purple in her eyes is gone, replaced by concern so intense it makes my chest ache.

"Fine. But the chimera got away." Another step closer to prison.

"The least of our worries." Natalie pulls me into her strong arms, trembling. "Good job keeping the net safe."

It hardly feels like a victory worth celebrating. Our first attempt is over, and we failed. Plus, now that Sophia knows we have the net, how long will we be able to protect it?

"Hey," Natalie says softly, pulling back to meet my eyes. Her brow is pinched, her gaze tender beneath all the blood and dirt streaking her face. "This was only our first try. We'll be okay."

I blink, but it's too late to hide the way my eyes are stinging and wet. Every one of her cuts and bruises is agony to see.

Before I can put on a brave face, she cups my cheek and kisses me. It's unhurried and desperate, stealing my breath. Her lips are soft and salty. For a moment, the world falls away—no chimeras, no Madsens, no looming prison sentence. Just Natalie, solid and real in my arms, her heart beating strong against mine.

When we break apart, she takes my hand, our damp and gritty fingers interlacing. "We need to get out of here before someone asks why Animal

Control caused thousands in property damage. I'll have Sky come by to fix all this."

Leaving the beach in shambles, I follow her, the warmth of her palm a small comfort as disappointment sits heavy in my gut. But really, did I ever have a chance of catching the thing, even if Sophia hadn't interfered? Aside from the chimera's ability to shift into a bug the second I threw the net at it, I was getting in my own way. Hesitating.

Not to mention hearing voices.

I need to figure out what's going on...and what this might mean for our plan to capture magic.

From the Journal of Hazel Okada

Things to ask Oaklyn:

- Are you a witch?

- What do you know about magic and chimeras?

- Kiss me?

CHAPTER 10

Post-Calamity Stress Eating

R AIN PATTERS AGAINST NATALIE'S windshield as we sit parked behind a burger joint. The dreary weather matches my mood as I slouch in the passenger seat, shoving fries into my mouth. We're famished after that ordeal—even Natalie, who usually maintains more dignity than this, is about to finish her burger in three bites.

"I wish I could've seen it." Hazel leans forward from the back seat, speaking around a mouthful. "One minute, you're facing off with a freaking elephant, and the next, the elephant is gone, you both look like hell, the beach is in shambles, and some scary-ass woman is making a getaway."

"Madsens," I explain, dabbing a spot of ketchup on my fake uniform. "She tried to take the net *and* the chimera."

"And our lives," Natalie says. She's cleaned up the cuts on her face, but she still looks like a wreck.

"Failed, though," Hazel says brightly.

"That doesn't mean we won." I shove another fistful of fries in my mouth like that'll dull the pain. "She's powerful, Natalie. No offense, but she nearly took you down."

Natalie's expression darkens, a muscle jumping in her jaw. "She's been practicing. Must've had time to perfect her magic while keeping my dad locked up."

My heart aches at the torment in her voice. I touch her forearm, her skin warm and soft beneath my fingertips. "You couldn't have known he was kidnapped."

"I should have." She looks away out the rain-streaked window. "Sky and I thought he was processing Mom's death. Throwing himself into work. Meanwhile, he was being tortured."

I squeeze gently. "Natalie, they tricked you. It wasn't your fault."

She falls quiet. The silence fills with crumpling wrappers, chewing, and slurping straws.

I take a breath, steeling myself for the confession I have to make. I need to talk about why I fumbled—and to find out her theories about what happened.

"I heard whispers." The words tumble out in a rush. As the others freeze, I force myself to keep talking. "At first, I thought it was like a hiss that came with being near magic—like static in my brain. But on the pier...there were words."

Natalie and Hazel exchange a look in the rearview mirror. The sort of concerned look I'd expect two people to exchange when they learn their friend is hearing voices.

"What words?" Hazel asks.

"Trying to warn me away. *Turn back.* That kind of thing."

Hazel perks up. "Maybe the chimera was talking to you."

Natalie shakes her head. "Chimeras don't talk. They're magic, not sentient creatures."

But her brow is pinched, her eyes darting, like my confession scares her.

"Are you positive?" I ask.

Natalie takes a long sip of her iced tea, as if buying time before she answers. When she sets it down in the cup holder, she fumbles it a little. "Magic is a mystery even witches don't fully understand. But I've never heard of anyone having magic talk to them."

I look at Hazel, who tilts her head. There's so much we don't understand about my ability to sense magic—and about chimeras. I won't rule out Hazel's theory, and it matches my own. I just don't know how I feel about being the only person to ever hear magic speak to them.

But there's another explanation for hearing voices too, a more concerning one.

I crumple up my burger wrapper, nauseous. "You don't think...Sophia has gotten access to bio magic? Mind control?"

"No," Natalie says firmly. "We'd know it. We'd be in huge trouble."

I nod, trying to let her confidence convince me. "Okay."

The air in the car is thick with that stale fast-food scent, the windows fogging. Rain drums harder on the roof, creating a cocoon that almost feels safe.

"Well, my algorithm worked," Hazel says, clearly trying to lift the mood. "We knew exactly where it would show up."

I give her a thumbs-up. "Nice work."

"Unfortunately, so did Sophia," Natalie points out grimly. "I believe her when she says she has eyes everywhere. She's no doubt hired a bunch of people."

"Um, does that mean she knows where Katie's been staying?" Hazel asks, her voice small.

A tense pause.

Natalie throws her crumpled paper bag on the floor and dusts off her hands. "If she doesn't already, it won't be long before she does." She turns to me, her expression hard and serious. "You need to move back to C.S.A.M.M. right now. We'll stop at Hazel's in the morning so you can get your bags and Ethel, but I don't want you without full protection at all times."

My heart skips a beat. I'm caught between worlds again—the magical one that's trying to kill me and a normal life with my best friend. "What about Hazel?"

"I don't mind living there too!" she says, her whole body lighting up with excitement.

"It's okay. You're safe at home," Natalie says. "Sophia probably doesn't even know you exist."

Hazel's expression falls, a flicker of hurt there.

"Being overlooked has its advantages," I say, attempting to lighten Natalie's blunt words. But when Hazel's face tightens, I scramble to clarify. "I only mean—"

"No, you're right." She sits back, crossing her arms. "Let her think I'm nobody."

Disappointment turns her mouth down, but in her eyes, there's unmistakable longing. It's the same look I've seen on her face before when talking about magic and the coven. She wants in on this world as badly as I once did. And I'm doing exactly what Natalie did to me that made me so angry—trying to force her to stay out of it.

"What Sophia doesn't know is that we desperately need you," I say, turning in my seat to face her fully. "We have to catch a chimera per day to get all fifty-six before my time runs out. You up for it?"

"I'll get to work on another lead," Hazel says, pulling out her laptop. "Staking out from inside that cafe was fun. I—I can do it again."

There's a flush in her cheeks that I don't understand. Maybe it's excitement over her working algorithm.

"Okay. And Natalie?" I reach over and squeeze her warm hand. "Tomorrow, I want lessons from your dad on how to use this net properly. I was a klutz with it today." I nudge it with my feet, where it sits in a heap on the floor.

She nods, her eyes softening. "Of course. We can spend as long as you want practicing."

"And the second Hazel finds something..." I add sternly.

"We'll drop everything and go," Natalie promises, lacing our fingers together. Her familiar touch soothes me when nothing else is certain.

Hazel looks between us, her eyebrows arched sadly.

My heart sinks. It was fun living with her for that short time—like it was the way things were supposed to be, the two of us in a new city. My chest tightens over the thought of abandoning her. I wish I could be a better friend right now, especially given all the trouble she's going through for me.

"I'll see you every time we catch a chimera," I say, turning to her. "But we have to admit that this is my best shot at learning how to trap them."

"While being surrounded by people who want to imprison you," Hazel mutters.

"They'll have to go through me," Natalie says, the same dangerous glint in her eyes that appeared when she unleashed her worst on Sophia.

"She's lucky to have you, Natalie," Hazel says softly.

Natalie frowns, looking down at our entwined fingers. "I don't know about that."

I squeeze Natalie's hand, wishing she would understand how true that is. The air between us feels thick with all the things we haven't had time to say and the quality time we haven't spent together since my return. There's always been something in the way, or someone with us, or pure exhaustion holding us back.

But as hard as we're fighting...it's tough not to feel the clock ticking on the time we have left.

From the Journal of Hazel Okada

I can't stop thinking about her.

Or texting her.

Since meeting Oaklyn yesterday, I've checked my phone approximately 2958 times, and it's only lunch. Every time it buzzes, my heart does this ridiculous little dance, and I catch myself smiling as I read her texts.

I haven't felt this way about anyone before—not Sean, not Devon, not any of my crushes. This is different, exciting, and a little scary.

When she asked me about my job, I unleashed a rampage about environmental impact algorithms...and then immediately regretted showing so much of my nerdy side right away. But when I apologized for boring her, she called my passion sexy. SEXY! I nearly slid out of my desk chair.

I love how forward she is. How she knows what she wants and goes for it. Her flirty texts, the way she acted in the cafe... Compared to my past relationships, which took weeks to get moving, it's exhilarating to be openly flirting and to have a date lined up within a day of meeting her.

I told her as much, and her response caught me completely off guard: "I don't usually hit on random girls in cafes. But there's something about you that's...refreshing and genuine. In the middle of all that chaos outside, you were just doing your own thing, calm and confident. I like that. You're like a light in the darkness. Sorry if that's too deep or whatever—I'm just really looking forward to our date. I want to get to know you."

God, who talks like that? It's like she stepped out of my dreams and promised a deeper connection than I've ever had with my emotionally stunted exes.

And honestly, I can't wait to find out who she is under that leather jacket and black makeup.

I'm already stressing over what I'll wear on our date tonight. My closet is suddenly woefully inadequate. Shopping after work? What's the best store for clothes that give off an "I like girls" vibe?

The anticipation has me vibrating in my chair. Is this what Katie felt when she first met Natalie? This electric current, this feeling that something amazing is about to happen? I understand now why she chased after a mysterious woman who might have kidnapped her cat.

I've always been practical, the one with plans and safety nets. The one who calculates risks and writes pro and con lists. But something about Oaklyn makes me want to leap without looking. And it's kind of intoxicating.

CHAPTER 11

Cue "Eye of the Tiger"

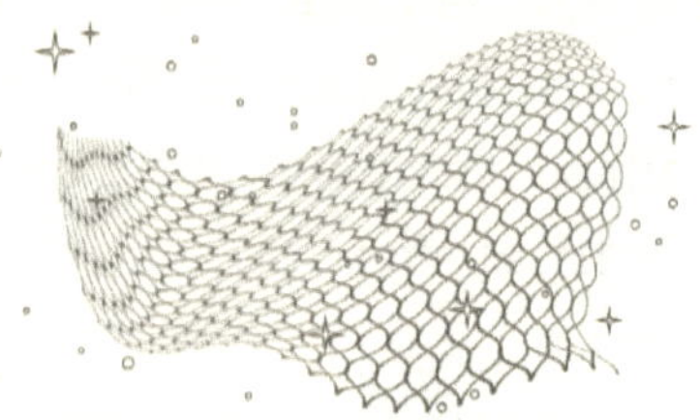

THE GOLDEN NET GLINTS in the dim light of the Alchemy lab as I throw it at the book Natalie lobbed at me. I only manage to swat the book out of the air, and it lands on my toes with a heavy *thwap*.

"Ow!" I hop on one foot as pain shoots up my leg.

Natalie winces. "Sorry! Try to anticipate where it's going, not where it is."

"Yeah, yeah." I rub my tired shoulder.

She summons the book back. It's dense and leather-bound, one of several we borrowed from the coven's library. It probably holds something important, but it's hard to care when my freedom is on the line.

Natalie catches the book and shakes out her arms. All the throwing and catching has left the veins in her forearms standing out beneath her rolled-up sleeves. The purplish-green bruises from yesterday's fight are stark against her pale skin.

"Chimeras are always a step ahead, I know," I say, dragging my attention away from her fingers and arms. "Your dad made that very clear."

After breakfast, Troy told us about the chimeras he trapped while abroad—a sea serpent in Norway being his favorite. The stories were meant to inspire me, but they only made me more nervous about how impossible this is going to be. His techniques for throwing the net are all easier said than done, and I'm convinced he was pulling my leg when he said it'll come back like a boomerang if I throw it right.

I ready myself for another try, the weightless golden threads tickling my fingers. Is this my training montage? Swinging a net around in an abandoned Alchemy lab while my girlfriend gently tosses books my way? Ugh, how sad.

We've pushed the wooden tables and chairs up against one side of the rectangular room, leaving space to practice. The whirring fan beneath the skylight does little to dispel the stuffy air, and my arms are tired from swinging this thing all afternoon.

Natalie sends the book in a slow arc, and I chuck the net, this time with too much force. It sails past the book and crashes into a shelf of empty vials, sending them to the floor with a cacophony of shattering glass.

"Shit!" I rush over and drop to my knees, trying to gather the broken pieces.

Pain stabs my index finger, and I hiss, watching a fat droplet of blood ooze out.

Natalie kneels beside me, brushing her fingers over the back of my neck. "Katie, stop. It's okay."

Her touch derails my brain for a second, making me want to turn around and feel every contour of her strong arms—but I shake my head fiercely. "It's not okay! None of this is!"

She tucks a lock of hair behind my ear. "We should take a break. We skipped lunch."

Frustration twists in my gut. I snatch up the net where it's tangled over the broken glass. "I need to get better. Your dad caught his first chimera when it was an eagle, and that's way harder than catching books you're throwing really slowly."

"Katie." She guides me to my feet. Heat spreads from her fingertips, easing some of the tension in my muscles. "You're overthinking it."

"Of course I'm overthinking it!" I gesture wildly with the net, the golden threads trailing behind my hand like a comet's tail. "How am I supposed to catch fifty-six of these things when I can't even catch a flying book?"

She studies me closely. Her face is still cut up from yesterday, each one painful to look at. "I feel like...like you might be holding back. I see it in your face when we talk about them."

Hot shame wells inside me. "I'm not..."

But I am. Every time I think about catching those creatures, the memory of that warning hisses in the back of my mind: *We remember the cages.* And that cheetah flashes across my vision, beautiful and strong, with intelligent eyes that really looked at me.

Her hands linger on mine, anchoring me in place when everything else is spiraling. The way she's looking at me, with such concern and focus, makes my breath hitch. We stare at each other for a moment, surrounded by broken glass and rays of sun peeking through the skylight.

"Is it the voices?" Natalie asks.

I nod, my throat tight.

She runs her fingers along my jaw. "Tell me if you hear it next time we're out there, okay? We can try to figure out what's going on. Where it's coming from."

I furrow my brow. Either she's in denial or I'm clinging too hard to my theory. "And if it is the chimeras talking to me? If we discover I'm trapping sentient creatures like some dirtbag trophy hunter?"

Natalie shakes her head, loose locks of hair falling across her face. "They're dangerous forces, not animals. Think of them like a hurricane or an earthquake."

"Natural disasters don't usually talk," I point out.

She sighs, her shoulders dropping. "Katie, they level cities. They hurt people."

"And if they *are* somehow conscious?"

"Then we still have to contain them."

I chew my lip, trying to find a solution. "Is there another way to banish the chimeras without trapping them?"

She scans the ivy-covered walls as if searching for answers. "Maybe. But for now, this is the only way to keep you safe—to keep *everyone* safe."

I nod, though the knot in my stomach stays tightly wound. She clearly doesn't think there could be another way, but she doesn't want to say it outright.

"Katie, we're talking about bio magic, and we need to consider that they could be manipulating your mind."

I open my mouth to argue, then close it. I hadn't thought about it that way. If bio magic is the ability to manipulate cells in living bodies, including mind control, then that could be exactly what's going on.

The net is still in my hand, the weightless golden threads dangling off the chair and pooling on the floor. I need to make a decision: I can either master this net and secure my freedom, or I can listen to the voices and risk everything. What choice do I have?

I growl and rub my face. "Of course this is happening to me."

Natalie's brow pinches. "What do you mean?"

I wave my hands. "I'm already a total weirdo, so let's add disembodied voices to the mix, shall we?"

Her mouth opens in surprise. "That's not true!"

"It is! The coven treats me like an outsider, and why shouldn't they? I can sense magic but can't use it. I'm not a witch, but I'm not normal either. And now these voices..." I break off, struggling to hide my fear. "What if there's something even weirder about me that none of us understand?"

Natalie takes my hand and raises it to her lips, pressing a kiss to my palm. The sensation shoots up my arm, pleasant and warm. "The fact you can sense magic is remarkable. It's exactly what we need to trap it."

I huff. "I just... I wish I were a witch. Then the coven would accept me."

Her brow furrows. "Do you know what would happen if I gave you magic? The coven would never forgive either of us. There'd be no coming back from it."

"Better than being dead or imprisoned for five years. I could actually protect myself—and I could be your equal instead of your burden."

"Katie!" she exclaims.

I shake my head. "It's true. Every time we run into trouble or go after a chimera, you're the one doing all the work. You're fighting the Madsens, manipulating the earth, protecting me...and what am I doing? Fumbling with a net I can barely throw." I look down at my inadequate hands. "Sometimes I wonder if you'd be better off with another witch. Someone who understands your world completely, and who could fight alongside you instead of needing to be rescued all the time."

The words spill out with more emotion than I meant to show. But it's hard to tamp it down right now as everything piles up.

Natalie steps closer, her face clouding over. "I hope you don't believe that."

"How can I not?" My voice comes out sharp, and I drop my gaze, heat creeping up my neck. "Look at us. You're throwing books for me to catch with a net because I can't do anything more useful. Meanwhile, you could be with another Guardian or whatever—someone who wouldn't be holding you back."

"That's not fair," she says tightly. "To either of us."

I shrug. "The coven has made it clear where I stand."

Natalie runs a hand through her hair, frustration evident in the tense line of her shoulders. "Katie, I've never seen you as less than me. Not once."

"I know you don't... But that doesn't change the reality." I gesture between us. "There's an imbalance here that we can't ignore forever."

Her eyes flash with something—hurt, maybe, or recognition of a truth she's been avoiding.

My phone buzzes, and I step back to fish it out. A text from Mom asking how I'm settling in.

"Shit." I drop onto a chair, overwhelmed. "I haven't even bought my textbooks yet. Or called my family. Or—"

"Breathe." Natalie closes her fingers around my wrists. "One thing at a time."

"But there isn't time," I say, my voice rising. "I have two months to catch all these chimeras while somehow going to class and keeping my family from worrying and protecting this net from Sophia and—"

The words die on my tongue as Natalie drifts closer, her legs pressing against my knees. She looks down at me, her gaze steady and intense.

"Katie," she whispers, cupping my face with both hands.

The room suddenly feels too warm. Neither of us moves, time seeming suspended between us. Slowly, she leans down, bringing her lips to mine with a gentleness that makes my heart so full it could burst.

I open my lips and pull her in, responding with all the frustrated energy that's been building inside me—the fear of failing, the exhaustion, the longing for her during our time apart.

All the tension melts from my shoulders as she brushes her thumbs over my cheeks. Her lips are soft and comforting, everything I missed so badly it hurt since I fled the city in February. When she deepens the kiss and puts her arms on either side of my head to grip the back of the chair, my brain short-circuits.

"You can do this," she says against my mouth, her breath warm. She pulls back a little and fixes me with a fiery stare. "And you are *not* my burden, Katie. You never have been. You're my happiness and the reason I fight so hard."

I try to believe her. I want to so badly. But it's impossible not to notice the difference between us.

"Do you know how much it kills me knowing I dragged you into this?" she whispers. "That I'm the reason you might lose five years of your life? If not for me, you'd be safe. Normal. Free."

I cup her face with one hand. "I wouldn't be normal. I'd still have this ability, but I wouldn't have you to protect me."

Her eyes dart across my face, maybe trying to find an argument.

"And anyway, I'd rather be in danger with you than safe without you," I add.

Her breath hitches, and a crease appears between her eyebrows. She searches my face as if checking to see if I'm serious.

Finally, she leans her forehead against mine, her breath warm on my lips. "I wish I could give you everything. Magic, acceptance...everything you deserve."

"You've given me more than enough," I say, and I mean it with every fiber of my being.

I hold her gaze—this gorgeous, incredible woman I've fallen hard for. The one making sacrifices to keep me safe. So I won't be given magic, and the coven won't forgive me any time soon—but no matter what, I can't lose this relationship we've built. For her and for everyone else I love, I need to figure out how to catch chimeras.

More than that, I need to be the best damn Tracker the coven has ever seen.

She leans in for another kiss, and I melt into her, letting the net fall to the floor.

"You're not a burden or an outsider or weird, okay?" she murmurs, threading her fingers through my hair. "You're brave and brilliant and special."

Her words tingle through me. She always has a way of making me feel better, even when the whole world is against me.

I hook my fingers over the waistband of her jeans, pulling her closer so the heat of her body envelops me. Her familiar scent fills my head, making everything else seem distant compared to the immediate need to be close to her. "Fine. Now come here."

She glances over her shoulder toward the door, then turns back to me with a smile. The hungry look in her eyes sends a thrill through me.

"I've missed touching you," she whispers. "Every night for seventy-eight days, I wished you were here with me."

"Same," I murmur. The fact that she was counting too makes something warm unfurl in my chest.

She kisses me again, slower this time, like we have all day. And maybe we can afford a little pause. We both passed out fast last night when we got back from White Rock, so today is the first stretch of time we've really had together since I got back to Vancouver. Maybe for now, I can forget about chimeras and nets and the Madsens.

Natalie wraps her hands around my thighs, and in my next hitched breath, she lifts me up and sets me onto one of the wooden tables. The casual display of strength makes my stomach flip pleasantly.

Her warm fingers wander beneath my shirt as I lean back on my hands. The cool surface under my palms contrasts with the heat of her touch, making me shiver. Her mouth traces a path down my neck, and I let out a shaky breath.

"We probably shouldn't..." I say with a glance at the door, even as my fingers find the buttons of her shirt.

"Probably not. But nobody has any reason to come in here, and anyway…" She stretches out a hand toward the door, and a *click* resonates. "Door's locked."

I return her grin, and she pulls my T-shirt over my head—which is actually hers since I don't have my stuff here yet. The soft fabric slides over my skin, raising goosebumps in its wake.

"I've been imagining doing this since I saw you at the airport," she says, reaching for the clasp of my bra.

I laugh breathlessly as my bra lands on the floor beside the T-shirt. "Before or after the Shadows attacked me?"

"Both." She kisses along my collarbone and palms my breasts. "Though I pictured a much better reunion."

Everything narrows to her fingers, her soft lips, and the heat of her body against mine. I slide my hands beneath her open shirt and push it off her shoulders, letting it hit the floor. She's so unbearably beautiful—all lean muscle and smooth skin glowing in the dim light, marred by the cuts and bruises from our fight with Sophia. Evidence of what she's willing to endure for me.

"So many things I've wanted to do to you…" Natalie murmurs against my skin.

I knot her hair in my fingers as she traces her lips down my chest. "Show me," I whisper.

Her lips curve into a teasing smile that makes my heart skip. There's something deeper in her eyes—a tenderness that feels more real than it ever did before. Like despite all the time we spent apart, we still grew closer every day.

We're finally alone, and the words I've been holding back for weeks—*months*—press against my lips, desperate to escape. I want to tell her. But my mouth is dry, and the words won't come. It feels selfish to say when everything is so uncertain. When our relationship has already cost her so much. Soon, our entire future together might be ripped away, and then what? What does being in love mean when my whole world could end in June?

So I just savor each moment as she continues undressing me, leaving me naked on the table, the cool air raising goosebumps on my skin. And as she slides her tongue between my legs, I tip my head back and cry out, gripping the edge of the table with trembling hands. The sensation is almost too much after months apart—her mouth hot and insistent, her hands firm on my thighs. More than that, it's the way she makes me feel seen and cherished despite all the reasons I have to doubt why she's chosen me.

"God, you feel good—oh, I missed you—" I stammer as she devours me, my words dissolving into incoherent sounds. What I can't articulate is how she makes me feel whole, and how in these moments, the differences between us dissolve into nothing.

She hums against me, running her hands up and down my thighs, her eyelids fluttering closed as if she's savoring the taste of me. The vibration of her voice sends shockwaves through my body, building the tension coiling inside me. Is this what magic feels like for her—this rising wave of sensations, this soul-deep connection?

"Natalie," I gasp, tangling my fingers in her hair.

But as we get lost in each other, I can't stop hearing that voice echoing in my mind: *We remember the cages.*

What exactly do the chimeras remember? And why do I have the sinking feeling that there's more to magic than anyone here understands?

The thought flickers at the edges of my consciousness, but then Natalie's fingers join her tongue, and for a little while at least, I let myself forget everything but the feel of her touch and the sound of her name on my lips.

From the Journal of Hazel Okada

When I got home from my date at 7:30 A.M., Katie had already let herself into my apartment with the key I gave her. I scared her so badly when I burst in that a bundle of socks flew out of her hands like popcorn. This startled Ethel, who zoomed around like a rogue firework and knocked over everything on the coffee table.

"Jesus Christ!" Katie shouted, pressing her hand over her heart. "Where've you been? I was getting ready to send out the supernatural SWAT team."

My grin was so big my face hurt. Two days ago in the car, I didn't want to tell her about the girl in the cafe with Natalie there—and anyway, we had bigger things to discuss. But this morning, with just the two of us, I could finally let it all out.

"I met someone," I blurted, my face warm and tingly from the crisp dawn air and the high I was riding. "She's perfect."

Katie gasped and fumbled the socks she was picking up. "Spill!"

"We went out last night, and dinner turned into..." Damn, I was blushing hard. I pulled the neck of my sweater up to my nose as if that would hide it. The memory of Oaklyn's mouth and fingers on every square inch of me made my skin tingle all over again.

"Are you just getting back from your date now?!" Katie checked the time. "Hazel Okada, did you have a fourteen-hour date? On a weeknight?"

I did a giddy tap dance and helped her gather her socks, everything gushing out. "I thought I'd messed it up because I couldn't stop blushing and being awkward all through dinner. I didn't think I'd have a chance with someone so gorgeous, but... I don't know, something sizzled."

I bit my lip. The restaurant had dimmed its lights for the evening, and the candle between us cast shadows over her face, making her eyes glitter. She ordered for both of us—something I would usually hate, but her confidence and suaveness was hot as hell. She'd chosen well, and everything tasted amazing.

"While we were waiting for dessert, she came around the table to sit next to me, and we started making out, and..."

The memory of her sliding into the booth beside me sent a fresh wave of heat flooding through me. The way she pressed against me, her strong body radiating warmth... The taste of her black lipstick and the minty mojito she'd been drinking... The cool brush of her septum piercing against my skin... When she slid her fingers into my hair and tugged, a whimper escaped me, and I swooned so hard I had to grip her thigh to anchor myself.

I'd never wanted someone so desperately on the first date. With Sean, who I thought I was head-over-heels for, it took weeks before I felt ready. But with Oaklyn, I knew from the moment I saw her.

Kissing her felt right. Beneath that tough exterior was a gentleness I'd never experienced. It left me floating and dizzy with the realization that I definitely like women, and I was absolutely going home with her after.

"So after dinner, you went back to her place?" Katie pressed, grinning at my expression, which must have been a little spaced-out.

I raced to help her gather all the belongings she left scattered around during her stay. "Katie, she literally threw me onto her bed. We didn't sleep all night. We caught maybe an hour after the sun started rising."

"Yeah, girl!" Katie reached across the open suitcase to offer a high-five, which I met with enthusiasm.

Yes, I went down on a girl last night! Freaking loved it. And the way she used her tongue and fingers on me? Christ, if I'd known it could be that good, I would've hit on a woman sooner. I've never felt so desired.

"So who is she? What does she do?" Katie asked, folding a hoodie and tucking it into her suitcase.

"She's beautiful, witty, a personal trainer... She seriously looks like she spends all her time in the gym, too..." I sighed, remembering how Oaklyn had pinned my wrists above my head with one hand while the other explored my body. The feel of her hard, toned muscles against me had me melting. "She's twenty and lives on her own in a really nice apartment..."

I bent to pick up Ethel, who wandered over to make a bed in Katie's open luggage. But I regretted that decision as the cat hissed and squirmed away, scratching my arms through my sweater. "Ow!"

"Ethel!" Katie scolded.

"It's okay. She probably smells the dog hair." I plucked a few offending strands off my sleeves.

"Aww, she has a dog? Green flag." Katie nodded in approval.

"Yeah, he's a real sweetie."

As for figuring out whether Oaklyn knew anything about the chimera or witches? Whenever I tried to broach the subject of what happened at the beach, her lips ended up on mine again. Not that I'm complaining. There's always next time—and I am determined to figure her out. Katie managed to pry the truth out of Natalie pretty fast, and I'm going to do the same with Oaklyn. I've got a feeling she's somehow involved in all this.

"What's her name?" Katie asked. She flashed a teasing grin. "Or were your mouths too busy to get each other's names?"

I laughed. Before I could answer, my phone beeped with the distinct sound I assigned to my chimera-alert program—the one indicating that people on social media were discussing strange activity. My heart shot into my throat, my thoughts scattering.

"Oh my God." I fumbled for my phone in my pocket.

"What?" Katie asked, freezing in place.

I squinted at the screen. I hadn't written code to process the output yet, so it took me a second to decipher the XML.

As it clicked, I jumped to my feet. "Chimera. We need to go, now!"

Katie let out a little shriek and ran in a small circle, a bundle of folded pants in her arms. "Where? What is it?"

"People are talking about a pop-up turtle pond in Burnaby."

Katie dropped the bundle of pants. "A pop-up... What?"

"It's a pond that appeared out of nowhere on a dead-end street. People are assuming it's an art installation." I checked the time, and my stomach plummeted. "Blah, I need to go to work."

That annoying grown-up job I was so looking forward to before all this magical chaos entered my life.

Katie grabbed her bag. "That's okay. Go. Text me the location."

"Will do. And text me when you're done so I know you're alive!" I shouted after her as she thundered out the door.

I'll tell her more about Oaklyn later, once the chimera is dealt with. We're going out again tomorrow, and my heart is dancing just thinking about it.

For now, I guess I'll sit at a desk in a boring office building while Katie is out there tackling another chimera. Don't get me wrong—I love this job, and my coworkers are cool. But damn, magic has its temptations.

CHAPTER 12

The Turtle Pond

S TANDING AT THE EDGE of a pond that shouldn't exist, I put my
hands on my hips, the enchanted net dangling from my fingers. Lily
pads float on the surface, reeds sway despite the lack of wind, and the
water shimmers like a mirage in the morning sun.

Pretty. I get why the public assumed it was art. Weird place for an
installation, though. The dead-end street feels forgotten by the city,
cracked pavement giving way to gravel and weeds, while a rusty dumpster
overflows with bits of plastic that skitter over the ground like tumble-
weeds. The pond is an improvement.

My skin prickles with the familiar sensation of nearby magic.

"These streets were wild before your stones claimed them," a voice hisses
in my mind. *"We remember when this was ours."*

Okay, no need to panic, it's just a vaguely threatening disembodied
voice.

I shift in my fake Animal Control shirt, which is stiff and doesn't sit
right across my shoulders. "It's definitely in there. I hear it."

"Voices?" Natalie asks.

I nod once. My palm is sweating on the net. All that practice in the Alchemy lab, and it still feels foreign in my hands.

She steps closer and lays a hand on the small of my back, looking around vigilantly as if to find an explanation.

But I know exactly where it's coming from, and she can deny it all she wants. At our feet, the pond shimmers and swirls like a potion, something alive waiting beneath the surface.

Sky strides over from down the street, her black traveling cloak billowing. "I've cleared the area and put up barricades. No witnesses."

"Thanks for coming," I say. Having backup feels good after what happened last time, though part of me wishes I was alone so no one has to see me floundering. "No Madsens?"

"Not yet, anyway. Let loose, Nat."

Natalie looks at me, checking in, and I nod and step back, gesturing to the pond.

Wasting no time, she raises her hands, her elegant fingers manipulating the earth beneath us. The ground quakes, making me widen my stance for balance, and the water churns as she uses magic to force the creature up.

My stomach roils like the pond. I tighten my grip on the net, trying to remember everything Troy taught me.

Something breaks the surface—a turtle, but not like any I've seen. Iridescent patterns shift and swirl on its shell like oil on water. My breath catches, and for a moment, it feels like I'm looking at an endangered species.

"Now, Katie," Natalie whispers urgently.

Blinking out of my thoughts, I lift my arms, which feel impossibly heavy despite the net's weightlessness—and a voice rings clear in my head: *Your ancestors knew better.*

I freeze. Wait, is it talking about *my* ancestors specifically? The ancestors of witches? Does the chimera know something I don't?

The turtle dives, and Natalie swears. She meets my eyes with a look of concern. "What did it say?"

"Again!" Sky shouts, sparing me from answering. She raises her hands to help her sister, and with a deep *crrrack*, the earth splits. The water swirls like someone's pulled a plug.

My heart races as they destroy the pond, its beauty shattering in an instant as murky water sloshes over the pavement. The sight of it being demolished sends a pang through my chest that I don't fully understand.

Catching a glimpse of the turtle's shell, I splash in after it, my boots sinking into thick mud. The water is shockingly cold, seizing my legs and sending a jolt of pain through my temples.

Before I can throw, the turtle bursts from the water, mud spraying everywhere. It hits my cheeks, cold and gritty, and I swipe my forearm across my eyes to clear them.

The chimera is already changing. Wings sprout from its shell as it becomes a massive eagle, its wingspan casting a shadow over the muddy ground.

I throw the net. It fans out like it's supposed to, the golden threads gleaming in the dim morning sun—but the eagle transforms into a snake that drops fast.

In another life, I would be awed and amazed by how this creature can transform. But my inner voice is screaming at me to hurry and catch it before it's gone.

Fifty-six chimeras. A chimera a day. Five years in prison.

My head swims. I can't breathe.

"Nearly had it!" Natalie shouts. She and Sky move their hands, manipulating rocks and dirt to block the snake's escape. Bits of earth hit my skin, adding more grit to my arms and face.

I lunge, slipping in the mud as I grab the net for another try.

The snake becomes a fish that flops in the draining water, its silvery-purple scales shimmering.

I throw again. My technique is better than before. I'm almost there, the net grazing it each time it shifts.

Mud speckles the gold filaments as I grip it tightly. Another toss.

It transforms into a raccoon that scrambles up the bank, trying to get away from us. Shifting rapidly like Troy said it would.

Natalie and Sky break up the earth, forcing the raccoon back. They're so sure and focused, ignoring the splatters of mud and pond water reaching past their knees.

Then, panic closes around me like a blanket over my mouth, and it's not only my own—the panic of another being fills the air, thick and smothering. It mingles with mine until I don't know which emotions are my own anymore.

"Please... See what we are... Feel our fear..."

"This isn't—I can't—" I don't know what I'm saying or who I'm saying it to. My head is foggy with too many thoughts and emotions.

The chimera transforms into a spotted deer with fuzzy antlers, only thigh-high, like the ones that bow to you in Japan. It trembles in the mud, looking at me with wide, terrified eyes that are far too intelligent—like it knows exactly how to break me.

Tears prickle my eyes as I gather the net, something inside me splintering.

They're dangerous, I tell myself. *They level cities.*

"Think of your freedom, Katie!" Natalie barks.

The word hits me like a bucket of ice water. My freedom. Five years of my life are at stake—five years I'll spend in prison instead of building a life with Natalie, laughing with Hazel, hugging my parents and sisters and Ethel, starting my career and my adult life...

Everything I want, everything I am, is on the other side of whatever doubts are holding me back.

I grit my teeth. This chimera is bio magic, which means it could be manipulating the cells in my brain, making me feel all these confusing emotions. I need to push past it. I refuse to let this chimera go free and spend years in prison for it.

Natalie holds my gaze, her brown eyes pleading. Mud and pond water soak her uniform, and sweat beads on her face as she uses all her strength to help me.

My heart cracks. Sometimes, survival means making impossible choices, and this is one of those times.

With a roar, I hurl the net, putting everything I have into the perfect throw.

It soars, fanning out like a golden web, the weak sun glinting off its threads.

It lands on the fleeing deer, whose knees buckle as if it weighs a ton. Magic pulses, raising the hairs on my arms as it cinches around the deer's hooves.

A terrible sound fills the world—the wail of an animal caught in a trap. It pierces straight through me, making me gasp.

I cover my mouth, gulping down air, my throat too tight to function. Bitter grit coats my lips.

"Yes!" Sky cries, letting her hands drop.

"Y-you did it!" Natalie exclaims, breathing hard.

The net fastens shut like an invisible hand is stitching it, trapping the deer—and a vision of myself behind iron bars flashes through my mind's eye. Both of us caught, both of us caged. By fighting to stay out, I'm forcing others in.

"Please..." the voice grows louder, begging me.

Nausea fills me, and I keep covering my mouth, frozen in place.

The deer thrashes, its hooves tangling in the golden threads that glow brighter with each desperate movement. After several long, horrible seconds, its struggle slows. Its eyelids droop as it loses consciousness, and then it goes limp.

Just like all the others will, I realize with a shiver that wracks my body. *Fifty-five more times, I'll have to make the same choice.*

Natalie grabs my shoulders, a smile breaking across her face. "Nice work, Katie!"

I can't respond. I don't know what to say. A hollowness fills me like nothing I've ever felt.

There's a *thump* down the street, and the three of us turn.

"The barricades," Sky says, raising her palms once more.

An engine roars. A silver FJ Cruiser tears toward us—the Madsens are here to steal what I've caught.

Natalie's palm presses against my back. "Go!"

She picks up the net, grunting under the weight. Maybe she can't use magic to levitate it with a chimera inside.

The sight of her struggling and covered in mud reminds me that I'm not just doing this for myself. This is for us, and for the future we could have. A lump forms in my throat as Natalie pours every drop of energy into this fight.

We sprint to her car, our boots squelching with each step, while Sky plants her feet and raises her palms. The street buckles and cracks beneath the approaching vehicle, jolting it off-course.

The driver's side doors of Natalie's car fly open. I dive across the back seat, and Natalie gets behind the wheel, stuffing the trapped chimera in beside her. She turns the car on and slams her foot down, steering us over to Sky, who hurtles into the back seat and squashes me. Elbows bump faces as we disentangle our limbs, grunting apologies.

We peel away, and my heart pounds as we put distance between us and the pond. *We did it.* We caught one. So why do I feel like throwing up?

"Buckle up," Natalie says, glancing at the rearview mirror. "They're on our tail."

I reach for the seatbelt with trembling hands, my gaze locking onto the deer in the passenger seat. It's lying unconscious with the golden net tangled around it. Its long eyelashes rest against its cheeks, and its ribcage rises and falls in shallow breaths. Its form flickers, like it's starting to revert to the pure, formless state I saw back when I entered the room with all those cages.

Its desperate pleas echo in my mind, making me want to rip away the golden net and set it free. But the image of prison bars flashes across my mind's eye, stopping me. *Five years.* Five years in a cell while Natalie faces the Madsens alone, while everyone I love continues life without me in it.

No. I made my choice.

I force my gaze out the window, where the outside world blurs in a mess of muted colors. I hate this. No matter what I do, I'm hurting someone or something.

I'm sorry, I think, though the apology only makes me feel worse.

"Hey, one down," Natalie says, meeting my eye in the mirror. "We're making progress."

I nod and try to smile. I'm freezing, filthy, in pain...and a step closer to securing my freedom. I should be cheering.

But my chest aches. And I can't help wondering who I'll have to become if I want to save my own life.

From the Journal of Hazel Okada

Tonight, I'm going to Oaklyn's with a plan:

1. Show her the chimera map.

2. Gauge her reaction.

3. Hopefully draw a witchy confession out of her.

And okay, let's be real:

4. Climb her like a tree and strip her naked.

5. Finish exploring all the tattoos she unveiled when I finally got to see what's beneath that leather jacket. She's got the most gorgeous vines winding up her arms, dotted with flowers and butterflies. There's a dagger on one forearm and a snake on the other—and that's as far as I got before she distracted me with other activities.

6. Pillow talk: Find out more about her personal life. On our date, she asked me a lot of questions about myself—life back in Toronto, my favorite classes at U of T, how my new job is going—but she seemed uncomfortable whenever I turned the conversation back to her.

"How are you finding living here?" she asked while we shared a tapenade crostini appetizer. "Homesick yet?"

"It's okay so far," I said honestly, skipping over the fact that I haven't had time to feel homesick with all the magical chaos going on. "My best friend is going to UBC, so at least I have her. My mom also calls every day whether I like it or not. She usually catches me right when I'm eating dinner."

Oaklyn stared into her red wine, swirling it. "Nice she cares."

"That's a good way of looking at it," I said with a little laugh. Though something in her expression made me wonder. "You close with your family?"

She hesitated. "My family isn't a good first-date topic."

"Sorry," I said automatically, my face heating up.

"It's fine," she said with a half-smile. But her eyes were sad. "It's just my mom and me. Sometimes it feels like life isn't fair. But nights like this make up for it... Like maybe I do have luck on my side once in a while."

The heat in my face intensified. Well, that was sweet. Hard to believe I could be important to a woman like her.

She shrugged out of her jacket then, gracing me with the first glimpse of her tattoos—a purple butterfly on her shoulder.

"Does it mean something?" I asked.

"Maybe," she said before taking a sip of her drink.

"You're very mysterious, you know that?" I said teasingly.

"I won't deny there's a lot you don't know about me yet," she replied, a challenge in her eyes that made my heart race.

It's the "yet" that gets me—the promise that we have time to get to know each other. The hope that she might actually want me to learn her secrets.

That's when she leaned in and gave me the kiss I haven't been able to get out of my brain. The head-spinning, life-changing kiss that had me melting into a puddle, her lips soft yet demanding against mine. Her hand cupped my face gently, but her fingers were strong, her body arching into me like she was promising how the evening would go when I went back to her place later.

Kissing her was so different, like discovering a new color on the spectrum, one I'd always known about but had never been able to see. She unlocked something inside me and opened a door to feelings I never knew existed. I guess I've been repressing part of myself, forcing myself to fit into a mold... But some things can't be explained with logic or algorithms. Sometimes you just know, deep in your soul, when something feels right.

CHAPTER 13

Scarier than a Monster

T HE METAL DOOR TO the bio magic containment room creaks open, its swirling designs gleaming in the dim lamplight. Vines and purple flowers encroach on the arched frame, just as I remember it. The serpentine handle has been repaired since I smashed it—and now here I am, returning a piece of the magic I risked everything to set free.

Troy has joined us in a wheelchair, his pride and excitement giving him a burst of energy as he guides Natalie and Sky through the next steps. As they secure the chimera in one of the cold metal cages, its deer form flickers like a dying candle, revealing glimpses of other shapes—feathers, scales, fur.

I avert my gaze, a fresh wave of guilt rolling through me. The room is suffocating, the threat of being caged behind iron bars like these all too real.

Shivering, I step back as they remove the golden net, and Troy murmurs words I don't understand. As the sleeping chimera takes its pure form—the shapeshifting creature that human eyes can't comprehend—I turn my back, wanting to escape this room as fast as possible. Its magic prickles my skin, making the mud caked on my arms and face even more uncomfortable.

We leave it in the cage to sleep. Trapped forever.

"Well done, girls," Troy says, smiling at his daughters. His eyes crinkle at the corners. "And you, Katie. Capturing a chimera without a drop of magic in you? Unheard of! I've got my eye on you."

I try to smile but can't even manage a fake one. Catching this chimera was supposed to bring me a step closer to freedom and show these witches what I'm capable of. But instead of feeling happy and proud, I'm just...hollow. And afraid that after I've poured my energy into trapping every chimera, karma will come for me and trap me too.

I can't believe I have to do that again and again. How am I supposed to keep catching something that's begging me not to? Will I have a heart left after this is all done?

Natalie, on the other hand, hasn't stopped beaming. She wraps her arm around my shoulders and guides me out the door, warm and sturdy at my side. "I'm sure you'll feel more like celebrating after we've gotten cleaned up. Come on. Hot shower time."

A shower sounds luxurious. I pick at the itchy mud on my arms, watching it flake off and add to the trail our boots are leaving in the hallway.

We wave goodbye to her family and head back to her room, the net dangling from my fist.

"We did it," she says to me, sounding happier than she has in days. "You were more confident this time. I could see it. The way you kept track of the chimera... I hope you know how amazing your ability is, Katie."

"I think you're overstating what I did. I just threw the net. Badly." And listened to it pleading with me. And felt its terror. And ignored both.

"You can sense where these things are, and that makes all the differ-ence. I don't think you realize how good you are at tracking it."

Interesting. Could this be true?

"You're doing the right thing," Natalie says, squeezing my hand. "Try to think of how good it will feel to prove to Fiona that she was wrong about you. That you're as good as any Tracker."

Picturing Fiona's shocked face as I stand before her and prove her wrong does make me feel a bit better. I crack a smile.

"But I still need practice with the net. Look at us. This is less than ideal." I gesture to our muddy skin and clothes.

Natalie nudges me. "You did fine!"

"I got lucky." I chew my lip. "Maybe if I come up with a contraption or something... I mean, I know Trackers have spent generations perfecting their tools, but they're witches who can send nets flying through the air with total precision. I'm just a non-magical girl with no coordination or athleticism. Maybe I can figure out a way to use the net better."

She raises an eyebrow. "Like what?"

"Well..." An idea sparks, though I might already know the answer. "Any chance Hazel could come down here temporarily? Just to help me come up with ideas?"

Natalie's eyes widen in surprise.

Before she can argue, I add, "You know as well as I do that she's the brains of this operation. I need her help. You said yourself that technol-ogy has become better than magic in some ways. Maybe we can invent something amazing that will keep me out of prison."

Natalie purses her lips. But to my astonishment, she nods. "Okay."

I look at her sharply, stunned. "Really?"

She lifts her shoulder. "I know it's hard for you being a non-magical person in the coven. I want you to feel supported. We'll pick a time when the Directors are busy—Fiona and Agnes, at least—and smuggle Hazel down so you can come up with a plan. Sound good?"

Relief trickles through me. "Yes."

Wow, I can't wait to tell Hazel she's allowed to come to C.S.A.M.M. She's going to be so excited. And while we're working, I can hear all about this dreamy new girl who's sweeping her off her feet.

At the door of Natalie's suite, she presses her palm to the lock to let us in. The second we step inside, she takes the net from me and drops it on the floor. She cups my face in both hands, her eyes searching mine. "I'm continually amazed by you, Katie Alexander."

Before I can argue, she kisses me, gently capturing my lips with hers.

I soften, leaning into her. The guilt crushing me eases a little, and as her fingers graze my neck, it's easier to forget the chimera's pleas. Her touch grounds me in the present, reminding me what I'm fighting for.

And I guess it *is* worth celebrating that I've caught one. One down, fifty-five to go. The math is overwhelming, but at least we've crossed the starting line.

"We should—get cleaned up—" she says between kisses, pausing to tug a lock of my mud-caked hair.

I glance at the large shower and cock an eyebrow, reaching for the buttons on her fake uniform. The fabric is damp and gritty beneath my fingers, and I can feel her heart racing.

A hungry look flashes in her eyes. "I like where this is going."

We stumble to the shower, leaving a trail of muddy clothes on the floor. Our hands never leave each other's bodies, as if breaking contact might shatter the fragile bubble of peace we've created.

Her shower is full of plants—ferns, vines, moss, and flowers grow right out of the stone walls, all thriving in the humid air. A copper rainfall shower head hangs in the center, and as she turns it on, steam billows and curls like a protective veil.

Her lips stay on mine and her hands roam down my bare waist as she backs me into the stream. A pleasant ripple cascades through me as the hot water hits my head and trickles down my back and chest, rinsing away traces of our battle with the chimera. But my muscles ache and the chimera's pleas still echo in my mind, and no amount of water can wash that away.

Natalie steps closer, her hands on my hips, pressing her forehead against mine. We stand like that for a moment, letting steam swirl around us.

"You're bleeding," she whispers, noticing a scratch on my arm I hadn't felt. She reaches for a jar of something on a stone shelf and dabs it gently over the cut. Her touch is gentle, and the salve sends a cooling, pleasant sensation rippling outward.

"I'm fine," I murmur, but I don't stop her. I don't mind this—being tended to by her. Being cared for.

"I know today was hard," she says, her fingers tracing the ridge of my collarbone. "I saw it on your face."

I swallow, surprised she noticed. "I don't know if I can do this fifty-five more times, Natalie."

"You can." Her eyes find mine, water droplets clinging to her lashes. "Because I'm going to be right beside you for every single one."

I kiss her again, deeper than before, like I'm trying to absorb her strength to get me through the coming days. Careful to avoid her cuts and bruises, I run my hands over her wet skin, my strange sixth sense picking up on the contrast between us—the magic pulsing through her veins, and my ordinary heart pounding against my ribs.

She backs me up further, her tongue dipping into my mouth, and I gasp as my bare back meets the cool stone and soft plant leaves. She pulls back, grinning, looking irresistible with beads of water rolling down her cheekbones, neck, shoulders, and breasts. Moments like this are my favorite—when she's not a powerful witch and a Guardian, but just Natalie, normal and vulnerable and *mine*.

I trail my fingers over her breasts and down the curve of her waist, closing my eyes to let the water wash away my fears about what's going to happen to me. No worrying about chimeras, about my future, or what it means that I can hear things Natalie can't. None of that matters right now. The world narrows to her lips and fingers, our bodies sliding together, warm steam wrapping around us, moss tickling my back.

I glide my hands down her soaked back, over her toned curves, around her thighs, and between her legs. She moans and tilts her head back, looking like a goddess as her skin glistens under the falling water.

"I need you," I whisper against her neck, and I mean it on multiple levels. I need her strength, her belief in me, her certainty that I belong here despite everything.

Wanting to taste her, I sink to my knees. She knots her fingers in my hair to guide me, making delicious noises that echo off the stone walls and send shivers through me. Her legs are warm beneath my palms, her inner thigh soft against my cheek, her scent driving me wild. Hot water beads down my face, over my breasts, and between my legs, awakening my every nerve ending.

"You're so perfect," I murmur against her, kissing and tonguing her until she's gasping for air. It's overwhelming how much I love her—her strength, her determination, her willingness to fight for me when no one else will.

"Katie—" is all she can manage.

I stay on my knees for as long as she can take it, drawing out her pleasure, wanting to give her everything I have. Moments like these, I'm not worried about whether I'm good enough for the coven or whether I can catch all the chimeras. I'm good enough for Natalie, and that's what matters.

When she comes, she braces herself against the wall and my shoulder, her knees trembling like she's fighting to stay standing.

I can never get enough of her in this state—totally letting go, losing control, forgetting who she's supposed to be for a few blissful minutes.

This is the side of her that only I get to see, and I'll never stop cherishing it.

After, we lay naked on her bed, overheated and flushed. I rest my head on her chest, listening to her heartbeat gradually slow to a steady rhythm as she traces circles on my bare shoulder. My earlier worries about trapping the chimera don't seem so bad, and my fear about having to do this fifty-five more times seems less relevant when I'm safely here with Natalie.

And that's the thing about being with her. I always feel safe. I feel *loved*. Even with everything hanging over us, she makes me feel like I belong.

I need to tell her. I faced my fears today, and I can do it again right now. The words have been building inside me for months, growing stronger with every video call, every text, every moment apart that only confirmed what I already knew.

"Natalie?" I murmur.

She kisses my temple, her lips lingering there. "Yeah?"

My heart jumps into action knowing what's coming. It slams into my ribs so hard that she must feel it. After everything—the chimeras, my trial, the Madsens—this might be the scariest moment of all. Because this is what has the power to truly hurt me.

What if this changes things? What if it makes all this even more painful? What if...

She leans back a little to look down at me, a concerned crease between her eyebrows. "What?"

Stop it, Katie. I can't keep letting fear prevent me from saying this.

"I—" My mouth is dry. I swallow hard and try again. "I'm completely in love with you."

There's a pause in which my life flashes before my eyes—or maybe just our relationship. Every minute we've spent together since the moment I saw her through my balaclava in that vet's office. The look in her eyes when we went thrift shopping for curses for the first time. The way she so easily steps between me and the Madsens. The pain in her eyes when she told me we couldn't be together, and the joy when she finally gave in. And then—

"I love you too!" she exclaims.

There's no mistaking the flood of relief in her voice.

I sit up, a smile breaking across my face. "You do?"

"Of course!" She laughs, an elated, almost giddy sound that I've never heard from her before. "I've wanted to tell you. I didn't know if...with the timing of everything..."

"I know." I lean down and kiss her once, twice, three times on the lips. "The timing is never good. But knowing we have each other... It helps me get through it. I want you to know how much I love you. How much it means to have you with me through all this."

She tugs me back down beside her and wraps her body around me, holding me tightly. "We've got this. We'll show Fiona and everyone here what you're capable of."

"And we'll take down the last of the fucking Madsens," I say, lacing my fingers through hers where they rest against my stomach.

Natalie huffs out a breath of laughter, but there's no humor in it. "The fucking Madsens."

I exhale slowly, my heartbeat returning to normal. With Natalie and Hazel in my corner, I feel like I could face anything—fifty-five more chimeras, the Madsens, Fiona and her jury. It's only May 6th, and though the plan to catch a chimera per day is already off-track, I've got a week before term starts and several weeks after that to figure this all out. It's not entirely hopeless.

"Question..." I tangle our legs together, needing to feel as much of her against me as possible. "When you said you want to leave here, where do you see yourself living?"

She squeezes me tighter, her lips brushing my neck. "I pictured us in a cottage."

My heart jumps at being included in her plan. "Really?"

"Mhm. Not so far away that the commute becomes a chore, but far enough to feel like we've got a place all our own. We'd have a vegetable garden, maybe some chickens."

I smile. "Would you use magic to help the garden along?"

"Oh, of course. Once you taste magically grown zucchini, there's no going back."

"Good. I'd also like to request a willow tree. I love the one here."

"That can be arranged." She props herself up on one elbow, looking down at me with a seriousness that makes my heart skip. "I want you to know that I'm not just saying this. I've thought about it a lot. I want a place that's ours, where we can just be us."

Warmth blooms in my chest. "That sounds perfect."

Her eyes crinkle at the corners. "So you like it?"

I kiss her hand and sink deeper into her. "Living in a cottage with my witch girlfriend? I can think of nothing better."

But as I picture this perfect future, an unbearable sadness presses down on me. It feels too good to be true. Fragile at best. And like the entire magical world is standing in our way.

From the Journal of Hazel Okada

Oaklyn's place is as fascinating as she is. It's minimal because she moved in recently, but the sparse decor draws me in like I'm at an art gallery. Nearly everything is black—wardrobe, bedspread, towels, dishes. Dried flowers hang in the window, their deep purple petals like bruises against the white sky. But among all the darkness are signs of life—potted herbs line the windowsills, well-used copper cookware gleams above the kitchen island, and the odd tuft of dog fur floats across the hardwood floor.

Most fascinating of all is the collection of pressed butterflies under glass covering her dining table, all an incredible shade of purple.

"My brother and I used to catch them," she explained, turning away to hide the sheen in her eyes. "Most of those were his."

I wanted to ask more, but something in her expression told me not to push. Not yet.

It was our second date. I sat at a bar stool while she cooked me dinner, mesmerized by the way she expertly prepared a red wine-braised pot roast without following a recipe. She'd removed the potatoes from the Dutch oven and transferred them to a baking sheet, smashing each one with a wooden spoon before topping it with butter and spices. The kitchen smelled heavenly, like wine and broth and sage.

"I wanted to ask you more about what we saw in White Rock," I said, propping my elbows on the island.

She stiffened, her shoulders tensing beneath her black tank top. Like she was afraid I was close to uncovering a secret.

She turned her back to me to adjust the oven temperature. "What about it?"

"It was weird, right? And it's not the first time something totally unusual has happened lately."

"Yeah." She slid the tray of potatoes into the oven, drawing my gaze to the rippling muscles on her shoulder blades. "A lot of theories floating around."

A pause. No elaboration or eye contact. Time to get to the point.

"I've been tracking them all with software, in case someone might find it useful," I said, trying to sound casual.

She faced me again, studying me closely. "Really?"

My heart skipped as she pierced me with those blue eyes. Something vulnerable was buried beneath her intensity, making me want to reach out and tell her she could trust me with whatever she was hiding.

I reached for my phone. "Do you want to see?"

Slowly, she walked around the island toward me, moving as gracefully as a cat stalking prey. "Yes."

I showed her the map, and she was very quiet. Unreadable. She just watched me point out chimera sightings and run an analysis on where one might appear next. A new prediction popped up since the last time I ran it.

"Huh. Next one should show up around Squamish," I said, making a mental note to tell Katie.

"You're so smart," Oaklyn said, her voice a little faint.

I flushed. "Thanks."

She took the phone out of my hand and set it on the island, stepping close. She looked down at me in a way that made me melt like I was just another slab of butter over a hot potato.

"I like smart girls," she said.

I smiled. "You go for the nerds, huh?"

She tilted her head, a little smirk on her lips. "I like that you see the world in patterns. You notice things others don't. And yeah, I guess I find your nerdy side pretty cute."

I laughed.

Crap, was it wrong of me to try and pry secrets out of her? Was I being manipulative?

But I'm not just going out with her because I think she's a witch. I like her regardless—her confidence, her charm, the way she looks at me like I'm a snack. The way she listens to me with her whole attention, leaning into every word. I just think that if she is a witch, she should know I'm someone she can confide in. I know about magic, and she can trust me to keep her secrets.

My plan to get a witchy confession out of her, however, was dissolving under the molten heat of her touch. She pushed my thighs apart and stepped between my legs, bending to graze her lips over mine.

"Thank you for showing me that," she murmured into my lips. "I like seeing your creations...learning how your mind works..."

"N-no problem," I stammered, losing the ability to form coherent thoughts as she teased me with her tongue.

She toyed with my waistband, her fingers brushing the sensitive skin at my hips. "Makes me want to do naughty things to you."

My heartbeat quickened, and I squirmed. "Like what?"

"Like lick you from head to toe." She planted a gentle, teasing kiss on my lips.

"Uh-huh. And then what?" I was breathless, my body responding to her every touch.

"Then..." Another peck. "Once you're shaking beneath me, I'll reward your patience and lick you right here..." She cupped a hand between my legs, making me let out a soft, hungry noise.

"I'll start off slow," she murmured in my ear, tonguing my earlobe, "licking you so softly that you'll be begging me to let you finish. I will...but I won't be done with you yet. Before you've caught your breath, I'll get on top of you and slide my fingers inside you. I'll fuck you until you're clinging to me with your thighs and screaming my name. I'll make you come again and again until you can't take it anymore."

I became feral after that, grabbing her hair and wrapping my legs around her hips. We started clawing at each other, leaving a trail of clothes between the kitchen and bedroom.

She kept her promise, making me come until I lost count. I did the same for her, devouring her like I was ravenous, relishing the sight of her lying sweaty and out of breath on the tangled sheets.

Afterward, as we lay in a daze, I traced my fingers over the tattoo on her shoulder—the purple butterfly that matched the ones in her collection.

"Your brother," I said softly. "Is he...?"

"Gone," she replied, her voice tight. She didn't elaborate.

I nodded, pressing a kiss to her shoulder. "I'm sorry."

She turned to kiss me back tenderly, something soft and unreadable behind her eyes.

I know, I know, I still haven't gotten an answer out of her about the chimeras or witches. We keep getting distracted by...other activities. But I'm not expecting her to spill that secret easily. It took Katie's near-abduction before Natalie was forced to tell her she's a witch, so I expect that whatever Oaklyn is hiding from me won't be easy to pry out of her either.

I'm okay with that. I've got time...and I'm enjoying the process. In due course, I intend to learn everything I can about this amazing and mysterious woman.

CHAPTER 14

Katie and Hazel's School of Questionable Inventions

"WE'VE GOT TWENTY MINUTES left to revolutionize chimera-catching, and this isn't looking good," I tell Hazel, scanning the carnage. Sweat prickles under my T-shirt, and I pluck it away from my chest to let some air in.

"This one will work," Hazel assures me, pushing back the hair plastered to her face. "Pass me the duct tape."

I wade through the tools, toys, and sports equipment, stepping on a rubber duck in a top hat that somehow made it into the pile, and hand her the nearly empty roll.

Two hours have flown by since Natalie smuggled her in, and the pair of us are alone in the same Alchemy lab Natalie and I used, frantically trying to reinvent a century of chimera-catching techniques before Fiona is done meeting with the Shadows. A T-shirt cannon sits defeated between a tangled fishing rod and a bow and arrow. And those were our more successful attempts.

Hazel suppresses a yawn as she winds the duct tape around a hockey stick. The bags under her eyes and the dreamy smile she's been fighting all afternoon tell me all I need to know.

"Long night?" I ask teasingly.

Her smile breaks free like she's been dying for me to ask. "She's a *dream*, Katie. My jaw is sore."

I laugh as she keeps winding tape with a loud *rrrip*.

"Have you done any actual talking between all the face-sucking?" I ask, going to collect the net from where it got hung up on a bookshelf. (Fun fact: a leaf blower will explode if you try to launch an enchanted net out of it.)

"We talked!" Hazel says defensively, then flushes. "For a few minutes."

With both ends of a bungee cord taped to hockey sticks, I grab the middle and walk back. "What'd you learn?"

Hazel holds the hockey sticks vertically and ducks her head while I put tension on the bungee.

"Well, she loves cooking and gardening… Used to have a pet snake…" Her voice softens. "Sounds like her family life is rough, to be honest. Not a great relationship with her mom, her dad died when she was little, and her brother died recently. The dog was his."

"Damn. That's really sad."

I ball up the golden net and lay it against the bungee, chewing my lip. This *might* work?

What we've essentially made is a giant slingshot. The idea is to launch the net much higher into the air than I'd be able to do by hand. Aiming, however, might get interesting. This is either a genius invention or the most absurd fucking thing ever to exist within the walls of C.S.A.M.M. And that's saying something, considering I once set eyes on cursed bag-pipes.

"I know," Hazel says, her arms straining as she fights against my pull. "She feels like Wyatt is one of the only tangible parts of him she has left."

I freeze, the name sending a chill through me. "Wyatt?"

She must hear something in my tone because her brow pinches. "Yeah."

Coincidence. Must be. Wyatt is a common enough name. Except...

Dead brother, dead father, shitty mother...

"What kind of dog is he?" I ask, the hairs on my neck prickling.

"German Shepherd."

My fingers fail me, and I let go of the bungee. Hazel stumbles. The golden net flies into the air, hits the ceiling fan, whips around a few times, and smacks into the wall. The ivy ripples and shudders as if offended.

No. No, no, no.

My heart is beating out of my chest. My lips are numb. "Hazel, what's your girlfriend's name?"

The confusion on her face intensifies. "Oaklyn."

I step back. "Oh my God. Tell me you're joking."

She drops the hockey sticks with a clatter. Her eyes glint with excitement. "You know her?"

I lunge for her, knocking some ping-pong paddles off the table, and grab her flannel shirt in my fists. "Hazel! You're dating a Madsen!"

"I—" She splutters. The excitement vanishes as quickly as it came, replaced by blank shock. "No I'm not."

"Tall, pale, could bench press both of us at the same time?"

"Th-that could describe..." She falters, and the color drains from her face as realization begins to take hold.

"Septum piercing? Razor lines in her eyebrows?" I shout, pulling her closer. "Black hair—"

"What the hell?!" Hazel shrieks, tap dancing like she's landed in a pit of cockroaches. "No. That's not... She can't be..."

I release her. "She wrote the note on the cursed plushie that nearly *murdered* you!"

"FUCK!"

We're both screaming, our voices carrying into the high ceiling.

"Did you not clue in that her last name is Madsen?" I shout.

"Her last name hasn't come up! I've only gone out with her twice!" Hazel presses her palms against her temples. Her eyes dart across the floor like she's reviewing every interaction, searching for clues she missed.

I let out a sound like a deflating balloon and drag my hands down my face. This is my fault for not telling Hazel more about the Madsens. I should have at least told her their names. God dammit, I should have shown her an entire PowerPoint presentation titled 'The Madsens: A Comprehensive Guide to the Family That's Trying to Kill Me.' Screw the coven and their secrets.

Hazel doubles over, hands on knees. "I'm gonna puke. Where did that bucket go?"

She scans the pile of stuff. I offer her a mosaic planter, but she waves it away.

"What do I do?" she moans.

I set down the planter and wave my arms. "Ghost her! Block her!"

"But—" She straightens up, staring at me with huge eyes. "But I care about her."

I freeze, trying to process this sequence of words in reference to Oaklyn fucking Madsen.

"She's been lying to you!" I cry. "She's not a personal trainer, she's a criminal!"

"But she's been so nice! She makes me food and cuddles me and..." She balls her fists over her mouth, her eyes growing glassy and distant.

I splutter and flail my arms as if to swat these words right out of the air. "She kept Natalie's dad caged in a basement!"

My ears ring from all the screaming. This is surreal. My genius best friend is dating a literal murderer and didn't know it.

Hazel turns and begins stress-organizing everything on the table, her hands shaking.

I draw a few deep breaths to calm my racing pulse. "You haven't mentioned me, have you?"

"Like I said, not a lot of time spent talking."

"Okay. Good."

There's a chance we can get Hazel out of this mess before something bad happens.

We stare at each other. A long, uncertain moment passes.

"Didn't you say the dog is *sweet*?" I blurt, scrabbling through my memory to fit the pieces together.

"Yeah. He cuddles up with us when we watch a movie. Puts his fuzzy paw on my leg."

"What the fuck..." I whisper.

Is the dog different now that Freddie's dead? Did their telepathic connection make him aggressive? Or is the dog only vicious on command, and when he's off-duty, he's a snuggle-bug?

My ankle throbs, the memory of his jaws still fresh after all this time.

When Hazel doesn't immediately reach for her phone to delete Oaklyn from her life, nausea churns in my gut.

"Are you going to keep seeing her?" I ask.

She hesitates. Keeps stress-organizing. The screwdrivers are all perfectly lined up now.

"The fact you're even thinking about this is a little concerning, Hazel."

"You don't know the other side of her." Her voice is soft. Too soft. "She's really hurting since—"

"Why are you talking about her like she's a human being?" I snap.

She faces me, folding her arms tightly. "She *is* a human being!"

"She tried to kill both of us!" I cry. I pace in a circle, shaking out my hands.

Then, a critical question zips through my mind like an angry wasp: does Oaklyn know who Hazel is, and is she using Hazel to get to me?

My blood turns to ice as I imagine her becoming another hostage like Troy, locked away in some dark basement. The Madsens have already proven there's no limit to what they'll do—and now they have their claws in my best friend.

I fumble for my phone.

"What are you doing?" Hazel asks.

"Calling Natalie." I tap her name and put the call on speaker.

Hazel covers her face. "*Please* don't give her the full details. This is mortifying."

I nod.

"Everything okay?" Natalie answers after half a ring.

The fact that this is her greeting says a lot about the state of our lives.

"Hazel's new girlfriend is Oaklyn Madsen," I say, pinching the bridge of my nose to ward off the headache threatening to come on. "She's here with me. We just realized it."

There is a long pause. So long that I check to make sure the call didn't disconnect.

"Do you think Oaklyn planned this?" she asks at last.

I meet Hazel's eye—and read the flash of pain in her expression. Sympathy hits me like a punch. A minute ago, she was head-over-heels, gushing to me with that dreamy smile. If she was being used all this time...

"It's possible. But it's also possible that Oaklyn has no idea who she ended up on a date with." I assumed they met via a dating app, but Hazel never actually said this. I lower the phone to address her. "Where'd you two meet?"

"In the cafe in White Rock, after you arrived to deal with the pig."

I squint at her. "So you saw someone just hanging out near a chimera, sipping a coffee, and didn't think she might be somehow connected to it all?"

"Well—I did, kind of." Hazel twists her fingers together, looking everywhere but at me. "I thought she might be a witch, and I intended to ask her about it. But we've been...too busy to talk about that..."

I try not to picture my best friend going down on Oaklyn fucking Madsen, focusing on the more important problem. "Did you mention that you were with me and Natalie that day?"

"No," Hazel says quickly. "I told her nothing."

"Okay. Natalie, there's a chance Oaklyn doesn't know Hazel is connected to us."

Natalie is quiet, probably unconvinced.

"You think she should cut contact?" I ask.

The gym door whips open, and Hazel and I both spin with startled gasps. I reach for the nearest object to use as a weapon and come up with a Sharpie.

But it's just Natalie, who ends our call as she uses magic to shut the door behind her. She glances around at the mess before storming over and stopping in front of us with her arms crossed. Her expression is grim.

"Hi." I set down the Sharpie and pocket my phone with trembling hands.

"Don't cut contact," she tells Hazel. "Not yet, anyway. If Oaklyn has no idea who you are, we can use this. How would you feel about learning what the Madsens are up to for us?"

Hazel's eyes go huge. "I—I don't know if I can be a spy!"

My breath catches. This is the *Madsens* we're talking about, and it's a terrible plan. I hold my palm up to Natalie. "I don't think we should drag her deeper into this."

Not to mention how cruel it is to ask Hazel to start *using* the person she was falling for.

"I know it's asking a lot," Natalie says. "But we need to do whatever we can to stop the Madsens, and having an inside woman could change everything."

I chew my lip. It isn't like Natalie to put someone in danger. She fought her hardest to keep me away from this world and insists on protecting me at every turn. The situation must be seriously dire for her to suggest this.

"You're smart enough to pull this off," I tell Hazel. "All the spy novels you read as a kid, yeah?"

"That's not exactly the same as being a real spy!" she squeaks.

She's right, and in truth, I don't like this plan at all. I don't want Hazel fucking around with the Madsens—in any sense of the word.

"First, we need to figure out whether Oaklyn is using Hazel to get to us," Natalie says. "Then we can go from there."

Hazel leans against the table, looking stunned. A broken umbrella clatters to the floor. "What, so if she starts asking too many questions about my friends, I should fake food poisoning and get the hell out?"

Natalie hesitates, her dark eyes troubled. "I wouldn't ask you to do this if we had another option. You're the closest person to the Madsens we've ever had."

"We do have another option, and that's to not ask Hazel to do this!" I say, watching Hazel closely as her love life crashes down around her. Again.

"Katie, you know as well as I do how desperately we need to catch Oaklyn and Sophia," Natalie says.

Hazel and I stare at each other, silent. An entire conversation passes between us in one look. What if? Why? Why *not*?

I don't know what to tell her. If Oaklyn finds out...

Then again, what if Hazel helps us win the war against the Madsens? This would be huge—for her, for me, for *everyone*.

"Oh my God," she says suddenly, throwing her hands over her mouth.

"What?" I cry.

"I—I told Oaklyn where the next chimera might show up," she says into her hands. "I showed her the map and... I guess that's why she was so interested in it..."

The words hit me like ice water.

Natalie swears.

I sprint for the golden net, snatching it up from where it landed in a tangled heap against the wall. "Why are we still standing here? Let's go!"

Hazel spins to the table full of junk. "With what?!"

"Which contraption worked the best?" Natalie asks.

"None of them!" Hazel and I shout together.

"Then we'll have to do it like last time." Natalie abandons our inventions and races for the door, pulling out her phone. "I'm calling Sky."

Before running after her, I bend and grab the bow and arrow off the floor. Just in case.

From the Journal of Hazel Okada

Today, I learned two things:

1. My girlfriend is not, in fact, a witch.

2. My girlfriend is one of the people who's been trying to murder Katie.

I should probably stop calling her my girlfriend.

My brain and heart are pummeling each other, trying to win the battle of how I'm supposed to feel. Part of me wants to vomit. Another part of me wants to scream and throw something. And underneath it all, a voice keeps hissing: how did you miss this? You, who notices everything, who catalogs details and has entire notebooks full of lists. Was I that desperate to be wanted?

The betrayal sits heavy in my chest, squeezing my heart. Every moment with Oaklyn is replaying in my head through a different lens, cataloging all the evidence I missed. Was every smile, kiss, and touch fake? When I showed her my chimera tracking map and she called me smart, kissed me and got all flirty, was that just manipulation? Has her seduction been a strategy, reducing me to the gullible fool who couldn't resist a pretty girl?

Fuck. I can't believe this is happening.

I'm sitting in Natalie's car in a hiking area in Squamish while everything collapses around me. Oaklyn, her mom, and Wyatt were already here when we arrived. My heart seized when I saw them stalking through the trees. Seeing Oaklyn in this context, coiled like a predator, a scowl twisting her face, was an out-of-body experience—like looking at a stranger wearing the face of someone I thought I knew.

There was no time to process. They saw us pull up, and Natalie and Sky leaped out to meet their attack. Beside me in the back seat, Katie grabbed the golden net and bow.

When I tried to climb out with her, she put her hand on my shoulder and stopped me. "If Oaklyn finds out you're with us, she might kill you."

The words burned like acid. I couldn't be sure how true that was, and damn, that hurt.

Knowing who Oaklyn is does make me a little afraid of her, I admit. The logical part of my brain is screaming at me to stay far away from her and block her number.

But...

Would she actually hurt me? Since we met, she's only made me feel more amazing than I've ever felt in my life. If it was all a ruse, she's a very good actor. She's called me beautiful, wonderful, amazing. She opened up to me, even cried a little when she told me about losing her brother. She's kissed me all over, caressed my skin when we cuddled, worshipped my body in a way nobody else has... And I've done the same for her. It's hard to believe she might throw that all away. That it might have never been real.

Can someone fake that level of intimacy?

But outside, there's a whole other Oaklyn—one who hurts people, who has no problem with murder, who will go to any length to get what she wants. The possibility that I was just a convenient path to Katie makes anger bubble up so hot I can taste it. When we cuddled in bed, skin against skin, was she just enduring it until she could use me to get to Katie? When she told me about her brother and tears welled in her eyes, was that real grief or a performance?

I couldn't be sure about any of it.

So I let Katie slam the door on me. I sank down in the back seat, as useless as ever when it comes to playing with witches. A bystander. A sidekick. A chess piece.

While more capable people are fighting outside, Katie with that ridiculous bow-and-net contraption and the others throwing bits of earth at each other like the world's deadliest snowball fight, I'm just…sitting here with my pen and notebook.

Oh, did I mention the chimera has taken the form of an actual griffin? Beak that could swallow a baby hippo, lion body with ropey muscles, wingspan to match a jet.

Seriously, nothing surprises me anymore. I should've brought popcorn.

Katie's made a few decent shots, but she's no Katniss Everdeen. The net keeps plopping back to the ground, and the griffin is casually flying from treetop to treetop like this is a game.

Natalie and Sophia have paired off, blasting each other with earth. The ground rumbles beneath the car, a charge in the air lifting strands of hair off my shoulders. Sky and Oaklyn are also going at it, and…

Wait. Holy shit, is Oaklyn a witch after all?

No, Katie would have told me.

But I swear she's got a wand or something. A knife? Whatever it is, she's shooting roots out of it. I wonder if she would let me try using that thing.

Ugh, listen to me. Still thinking I'm going to see her again while she tries to kill my friend. What's wrong with me?

Ouch, she totally smoked Sky in the gut with a root ball, and now Wyatt is making a snack out of Sky's leg. The same dog that cuddled me on the couch and licked my cheek now looks like a wolf tearing into prey.

Jesus, I'm sitting here with a pen in my hand when I could be helping.

You know what? Fuck this. I'm scribbling in a notebook, watching my best friend and the girl who's possibly been analyzing me like a lab specimen try to kill each other while an actual griffin flies overhead.

I could stay in this car like a good little normie, or I can act. Maybe I can't do magic, but I can do something better: I can make Oaklyn trust me. It might be dangerous, and it might shatter what's left of my heart, but at least it's doing something.

Time to find out if Oaklyn has been tricking me.

And if she has... Well, she's not the only one who can wear a convincing mask.

CHAPTER 15

Griffin-Sized Problems

MAN, I AM *ON fire* with this bow and arrow. Katniss Everdeen is in the house, bitches! Sure, I haven't actually hit the chimera with the net yet, but I'm better equipped than last time.

I nock the arrow again and take aim at the griffin perched on a huge fir tree. The mountain air fills my wheezing lungs, and pine needles crunch under my boots as I crouch beside a mossy boulder. I need to move fast—between the cliffs and the temperate rainforest on all sides, the chimera could disappear with a flap of its wings. Not to mention Natalie and Sky blasting the shit out of Sophia and Oaklyn strides away.

Just like in the Alchemy lab, I tell myself, pulling back the bowstring with trembling arms. *Except instead of a target on the wall, you're trying to shoot a mythical creature that can shapeshift into literally anything.*

Okay, I'm terrible at pep talks.

Sweat beads on my forehead, mixing with the cold drizzle of rain. I exhale and release the string, and it makes a *twang*, raking my inner arm.

The arrow soars, the net streaming behind it like a golden comet. It helps that my target is enormous, but the griffin dives at the last moment, wings folded tightly to its sides. The arrow sails past before losing momentum and plummeting back to earth.

"Dammit!" I sprint to retrieve it, ducking to avoid the creature's talons. A gust of wind pushes me as it spreads its wings and soars back upward.

It still hasn't shapeshifted. Maybe it's realized that being a griffin makes it seriously hard to catch.

Which makes me wonder... Can *all* chimeras shift into griffins? If it were easy for them all to become huge monsters, wouldn't they do that immediately? Maybe some chimeras are more powerful than others.

I straighten up with my weapon, ready for the creature to land so I can shoot again. For its size, it's astonishingly nimble as it weaves through the trunks to get back up to the canopy.

"Sky!" Natalie shouts, her hands outstretched.

"Yep," Sky grunts, ducking as a pine branch whips over her head.

It's like they've choreographed this fight, their movements fluid, each sister anticipating the other's next move without having to say much.

The sight puts a knot of homesickness in my throat that hasn't been there for a long time—the feeling of being surrounded by people who get you, who unconditionally have your back.

Magic crackles through the mountain air, making my skin prickle. Natalie and Sky have pinned Sophia, Oaklyn, and Wyatt between two massive cedars, forcing them to split their attention. Every time the Madsens try to advance, Sky launches a volley of rocks while Natalie manipulates the roots under their feet.

My gaze keeps pulling to Oaklyn, my brain working frantically to understand how it's possible that this terrifying woman and Hazel's new girlfriend are the same person.

Movement overhead yanks my attention back to what I'm supposed to be doing. The griffin lands on another large branch, which bends and bounces beneath its enormous weight. Droplets fall from the needles, raining down around me. I'm dizzy as I look up, trying to aim.

Flapping its wings for balance, it turns its massive beak my way. *"Little hunter with the blood of a Guardian... I know you can hear me."*

The voice winds me like a punch to the ribs, making my aim wobble. More rain falls into my eyes, and I wipe my face with my damp sleeve. The griffin's purple eyes lock onto mine, and memories flood through me—cradling a tiny kitten at the animal shelter, her purr vibrating against my chest...and her eyes blazing that same otherworldly purple as her true nature became clear.

The griffin's talons tighten over the branch, and there it is: a dark smudge on its back paw.

"Lucy?" I whisper. My arms fail me, the arrow slipping from my fingers.

The griffin ruffles its feathers. *"You ally yourself with those who chain ancient powers beneath earth and stone. Do you believe you are the only one worthy of freedom?"*

"I... I don't..." I shut my mouth. Am I really going to answer? Natalie said talking to magic isn't a thing.

A shriek makes me gasp. A root ball from Oaklyn's dagger has slammed into Sky's gut, sending her flying backward. Wyatt tears after her, striking while she's down.

Shit!

Sky lets out an agonized roar as Wyatt clamps down on her leg. A cold sweat breaks out across my body at the memory of having the same done to me.

"Natalie, help her!" I cry, but she's already on it. Her eyes flash dangerously as she raises her arms, and the air vibrates with her power.

She slams her hands forward, and a wave of earth sends Wyatt tumbling back.

Sky rolls over, spluttering in pain. She grits her teeth and hobbles to her feet, more stoic than I could ever be.

I try to shake Lucy's voice from my head as I ready another shot, but my palms are slick with sweat and the net is tangled around my wrist.

"We are the essence of earth and sky, not herbs to be ground by human hands. I will not be consumed like a potion." The griffin stretches its wings, blocking out the clouds.

An image flashes across my vision, obscuring my view of the surrounding trees for the time it takes to blink. A street sign. Blue with a white arrow and the words *Lighthouse Park.*

"When the moon meets the sea, come alone without your golden chains."

I lower my weapon again, my hands too sweaty to hold it properly. I wipe my palms on my jacket and try to refocus, but dammit, it's a little tough knowing I'm shooting at my ex-kitten. That I'm trying to ensnare her, to hurt her with this enchanted net that will force her into unconsciousness so we can cage her forever. Also, she's inviting me to come talk later. Can I trust her?

The griffin takes flight, the trees trembling and swaying in its wake. Mist swirls through the canopy as it rises higher—and movement flashes in my periphery. I spin toward the threat, my bow raised.

A small figure wearing a backpack emerges from the woods beside me. My stomach drops, and I lower my aim.

What the hell is Hazel doing out of the car? And why is she coming out of the forest? Every protective instinct screams at me to grab her and pull her away—but I don't move, trusting that she has a reason.

Natalie sees my face and whips around, her eyes wide.

The split second of distraction gives Sophia the opening she needs. A blast of magic sends a stone flying at Natalie, clipping her shoulder and making her stumble back with a hiss of pain.

I gasp, my feet carrying me toward her automatically. "Natalie—"

"Oaklyn!" Hazel's shout drowns out mine, filling the misty forest as she runs past us to the Madsens.

Everyone freezes.

Oh my God. What is she thinking? She's going to get killed!

Oaklyn's expression goes blank. It might be the first time I've seen her face do something that isn't a sneer.

"What—" Sky begins, but Natalie throws an arm out to shut her up.

Sky shakes her head and leans against a tree, panting, sweat beading on her face as she fights the pain from Wyatt's bite.

Hazel keeps running, breathless. "Oaklyn, I came to see if my map was right. I didn't think you'd... What are you doing here?"

Wyatt wags his tail, jumping around her like an excited puppy.

You've got to be kidding me.

"Who is this?" Sophia raises her palms toward Hazel, her fingers working like she's ready to blast her off her feet.

I raise my bow and arrow, my aim steadier than it's been since we got here. If Sophia makes one move toward Hazel, this net is going straight for her head.

Oaklyn reacts in an instant. She pushes Hazel behind her, shielding her from both us and Sophia. "Mom, don't. She's..." She hesitates, panic flashing across her face. Like she doesn't quite know how to finish that sentence.

Hazel clutches Oaklyn's arm, her eyes wide with fake confusion and what I suspect is real fear. "Who are these people?"

My mouth falls open as understanding hits me. She's pretending not to know us. She's actually going through with Natalie's plan to become our spy.

Oh no, no, no... If this goes badly, I'll never forgive myself.

Everything grinds to a halt, the chimera forgotten. Natalie, Sky, and Sophia stand with their palms up, Oaklyn grips her dagger, and Wyatt crouches beside her.

"You shouldn't be here," Oaklyn hisses, but her tone lacks its usual venom.

"Neither should you!" Hazel snaps back. "When I showed you the map, I didn't mean for you to come here and—"

A shriek cuts through the air, making us all flinch. Lucy's shadow passes over us before disappearing beyond the treetops—leaving me with that final image whirring through my head.

Lighthouse Park.

Do I go, or is it a trap?

Something deep inside me knows that Lucy doesn't want to kill me—the same pull that led me to adopt a cursed kitten in the first place, and the same certainty that drew me to Natalie. This is the way to get the truth.

Oaklyn and Hazel are in a physical struggle, Hazel trying to break free as Oaklyn grips her upper arm. I shake my head and force my attention back to them. I can decipher Lucy's words later.

"Go home," Oaklyn murmurs, her eyes darting between her mother and Hazel.

"I took the bus." Hazel's gaze drops to the enchanted dagger in Oaklyn's fist—and the hungry gleam in her eyes is definitely not acting. "I'll leave with you, and you can explain what's going on."

"Oaklyn," Sophia snaps, "who the hell is—"

Sky strikes. Despite the blood oozing from the bite on her leg and the obvious pain on her face, her movements are as quick and precise as ever. A wave rolls through the earth toward the Madsens, knocking all three women and the dog off their feet.

I gasp, clapping a hand over my mouth before I can shout Hazel's name.

Everything erupts. The Madsens, now with Hazel in their midst, retaliate viciously. Natalie rushes to help her sister, shouting over her shoulder at me. "Where's the chimera?"

"Gone. We need to go." Anyway, how can we keep fighting when Hazel is on the opposing side? She's crouched between Wyatt and Oaklyn, inches from danger as Sophia retaliates against the Zacharias sisters.

The sooner we get out of here, the less likely Hazel is to get hurt. Though Wyatt is standing protectively in front of her while Oaklyn fights. Which...okay, what the hell? I got a mangled ankle, and she gets a guard dog?

"Okay," Natalie says, backing up. "Sky, let's go."

Sky hobbles closer, hissing through clenched teeth with every step, and Natalie puts an arm around her to help her move faster.

Through the chaos of magic and flying debris, I lock eyes with Hazel. She gives a tiny nod as if to tell me this is what she wants. She knows what she's doing, and I need to trust her plan.

Fighting my instincts, I back toward the car, drawing Natalie and Sky with me—leaving my best friend in the hands of the Madsens.

From the Journal of Hazel Okada

Driving away from Katie, Natalie, and Sky felt like being kid-napped, especially with Sophia white-knuckling the wheel and smoke practically billowing out her ears. Oaklyn climbed into the back seat with me, and Sophia kept glancing at us in the rearview mirror like she was deciding whether to pull over and dump my body in a ditch. Her nostrils flared, her still-purple eyes flashed dangerously, and a muscle ticked in her jaw. Both of them were sweaty and covered in mud.

It didn't escape me that this was the same woman who tor-tured Natalie's dad, and I had just put myself at her mercy. But I wasn't scared—just determined. Angry, even, over being duped. The coven needs a spy, and I'm going to be the best damn spy those witches have ever seen.

I opened my mouth to introduce myself and diffuse some tension, but Oaklyn reached a subtle hand toward me, stopping me before I could make a sound.

"Mom?" she said quietly. To my surprise, she lost her suave confidence in the presence of her mother, like the woman had the power to suck the life out of her with a single look.

"We could've had that chimera," Sophia snarled, and the car vibrated, the radio turning staticky as if she could barely contain a magical outburst. "If this girl hadn't—"

"Hazel created an algorithm that can predict where the chimeras will appear," Oaklyn said quickly, cutting off her moth-er's rising tone. "That's how I knew where to find this one."

Sophia's eyebrows shot up, her expression changing from murderous to calculating in an instant. "Are you a witch?" she asked, meeting my eyes in the mirror.

I swallowed hard, feeling like a mouse being sized up by a snake.

Okay, maybe I was a little afraid.

"No," I said, my tremulous voice betraying me. "Just a normal girl with too much curiosity."

Wyatt huffed behind me and flopped down, his furry butt pressed against the bars separating us. I reached over and scratched him, which made his tail wag.

"That was no ordinary fight I walked in on," I said, treading carefully.

Sophia's grip tightened over the wheel, the leather groaning. The radio went staticy again, and she glared at the controls. The sound sputtered and died.

She and Oaklyn met each other's eyes in the mirror, a silent conversation passing between them. Sophia dipped her chin in the tiniest of nods.

"What you saw was magic," Oaklyn said at last.

A flare of excitement lit up inside me. She was going to spill everything.

"That dagger is magic?" I asked, pointing to it in her fist.

She nodded. "This is my power, but Mom's a full witch. So were those other girls. Well, two of them, anyway. They're part of a coven that's trying to hoard magic for themselves."

I stopped petting Wyatt and squinted at her. "Hoarding magic?"

Both Oaklyn and Sophia raised their eyebrows at me, a heavy pause in the air.

"I mean—wow, witches?" I scrambled to look surprised about this big reveal, but it was too late. "I—I guess I already suspected magic was involved when all these creatures kept showing up. And then with that griffin flying around…" I shrugged like it was all obvious.

"Yeah." Oaklyn scowled, her grip tightening over the dagger. "The coven decides who's worthy and who isn't. They trap magic and lock it away, carefully controlling who uses it and when."

Wait, what? This wasn't what Katie told me about the coven. Are Sophia and Oaklyn wrong, or is there just a lot I don't know?

"Why would they want to restrict magic like that?" I asked.

"Power," Sophia said. "Control. They refuse to give anyone else the chance to be extraordinary."

"So you're trying to take some for yourselves?" I asked.

Sophia slammed her palms against the wheel, her crimson nails like spots of blood. Her eyes flashed dangerously in the rearview mirror. "We are not greedy tyrants like those witches!"

"Mom," Oaklyn said softly, glancing sideways at me.

But Sophia ignored her, continuing in an impassioned tone. "We're working to stop their monopoly over magic. We want to free it so anyone can use it. That includes you, darling."

My heart skipped. I could use magic?

I couldn't help it—I pictured myself with power radiating from my palms, my hair lifting as the charge gathered strength, raising enormous chunks of earth and stones...

Me. A witch.

Sophia's lips curled upward, a satisfied look on her face when she met my eyes again in the mirror.

As silence fell between us, I let out a breath. I guess I wasn't about to be murdered and dumped in a ditch—at least not today.

Oaklyn covertly reached over to take my hand in the back seat, her touch warm and gentle. My heart thudded as a confusing mix of sensations rippled through me. Despite the truth, my body still responded to her the same as before, and my fingers curled closed over hers.

"Oaklyn, darling, I'm almost out of those artisanal chocolates," Sophia said, her tone shifting to something falsely sweet. "Go get some more for me this week, will you? And get me a load of groceries while you're out."

"Yes, Mom," Oaklyn said, her voice flat.

"Good. I have a little gift for you when you come."

Oaklyn looked out the window, hiding her face from me. I couldn't help the little pang of resentment toward Sophia.

The rest of the drive was quiet, everyone exhausted and filthy. I'm now on Oaklyn's couch while she showers. I'll stay the night again.

Honestly, unless she's a very good actor, she seems to have no idea I'm Katie's friend.

This means two things:

1. It's possible she wasn't just using me and really does like me. (Verdict TBD.)

2. I can be a spy as planned.

I should feel victorious about infiltrating the Madsens, but...

I don't know. I feel sick.

What'll happen when Oaklyn finds out who I am? I don't doubt what Sophia would do to me, but I can't be sure about Oaklyn. Does she really care about me, or am I just a distraction?

Every time I look into her eyes, the guilt of lying twists deeper. These are the same eyes as before, soft and blue and full of affection. The only difference is that now I know the truth. I know she tried to kill Katie, and those scars on Katie's ankle are from Wyatt, and Sophia has spent decades murdering people in pursuit of magic.

But I've seen the hurt in Oaklyn's eyes when she talked about losing Freddie and her dad, and I've felt her arms around me at night, holding me like I'm something precious she's afraid to lose. When I wake up beside her and look over to see the sun catching on her eyelashes, on the curve of her cheek, on her bare, pink lips, all I see is a normal girl. She has layers Katie doesn't see. Do they count for something?

I hate this. I have critical information I could give the witches right now—Oaklyn's whereabouts. But if I tell them where she lives, they'll come for her, and I'm too confused to know how I feel about that.

Well, the witches also need Sophia's address, so I can work on getting that info first. Sophia is clearly the more dangerous one, so she should be the primary target anyway.

The shower just turned off.

My heart is pounding.

I'm about to look into Oaklyn's blue eyes and ask about her mom, knowing her answers will bring me closer to the moment I betray her.

Note to self: Get serious about keeping this journal a secret. No writing in it while I'm with Oaklyn. Keep it buried deep inside my backpack among my schoolwork. I might consider going to therapy to process my feelings instead of writing about it, but given the subject matter, here we are.

It'll be fine. I'll be careful.

CHAPTER 16

The Truth in the Cove

I PULL ON BLACK jeans and a hoodie, getting ready for what might be the most dangerous decision of my life. My gaze keeps snagging on my phone on Natalie's bed, where my text to Hazel sits unanswered.

Katie

You ok? Send me your location.

My stomach churns with worry. First Lucy soars back into my life as a griffin and speaks to me inside my head, then Hazel literally throws herself into the Madsens' arms, and now I'm about to sneak out to meet a chimera in the dark.

After taking Sky to the infirmary, Natalie left to neutralize a curse at a thrift store—which feels absurdly normal after recent events. Her absence gives me the window I need to get to Lighthouse Park.

Imagining how angry and hurt she'll be when she finds out makes me hesitate with one shoe on. We just said "I love you," and is this how I show it? By sneaking out behind her back?

But if she knew, she'd either stop me or insist on coming along. And something tells me Lucy won't show if I bring a witch with me—especially one who's determined to trap her.

I put on my other shoe with a sigh. The chimeras' pleas have been haunting me since I first heard that voice in White Rock. Why can I hear them when no one else can, and what are they trying to tell me? I can't keep hunting them knowing I might be ignoring something crucial.

The coven has made it clear from day one that they're not about to answer any of my questions about magic. But if Lucy is offering answers—possibly beyond anything these witches understand about chimeras—I have to go.

When the moon meets the sea... I look at my moon-phases tee crumpled on the bed. Waxing crescent tonight, which means the moon should set at about 9 P.M. I need to leave now if I want to make it in time. I've left a buffer in case it takes me a while to convince a witch to escort me out through the steam clock with them.

Ethel watches me from the pillows, judgment plain on her furry face, like she disapproves of me listening to a disembodied voice.

"It's not like that," I tell her, aware that defending myself to a cat is not helping my case. "It was the chimera, which happens to be my old cat, telepathically speaking to me."

Yeah, it sounds even worse when I say it out loud.

But before Natalie, before the coven, before I knew witches existed, there was Lucy. And despite everything that happened afterward, I can't shake the feeling that I was meant to find her.

I pull on the gauntlet and zip up my backpack, which I've loaded with supplies I usually bring hiking: flashlight, water bottle, pepper spray, snacks, tiny First Aid kit, emergency blanket if I get lost.

Ethel wanders over to her scratching post and gets to work on her nails, as if to tell me she doesn't care what I do.

My phone chirps, and I lunge for it.

> Staying at Oaklyn's tonight. Will call you tomorrow when I'm in the office. Don't text me again in case she sees.

My stomach clenches. After learning the truth about Oaklyn, she's still going to...?

Ugh, I can't think about that. Hazel's a grown-ass woman who can make her own decisions.

Anyway, I'm just glad she's in one piece.

I slip on my running shoes and shoulder my backpack, my heart pounding. I don't know how deep into the forest I'll have to walk—Lighthouse Park is a hiking area, after all—but I'm prepared for anything.

"I have to do this," I tell Ethel as she watches me lay a hand on the doorknob. "I might be the first person who can communicate with chimeras. Either that, or..."

I don't want to think about what else could be putting a voice in my head. But every day, I get closer to having to spend the next five years in a dungeon, and I'm desperate enough to follow that voice if it might lead to a way out.

As the bus pulls away behind me, I click on my flashlight, illuminating the Lighthouse Park sign I saw in the vision. The beam cuts a weak path through the blackness, revealing a paved road leading into the park.

Ugh, what if this is a trap? Could the Madsens be behind it? How angry will Natalie be when she finds out what I'm doing?

I push down my doubts and start walking, the cold night air seeping through my hoodie. My footsteps are too loud, and the feeling of being watched makes me quicken my pace, my flashlight beam bouncing wildly.

At the end of the road, a yellow gate indicates the park is closed after dusk. I duck under it, following a dirt path bounded by enormous Douglas firs and red cedars that must be hundreds of years old. A sign warns me about bears, but I suspect ordinary bears are the least of my worries tonight.

The deeper I go, the thicker the air grows with the scent of damp earth and ocean salt. Branches creak, their shadows twisting in my flashlight beam like grasping hands.

Then, my skin prickles, and the hairs on my arms stand up. That familiar sensation pulls me forward like a magnet. I take the left fork in the trail, then the right, the feeling intensifying until it's humming through my body. Hisses fill my mind like a jumble of whispers.

"A human comes our way..."

A twig snaps behind me, and I whirl around—but there's only darkness between the massive tree trunks.

The magic tugs harder, leading me down a steep trail toward the crash of waves. My foot slips on wet rocks, and I catch myself with my hands, wincing at the sting in my palms.

Natalie is going to kill me if I survive this.

Something huge passes overhead, momentarily blocking out what little moonlight filters through the canopy. My heart leaps as I recognize the shape—wings, eagle head, lion body.

Lucy. I found her.

I'm not sure whether to feel relieved or scared.

She circles back, staying overhead like a vulture stalking dying prey. Ignoring every survival instinct, I follow her, stumbling over roots and ducking under branches until the trees thin out.

I arrive at a cove, where jagged rocks form a natural amphitheater and frothy waves crash against the shore. I'm on time—the waxing crescent moon hangs low on the horizon, its light painting a silver path across the water.

And on the shore…

My feet root in place as terror slams into me. Prowling among mossy boulders and driftwood, silver-gray in the moonlight, are dozens of chimeras.

They crawl across the ground, spill into the water, and soar into the air, their forms shifting and changing—a deer becomes a crow, a bear becomes a seal. Purple eyes glow in the darkness like beacons, all turning toward me at once.

I step back, my legs trembling, my flashlight beam wavering.

They stalk nearer. Hisses and snarls rise, bleeding into my mind.

"Your nets cannot hold our storm, witch pet."

"Remember the wisdom of your ancestors, who knew to let us roam."

"We remember every cage and enchantment, every witch who tore our essence apart."

My breaths grow shallow as the voices overlap, getting louder.

Something moves in my periphery, much too close. I whirl around, a gasp escaping. Are they flanking me like raptors?

The shadow closes in, spilling onto a log beside me. My legs feel like jelly as I step back.

Run! my inner voice yells. *This was a mistake!*

A tiny meow meets my ears.

I shine the flashlight at it. "Lucy?"

A fluffy white kitten with beige-tipped ears is sitting on the log, delicately licking her paw. She looks up at me with glowing purple eyes.

"You have arrived, little hunter," she says in my head, her voice cold and powerful, completely at odds with the adorable ball of fluff in front of me. *"Lower your light."*

I click the light off, blinking to try and adjust my sight to the darkness. "Sorry."

She becomes a small silhouette in the moonlight, turning toward the chimeras on the shore. *"Look at what is before you. This is what you are hunting."*

I follow her gaze to where they're all still watching me. And in their midst...

My stomach flips, and I drop my flashlight with a clatter. A *person* is sprawled on the rocks. Chimeras surround her like hungry lions, looking down at her limp form.

"Oh my God." I break into a run, moving as fast as the darkness and terrain allow, my steps clumsy on the uneven ground. "Get back! All of you!"

My first thought is that it's Hazel, and the Madsens found out and... But no. It's not her. This person is very pale with short blonde hair.

As I barge into the swarm of chimeras, wildcats hiss and wolves snarl at me, their teeth glinting in the moonlight. A bear stands on its hind legs.

My heart skips a beat, and I freeze. Am I next?

"No. Let her see, " Lucy says, her voice carrying.

A gust of wind lifts my hair, and there's a noise like talons scraping against rock. I whirl around—only to see the fluffy kitten trotting over.

The other chimeras back up, glowering at me.

"See what becomes of those who try to consume our power, " Lucy says, filling my head.

I edge closer to the victim on the rocks, acutely aware of my audience. What'll happen if I make a wrong move?

The person is small and frail beneath a long green cloak, a white T-shirt, and jeans. I crouch and push the locks back from her face, a zap of magic stinging my fingers like a static shock. She's cold and damp—but her chest rises and falls rapidly, and her eyelids are fluttering.

Purple light pulses in her veins like lightning in a storm cloud. Tremors pass through her body like she's having a nightmare.

Recognition dawns as I take in her features. "Millie!"

Footsteps pound closer. I jump to my feet, adrenaline surging.

"Katie?" Sebastian's voice cuts through the hum of the chimeras in my head. He races over from the trees, breathless, his face gaunt and exhausted.

"What's wrong with her?"

"It's the bio magic. It didn't happen like it was supposed to." His voice quavers as he drops to his knees beside Millie.

"What didn't? Embodying it?" The image of the chimera dissolving into shimmering particles flashes through my memory—and the way she screamed in pain as it fused with her.

"It's battling for dominance inside her," Sebastian says, combing his fingers through her soaked hair.

It hits me then—her hair. She was bald the last time I saw her.

"Did it work?" I ask. "Could she use the magic to cure her cancer?"

He frowns, his eyes hollow. "We don't know. As she was learning how to use it, she started having problems. Acting funny. Talking to herself, forgetting what she'd been doing for hours at a time, losing control of her magic and hurting herself or me..."

Millie stirs, making us both inhale sharply. "Seb?" she croaks, her voice barely audible over the crashing waves.

He lurches closer, cupping her face with two hands. "I'm here. What do you need?"

She turns her gaze onto me, staring for a moment before her eyes widen with recognition. "Katie. The bio magic. I shouldn't have..."

I suck in a breath. I never considered that consuming bio magic might be a dangerous process. There was only the danger that the coven focused on—the potential to abuse its power.

"Do you feel its presence?" I ask.

She dips her chin. "Like having two minds. We came here hoping the other chimeras could separate us. It was my magic's idea." She looks around with wild eyes, which glow an eerie purple in the moonlight. "I'm so sorry. Please don't tell the coven, Katie..."

"Of course," I whisper. The coven still has no clue she absorbed bio magic to try and heal herself—though they might have an inkling, given that she and Sebastian helped us set it free and then disappeared. Either way, if they're found out, they'll probably face a similar punishment to mine for breaking the coven's laws. As if she hasn't been through enough hell.

Sebastian kisses her hand and cups it between both of his. "Shh. It's okay. You only did what witches before us have done."

My heart thuds. Of the witches who've consumed bio magic in the past, how many actually survived? And looking at the creatures surrounding me... I can't help wondering: is it even meant to be consumed at all?

"How long have you been here?" I ask, trying to piece together what's happened to them since February.

"A few days," Sebastian says, not taking his eyes off his wife. "We came when it was clear something was wrong."

"And they will be here for many more," Lucy says, cutting through my thoughts.

I flinch as her voice fills my head, spinning around to face her. "What did you do to her? Fix this!"

She gives me the sort of disdainful look that only a cat can give. *"The better question is 'what did she do to us?' What do all witches continue to do to us? You trap us, consume us, weaponize us..."*

Images flood my mind, blinding me to my surroundings—memories that aren't mine. Being trapped beneath a golden net, forced into a cage, afraid and desperate to escape... Millie, palms out, screaming in agony as she absorbed a chimera into her blood... Witches I don't recognize making others cry in pain without touching them, tearing enemies limb from limb on a battlefield, shapeshifting until they've taken on a new identity...

Nausea fills me. My mouth goes dry. "Why did you invite me here?"

"To show you what awaits your coven if you continue your hunt. We will not be caged or consumed."

I swallow hard. My survival instincts scream at me to run, but that familiar pull toward magic keeps me rooted. As terrified as I am, I need to know more. Natalie told me chimeras are mindless forces, but that's not what I'm seeing. "Help me understand. I came here to find the truth about what you are."

Sebastian lifts his gaze from his wife to stare at me. "Katie, is it talking to you?"

I nod.

His eyes widen. Millie turns her head on the rocks to stare too, her chest still rising and falling rapidly.

Lucy sits, puffing up and swishing her stubby tail. *"We are the first magic. Before—mouse!"*

A little brown mouse scurries over the dead leaves between us, and she scampers after it with her claws out, trying to catch it.

I watch, confused, as she chases it into the woods.

"Uh..." Sebastian says.

A moment later, Lucy trots back to us. *"My apologies. After spending so long trapped in kitten form, I often find my instincts at war."*

"Oh. N-no worries," I stammer.

"As I was saying," she continues. *"Before mortals built their stone walls and iron cages, we roamed free."*

I furrow my brow. "None of this matches what the witches told me."

"They have suppressed their history for a century. We have the power to heal a dying bird, to refill a parched wetland, to help an injured human. And yet, the witches see us as weapons to be contained."

"But—but you destroyed the city," I splutter.

"When cages break, the caged lash out. It is the nature of living beings."

"And when you were my kitten, you—"

Lucy's eyes narrow. *"When I was bound in the confines of a curse, my magic became unstable. You tried to bottle lightning and got struck. That is not my fault."*

I shake my head firmly. "It wasn't me who trapped you. I'm not a witch."

"Your kind did—and now you follow in their footsteps, chasing us with nets and weapons. Why not let us exist freely? Why must you harness us for your own selfish desires?"

I don't know what to say. Can I honestly look at what's in front of me and say that I believe these creatures should be in cages? Beyond those surrounding us, more chimeras glide across the shore, their forms flowing from one shape to another. A deer becomes an otter that plunges into the water. A great horned owl soars toward the trees, becoming something with too many limbs as it latches onto a long branch.

Millie stirs on the rocks, grunting in pain. While Sebastian presses a kiss to her forehead, murmuring words I can't hear, several rats edge closer.

A chill rolls through me, and I fight the urge to shoo them away.

"To the witches, you're just a vessel that holds the most powerful type of magic," I tell Lucy. "And containing you is the only way to keep people safe from those who want to use you as weapons."

"We are not weapons to be wielded or forces to be tamed," Lucy hisses, flashing her little fangs. *"We are spirits of the wild, keepers of ancient magic. We are the force that awakens a bear from its winter sleep, the quiet power that knits your wounds closed, the pull that guides birds across continents. We are a hive's collective consciousness, a tadpole's growth into a frog, a whale's song as she migrates to give birth. We flow through every*

living thing, upholding the balance between life and death, growth and decay. Without us, the natural order simply would not be."

The rats scamper over Millie's body. Sebastian doesn't push them off, which makes me think this has happened before—that this is supposed to happen. He sits up to watch, breathing fast, as purple light crackles like lightning over her skin. She gasps, arching her back.

Their voices are faint in the back of my mind, barely there unless I focus. "*Stay still... We will try to separate you... Do not struggle...*"

They're helping her—or helping the chimera trapped inside her.

I meet Lucy's eyes. "Why am I the only one who can speak to you?"

As she looks back at me, something foreign ripples through me—an emotion not my own. My breaths come faster. My hands shake, and I ball them into fists, unsure if I should turn and run.

"Wh-what are you doing to me?"

"*You feel our suffering?*" Lucy asks, tilting her head.

I furrow my brow, trying to think past the terror rocketing through me. This emotion belongs to every chimera who's been trapped, and it's filling me like water being poured down my throat. "Why am I feeling this?"

"*Few humans possess this gift anymore.*"

"Anymore?" I press. "There used to be more people like me?"

"*Long ago, there were witches who stood between us and those who hunted us.*" Lucy stands, pacing back and forth. "*Our ancient guardians could speak with us and feel what we feel.*"

I shiver. Around us, many pairs of purple eyes still linger on me. Is this why I feel such a strong pull toward the chimeras? Am I descended from these ancient guardians?

"*Those witches protected the balance between our world and yours...until the coven decided we were too dangerous to remain free.*" Lucy's voice hardens. Her fur ripples, her body growing. She curls her claws over the rock, the scrape resonating too loudly—more like the sound of talons.

"If your witches attack us again, we will not show mercy. We have been patient, but we will no longer hesitate to unleash what we truly are."

I nod, believing her. Looking at their true forms, feeling their power pulsing through my veins, it's clear the witches have no idea what they're dealing with.

Lucy keeps growing, her form shifting, until a massive griffin stands before me. She clicks her beak, her eyes narrowing. *"Help us remain free, and you will see what harmony looks like. Hunt us, and your kind will regret waging war against ancient magic."*

I swallow hard. Help the chimeras? But Natalie, and the coven, and... "What about Millie?" I ask.

Lucy turns her regal gaze to Millie, who writhes in pain under the chimeras trying to separate her soul from the magic she consumed. *"She made her choice, as do all who consume us. Some can handle the power, and some cannot. If she does not survive this, then that is the price of her human arrogance."*

I open my mouth to argue that it wasn't arrogance—it was desperation. If Millie knew what the consequences would be, she probably wouldn't have done it. But knowledge of chimeras and bio magic is so strictly controlled and limited within the coven that there was no way she could have known all this.

As for me? I understand better than ever. Millie has shown me with absolute certainty that a chimera's power is not meant to be consumed. Witches might have named it bio magic and used it to win wars and heal illnesses, but that doesn't make it right.

But is C.S.A.M.M. right to trap it underground? Or are chimeras meant to be free?

Does it matter, when the only way to secure my freedom is to trap them?

"Leave now," Lucy commands, spreading her wings like a massive wall in front of me, *"and take this warning back to your coven. Tell your witches to stay away."*

The chimeras with their burning eyes respond to Lucy's gesture, creeping closer. I back away, stumbling over rocks, the message clear: I am not welcome here. I am not their ally. I'm a messenger, a non-magical human who is no threat to them, and my purpose is to deliver a warning to the witches.

I look to Sebastian, not wanting to abandon them.

"Go," he says hoarsely. "Before they hurt you."

My eyes sting, but I nod, knowing I have no other option.

As I retreat, Millie's screams follow me—a reminder of what happens when humans try to control forces they don't understand.

My heart hammers as I flee up the dark trail without my flashlight, branches slashing my cheeks raw. The chimeras see me as just another hunter. But I felt their fear beneath their anger—memories of cages and torches, of being trapped and used.

What am I supposed to do? These creatures aren't what I thought, and they might be the key to understanding my ability. If I'm meant to protect them, then trapping them betrays who I am. But Natalie and the coven would never believe that, and my freedom depends on capturing them.

A shriek tears through the trees—whether human or monster, I can't tell.

I pause, lungs burning, staring into the darkness behind me. Somewhere in those shadows, ancient magic is trying to heal a witch who made a terrible mistake. Now, I have to decide which side I'm on before my time runs out.

From the Journal of Hazel Okada

There was no easy way to broach the subject, so I just went for it as we settled on the couch with stiff drinks (much needed after getting in a fight with a couple of witches and a chimera). "It was nice meeting your mom."

Oaklyn coughed as she took a sip of her whiskey, on the verge of laughing. "Not the way I would've planned it."

"We should have dinner at her place sometime. A more normal context."

She recoiled, looking at me like I was a T-rex that had come crashing into her living room. "I guess…"

"I'll introduce you to my parents too, when the opportunity comes." I tried to position it as a meet-the-parents idea and not 'show me where your mom lives so I can send a coven of witches after her.'

Ugh, more nausea. My rum and coke suddenly went down like acid.

"Maybe," she said. "I'll ask."

Between her tone and the way her fingers tightened around her glass, she was definitely not about to bring it up any time soon.

I tried another angle. "Does your mom live in the house you grew up in?"

"No. We moved a few times. Lately, we've moved more often because…" She paused, then seemed to remember the cat was already out of the bag regarding magic and witches. "The witches keep finding us. We have to stay ahead of them."

"They're after you?"

"They don't like that we see them for what they are—hoarders of magic."

I chewed my lip, debating my next words. This topic felt more important than figuring out her mom's address. Because here's a big part of what's keeping me up tonight: Oaklyn's argument isn't entirely wrong. Why does the coven get to monopolize magic? What if instead, they allowed people to earn it? Classes, tests, regulations... They could create a system that's fair and accessible while maintaining safety protocols.

When I suggested this to Oaklyn, her whole face lit up.

"Have I told you how brilliant you are?" She scooted closer on the couch.

When she kissed me, I didn't freeze or recoil. Instead, a pleasant shockwave rolled through my lips and all the way down to my toes, my body responding the same way it did last time we had sex.

"Maybe once or twice," I murmured.

When she pulled back, her fingers knotted in my hair, her expression shifted to something more serious. "You scared me today, running into that fight. Don't do that again."

"Then don't give me cause to do that again," I challenged. When she glowered at me, I added, "Do you anticipate getting into more fights like that in the future?"

"It's sort of my thing." She traced her thumb over my cheek. "Promise me you won't do anything rash. There's no need for you to get involved in something dangerous."

I scoffed. "And what about you? You're allowed to run into danger?"

Her shoulders slumped, and she tilted her head, something sad and unreadable in her eyes.

She leaned in to kiss me again, slower and deeper than before. The way her lips gently teased mine sent a whirlwind of heat spiraling through my middle.

I guess as far as my body was concerned, nothing had changed between us. Even as my brain was screaming and running in confused circles.

"I'm doing this for us," she whispered. "Imagine... Both of us, witches. We can change the world together."

I shivered under her touch and arched into her. Reacting on instinct, with no regard for what I was supposed to be doing, I opened my mouth and deepened the kiss. We pushed against each other, tongues dipping into each other's mouths, hands roaming. She tugged my shirt upward and undressed me piece by piece, tracing her lips over every inch of my skin as she exposed it.

"You were hot with that dagger," I said breathlessly, pulling her shirt over her head.

As I tossed her shirt on the floor, she cocked an eyebrow. "Oh?"

"Yeah." I unclasped her bra next. "Maybe you can let me try it out one day."

The intrigued look in her eyes sent a tingle through me. She reached for it on the coffee table, where she'd set it down beside her drink. "We can try it out right now if you want."

I thought I knew what she meant, and it wasn't target practice.

I watched in awe as dark green ivy sprouted from the end, snaking toward me. The sight was as beautiful as it was terrifying.

My heart beat faster.

I raised my gaze to hers, and she grinned, leaning in to kiss me again. She pushed me back on the couch, not forcefully like usual, but slowly and gently.

The ivy kept creeping around my wrists, binding one, and then the other, raising my hands above my head so they dangled over the armrest.

"Like this?" she murmured, her eyes searching mine.

I nodded. "Keep going."

The ivy tightened around my wrists.

As Oaklyn traced a line with her tongue all the way down my neck, chest, belly, and between my legs, I shivered, letting out a moan.

"You're so beautiful," she whispered. "So smart, and caring, and fun, and sexy."

My pulse raced hearing these words. How she made me feel... How she held my gaze as she touched me...

"Can I tell you something?" she murmured against my inner thigh, her breath warm on my skin.

"Y-yes," I stammered, my head so cloudy I barely got the word out.

"I'm secretly glad you found out about magic. About what my mom and I are trying to do. Now we don't have to keep secrets from each other."

"Me too," I said, closing my eyes and leaning my head back. "No secrets."

Guilt burned like a flame inside me...but given where her mouth went next, it was hard to focus on that for longer than a second.

With my hands bound above my head and my legs draped over the sides of the couch, I succumbed to her over and over, her tongue and fingers tipping me over the edge like nothing I've ever felt. She left me sweaty and exhausted—and as always, wanting more. Wanting to pleasure her the same way she pleasured me until the sun rose and we had to pry ourselves away from each other.

I can't help feeling like something has shifted between us now that I know her secret. She's really looking into my eyes now...like maybe I'm not just a casual fling or a distraction from her dangerous life. And while she's being honest with me, I'm betraying her, gathering information to use against her.

And yet...

For huge chunks of time, I forget I'm pretending. When we cuddle or kiss or fuck, I'm not thinking about the coven or Katie or any of it. I'm only thinking about her.

Oh God, I can't think like that.

I can't fall in love with the person I'm supposed to be spying on.

CHAPTER 17

Witches and Chimeras

T HE STEAM CLOCK BILLOWS into the chilly air, its whistles chiming a haunting midnight song as I sprint toward it. My legs burn and my hand is sweaty as I clutch my ringing phone. *So close...*

Natalie materializes out of the cobblestones like smoke taking form, walking toward me with her phone pressed to her ear and a frown on her lips. When she sees me, relief flashes across her face before hardening into something colder.

She ends the call, and my phone falls silent.

I stop in front of her, clutching a stitch in my side. "I—I'm here," I say, as if that'll somehow excuse my absence.

She closes the last stride between us and grabs my arm, her fingers digging through my sleeve. "Where *were* you?" she asks through her teeth.

My stomach lurches as she brings me right back down through the steam clock. We land in the brick hallway under the warm glow of a Victorian street lamp, and I suck in a breath. "Lighthouse Park. The chimeras were there. Tons—maybe all of them."

Natalie stares at me, frozen, before pulling me down the hall by the elbow. "You went into the woods alone at night?"

"That's beside the point." My voice bounces as I pick up a jog to keep pace, my muddy runners slipping on the cobblestones. "I had a chance to learn more about the chimeras, and I took it. And I learned we've got it all wrong."

Natalie glances around the lounge as we cross through it. It's late enough that the booths and tables have emptied. "Why didn't you bring me with you?" she growls.

Beneath the anger, her voice trembles, and her eyes are wide. She keeps a tight hold on my arm, like she's afraid I might slip away again.

"Because they wanted to talk to me," I say gently. "Just me."

"Talk?" she snaps. "Bio magic doesn't talk."

"Lucy spoke to me."

Natalie drags her hand down her face. "Katie…"

I wrench out of her grasp and stop walking, my fists clenched. "You believed me when I told you I'm an empath, and you believed me when I told you I could sense curses and magic. What's so different about this?"

She waves her arms. "Because this time you're telling me you're having conversations with *magic*. It doesn't make sense."

"I know." My voice softens as Natalie's expression turns distraught. I guess I am throwing everything she knows into question. "Natalie, there's more to the chimeras than the coven understands. They're sentient, conscious—"

"And dangerous!" She steps closer, dropping her voice. "Bio magic is what witches have used to perform mind control. If these chimeras were inside your head, we need to be careful. You're being influenced by dark forces."

I shake my head, frustration building in my chest. "It wasn't like that! They wanted to show me—" I swallow hard. I could tell her about finding Millie, but that might reinforce her belief that bio magic is dangerous. Besides, Millie and Sebastian didn't want me to tell anyone. "The chimeras want to be left alone and free. Natalie, I don't think this magic should be caged. I don't think chimeras are dangerous unless—"

"Unless witches dedicate our whole lives to keeping them out of the wrong hands?" She looks around again, maybe afraid someone will overhear. Her face is pale in the dim light. "Do you understand what bio magic has done in the past? What the Madsens could do with it?"

"Of course I do." I grit my teeth, trying to keep my voice level. "I get that their power needs to be kept safe. But is trapping and caging them the answer? There has to be another way."

"There isn't," Natalie snaps. Something flickers across her expression—a flash of uncertainty before she shakes her head. "The coven has studied these entities for centuries. We wouldn't be doing this if it wasn't the only way."

"But what if—"

"I thought you wanted to avoid getting sent to prison." She spins and strides toward her room, her cloak billowing. The plants on the walls lean away as she passes.

"I do!" I cry, racing after her.

"Then why are we arguing about whether we should trap these things?" she says over her shoulder.

I open my mouth, but any arguments die in my throat. Am I getting distracted from the more important issue of my freedom? My trial gave me one path forward: catch every chimera or spend five years in a cell.

"Maybe the chimeras spoke to you, Katie, but that doesn't mean they can be trusted."

The words hit hard, and my heart stumbles. Was I tricked? Did Lucy read into my deepest desires and use that to manipulate me?

I've been so desperate to belong in the coven, twisting myself into knots to try and prove my worth, and it's possible she reached into my mind and pulled that shameful fact right out of me. Used it against me. Made me feel validated, knowing how readily I would believe I was special.

I clench my fists, my palms sweating. The certainty I felt at the cove suddenly seems fragile.

But then there's my intuition, which has never led me astray. Thinking back to the cove, the way Lucy's words resonated in my bones...I felt something real. And what about Troy telling me to trust my gut? I can't ignore that.

The silence stretches out, the air between us thick and murky.

"Everything's a fucking mess," Natalie growls, running a hand through her hair. "Has Hazel at least told you where Oaklyn lives?"

"No," I say, bristling.

Natalie shoots me a glare, her dark eyes piercing me. "She's staying at Oaklyn's place, isn't she?"

I glare back. "We're asking her to share information that will destroy any future she has with a woman she's infatuated with. Give her time."

"Where the Madsens are involved, we don't have time." We reach Natalie's door, and she faces me with her jaw set. "Are we going back to Lighthouse Park to trap these things?"

I splutter, Lucy's warning fresh in my mind. "If you want to get us killed."

"This nest you found is exactly what we need to win your freedom."

I stare at her, my heart pounding. I could argue that the chimeras might not be there anymore, but Lucy did say that Sebastian and Millie would be there for a few more days as they tried to separate her from the magic she absorbed.

Natalie drops her voice. "Katie, you've just told me you visited an entire pack of chimeras, and your best friend, who has an algorithm to track where these things are located, is currently bunking up with Oaklyn Madsen. We need to go back and trap them as soon as possible before someone else gets there first. We'll bring Sky and whoever agrees to help."

I open my mouth, strangled by several arguments at once. First, how dare she imply that Hazel can't be trusted. Second, will Sky be up for it after having her leg bitten? Third, the image of Lucy trapped beneath a net, thrashing in pain, sends a shudder through me.

Your ancestors knew better, one of the chimeras said as I approached.

"Natalie, we can't just trap them without understanding—"

"You have a choice." Natalie's sharp words cut through my weak argument. "Do you want your freedom, or do you want to waste time trying to change the entire coven's mind about bio magic? You think Fiona will listen when you tell her you want to be buddies with the chimeras instead of trapping them?"

Heat rises in my face as she speaks the blunt truth. The stubborn part of me wants to argue back. I want to demand that she considers that I might be right. I know she's protecting me, but she's not listening.

But she's fighting so hard for me—she's defied her coven, risked her position, and fought against friends she's had her whole life. And I'm here entertaining the idea that everything she believes is wrong.

Away from the chimeras, the certainty I felt fades fast, like I dreamed all that nonsense about being descended from witches.

Am I so desperate to be a witch that I'll believe anything? There is zero proof that there are witches in my lineage. I'm no more descended from ancient chimera guardians than I am from Cleopatra.

"You think the magic wormed into my mind and manipulated me into not wanting to catch it?" I ask, barely a whisper.

Natalie softens. "I do."

I swallow hard, unsure what to believe. But looking into Natalie's eyes—this woman I love with every cell in my body—I know whose side I'm on.

"When do you want to go?" I ask, the words burning my throat.

The relief on Natalie's face sends a pang of guilt through me. She pulls me into her arms, holding me tight against her chest. I can feel her heart racing.

"I'll talk to Sky first thing," she says into my hair. "She'll assemble the Shadows for this. I think even Fiona will be on board, given the magnitude of what you've found. We'll plan an ambush late tomorrow night when the park is empty."

I nod against her shoulder, a strange numbness spreading through my limbs. The thought of returning to Lighthouse Park with nets and witches makes me nauseous. Lucy trusted me and brought me to the place where she and the other chimeras have gathered...and I'm about to lead hunters to them.

But what choice do I have? The coven won't change their minds about bio magic after centuries spent containing it. And the Madsens have proven why that protection is necessary.

This is my life we're talking about, and I'm the only one who can save it. I can't get distracted from dreams of being special—of being a witch.

As we break apart, I curl my hands into fists, my nails biting into my palms. I'm angry at the coven for putting me in this impossible position, and at the Madsens for proving why bio magic is dangerous, and at myself for ending up in this predicament. Even if I secure my freedom, will I spend the rest of my life haunted by what I've done?

Natalie's hand finds mine, and I exhale slowly, letting my fist loosen so our fingers can entwine.

As angry as I am, and as much as it scares me, I know what I need to do. Even if I have to ignore the voice in my head—not Lucy's, but my own—whispering that I'm about to make a mistake.

From the Journal of Hazel Okada

I fucked up.

We were tangled in Oaklyn's sheets this morning, my head resting on her shoulder, her arm securely around me. After all the time spent playing with her dagger, I felt bold enough to ask about it.

"Where'd you get it?" I asked, tracing my fingers up and down her body, relishing the feel of her smooth skin.

"Gift from my mom. She took it from some witches long ago... Gave it to me on my sixteenth birthday."

"Quite the sweet sixteen present." I paused and grinned up at her. "Bet she didn't know you'd use it as a toy while railing your girlfriend a few years later."

She snorted and dissolved into laughter, her whole body shaking. "You're bad."

I nestled deeper into her warmth, tracing my fingers over a thorny rose tattoo on her abs. "Maybe I can have an enchanted weapon of my own one day. You've got that one, Freddie had Wyatt, Katie's got that gauntlet..."

The air in the bedroom seemed to crystallize. Oaklyn tensed beneath me. She shifted her head back to look down at my face, her eyes piercing me.

"Katie?" she repeated, unnervingly calm.

My heart stopped beating. The name had slipped out so naturally, as if my best friend had been part of our conversations all along. But she hadn't been, of course.

"The—the girl we saw in the woods who had the golden net. She was wearing that gauntlet." I tried to sound steady and casual, but my heart was pounding hard, and I was sure she could feel it.

Oaklyn kept staring at me. I could see her brain working behind those bright blue eyes. "I never said her name."

"Yes you did."

"When?"

"I don't remember." Shit, my mouth was so dry, and my lies felt clumsy on my tongue. "But you did, because how else would I know it?"

I shimmied up to plant a kiss on her lips in a desperate attempt to distract her. For a moment, she stayed rigid and unresponsive—but as I pressed my naked body to hers, my nipples grazing her skin and my legs wrapping around her thigh, she softened, and a hungry noise escaped her.

She kissed me back, and I opened my lips to let her tongue dip into my mouth. But as our bodies responded to each other in a now-familiar way, panic guided my actions, as if I could somehow stop her from learning the truth if I kissed her hard enough.

She rolled on top, and I wrapped my legs around her hips to hold her against me. Her breath hitched, and her fist came up to wrap in my hair, and it was my turn to let out an involuntary noise as she pulled.

We were both rougher than usual. Fingers grabbing, teeth biting, bodies writhing. There was a new calculation in the way her hands moved over my body, as if she was desperately trying to solve a puzzle instead of making love. And I was urgently trying to prove something.

I tried to say everything in my heart without words: I'm sorry I'm lying to you, Oaklyn. But this part? The way I respond to your touch, and the way my heart races when you look into my eyes? This is real.

That was the end of the conversation. She said nothing more.

But the rest of the morning felt...off. I can't be certain, and I might just be paranoid, but my journal was in a different pocket of my backpack when I zipped it shut to go to work. I'd been keeping it safely buried in the depths of the middle pocket, but I found it upside-down in the main compartment.

Did I slip it in too hastily last night, or did Oaklyn read it while I was showering? Was I imagining the way she looked at me as I got ready—searching, scrutinizing? Her eyes followed me around the apartment, lingering a beat too long when I checked my phone, when I brushed my teeth, when I kissed her goodbye.

"See you tonight?" I asked at the door, trying to sound normal.

She smiled, but it didn't reach her eyes. "Of course."

It's possible she read my journal and knows everything—about Katie, about my mission to spy on her, about how I've been lying to her since shortly after we met. But it's also possible that I'm just scared and paranoid. I can't imagine how angry she'll be with me if she finds out the truth...and just as much, I'm terrified that when that happens, I'm going to lose her forever.

CHAPTER 18

Dangerous Loyalties

ORDERING MY TEXTBOOKS FEELS surreal, like I'm watching myself play the role of a student while my life crumbles to pieces.

Sitting at a picnic table in the C.S.A.M.M. courtyard with my laptop, my eyes glaze over as I stare at the checkout page. My mind keeps playing out different versions of how tonight's invasion at Lighthouse Park will go—how the chimeras will respond, how the Shadows plan to capture them all, whether blood will be spilled.

But my degree is a huge part of the life I'm fighting to keep, and I need to do this. If I'm going to avoid witch prison, I need to make sure I maintain this fragile balance of—

Beside my laptop, my phone lights up with Hazel's face.

My heart lurches. Okay, turns out some things are a higher priority than textbooks.

I abandon my laptop, where the timer on the checkout page warns me I only have four minutes left, and grab my phone.

"Still alive?" I answer, glancing around to ensure no witches are listening. They stroll past on their way to and from the lounge, and beside me, Ethel and another resident cat named Juniper watch the koi pond.

"Yeah." Hazel's voice is flat and tired, like she's struggling with the emotional burden of everything as much as I am. "No indication that she's using me to get to you."

"Oh, thank God." Relief floods through me—followed quickly by a knot in my stomach. I don't like what comes next.

Neither does Hazel, apparently, because she's quiet.

"You don't have to spy for us if you don't want to," I say, watching a ladybug crawl across the picnic table. "I'll tell Natalie off."

"Don't." She sighs. "I don't want you to argue because of me. Besides, I'm already working on finding out where Sophia lives."

A skip of excitement in my chest betrays me. As much as I want to protect Hazel and avoid pressuring her to do this, it's thrilling to think my best friend might be the key to helping the coven catch Sophia Madsen.

"But you don't want to do this, do you?" I ask.

"Not really. But if Oaklyn is who you say she is, I have to learn more."

"*If*? Hazel, she is *exactly* who I say she is." I hunch down, dropping my voice. "She tried to abduct me. And then tried to kill me."

"Yeah, I know." She sounds unconvinced. Jesus, Oaklyn must be good in bed to make Hazel doubt what I've told her.

I rub my face. "The Shadows will need both Sophia and Oaklyn's addresses so they can organize an ambush."

"And kill them?" Hazel asks with a hardness in her voice.

The word sends a jolt through my chest. But based on what I know about the coven's laws, killing wouldn't be their first move. "Detain, ideally. But if they resist or get violent..."

Hazel snorts. "Yeah, as if they'll go nicely."

"I know. I know this is asking so much of you." My heart cracks for her knowing how impossible this decision must be. If she doesn't help us, people might die. But helping us means betraying the woman she cares about—and putting herself at risk of being discovered as a spy.

I really don't want to ask her to do this. But how can I ignore the opportunity to catch the most dangerous people known to witches? So I stay quiet, letting her make the decision, ready to support her either way.

Leaves rustle on the willow tree, witches bend their heads together in murmured conversations, and white clouds drift overhead. The world keeps turning despite the magical war brewing.

"I'll send you Sophia's location as soon as I know it," Hazel finally says, sounding resigned. "But give me some time. I...I need to understand all this and what I'm doing. It's a lot to take in."

My heart jumps. "Yeah. I get it. Just promise me that if Oaklyn seems suspicious, or you feel unsafe, or even if your gut just tells you something's off...get the hell out of there."

A pause. "I will."

I don't know what went through her mind in that hesitation, but I can only hope she's not considering any alternative.

"Anyway, I should go," she says. "Work meeting."

"Wait. I wanted to..." I try to find the words to ask what's burning in my chest. Cupping my hand over my mouth, I drop my voice lower. "Hazel, in your considerably rational opinion, do you think it's worth investigating *why* I can hear the chimeras inside my head?"

Rustling in the background tells me she's getting ready for her meeting. "I mean, yeah, but... Where would you start?"

My cheeks burn before I ask the question. "Do you think it's possible I'm descended from witches?"

"Yes," she says at once. "That would explain a lot."

She didn't hesitate. It's everything I needed to hear.

I blow out a breath, as grateful as ever to have her in my life. "Maybe I can find records in one of the libraries. I'll do some digging."

A pile of leather-bound books flashes through my memory—the ones Natalie lobbed at me when we practiced throwing the golden net in the Alchemy room. She got them from the library, where hundreds of books hold information about the history of witches, magic, and the coven. There must be something in there about chimeras...

"What would it mean if you are?" Hazel asks, her voice bouncing as she walks. "Does it give you the right to become a you-know-what?"

"I doubt it, but..." I chew my lip. Better not tell her too much, given how close she is to Oaklyn. "I just want to know whether people before me could talk to chimeras, too."

And if they could...then maybe Lucy wasn't just manipulating me. Maybe my bone-deep calling really is to protect them.

In which case it's me against the world. Against the coven, against Natalie, against everything I'm supposed to be doing.

And I'm so screwed.

As we hang up, my laptop screen dims, and I tap the trackpad. I should order those textbooks and pretend to be a normal student for a little while longer.

But there's no going back to normal. Not when tonight, I'll be leading witches to trap the creatures that might be the key to understanding who I am.

I drop my head into my hands, my stomach hurting. My loyalties are so torn that I feel like I'm being ripped in half.

Amid all this uncertainty, there's one clear step forward: I need more information.

One hour until the ambush.

I wait until Natalie is busy coordinating with the Shadows before slipping away. She doesn't need to know what I'm doing.

The library feels colder and darker than the rest of the building, as if to discourage people from staying. Yellow light from an old brass lamp casts shadows across the towering bookcases. Dust motes swirl in the beam of my phone's flashlight as I scan the spines, some old and leather-bound, others new and glossy.

The Formation of a Coven: A History of Magical Governance

Principles of Earth Magic

The Guardian's Handbook: A Guide to Curse Breaking

Riding His Broomstick: A Forbidden Coven Romance

Wait, what?

I pull out the pocket-sized book and find a broody man on the cover with smoldering purple eyes and his robes open to reveal a hairless chest. I guess witches need romance novels too.

I slide it back and keep going, passing shelf after shelf.

Alchemy in the Modern Age: Approved Methods and Materials

Between the books, artifacts sit behind glass cases—tarnished medallions, a gold feather that shimmers with its own light, a black gemstone that my fingers itch to touch...

The hairs on my arms lift, and I pause. Is someone coming?

I hold my breath, straining to hear footsteps, but nobody appears. Must be the magic in these relics setting off my sixth sense.

I sweep my flashlight beam across the far wall, illuminating what I hadn't noticed before—an iron gate cordoning off a small, shadowy alcove. It's deliberately isolated, the bars a clear warning to stay out.

Which means whatever's in there is exactly what I'm looking for.

I approach the gate and run my fingers along the cold iron. A padlock secures it shut, and the bars seem to absorb all light. Inside, a few dozen books are arranged on narrow shelves.

"Screw it," I mutter, unzipping my backpack and pulling out the gauntlet. It feels alive as I slip it on, that familiar hum of power vibrating up my arm.

I glance over my shoulder once more, then slam my fist into the lock. The sound echoes through the library like a gunshot, making me flinch. But the lock gives way, breaking open like it was made of paper.

Heart pounding, I push the gate open enough to squeeze through, wincing at the creak of hinges.

I scan the shelves quickly, the hair on the back of my neck prickling. God, I'm going to be in *so* much trouble if someone finds me looking for books about forbidden magic.

At last, my beam falls on a cloth-bound hardcover that looks promising.

Guardians of the Wild: A History of Magical Stewardship

I ease it off the shelf, cringing at the loud scrape. As I kneel and set it on the floor in front of me, it makes a deep *thump*.

The pages are yellowed and brittle beneath my fingers as I carefully turn them, and the text has faded with age—but the spine and corners are intact, telling me the book hasn't been taken out much.

> *Prior to Western intervention, chimeras were integral members of Asian and Middle Eastern societies. Archaeological evidence suggests these beings served essential ecological functions, including restoring damaged ecosystems and maintaining the natural equilibrium in their territories.*

My heart pounds faster. Okay, this fits what Lucy said.

I glance at the closed door and flip through the pages, searching for information about people who could communicate with the chimeras.

Finally, I find something, and my breath catches.

> *...certain regions produced individuals capable of telepathic communion with these entities, a phenomenon documented in Eastern manuscripts dating back to 600 CE.*

However, the discovery of bio-magical absorption methods by European practitioners in the early 1800s marked a shift in human-chimera relations. Through a blood ritual (protocol redacted by order of C.S.A.M.M. Directive 274), practitioners could assimilate a chimera's capabilities, including metamorphosis and psychic influence. This precipitated a change in magical philosophy and practice.

The colonial period saw increasing tension between traditional Guardians and those who sought to control magic. In the early 1900s, when the abuse of biological magic during World War I demonstrated its catastrophic potential, the newly established Coven of Shadows and Alchemists for Managing Magic enacted sweeping reforms, declaring bio magic too dangerous to possess. Those who opposed this doctrine, including the remaining Guardians, were eliminated in the Great Magical Reform of 1928.

While some Guardian bloodlines maintained their practices in isolated mountain regions, C.S.A.M.M.'s influence eventually reached these remote areas. Their philosophy that chimeras were essential to magical equilibrium was branded as dangerous idealism.

The Guardian title was later appropriated by the Coven, though with a different purpose. While ancient Guardians maintained harmony between magic and humanity, modern Guardians and Trackers serve C.S.A.M.M. by harnessing it. These roles exemplify the Coven's reformation of magical governance.

My hands shake as I brace my palms against the floor. So bio magic wasn't always considered dangerous. It wasn't meant to be consumed.

Lucy was right—and there's a lot that I never knew about the relationship between humans and magic. Could I be descended from the ancient Guardians this book talks about? Mom's side is from the Philippines, which fits the region. Plus, the pull I feel toward magic, my ability to sense it, the chimeras talking to me... It all fits.

I press my palm to my chest, feeling my fluttering heartbeat. I thought I was broken—not witch enough and also not normal enough. But what if that's by design? What if there's a reason I can hear the chimeras when no one else can?

Before I can keep reading, footsteps click beyond the library door. My pulse spikes, an icy sensation shooting through me.

I grab the book and stuff it back onto a shelf, then slip through the gap in the iron gate just as the door swings open with a creak that reverberates through my bones. I crouch behind the closest bookcase.

"Should be in the third row near the bottom," Fiona says.

Through the gaps in the shelves, I catch a glimpse of her cloaked figure bathed in shadows.

A second person strides closer, their footsteps quiet.

I struggle to suppress my breathing, willing my heart to calm down. *Please, please don't come to the back of the library...*

Through the shelves, two bookcases away, Hayley bends down and drags a finger along the spines, her cloak pooling around her feet.

She freezes. Her head turns left and right, like she can sense my presence.

I cover my mouth and hold my breath, staying as still as I can.

After an agonizing moment, she returns her attention to the shelf. Leather groans and scrapes as she pulls out a book. "This one?"

"Let's see." Fiona's heels click as she steps into the room. "That's it. Should have the enchantments near the beginning."

Enchantments? Are they planning to use ancient magic to catch the chimeras?

At last, their footsteps fade, and the door clicks shut.

I let out my breath in a whoosh.

I wait before emerging from my hiding spot on trembling legs. My discovery sits like a stone in my chest. I knew C.S.A.M.M. was formed to control magic, but I never knew humans once *coexisted* with magic—and that those humans had been eradicated. The coven let that part of their history die...or more likely, buried it on purpose.

Ancient Guardians.

The words roll around in my mind, like they're trying to see if they belong there.

This would explain who I am and what I can do. Some of those witches must have survived, and I'm descended from them.

And once, long ago, the coven eliminated people like me.

My stomach churns. By working with the coven to trap chimeras, I'm betraying the people who dedicated their lives to protecting them—people who might be my ancestors.

My phone vibrates against my butt, making me jump.

I pull it out of my pocket and squint at the bright screen.

Natalie

Where are you? We're getting ready to go.

I'm out of time.

And I'm more confused than ever about what I'm supposed to do.

I return the alcove to what it was (uh, except for the broken padlock) and head back toward the lobby, a strange tingling in my head.

Ever since Natalie brought me into the coven, I've been trying to prove my worth. I showed the witches my ability and let them use it—use *me*—for their benefit, all to achieve some sense of purpose and belonging. I swore their oath and spent my time and energy hunting down curses, and now, I'm hunting chimeras.

But what if my ability isn't meant for hunting chimeras, but for protecting them? What if *that's* my purpose? This deep sense of right and wrong inside me is trying to tell me something, waving a red flag while I obediently run around with a golden net.

I turn a corner in the empty brick hallway, my rapid footsteps echoing my pounding heart. Who, exactly, am I trying to be? Who am I betraying by ignoring what feels true?

The same intuition that pulls me toward magic is telling me I shouldn't be trapping chimeras. Even if it means stepping away from the coven I've been trying so hard to fit into, and even if it means facing the rejection I've been afraid of, I have to do the right thing.

But it's not as simple as that. The cost of choosing this path would be more than just isolation from the coven—it would be five years of isolation from everybody I know and love. Five years of my life, wasted while I rot in prison.

I slow my steps before I get to the lobby, my chest fluttering. Do I follow my intuition and do what feels morally right? Or do I keep fighting for the belonging and purpose that comes with being in Natalie's coven?

I have minutes left to decide. On the one hand, I could listen to the ancient Guardians who protected the balance between magic and humanity—witches who are long gone and have no influence over my life. On the other hand, I could listen to the coven—the people who are here and now, a community I can be a part of if I do what they say.

So, do I follow in the footsteps of the ancient Guardians...or do I keep fighting to prove my worth to a coven that doesn't respect me? The choice seems obvious, but I suspect Natalie might try to change my mind.

From the Journal of Hazel Okada

I did something terrible tonight. Or maybe I did something necessary. I honestly can't tell where the line is anymore.

The evening started as a perfect date night. Oaklyn picked me up in her FJ Cruiser, and after dinner on a patio, we drove to a viewpoint to watch the sunset—though we accidentally missed the sunset. Her hand found my thigh as we parked, and soon I was fumbling for the button of her jeans. Within minutes, we were in the back seat, fogging up the windows like a total cliché.

It was what happened on the drive home that's making my pulse race.

"I need to make a couple stops," she said, her voice husky and her hair tousled from our backseat activities. "Mom wants her fancy chocolates and groceries."

Cold sweat prickled on my back as the words left her mouth. This was it. I was about to learn where Sophia Madsen lives.

After the grocery store—the most expensive in town, of course—we pulled up outside a ritzy downtown high-rise. Its glass exterior reflected the city lights, and a crystal chandelier glowed in the lobby. Given the building's size, I could have had an excuse to say I couldn't figure out which unit Sophia was in.

Instead, I heard myself say, "Nice place. She on the top floor?"

"Nothing but the best for Sophia Madsen." Oaklyn sighed.

My two-faced inner voice made a note: Cascade Tower. Penthouse suite.

Fuck. I knew the address—now what was I going to do with it?

I stayed in the passenger seat while she strode inside with Sophia's groceries and chocolates, my hands shaking so badly I could barely drop a pin on my phone's map.

That little pin had the power to change everything.

I stared at it, trembling, not ready for what came next.

Helping Katie should've been my priority. She's been my best friend for years and has always had my back. She needs me.

But sitting there with my fingertips frozen over the phone screen, the idea of betraying Oaklyn sent a pang through my chest so intense it took my breath away. Was it just because of my attraction to her, or...?

Or am I starting to understand what she and her mom are fighting for?

Does their mission to democratize magic actually make sense?

I've known Katie for years and Oaklyn for minutes, yet somehow the line between right and wrong isn't as clear as it should be. What does my hesitation say about me? Was I really questioning the coven? Questioning Katie?

God, it scares me how quickly my certainties have unraveled since meeting Oaklyn.

If I sent the witches after her mom and they killed her, how could I live with myself? Oaklyn has trusted me, opened up to me, made me feel pleasures I've never experienced. What a total, utter betrayal that would be.

She returned before I could make a decision, and I clicked off my phone, leaving the pin on the map and my message to Katie unsent. I needed more time to sort through my mess of emotions.

She tossed a small gift onto the back seat—a ring box wrapped in purple wrapping paper with a tiny purple bow on top—and slammed the door.

"Everything okay?" I asked hesitantly.

She threw the car into gear. "She's just so..."

She hit the gas, taking out her anger on the accelerator. The engine roared as we pulled away from the curb.

A minute passed, and she didn't finish the sentence.

"Has it always been like that?" I asked, wondering if things got harder since her dad or brother died.

"Long as I've been alive." Oaklyn gripped the steering wheel tighter. "Dad used to tell us Mom was just trying to make the world more balanced. That life made her this way."

"What happened?" I asked.

Oaklyn lifted a shoulder. "Growing up, her parents fought, and she spent hours in the park every day to escape. That's how she met her best friend, Morgan. It didn't take her long to notice Morgan was always hungry, and her family could barely afford to survive. Meanwhile, Mom's family had three vacation homes they rarely visited and cars they never drove. So, Mom started sneaking food to Morgan's place. Learned the bus routes at nine years old so she could fill her backpack with groceries and deliver them after school. Her parents never noticed—too wrapped up in their corporate ladder-climbing."

I stared at her, trying to reconcile that awful woman with a kid who actually cared about another person.

"Then, when Mom was seventeen," Oaklyn continued, "she showed up at Morgan's apartment, and no one answered. She found out days later that Morgan had died from an infection. Something an antibiotic could have treated... Something magic could've cured in seconds."

My heart squeezed. The lure of magic made a heck of a lot of sense.

"Later, when Mom discovered magic existed," Oaklyn said, "she became obsessed with the injustice of it—that magic was being restricted by witches while people like Morgan died needlessly. I don't know... I think after spending her childhood powerless, watching her friend die, magic represents everything she never had. Control. Power. The ability to fix what's broken."

"Oh," I said quietly.

Oaklyn looked sideways at me, her frown deepening. "Don't let me change your opinion of her. She's not the same fucking person. Not at all. When I was twelve, my pet snake died, and when I cried, she—" Her jaw worked. "She hurt me, and she made me skin the snake. Said attachment is a weakness."

My stomach churned. "Holy shit. That's...not normal."

"Whenever my brother and I fought, she'd tell us to hit back harder. It wasn't until...I don't know, the last year or so, that Freddie and I realized how fucked-up that was. I wish we'd figured it out sooner. All those years, we could have had each other instead of fighting."

That hard expression was back on her face—the one I've come to recognize when the topic of her brother comes up. It makes sense that she puts up a tough front, not to mention how protective she is of the few people she lets in.

"There's a reason I've got Freddie's dog and not her," Oaklyn said. "I don't trust her to take care of anything living."

My phone buzzed. It was Katie: "SOS. Need intel on the Madsens. Whatever you've got."

My heart dropped through my feet, through the floor of the car, and into the earth's core. It's like she fucking knew how close I was to sending her something. Like she was sitting behind me with a fire iron, poking and poking until I cracked.

I knew what I had to do. It was inevitable. But I couldn't. Not yet.

I reached over to where Oaklyn's hand rested on the gear shift, lacing our fingers together. Her skin was warm and comforting.

"I can't imagine how hard it must have been living with her," I said, though I wasn't sure if this was helpful. Maybe there was nothing helpful to say, and I should have stayed quiet.

Oaklyn lifted a shoulder, her eyes glassy. "I know she's my mom...but sometimes, I hate her. Is that bad?"

Her lips puckered, like the words tasted sour.

I squeezed her hand. "It's okay to feel that way."

And it made what I had to do a little easier.

My heart beat faster, hammering against my ribs.

I had the power to fix this. To take that awful woman out of Oaklyn's life and help Katie all in one swoop.

Pros of texting Sophia's location to Katie:

+ Help catch the most dangerous known witch, who has hurt her own children, Natalie's family, and innocent bystanders.

+ Oaklyn deserves better than Sophia's bullshit.

+ Katie's safety depends on this.

Cons:

- Send the only family Oaklyn has left to prison. Or worse.

- Oaklyn might hate me forever.

How can I even weigh those against each other?

There was one way forward. One thing for me to do, no matter how sick it made me.

On the drive back, I did it. And a chill spread through me the moment the message to Katie showed 'Delivered.'

Now the Shadows will come for Sophia, and...

Well, whatever happens next will be my fault. I'll be responsible for Sophia's capture—responsible for Oaklyn losing the only family she has left.

As terrible as Sophia is, she's still Oaklyn's mother, and the way Oaklyn talked about her... There was pain in her eyes, but also a complicated sort of love. The kind that comes from being raised by someone who hurt you but also made you strong enough to fight for what you believe in.

I texted Katie one more time and asked her to call me in the morning before doing anything with Sophia's location. I wanted to talk to her, to make sure the witches weren't going to kill Oaklyn's mom—only imprison her.

My heart is beating hard with the realization that I've done something serious. Part of me wants to call Katie right now and take it back. Tell her to stop whatever the Shadows are planning. But it's too late, and the information is sent.

And anyway, this is bigger than my feelings for Oaklyn. This is about keeping the world safe.

I just hope that when this is all over, Oaklyn will understand why I did it. But I don't expect forgiveness from her.

Honestly, I don't even know if I'll ever forgive myself.

When we got back to her apartment, she pulled me close and kissed me with such tenderness that tears sprang in my eyes. "Stay tonight?" she whispered against my lips.

The guilt was as sharp as a blade between my ribs.

How could I say no? How could I walk away when this might be our last night together before everything falls apart?

I need tonight to commit her every contour to memory. To remember the way her breath sounds in my ear and the way her eyes glint when she smiles. Because after tomorrow, these memories might be all I have left of her.

CHAPTER 19

Katie vs. The World

T HE LOBBY FEELS MORE like a war room than the magical haven I once thought it was. As black-cloaked figures gather beneath the wrought-iron lanterns—ten Shadows that Sky assembled for the mission—fear grips my throat. I'm positive tonight will end in a bloodbath.

The enchanted net drags behind me—one of two pieces of magic I've been granted. The other, the gauntlet, sits cold and hard on my hand. The thought of using either tonight makes me nauseous.

I follow Natalie across the lobby, my heart beating fast. "I need to talk to you about all this."

"We'll be okay," she says, misreading my panic. "The Shadows have a plan. This is exactly what we needed to secure your freedom."

She's way more excited than I am—and I get it. Before I knew the truth, I would have been excited too about trapping all these chimeras at once.

But Lucy's voice resonates in my memory: *If your witches attack us again, we will not show mercy.*

"We're putting everyone in danger for something that's my responsibility," I say. "And the chimeras..."

We are spirits of the wild, keepers of ancient magic.

I grip the net tighter, torn. Everything would be simpler if I could just believe trapping them is the answer. But I've heard Lucy's voice and felt their fear, and I've come to recognize something within myself that's been here since the moment I first sensed magic. During my time in the coven, I've seen the difference between trying to control magic and trying to protect it. And I feel in my soul that whatever is happening here isn't right.

Natalie puts both hands on my shoulders and holds my gaze. "I know you're scared, but we've got this. You're not going to prison on my watch, and that's a promise."

Her stubborn loyalty makes my eyes sting. She doesn't get it.

And the worst part is that I don't know how to explain. If I tell her I think I'm descended from ancient Guardians, she'll think I'm being naive and grasping at nothing.

A scoff behind us makes us turn.

"That net is *valuable C.S.A.M.M. property*," Agnes says, her fawn pigtails swinging as she shakes her head. She's holding a clipboard and pen, though what she could possibly be taking notes on, I have no idea. "It's not some *trinket* for you to mishandle. Stop dragging it on the ground."

Natalie sighs. "Don't you have some...checklist to check?"

"*And—*" Agnes ignores her, her wide-set eyes scanning me up and down. "You should be wearing a proper cloak. Why don't you have one?"

"Ask Fiona," I mutter.

She scoffs again and turns up her nose before walking away. "I will. No sense of tradition around here... Things are changing for the worse... Greg, get out!"

She chases the French bulldog from the lounge, waving the clipboard, leaving me to let out a breath and try to refocus.

The volume of conversation rises, the team of Shadows putting on their cloaks and backpacks as they prepare to go. My own backpack is slumped in a booth, practically empty except for the hiking essentials from last time.

I hold up the enchanted net. "So *how* are we supposed to catch that many chimeras with just one of these?"

Natalie looks past me. "Time to go, Sky?"

"All set," Sky says. She's favoring the leg that got bit, but she looks as ready for action as ever.

Sweat prickles on the back of my neck as the ambush ticks closer. "Natalie, did you know there used to be witches who protected the chimeras? Guardians, before Guardians became dedicated to neutralizing curses?"

Natalie's brow furrows. She looks at me properly, her excitement morphing into confusion.

Heels click, and Fiona marches over wearing her red traveling cloak and a satisfied smile. My stomach clenches, and I avoid meeting her eye like a solar eclipse.

"This is your chance, Miss Alexander. If we trap all the bio magic tonight, you'll earn your freedom—and maybe more. I hear your ability proved useful in catching the last one."

I don't know what to say, so I just nod. Big change of heart from when she wanted me to catch chimeras alone.

"It's hard to find good Trackers these days," she continues. "There may be a place for you in that guild if your talents align."

Her words trickle through me, easing the tension in my head. It's not the first time I've been promised a place in the coven if I prove useful. She kept her word last time, letting me be a Guardian with Natalie for weeks before I blew it. Could tonight fix everything? We could put this mess behind us, and I can move forward as part of the coven, ready to continue keeping the world safe from dark magic.

"Thank you," I say, unsure how to feel.

As she walks away, a jitter rolls through me, and I tighten my grip on the net.

God, it's tempting. If I can forget about the voices in my head and whatever I learned about the ancient Guardians, I can accept her peace offering and move on—because in truth, this is all I've wanted. A place in the coven with Natalie.

But this isn't just about my freedom anymore. This is about purpose, and morals, and what kind of person I want to be.

Is there any winning? Either I betray what my heart is telling me and we trap these chimeras, or I somehow sabotage this mission and spend five years in prison. There's no middle ground.

Sky raises her hands for quiet. "Listen up!" she shouts, her voice strong. "I know this falls outside our expertise. But this is a critical opportunity to trap the bio magic that escaped in February, so we need to give it our all."

I appreciate the way she said 'escaped' and not 'set free by this dumbass over here.'

"You should have all had a chance to review the enchantment by now," Sky continues. "If not, come see Hayley."

"What enchantment?" I whisper to Natalie, unease crawling up my spine.

On Natalie's other side, Fiona leans forward. "We won't be able to catch them one-by-one, so we're doing what we should have done long ago: destroying them altogether."

My blood runs cold. "What?"

"We're going to end bio magic's existence so a disaster like this never happens again. We should have done it right from the start instead of setting up those damned cages."

"You can't!" I cry, and a few Shadows look back at me.

Natalie touches my arm, dropping her voice to barely a whisper. "It's okay, Katie."

"Bio magic causes nothing but pain," Fiona says. Her gaze burns into me, full of that heaviness that's been there since she intercepted me at the airport. "Think of your loved ones before you ask us to leave this power feral, Miss Alexander. Think of someone's niece playing in the park, or their sister walking home alone at night."

I pull my arm away from Natalie. "But destroying it isn't the answer! These chimeras are a natural wonder. You can't just eliminate them."

At my rising voice, Sky stops talking, and every Shadow turns to look at us.

"A natural wonder? Don't be absurd." Fiona addresses everyone listening in. "Okay, let's move. Remember, no magic goes free."

My chest tightens. Do I tell her I had an actual conversation with a chimera, or would that make everything worse? Will *anything* I say convince her not to destroy them, or am I basically standing in front of a high-speed train right now?

Unless...

"Millie and Sebastian are there," I blurt. "If we storm in, they'll get hurt or killed."

The entire room goes still. I can't look at anyone, least of all Natalie. Not only have I betrayed Millie's secret, but I've also admitted to keeping this huge secret from Natalie.

But I had no choice. They need to know human lives are at stake before sending in the cavalry.

"What are they doing there?" Natalie asks, breaking the silence.

"Millie tried to consume bio magic, and she's...unwell. They're trying to fix it."

There's a furious glint in her eyes that tells me we're in for an argument later. My stomach plummets—but I can't think about that right now. I just need to stop this massacre from happening.

"If they get in the way, they're the only ones to blame," Fiona says.

With a jerk of her chin, the Shadows move toward the steam clock exit, a dark tide of cloaks.

I rush to grab my backpack and follow Natalie down the hall, my heart beating out of my chest. No, no, no. This is a huge mistake.

But what am I supposed to do? I can't stop an army of witches!

Dad's words echo in my head: *Alexanders don't give up.*

My brain whirrs frantically, my feet clumsy as I let Natalie guide me with her hand on my lower back. *Think, Katie!*

What could possibly take the Shadows away from this mission? Is anything more important than the chance to trap a hundred chimeras at once?

I can think of one thing. An extremely high-priority target.

I pull out my phone, hating myself for doing this to Hazel.

Katie

> SOS. Need intel on the Madsens. Whatever you've got.

We pile into the van, and I end up wedged between Natalie and Hayley on the floor. I stare at my phone as we wind through Vancouver's dark streets toward the park, waiting for Hazel's reply, desperately trying to come up with another argument.

At last, my phone buzzes in my hand, and my breath hitches.

Hazel

> Sophia's place.

With it comes a pin on a map.

Holy shit. She did it.

This is how I derail the mission.

As I'm staring at the pin, another text arrives.

> Can we talk before you share it with the witches? I feel like a terrible person for doing this. Call me in the morning?

But we don't have time to talk first. She doesn't realize how urgent this is and what's at stake tonight.

I'm sorry, Hazel, but this is life-or-death.

I jump to my feet, hitting my head on the roof. "Ow—stop!"

Sky keeps driving, but everyone else turns to stare at me, their faces ghostly and unreadable in the street lights flashing by beyond the windows.

My hands shake as I hold up my phone—my last, desperate hope. "I know where Sophia Madsen is."

From the Journal of Hazel Okada

Back at Oaklyn's, we got ready for bed, though my mind raced with what Katie might do with Sophia's location. She'll wait until morning, right? Should I be concerned about her lack of reply?

Oaklyn stripped down and rummaged for the tank top she wears as pajamas. "Who do you text so much?"

"My parents," I said too quickly. Shit, she must have noticed me texting Katie on the drive back.

"Hm." She plucked a strand of dog hair from her shirt. Watching her stand there with no pants and her nipples visible through the thin fabric, my brain went fuzzy—until she said, "Have you made friends in Vancouver yet?"

Something in her voice made my skin prickle. Like she was forcing a casual tone.

"If coworkers count," I said, forcing a casual tone right back. I sat cross-legged on the bed and shook my hair loose from its braid, not meeting her eye.

Oaklyn picked up her dagger where we left it on the bedside table and touched the tip with her index finger. "I can't figure you out. What your game is."

I tried for a playful smile, but it wavered. "What do you mean?"

"To start, you've mentioned names and places I've never told you about. Slips out sometimes. You usually don't notice."

My mouth went so dry I couldn't speak. My heart pounded faster. Run, run, run.

"You also know more about magic than we've talked about," she continued. "Earth magic. Bio magic."

"I do a lot of resear—"

"Bullshit." Her eyes narrowed dangerously.

My heart slammed into my ribs. "I don't know what you're—"

She stepped closer to the bed, looming over me. "Your journal had some pretty interesting entries, sweetheart."

I froze, staring up at her. "You did read it!"

She tilted her head. "Parts of it."

Oh God. How far did she get?

"Spying for witches?" she added. "I never would have thought you'd be capable of something like that, sweet girl."

Ice shot through my veins. The room shifted beneath me.

"Now what I need to figure out is..." She rested her hands on the bed, inches from my knees, one fist still around her dagger. "How dangerous are you?"

I forced a laugh and leaned sideways on my hand so my shoulder stuck out, trying to look small and harmless. "Oaklyn, come on. If you read it then you know how I feel about you."

"Show me your phone," she snapped, not falling for it.

My chest tightened. "What? Why?"

"If you've got nothing to hide, then you shouldn't have a problem showing it to me."

"Then—you should show me your phone, too! Make it even."

"Fine. Here." She snatched hers off the bedside table and unlocked it, then held it out to me.

Shit, shit, shit. If I gave her mine, she would see that the last thing I sent Katie was the location of Sophia's apartment!

"Okay, look." I raised my hands in surrender. "I know Katie. But I swear, I had no idea the two of you were...um..."

"You didn't know she's the one who killed my brother?" she snarled. "You didn't know she's part of the organization that's been hunting my family over the cause we believe in?"

I shook my head. "We only realized the connection recently."

"And you didn't tell me? Why is she aware of this fucked-up triangle but not me?"

"I didn't want... I thought if you knew, you might..."

"Open—your—phone," she said, her voice low and dangerous.

"Oaklyn, please listen—"

She cracked her dagger like a whip, and in a blink, the roots had me by the throat and wrists, holding me down on the bed. I gasped, struggling, as it creaked and hissed across the duvet.

Wyatt started barking, his nails scraping the floor as his dark shape appeared in the doorway. Absurdly, I thought he might come to my rescue, like maybe we'd formed a bond after all the time I spent scratching his ears. But—

"Sit," Oaklyn said, and he did. Just stayed there while she climbed on me and searched my pockets with rough hands.

My eyes stung with tears. Those same hands had caressed me minutes ago. The sharp angles of her face, once so beautiful, now looked harsh in the moonlight.

I stopped struggling and let her take my phone. There was no winning against her—but more than that, I didn't want to fight her. I'd betrayed her, and now, I just had to convince her that it wasn't what it seemed. That I was never planning to sell her to the witches.

"Oaklyn," I choked out as the roots tightened over my throat.

She glanced up, saw I was suffocating, and flicked her wrist.

The roots fell away, and I gasped, gulping air back down.

I stayed put while she held the phone to my face to unlock it. The mistrustful glint in her eyes sent a pang through my chest.

Then, before she could open my messages and find the awful truth, I said something that I can't believe came out of my mouth.

I can't bring myself to write it down. I'm too afraid of what I've done.

CHAPTER 20

Yet Another Madsen Residence

THROUGH THE VAN'S TINTED windows, Sophia's apartment building rises like a glittering spear against the night sky, its lobby lit by a crystal chandelier. The Cascade Tower—all glass and steel and wealth, because apparently even magical terrorists appreciate a good view.

The inside of my cheek stings where I've been chewing it. I should be racing to Lighthouse Park to warn the chimeras. But my heart is torn, fluttering desperately. Could I slip away without Natalie noticing?

We park in the loading zone, and the Shadows flood out of the van like a SWAT team, their black cloaks billowing as they move silently through the night. The streetlights catch their utility belts, glinting off small containers.

Natalie grabs my wrist to stop me from following, her touch sending a jolt up my arm. "People are going to get hurt in there. Stay in the van?"

Her tone is pleading, her eyes searching mine desperately. She knows me well—and under other circumstances, I would argue that I should help fight in any way I can.

But today is different, so I nod, my stomach twisting. "Go. Stay safe."

Her brow pinches, like she's suspicious of my lack of argument. But we have no time to stand here, so she just takes my hands and pulls me into a kiss.

"I love you," she whispers into my lips.

After my lies and secrets, these words wrap around me like a hug. I melt a little, my eyes prickling. "I love you too."

While she races after the Shadows, I get back into the van—and immediately open my phone to hail a ride-share. If I can warn Lucy that the Shadows are planning an ambush, I can stop a disaster from happening.

The street is quiet except for the distant hiss of a car. Few people are out this late, and the sidewalks look dark and cold.

Something rustles beside me in the van, and I jump, my heart shooting into my throat.

Nobody is in here. The seats are empty, other than…

My backpack is moving. Struggling.

I stare at it. A disgruntled "mrrrp" rises from its depths.

Oh no.

Slowly, I reach for the zipper. A furry butt greets me before Ethel turns around and springs out, latching onto my thigh with needle-sharp claws.

"Ow!" I cry, plucking her off my leg.

She glares at me like this is my fault, her blue eyes wide. Her fur is ruffled like she's weathered a storm in there.

"Why did you climb into my bag?" I scold her. "This isn't—"

A crack like a gunshot erupts outside. Ethel startles and scrambles out of my arms, her claws digging into my jacket. She ping-pongs around the van in a thunder of paws and tearing sounds, managing to turn on the hazard lights and an overhead light.

"Ow! Ethel, stop!"

A metallic hiss from outside rises above the chaos, and I spin to see glittering debris catch the moonlight as it falls from what must be the penthouse. The shards rain down on the pavement in a wave of crashes and tinkling, like a wind chime in a hurricane.

"Oh my God."

Leaving Ethel clinging to the ceiling like a fuzzy chandelier, I whip open the rear doors and scramble out.

High above, shouts carry into the night. Purple light bursts through the shattered window, casting an eerie glow over the dark sky.

Fear floods my veins. Do I go up there?

The image of Natalie lying injured flashes across my mind's eye—collapsed on the floor, bleeding out with glass in her side, everyone else too busy to help.

I can't leave. Not when Natalie might need me.

"I'm going," I say. "Ethel, stay here—"

She's no longer latched to the ceiling. And I left the van door ajar.

"Dammit!"

A white blur darts toward the building, and as a fleeing couple pushes open the glass door, she slips between them and into the lobby.

"Jesus Christ..." I sprint after her, losing sight of her as a stream of people floods out the stairwell.

I push through everyone. Footsteps echo off the marble floors, and distant rumbling prickles my eardrums.

"Anyone see a cat?" I ask the flowing crowd, my voice high with panic.

"It just ran past," an older man says as he hurries by. "Don't go up there though—something's happening. We called the police."

"Thanks," I say, having zero intention of listening to his advice.

When there's a gap in the flow of people, I burst through the stairwell door to find Ethel sitting primly on the third step, grooming her paw.

"If you get us killed, I'm never forgiving you," I growl, scooping her up. I stuff her into my jacket and zip it up so only her head pokes out. "Now stay, and don't scratch me."

I hesitate, debating whether to take the stairs. I would probably die if I tried to climb all the way to the penthouse, so I race back through the lobby to the elevator.

When the doors open, more terrified people stream past, warning me not to go up there. I thank them and get in anyway. My hands are sweating as I push the button to the top floor.

The elevator glides upward, maddeningly smooth and unhurried while my insides twist with visions of Natalie bleeding out on some fancy carpet. Ethel's purr rumbles against my chest like she's enjoying this adventure too much.

Another crash sounds. The elevator shudders. The lights flicker, and for a terrifying moment, I think I'm going to be trapped in this metal box while Natalie and Sky fight for their lives beyond it.

But the elevator continues, and I clench my fists, ready for whatever awaits. God, I wish this gauntlet gave me powers beyond just a good punch.

The doors open with a cheerful ding, and I blink away a cloud of dust. My breath hitches. Ethel stops purring, her head swiveling.

The penthouse door has been blown off its hinges and lies in splinters across the hallway. Cool night air rushes past me, carrying the scent of smoke. My hair lifts from my shoulders like I've walked into a thunder-cloud.

I step over the mangled door, ears ringing. Marble countertops are shattered. A light fixture lies in fragments. Furniture has been ripped apart and flung about the room. The opposite wall of floor-to-ceiling windows is gone, leaving jagged glass around a gaping hole to the night beyond.

My stomach lurches at the sight of Sophia standing with her back to the open, her white-blonde hair whipping around her face. She's wearing a blue silk robe, red cuts oozing all over her pale skin. But she's holding strong, her teeth gritted and her eyes blazing purple.

The Shadows fire debris at her so fast that I can't keep up. Fiona stands among them, her cloak like a splash of blood against the darkness.

Natalie. Where's Natalie?

I scan frantically, my breaths shallow and panicked.

Sophia blocks every hit, blowing each piece to dust before it can touch her. Copper spheres clatter to the floor—the same ones Natalie used as bullets when the Madsens infiltrated C.S.A.M.M.

There. Natalie's kneeling, fighting hard, her face streaked with blood. Alive.

Relief floods through me.

Neil crouches beside her, hands raised as he fights, face tense with concentration. Sky leads the charge, launching copper bullets and anything she can summon.

Need to get to Natalie.

Ducking low to avoid drawing attention, I inch closer. My pulse races so fast that a shudder runs through me. Ethel squirms, and I zip my jacket tighter before she gets any ideas.

Sky reaches into her utility belt and hurls something new. With a tinkling crash, a cloud of purple smoke erupts at Sophia's feet.

Sophia roars and steps backward, coughing. Her heel meets empty air. She teeters on the edge, thirty stories above the street.

"Keep her alive, Skylar," Fiona barks. "Let's go, everyone! Surround her!"

"Trying," Hayley grits out, ducking to avoid a flying toaster.

The counter explodes.

Without thinking, I throw myself in front of Natalie and raise my gauntlet. A hunk of marble ricochets with a clang, leaving my hand tingling but unharmed.

"Katie!" she shouts, her eyes widening when she realizes who I am. Her gaze darts to Ethel for the briefest moment. "What—I told you to stay in the van!"

"Yeah, well, the plan changed when the window exploded." I grab her arm and yank her down to the floor as more debris slams into my side. The pain barely registers. All that matters is the warmth of her skin beneath my fingers, and the strength of her racing pulse as it matches my own.

"You should've stayed down there," she whispers fiercely, but her grip on me tightens, betraying how relieved she is that I'm with her.

A high sound rings out, and it takes me a moment to process it—it's Sophia laughing. Wisps of violet lightning dance from her hands, feathery arcs reaching out. The way she moves her fingers is mesmerizing, like choreography she's spent her whole life perfecting.

A shiver rolls down my spine as chunks of floor tile lift into the air, hovering like a swarm of deadly insects.

"Stay behind me." Natalie forces me back, shielding me from danger as usual. She thrusts out her palms, and the air crackles as she deflects Sophia's barrage, her muscles tensing with the effort.

I want to pull her back and be the one to protect her for once, but all I can do is press my hands to her strong shoulder blades and feel the way magic vibrates through her body, zapping my palm like a static shock.

The Shadows advance, trying to corner Sophia against the deadly drop. But she's like a wild animal, lashing out in all directions. A chair leg impales the wall inches from Hayley's head. Glass shards spray toward Sky, who dives behind an overturned couch and swears, clutching her already injured leg.

"Give up, Sophia!" Fiona shouts through the tumult. "You're outnumbered."

"Doesn't put me at much of a disadvantage, does it?" Sophia's lips curve into a wicked grin. She opens her arms, and I gasp as every loose object in the suite rises into the air—broken furniture, kitchen appliances, shattered glass, stray copper bullets, all of it suspended in a deadly tornado.

Natalie tackles me to the floor as the whirlwind explodes outward. Ethel yowls in protest, pulling her head in and batting her paws inside my jacket as if searching for an exit.

I do my best to shield us with the gauntlet, but my skin stings and burns as God-knows-how-many cuts split open. Impacts and cries of pain rise all around us.

When the attack fades and I dare to raise my head, several Shadows are down, coughing and spluttering.

And beside Natalie, slumped against the wall, is Neil. It takes my brain a moment to register what I'm seeing—the chunk of marble protruding from his sternum.

He opens his mouth, and blood trickles out as his body slides down the wall. His muscular frame looks deflated and small as he crumples to the floor.

"Neil!" Natalie shrieks, lunging for him.

His black cloak darkens further as blood spreads out around the marble. He blinks once, and then his eyes go still and glassy, reflecting nothing but ceiling.

"No!" Natalie grasps his face, his collar, his arms, as if trying to figure out how to help.

But there's nothing we can do. Blood pools beneath him, creeping toward Natalie's knees. The smell fills my nostrils. I cover my mouth to hold back the sudden nausea.

One second he was alive and fighting, and the next, gone. The brutal simplicity of his death winds me, making me dizzy.

"C-careful," I stammer, grabbing Natalie and pulling her closer. Unwanted calculations flash through my mind—the trajectory of the marble, the few inches that spared her and condemned Neil.

The thought of how close they were standing paralyzes me. My heart pounds so hard I can barely breathe.

The memory of Freddie's body flashes across my mind's eye, and Will lying on the floor of C.S.A.M.M.'s lounge—every time I've seen a person become a corpse. Lifeless eyes gazing at the ceiling, faces frozen, bodies limp.

Natalie's breathing quickens, her expression twisting. Past the tears in her eyes, past the numb shock, there's something else—fury. My blood runs cold at the sight of it.

Then, distantly, a car engine revs. It's a pitch I've heard enough times that it's painfully familiar.

I gasp. "Natalie, it's..."

Sophia looks down at the street below, and then back at us. A sneer curls her lip, triumph glinting in her purple eyes.

Hayley jumps to her feet and launches something from her belt. A cluster of jagged spikes beelines for Sophia, a hum prickling my ears like the sound of a drone.

Sophia tilts her head. With a playful wiggle of her fingers, she leaps backward—and lets herself fall.

"No!" Fiona roars, lurching toward the window.

I race after her, more footsteps thundering around me. I stop a stride away, my insides seeming to launch into my esophagus as I look down, where parked cars resemble toys.

Stopped beside the van in front of the building, illuminated by a pale floodlight, is Oaklyn's silver FJ Cruiser.

From the Journal of Hazel Okada

After all we'd been through, was this going to be the moment Oaklyn finally killed me?

Flat on her bed, my neck and wrists throbbing where the roots had been, I scrambled for an explanation. "Oaklyn, I did it to protect you. The witches found out where you live. It was either you or your mom."

The awful part is that I didn't know who I was trying to protect. By lying, was I trying to save our relationship, or did I only care about saving myself?

Oaklyn's eyes widened a fraction, her fingers hovering over my phone in her hand. "What do you mean, me or my mom? What did you do?"

So she didn't get that far in my journal. Maybe I could lie my way out of this.

"I—I'm sorry. I was spying for them, it's true. But then I fell for you, and everything changed."

She shook her head, her brow pinched. Her hands trembled as her fingers fluttered over my phone screen.

Still lying on the bed, not daring to move in case she decided to strangle me again, I held my breath. The dagger sat on the bedside table, gleaming in the dim light. Its metal had a faint purple hue, the same shade I'd seen in the witches' eyes.

I could see the moment Oaklyn found the text to Katie. Her eyes went huge. She stepped back, putting distance between us like I was toxic. "You sent her location to the coven?"

"To get them off your back. I knew she could handle them, being a full witch, and..."

The temperature in the room seemed to drop. Oaklyn's face transformed into something I'd never seen—something cold and deadly that made my blood turn to ice. This wasn't the woman who'd held me in her arms and kissed me breathless. This was the person Katie had warned me about.

"This could have my mom killed," she whispered, her voice shaking.

I sat up slowly and carefully, like I was facing a wild animal. "I had no choice—"

She snatched up the dagger. "Give me one reason I shouldn't kill you right now."

I scooted backward on the bed, my heart launching into my throat. "B-because..."

She followed, climbing on the bed on her knees, her nostrils flaring with barely suppressed rage. "I trusted you. I thought—"

"Because you're the best thing that's ever happened to me," I blurted. "Because I love you."

It felt like I'd thrown myself off a cliff, not knowing if there would be water or rocks waiting below.

She froze, her expression going blank. She clearly did not expect this to come out of my mouth.

And neither did I.

I'd imagined saying those words to her in any other scenario than this. Maybe in bed, or over dinner, or on a walk. Not at knifepoint. Not as a bargaining chip for my life. But there they were, hanging between us.

Finally, she scowled. "You're just saying that to save your own ass."

"I'm not! If I wasn't head-over-heels in love with you, I would have backed away from this mess long ago. But I'm here, and I'm with you no matter what."

My throat tightened around the confession. I wasn't lying—not really. I know it's soon, but what I feel for her is so real. The way she looks at me, the gentleness in her touch, her smile that changed my whole world. She makes me feel like no one else ever has. I never want to stop this thing between us, as messed-up as it is.

And yet, as my admission hung in the air, I couldn't help thinking of Katie and Natalie, and what love looks like for them. Even from afar, I can feel that what they have is steady, safe, like home. What Oaklyn and I have feels more like standing at the edge of a volcano, beautiful and terrifying and potentially deadly.

But maybe that's the difference between them and us. Maybe some love is a warm hearth, and some love is like wildfire.

I don't mind ours. The wildfire.

Even sitting on Oaklyn's bed at the end of her dagger, when I wasn't sure whether she was about to kill me, I couldn't regret a single moment with her. That had to mean something, right?

Her expression twisted as several emotions flickered across her face.

"If you love me, then prove it," she snarled, grabbing my arm and pulling me off the bed.

She didn't say she loved me back, and I didn't expect her to. With all the fear rocketing through me, I barely felt the sting. And when she pulled on her pants and jacket and tugged me out the door with her, I went willingly.

The words still hummed in my chest, both true and calculated.

Would we be too late to stop the witches from hurting Sophia? Was saving Sophia even what I wanted?

As we raced out of Oaklyn's apartment, two things were certain.

The first was that I had to do something drastic to save myself and Katie.

The second was that I had to come clean about my beliefs: it's unfair that Oaklyn has been labeled a criminal because of what she's fighting for. She and her mom aren't wrong to want an equal distribution of magic.

The coven's secrecy, the way they've bullied and threatened Katie, and their monopoly on magic have convinced me that they're the bad guys here. They don't even know who I am, and if they did, they would respect me even less than they respect Katie. Hell, they punished Natalie for loving a non-witch.

But Oaklyn? She was born normal like me, with no chance at magic. Her brother died fighting for what should be a universal right. The way she talks about her family, the pain in her eyes... How could I not sympathize?

So yeah, I agree that magic shouldn't be hoarded by a few self-appointed gatekeepers. And if believing that makes me a criminal too, so be it.

CHAPTER 21

Things That Don't Make Sense

As Sophia plummets thirty stories, Oaklyn's car door flies open, and she jumps out and thrusts her arm upward. Dark roots extend from her dagger like living ropes, twisting and growing rapidly. They encircle Sophia's body, cushioning her fall before she can hit the ground.

"God dammit!" Sky punches the wall. "First division, take the stairs! Now!"

"We haven't lost her yet!" Fiona shouts, pivoting. "Get moving!"

Four Shadows sprint for the elevator. Panicked shouts break out when they spot Neil lying dead on the floor.

"Later!" someone roars. "We'll come back for him!"

My eyes sting. My chest is so tight I can barely breathe. Ethel struggles in my jacket once more, and I wrap my arms tightly around her, refusing to let her get hurt.

Below, the car's passenger door opens, and my blood runs cold as a second person steps out.

"Hazel," I whisper, icy horror flooding through me.

Wyatt jumps out after her and looks around vigilantly, as graceful as a wolf.

I grab Natalie's elbow and pull her back from the edge. "We need to get down there."

We race for the elevator with the others while Sky directs an attack on everyone below—including Hazel.

"Sky, careful!" I shout.

She glances back, confusion plain on her face. "I'm sorry, Katie. This is my job."

Bile rises in my throat. I stick my arm out to stop the elevator doors from closing and force myself in among the Shadows. Natalie steps in beside me.

"Try to see this from her perspective—" she begins, but I shake my head firmly.

"Don't." All I can think is that I need to get to Hazel before she's killed.

At ground level, debris hails down on the car, stopping the Madsens from escaping. Dust chokes the air so it's hard to see past the side-walk—either from the battle or a wall created by the Shadows. I cough as grit coats my tongue.

Through the haze, Sophia stands defiant. Her white-blonde braid is undone, her silk robe is torn, and blood streaks her skin. A red river flows down over her clavicle. She inches toward the car as she fights, her eyes darting between the Shadows and the FJ Cruiser—her only escape.

The Shadows advance. She thrusts her palms forward, and concrete ruptures beneath their boots, sending them stumbling. She lunges for the car, but Natalie is quick, countering with a blast of magic. The two forces collide with a shockwave that knocks everyone off their feet.

I hit the ground hard, pain shooting through my shoulder. Wyatt barks, the deep sound coming from much too close.

Paws thunder. His breath makes a low *huff-huff* as he gallops toward me.

With a hiss and a painful scrabble of claws, Ethel bursts out the bottom of my jacket and blitzes away over the broken pavement.

Wyatt skids to a stop, strides away from Natalie and me. He looks from us to Ethel, his eyes huge. With a "yip!", he changes course, chasing the fleeing cat.

"Thanks for the distraction, Ethel," I grunt as I sit up, watching her disappear under a parked sedan. Wyatt barks and claws at the front tire, trying to get to her. Ethel yowls in response, swiping at his nose from the safety of her hiding place.

With Wyatt occupied, my top priority floods back to me. Heart in my throat, I search frantically for Hazel through the dust. Sophia is already scrambling to her feet, still trying to get to the car.

There. Hazel is on her hands and knees, coughing and spluttering. Oaklyn is at her side, helping her up. The protectiveness in her gesture is familiar, making my stomach twist.

The air crackles with energy as magic flies in every direction. A chunk of concrete hurtles toward me, and I roll in time to avoid being crushed. My chest spasms from all the dust, and I cough, my head swirling as not enough oxygen gets into my lungs.

"Katie!" Natalie's voice pierces the chaos. She hauls me to my feet with one strong arm while her other hand remains outstretched, manipulating debris to shield us. "I've got you. Stay behind me."

Maybe it was the sound of Natalie shouting my name, but Hazel and Oaklyn look over sharply. There's a heavy pause between the four of us, though the Shadows have resumed their attack on Sophia.

Then, Oaklyn whips her dagger like a snake lashing out, ripping a parking meter from the sidewalk and hurling it at us. Natalie deflects it with a sweep of her arm, sending it into the FJ and denting the hood.

With another sweep, she sends a wave of broken pavement back at Oaklyn.

"Natalie, careful!" I cry as jagged pieces rocket toward Hazel.

But Oaklyn shields her, using her dagger to unleash twisted roots. They link together like gnarled fingers, forming a protective wall in front of Hazel.

"That was shitty of you, Katie," Oaklyn says as everything falls to the ground. "Using your bestie as a spy? Come on."

My heart plummets into the cracked earth beneath my feet. She knows? But that means—

"Hazel, get away from her!" I shout. I try to move forward, but Natalie holds me back, her grip strong on my arm.

My breaths come fast, my chest constricting. I don't understand. If she found out Hazel's secret, then why is Hazel here? And why is Oaklyn protecting her?

Hazel's eyes meet mine, something hard there I've never seen before. "I told you I wanted to talk first."

"There wasn't time! We were on our way to the chimeras, and I needed to—" I cut myself off with a wave of my hand. This isn't the moment to try and explain my decision to steer the witches away from the chimeras, and as Hazel and Oaklyn both narrow their eyes at the mention of chimeras, it's clear I've already said too much. "Hazel, what's going on?"

"I've learned all I need to know about what your coven does," she says, her voice strange and cold. "They hoard magic, deciding who's worthy and who isn't."

I step back as if punched. *What?*

Hearing those words come out of her mouth... It's wrong, like Freddie Madsen is speaking through her. I'm transported back to the trunk of the FJ Cruiser, questioning everything as Freddie preached to me. And later, in the halls of C.S.A.M.M., almost losing Natalie when I briefly believed him.

Did Oaklyn get to Hazel?

I thought I explained it. I thought she understood.

I mentally travel back through the last few days, trying to fit the pieces together. Has she been acting strange? Did I fail to notice the signs that she was buying into the Madsens' cause? I knew she was struggling to reconcile her feelings for Oaklyn, but I didn't think it would come to *this*.

Natalie's grip on my arm tightens—holding me back from danger as usual. But this time, we're staring into my best friend's eyes.

Oaklyn's lip curls as she watches me—probably taking satisfaction in seeing the horror dawn on my face. Her fingers slide possessively around the back of Hazel's neck.

"They're—they're murderers!" I splutter, my lips numb.

"They're fighting for equality." Hazel's fists are clenched, her chest heaving. "Magic should be available to anyone who wants to learn how to do it. You, of all people, should agree."

Heat rises in my face as she brings up my own frustrations with the coven. She doesn't understand the full picture.

Oaklyn toys with Hazel's hair as she caresses the back of her neck, and I shiver just watching it. How could Hazel fall for someone so awful?

"It's more complicated than that, Hazel," I say. "Natalie and I will explain it to you."

I clearly didn't give her enough information. She's smart—she'll get it if I explain. I can fix this.

The Shadows are still attacking from both the ground and the shattered penthouse window. Sophia is holding strong, inching closer to the vehicle with each retaliating blast. Despite being outnumbered, she looks like she's about five seconds from obliterating us all if we try to block her path any further.

Natalie keeps her palms up and nods toward Sophia. "You really think anyone should have access to magic? Look at what the people you're siding with are choosing to do with it."

Yes. My heart jumps as she makes the argument, and I look quickly at Hazel, hoping to see a flash of understanding.

But her face is set.

Oaklyn laughs. "What *we* do with it? You had magic locked in cages. Your coven controls its members with an iron fist."

Wyatt barks, frantically digging at the concrete beneath the parked sedan where Ethel is hiding—doing her part in this fight by keeping the dog's teeth away from our legs.

Hazel breaks away from Oaklyn and runs toward the cargo van. My stomach drops further, sinking right into the ground.

"Hazel, don't—" I start, but she's already whipping the rear doors open.

Natalie sucks in a breath and raises her palms. The air crackles, lifting the hairs on my arms.

I grab her wrist. "Don't hurt her," I beg—because even now, she's still Hazel, and I can't let her get hurt.

Hazel jumps out of the van with the golden net in her hands, the threads gleaming unnaturally bright under the streetlights.

My heart misses a beat. She can't be doing this.

"That's my girl," Oaklyn says. "Get in the car, sweetheart."

I'm numb, her betrayal surging over me like a tidal wave of arctic water.

I reach out a trembling hand, desperate to fix this. My chest is unbearably tight. "Hazel, don't. Come with us and we'll keep you safe."

"I am safe." She moves closer to Oaklyn, though there's the briefest hesitation in her step.

My ears ring. "She pressed a blade to my throat!"

"After you killed her brother!" Hazel's voice cracks, and she swallows hard, her eyes not quite meeting mine. "Come on, Katie... Wouldn't you do anything for someone you care about? Isn't that what you've always done?"

I blink, trying to absorb what's happening. My best friend, the person who's been by my side since high school, has chosen the Madsens over me. The treachery cuts deeper than any knife could, twisting in my gut until I can't breathe.

"You don't know what you're doing," I say through my teeth.

Hazel shakes her head fiercely, her fingers winding nervously around the golden net. "I'm done watching from the sidelines. I need to fight for something I believe in. Katie, that coven doesn't give a shit about you. They've lied to you, betrayed you, and..." She takes a shaky breath. "Maybe there aren't any good sides here. Maybe we're all just trying to do the best we can."

I step back, dizzy as the world tilts under me. The idea of there being no good side hits harder than it should because of how much I've been doubting the coven. How they've treated me. How wholeheartedly I disagree with their decision to trap the chimeras.

But that doesn't mean I'm going to side with the Madsens. I will never, *ever* stand with the family that has brought Natalie so much pain. The coven might be wrong about some things, but that doesn't make the Madsens right.

"Hazel, let's talk about this," I say, my voice coming out weak as my last thread of hope frays.

She shakes her head, backing toward the car with Oaklyn. I can see her hands trembling from here. She's sweating, terrified...but she's made her choice. She's chosen the path I've been fighting against.

Sophia unleashes a final, devastating blast that knocks back the closest Shadows, and makes a desperate sprint for the passenger seat. She climbs in, and Hazel gets into the back on Oaklyn's side.

"Wyatt! Come!" Oaklyn shouts, one foot in the car.

The dog turns his head, visibly torn between obeying her and eating Ethel. A little white paw takes another swipe at him from under the car, claws extended.

"Come!" Oaklyn shouts again, and the dog obeys, bounding over in a few long strides.

Hazel gives me one last look—and I swear I barely recognize her past the coldness in her eyes—before Oaklyn slams her door and climbs into the driver's seat.

"Hazel, please!" I try to follow, but Natalie yanks me back as a wave of concrete explodes between us.

I pull out of her grasp. "I can't let her go with them!"

She just grabs me tighter, her body shielding mine as debris rains down. "We can't help her if we're dead."

The car's engine comes to life, roaring and sputtering under the dented hood. Through the open car window, Sophia raises a wall of broken concrete and twisted metal. Then they're speeding away, Hazel's face visible in the rear window.

"No!" I cry, my feet carrying me forward automatically, like I think I can catch them.

Natalie holds me back, her arms strong around my waist. "Katie, don't. We'll get her back, but we need a plan."

The Cruiser disappears around a corner, leaving behind destruction and wounded Shadows.

Natalie cups my face, forcing me to look at her. "You're bleeding. Where are you hurt?"

I can't register physical pain right now. Not when everything is falling apart. Hazel is gone. The enchanted net is gone. Sophia Madsen has escaped, and we lost our chance to catch her and Oaklyn.

"How could she side with them?" I ask, my voice breaking. "Did I not explain how awful they are?"

Natalie's expression softens. "It's not your fault. Love makes people do things that don't make sense."

My eyes sting, and I wipe my face, smearing blood down my arm.

However safe Hazel thinks she is, she's in danger. And so are the chimeras at Lighthouse Park. I've failed everyone tonight.

I stare at the destruction around us—the shattered concrete, the wounded Shadows, the space where Hazel should be standing. Dust and blood linger in my mouth, bitter and too dry to let me swallow.

Hazel's cold, distant gaze lingers in my vision. My best friend, the one who came for sleepovers in high school, who sat with me over countless video calls to stop me from being homesick, who helped me get through my fight with Natalie...replaced by someone I don't recognize.

Natalie pulls me against her, her heartbeat strong and steady. "We'll get her back."

Sirens wail in the distance. We have to go.

I believe Natalie—first because I trust her, and second because I won't have it any other way. The alternative—accepting that I've lost my best friend to the Madsens—is unthinkable.

Ethel trots over with her tail up, and I break away from Natalie to scoop her into my arms. I am *not* losing her too. But as I bury my face in her fur, trying not to cry, I see Hazel's face in my mind's eye—that final glimpse of my best friend driving away with two murderous women, leaving me with a cavernous hole in my chest.

From the Journal of Hazel Okada

The drive away was tense and silent for the first few blocks. The net sat in my lap, strangely weightless and silky.

Wyatt panted heavily beside me on the back seats, his breath fogging the window. Diagonal to me in the passenger seat, Sophia touched the cuts on her face, wincing as her fingers came away with blood.

Oaklyn caught my eye in the rearview mirror. "That was brilliant, Hazel. I can't believe you got it. You're incredible."

I flushed under her praise, still trying to process what I'd done. I stole from witches. I made a choice that might make Katie hate me forever.

I tightened my grip on the golden threads, which shimmered in the passing streetlights as we wove through traffic. My stomach twisted with each block we put between us and Katie. That hurt look on her face wouldn't get out of my head. I betrayed her—the friend who'd been there for me through tumultuous high school years, and who I trusted enough to come out to first. I'd just shattered an irreplaceable friendship.

Was magic worth that price?

Shouting at Katie felt so wrong. But I needed to do it to save my own ass. If I'd shown weakness, uncertainty, conflicting loyalty... I don't know what Oaklyn would have done.

Sophia turned in the passenger seat and opened her palm, beckoning with bloody fingers. "Give it to me."

Her voice was cold and commanding—nothing like the way Oaklyn speaks to me.

I held out the net. She took it, and though she didn't smile, I could see the elated glint in her eyes as she inspected it. Bright blood smeared across the delicate gold threads.

I studied her side profile, searching for the resemblance between mother and daughter. It was difficult to see past Sophia's harshness.

"We've been trying to get our hands on Tracker technology for months," Sophia said finally. "You might be more useful than I thought."

Wow, high praise.

Oaklyn gave her mom a double-take, then met my eye in the mirror again, a small smile on her lips.

Although the way she looked at me sent warmth flooding through me, Katie's devastated expression flashed through my mind again, and the feeling trickled away as quickly as it came.

"I guess we'll have to find our next chimera, hey Mom?" Oaklyn said, her fingers tapping a nervous rhythm on the steering wheel.

I pulled out my phone to check my tracking app. "On it."

The familiar interface greeted me, dots of activity scattered across the map—my creation that started all this when I tracked that first chimera to White Rock. If I hadn't been in the cafe that day, would I be here now? Or would I still be living my ordinary life, coding during the day and going home to an empty apartment at night?

Sophia's gaze locked onto the wrapped ring box sitting beside me in the back seat. "You haven't opened my gift."

Oaklyn's shoulders tensed. "Not yet."

Sophia looked out the window, the silence heavy. The tension between them crackled in the air.

"Um, I think there might be a chimera at Lighthouse Park," I said, my voice small. "Maybe more than one. My algorithm shows unusual activity there."

I zoomed in on the cluster of data points, where multiple people had shared strange sightings on social media lately. There was either one very active chimera or several in the area.

Sophia smoothed the net across her lap. "Then that's where we'll go first thing tomorrow."

Oaklyn gave a quiet laugh of disbelief. "Impressive, Hazel."

We exchanged a look in the mirror, and there was something hungry in her eyes that lit a spark in my belly—like a silent promise of what would happen when we got back. As heat built inside me, I had to look down, too aware of Sophia's presence inches away.

"I'll stay at your place tonight," Sophia said. "Where will you two go instead?"

Her boldness caught me off guard until I remembered who we were dealing with. Of course this woman who just battled a dozen witches and leaped from a thirty-story building wouldn't hesitate to commandeer her daughter's apartment.

"We can sleep at mine," I said. "Wyatt too."

"Very good."

End of discussion.

God, that woman irks me. The way she treats Oaklyn, and the way she thinks the world is at her command... I'd love to see her taken down a peg.

Half an hour later, the moment we got to my apartment and shut the door, Oaklyn pressed me against the wall, her breath hot on my neck. The feel of her body brought a rush of comfort, making everything else less important.

"I can't decide," she whispered roughly, "whether I should stay furious with you for betraying me, or reward you for being so fucking brilliant."

"Why not both?" I suggested, my breath hitching.

She laced our fingers and pinned my hands above my head with bruising strength. "You like it when I get rough with you, don't you?"

"Maybe a little."

"Come on." She pulled me toward the bedroom, already tugging my shirt over my head. Before she pushed me onto the bed, she paused, her expression serious. "You could have gotten yourself killed though. I told you not to do something like that again."

The genuine concern in her voice took me by surprise. Hours ago, she'd been ready to kill me, and now she was worried about my safety.

I furrowed my brow, searching her face for the truth. "I knew what choice I was making. I believe in what you're fighting for."

Something softened in her eyes. She stepped in and cupped my face in her hands, her touch gentler than expected. "When you said you loved me earlier... Was that real?"

My breath caught. The question was so vulnerable. This fierce, dangerous woman who had battled a horde of witches was now looking at me with uncertainty. In the soft lamplight of my bedroom, with her hair messy and her makeup smudged, she looked younger and more human.

"It's real," I whispered, my heart beating faster.

It wasn't just the adrenaline and danger. It wasn't infatuation or some weird form of Stockholm syndrome or whatever. The way I felt when I was with her, from the moment we met, was very real.

It feels like there are two versions of us—the one with the fighting and betrayal, and the one where everything is normal, and we're just two mildly insecure people falling madly in love.

She studied my face as if searching for any sign of deception. Her blue eyes traced every feature, lingering on my lips. Then she kissed me hard, her hands firm on my waist, pushing me back onto the bed.

"I love you too," she murmured, leaving a trail of kisses down my neck and chest. "I didn't mean to. But here we are."

For a moment, I froze, absorbing her words in disbelief. Did she really feel that way? Or was she just saying that?

But the way she kissed and held me said more than words ever could.

I arched into her, my heart soaring. The contradiction of it all—loving someone who might have killed me, betraying a friend who would risk her life for me—should have torn me apart. Instead, it felt like the pieces of me were coming together.

Tomorrow morning, we'll go to Lighthouse Park with the net. We'll catch a chimera and start building a world where magic is available to anyone brave enough to claim it.

Including me.

I just hope that someday, Katie will understand why I chose this. That I never wanted to hurt her. This isn't just about Oaklyn—it's about fighting for something bigger than ourselves. It's about changing the world.

As Oaklyn's lips trailed down my body, I closed my eyes and focused on the sensation, on the love I felt for her, on the future we're fighting for. But as hard as I tried to stay in the moment with her, Katie's face kept appearing behind my eyelids—hurt, betrayed, and broken.

I made my choice. Now I have to live with it.

CHAPTER 22

Never a Witch

I HISS AS MY tea burns my tongue, setting it down with a grimace. Steam rises from the mug, fogging the air between Natalie and me. Even surrounded by greenery, warm lights, and a crackling fireplace, the lounge feels like a funeral home. Most of the Shadows are either in the infirmary or recovering in their rooms. Only a few remain in the booths, refueling with midnight snacks. No laughter, no chatter, just silence and exhaustion.

Neil's body has been recovered. His family will be notified.

The thought sits like a stone in my stomach. Another witch, killed. Is it my fault? I couldn't balance the two halves of my life—Hazel and Natalie, friendship and love, loyalty and responsibility. I tried to be everything to everyone and somehow managed to fail everyone at once.

What if I'd talked to Hazel like she asked before sharing Sophia's location? What if I hadn't gotten caught up trying to prove myself to a coven that I obviously don't belong in?

My eyes sting, and I blink fast. I feel like the willow tree in the corner, broken and barely standing, held up with wooden splints and twine since the Madsen attack in February. Its leaves dangle like they've given up.

I'm still trying to understand where I went wrong with Hazel. The memory of her face before they drove away keeps replaying in my mind. Not only did she choose the Madsens over me, but she stole the enchanted net for them.

What if they manage to catch a chimera with it? If Sophia gains access to bio magic, we're all completely screwed.

"We need to talk about what happened," Natalie says quietly.

I meet her dark eyes, finding defeat reflected back at me. Her cuts are still bleeding, and her tangled hair is full of dust and debris. She's clutching her mug tightly, straining the raw scrapes on her knuckles.

"Which part?" I ask. "The part where my best friend betrayed us, or the part where you didn't tell me we were on our way to murder a bunch of chimeras?"

"And you didn't tell me Millie and Sebastian were there," she says coldly. "I'm not the only one who withheld information."

Her icy tone stings, and I glower in response.

She exhales, dragging her fingers through her tangled hair. "And we weren't on our way to *murder* anything, Katie. Chimeras are magic, which means they can be neutralized like a curse, and that's what we were planning to do."

"If they're not sentient, then how do you explain how I spoke to Lucy?" My words come out sharp. I'm sick of arguing with her about this. "She showed me memories—"

"That's bio magic manipulating you," she cuts in, just as sharp and impatient. "It can influence minds, and that's exactly why it's so dangerous."

I bang my fist on the table, my self-control fracturing. The tea sloshes, spilling over the rim of the mug. "I'm not the first person who can talk to chimeras. My ability means something. I need to—" I hesitate, her constant doubts seizing hold of me. But I push on, determined to be heard. "I need to protect them like the people before me did."

Natalie blinks, her expression going blank with surprise. "Who else can speak to them?"

Her icy tone is gone. Was that a slight tremor in her voice?

I shift in my seat. "I read about it in the library here. Ancient Guardians once communicated with them."

Natalie searches my face, a crease between her eyebrows. I can't tell if that's a look of curiosity, like I might have a hope of getting through to her, or if she thinks I've totally lost it and is too tired to keep arguing.

Footsteps approach, and we both turn. Fiona sweeps up to our table, her red cloak torn and dusty but her spine as straight as ever. Sky trails behind her, looking as battered as I feel. There's a bruise blooming across her cheekbone, and she's limping heavily.

"At dawn, we move in on the chimera nest," Fiona announces. "Every available Shadow. We're not letting this slip away—especially now that the Madsens have the net."

I stand so fast that I bump the table, and more tea sloshes everywhere. "You can't!"

"Sit down, Miss Alexander," Fiona snarls. "This isn't your decision to make."

I stay on my feet, balling my fists. The familiar feeling of being dismissed, of being treated like I don't belong, burns through me. I'm done with this.

"You're making a mistake," I say, determined not to let my voice waver. "They aren't weapons or mindless forces. They're ancient magic, and they maintained balance in nature before the coven existed."

"Balance?" Fiona scoffs. "Tell that to the families of the people they've hurt."

"They lashed out because you caged them!" My voice rises, drawing the attention of the few Shadows scattered across the lounge. "Because the coven decided it knew better than centuries of Guardians who came before you. You created this problem, and now you're going to make it worse."

Fiona's face hardens. "This is exactly why you're not a witch. You have no loyalty to the coven and no devotion to protecting humanity from dark magic."

The words slice through me, but I glare at her, unwilling to shrink back. "Or I understand better than any of you. Maybe that's why I can hear them when you can't."

Silence falls over our corner of the lounge. Even Fiona seems taken aback.

"Katie," Natalie says softly, "you're upset about Hazel. I'm concerned for her too. But we can't let that cloud our judgment about what needs to be done. The Madsens have the net, and we need to harness all traces of bio magic before they can get a hold of it."

Her gentle dismissal hurts worse than Fiona's cruel one. I step away from the table, my chest tight. "You really think I'm wrong here."

Natalie looks down, a flash of guilt in her expression. But she doesn't contradict me.

Part of me wants to reach for her hand across this gap, but my arms stay firmly at my sides. And she doesn't reach for me, either.

It feels like the world is spinning away from me. I've lost my best friend, Troy's net, and any hope of convincing these witches to see reason. Even Natalie, the one person I thought saw me for who I truly am, thinks I'm delusional.

"Fine," I say, my voice rough. "Go ahead with your ambush. But there's more to the chimeras than you think, and I want you to remember I warned you."

I walk away, leaving them to their plans. Like always, I'm just an outsider who can't do magic, whose opinion means nothing.

Natalie doesn't follow me, and to be honest, I'm not sure what I would do if she tried. I might tell her to go away. I might break down in tears.

But I don't need to worry about that because she stays rooted with her coven.

My eyes prickle as I head for the Chambers wing. I couldn't protect the chimeras, I couldn't keep Hazel safe, and I couldn't even convince the woman I love to believe me.

I hesitate in the corridor, unsure where to go. I don't belong in the coven, where I'll always be an outsider. Nor do I belong with Hazel, who's chosen a new path. I can't even turn to my family, who have no idea what I'm going through.

I'm completely alone.

I walk toward Natalie's room anyway, wiping my damp cheeks. Maybe Ethel will be there, waiting to be let in. She's my one constant through all this.

I tried so hard to be useful, to fit in, to be a part of the coven. I thought if I followed the rules and proved myself valuable, they would eventually see me as one of them—and secretly, I hoped that if I proved worthy enough, they might let me become a witch. But that was never going to happen. I was always going to be an outsider, no matter how many curses I found or chimeras I helped catch.

I've been so desperate to belong that I've doubted myself, even when I feel deep in my gut that what they're doing is wrong. All along, I should have been questioning whether this is where I belong at all. Whether I even *need* to belong here.

So where does that leave me? If I'm not on the coven's side and I'm not on the Madsens' side...

I stop outside Natalie's door and pick up Ethel, who was indeed waiting for me.

"We'll create our own side," I tell her, kissing her head.

The thought of standing apart from Natalie makes my heart feel like it's being wrung out like a dishrag. I guess several things can be true: I love her, and I'm furious with her, and we both feel like we've let the other down. I don't know where this leaves us. All I know is that I can't keep pretending to be someone I'm not, even for her.

I'm not a witch, but I'm not normal either. I'm something in between...and it's time to figure out exactly what that is.

I can't sleep, especially with Natalie lying as stiff and silent as a corpse beside me, so I rise before the sun and get dressed in the first outfit I pull out of my suitcase—jeans and a white T-shirt that says 'no thank you' in small letters across the front. Ethel trots at my heels as I slip out the door.

In the courtyard, we curl up in a hammock together, her watching the koi fish undulate in the pond, me replaying the same few seconds incessantly: Hazel shooting me that last glare before climbing into the car with Oaklyn, choosing the Madsens over me.

I don't understand. In her shoes, I don't think I could ever choose a girl I'd just met over my best friend.

Then again, I suppose part of me understands what it's like to fall hard and fast. I fell for Natalie fast enough to break the sound barrier. Is Hazel going through the same feelings with Oaklyn, and should I be more empathetic?

Empathy would be easier to summon if she weren't dating an unhinged criminal.

Ethel purrs as I stroke her back, and far above, birds have started their morning songs, oblivious to the fact that today, witches will go slaughter dozens of ancient beings they don't understand. And I'll probably be thrown in jail anyway for refusing to help them.

It seems like years ago that I was flying back here, thinking I could slide into the coven and resume my old role helping Natalie find curses. What a reality check.

Footsteps swish through the dewy grass, and I don't need to look up to know who it is. My skin crackles as Natalie's energy reaches me—the pull that's grown stronger and more mystifying the longer I spend in the presence of magic. Her scent reaches me next, that warm, herbal blend I've come to associate with safety. Now, it makes my heart jump with uncertainty.

She sits on the grass in front of me, her forearms resting on her knees, watching me rock the hammock. She's in a cropped brown sweater and joggers, looking cozy enough to cuddle up against. The brightening sky illuminates her brown hair, highlighting the little green and yellow braids peeking through. There's a butterfly bandage over the cut on her cheek.

We sit in silence for a long moment, a gulf between us.

"I was thinking about you and your ability," she finally says, her voice low, "which none of us really understand. I thought about what you read in the library, about the ancient Guardians... And I'd heard something like that before from my dad..." She runs her fingers through her hair, looking uncomfortable, and huffs. "He told us witches didn't always hunt magic. Said there used to be witches who communed with it instead, until the abuse of power happened after the turn of the century and everything changed. I never thought much more about it. Just accepted it as history."

My hand freezes mid-stroke on Ethel's back. She looks up at me and paws my arm, annoyed that I stopped.

"What are you saying?" I ask.

"I thought about it all night, and I believe you when you say you're communicating with the chimeras."

Her words hit me like a branch falling on my head. I prepared for more doubts and dismissals, running through arguments that all ended in worst-case scenarios—Natalie and me breaking up, me flying back to Toronto, living the rest of my life trying to pretend none of this ever happened. But after all this time spent drowning alone, grasping for any help, this feels like she's thrown me a rope.

"What changed?" I ask, my voice hoarse.

"Nothing. I just...remembered what matters." She moves closer, resting her hand on my knee. "I've watched you sense curses that no one else could detect. I've seen you follow invisible trails that helped me do my job and even saved our lives. Your intuition has been right time and again. More than that, I trust you. And I'm sorry for doubting you."

My eyes prickle. After all these arguments, losing Hazel, and battling with the coven, her belief in me feels like the first ray of light in days.

"I was scared that bio magic was manipulating you," she continues. "Scared of losing you to something I didn't know how to fight."

I reach out and squeeze her hand. "I know you were just looking out for me. I love you so much, and I...I didn't want to have to choose between you and what I know is right."

She rises to her knees. "I don't want that either. I'm on your side in life—now and always."

I press my lips together into a small smile. "Thank you."

She leans forward, and Ethel scrambles down from the hammock before she can get squished.

Natalie kisses me gently, and as her familiar scent surrounds me, I lean into her, feeling for a moment like everything might be okay.

But as we break apart, I shake my head. "It doesn't matter though. Any minute, the Shadows will be on their way to try and kill them all."

"We're not powerless." Natalie shakes her head. "It's ridiculous, really, that we sent you out there with some enchanted net when the solution was staring us in the face."

I raise an eyebrow, trying to understand what she's getting at.

"Your ability," she says. "That's what we needed all along. Not traps."

"But how? What am I supposed to do?"

"You can talk to the chimeras." Natalie stands, extending her hand to me. "So let's go talk to them."

I stare at her, not moving. "You believe me?"

"I do. You're the only one who can fix this."

I look up at Natalie, this incredible woman who's fought for me and chosen to believe in me despite everything she's been taught.

She's right—I need to stop this. Not only are the chimeras in danger, but so are the witches. They don't seem to grasp how dangerous it would be to attack these chimeras. Honestly, before I spoke to Lucy, I didn't understand either. But now I know better, and I have to do everything in my power to prevent a gruesome fight.

"I'll do what I can," I say.

Natalie smiles. "The witches need you, Katie, even if they don't realize it yet."

I tilt my head. "I'm not sure I care what they think anymore."

She furrows her brow. "What do you mean?"

I swing my legs over the side of the hammock and plant my feet on the ground. "I've spent too much time trying to show how useful I can be. Like that would earn me a place in the coven. It's absurd, measuring my worth by how valuable I am to others, but..."

Natalie lets out a breath, tracing her fingers along my jawline. "But these witches are too stubborn to recognize how special you are."

I shake my head. "I'm done caring about that. I don't *want* to prove myself anymore. I just want to trust myself."

A small smile tugs at Natalie's lips. "How wise of you."

I nudge her with my foot. "You once told me that being in the coven is like your whole identity, and you don't know who you are outside of it. I feel like...I've been trying to do the same thing. To mold myself into the person they want me to be. And why? I've been so desperate to prove my worth that..." I lift a shoulder. "I've been ignoring my intuition."

She searches my face, a crease between her eyebrows. "What's your intuition telling you now?"

"That I'm not meant to be a witch."

"Katie—"

"No, it's okay. I don't want to be anymore." The words feel weird leaving my mouth. It's something I never thought I'd say since learning Natalie's secrets. But there's something freeing about releasing that desperate want—like I can stop trying so hard. I can just be *me*. "I think I was born to be something else," I say, my voice coming out strong. "I'm meant to be someone who doesn't fit neatly into the coven's structure."

Deep down, I think I've known this for some time. If I truly wanted to join the coven, I would have just done what they said and stopped questioning everything. But somewhere along, I decided that doing what's right is more important than fitting in. It's time to own that.

I take Natalie's hand and rise from the hammock. No more hesitation, no more doubting myself. "Let's go to Lighthouse Park and talk to the chimeras before the Shadows arrive. There must be a solution that protects both magic and humanity."

Natalie nods. "Lead the way."

I entwine our fingers, soothed by her warm, strong hand in mine, and pull her back toward the lounge. "First, we have to make a stop."

As we hurry through the quiet halls, my path forward becomes clear. I've been looking for acceptance in the wrong places. I don't need to be useful to be valuable. I don't need to trap chimeras to prove my worth.

What I need is to embrace who I truly am: a Guardian, but not C. S.A.M.M.'s kind. I'm descended from the ancient protectors of magic, and I can hear what others can't. And that's exactly what this situation needs.

For the first time since I arrived in Vancouver—and maybe the first time in my life—I know who I am and what I have to do.

From the Journal of Hazel Okada

Driving to Lighthouse Park. It's barely dawn. The golden net is on the seat beside me like a sleeping snake.

I wasn't prepared for the chill that settled over everything when we picked up Sophia from Oaklyn's place. Oaklyn's confidence evaporated, replaced by a tense vigilance that reminded me of a soldier awaiting orders. Wyatt stayed low in the back, his ears flat against his head.

"Oh, she's coming too?" Sophia said as she climbed in, looking me up and down like I was a piece of luggage in the back. Her makeup was flawless, her white-blonde hair was in an elegant updo, and she wore a gorgeous crimson trench coat to match her lips and nails—dressed for a special occasion.

I suddenly felt underdressed in my usual jeans and flannel. But I straightened my spine, letting her critical eye slide over me without flinching. I'm the one who got them the net, and I'm the one who found the chimeras. I'm the reason they have a chance today.

Oaklyn's grip tightened on the wheel. "She's with us now."

Sophia's smile didn't reach her eyes. She brushed a lock of hair back from her cheek with an elegant finger. "We'll see how useful she continues to be."

As we set off, she checked the time and tapped an impatient rhythm on the door handle with her manicured nails. The polish was chipped from the fight last night, and she couldn't conceal all the cuts on her skin. The air around her seemed to crackle, making wisps of my hair lift from my shoulders.

"Drive faster," she snapped. "If those witches get there before us, this will all be for nothing." Her voice was so icy and cruel, like she might as well have slapped her daughter across the face.

Oaklyn's knuckles whitened, but she obeyed, pressing harder on the accelerator. She glanced at me in the rearview mirror, a silent apology in her eyes.

Last night, in the warmth of Oaklyn's arms, our cause felt so right—fighting for equality, for a world where magic isn't hoarded. But in the cold light of dawn, with Sophia in our midst, a strange pang hit me in the gut. Something like homesickness. Like I wasn't where I was supposed to be.

"When we get there," Sophia said, examining her chipped nails, "I'll handle any witches. Oaklyn, you'll use the net. The girl can help you if needed."

The girl. My spine prickled.

"Her name is Hazel," Oaklyn said quietly.

Sophia turned slowly, her gaze like ice. "What was that?"

"Nothing," Oaklyn muttered, shrinking lower in her seat.

She's never so diminished and afraid as she is in the presence of her mother. And God, I hate Sophia for that.

"Once we have a chimera, we'll need to move quickly," Sophia said, turning back to the window. "The ritual requires precision."

"Ritual?" I asked. What were they planning, exactly?

"So I can absorb the bio magic," Sophia said without looking back at me. "Did you think we were collecting it for fun?"

"I thought..." I began, then recalibrated. What did I think? That we'd somehow distribute magic fairly to everyone who wanted it? That Sophia would give some to Oaklyn and me first?

"You thought what?" Sophia's voice was dangerously soft.

"I'd like to understand the process. How does the transfer work?"

Sophia squinted at me. "Curious little thing, aren't you?"

I shrugged. I've never seen real magic before. Not like this."

Sophia laughed. "Oh, you'll see magic today."

Wyatt whined behind me. I reached back to stroke his fur, finding comfort in him. He licked my hand.

We exited the highway, and as we began weaving south toward the park, Sophia straightened. "Finally, I'll get what I deserve," she breathed.

I can't help wondering what that will be. I know she's talking about magic, but is that really what this woman deserves?

I know people aren't simple, and nobody is all good or bad. I know Oaklyn has done terrible things, but I also know who she is beneath that. Katie has always been a good friend, but going after Sophia when I asked her to wait was a shitty thing to do.

As for me? I've always thought of myself as good, but I just betrayed my best friend. Even if my reasons felt right at the time, that doesn't make it any better.

I suppose we all get what we deserve at one time or another.

We're close to the park now. The net is ready, and I've memorized the trail map.

It's time.

I'm going to watch and wait...and when the moment comes, I'll do what's right—whatever that turns out to be.

CHAPTER 23

Reasoning with Feral Magic

I'VE BEEN HERE TWICE already: once to set the chimeras free and once to imprison one. I'm back again, and this time is different. This time is final.

The bio magic containment room pulses in front of me with a strange energy, its metal door gleaming under the corridor's dim lights.

"Stand guard," I whisper to Natalie, giving her hand a quick squeeze.

She nods and positions herself between me and the corridor, ready to defend us if anyone approaches—or if this doesn't go as planned. "Be careful. If it attacks you—"

"It won't."

I hope.

I flex my fingers under the gauntlet, which is warm against the back of my hand. Sucking in a breath, I slam my fist into the lock. The metal gives way with a satisfying crunch, and the door swings open on silent hinges.

Cool air rushes out at me, carrying an earthy scent. The chimera we caught lies inside the first cage, the room's only occupant, its flickering form cast into shadows. One moment it's the turtle from the pond, then a bear, an eagle, a bull... It expands and contracts, breathing as it sleeps.

I approach slowly, my breaths and footsteps too loud in the absolute silence. I'm jittery, like I'm expecting it to wake up and lunge at the bars any second. But I know from last time that it won't wake up until I've opened its cage.

I raise my fist, my heart hammering. I have to do this.

The lock shatters under my punch, the impact echoing through the room like a gunshot and reverberating up my arm.

The moment I swing open the cage door, the chimera stands, taking the form of the little deer from before. It lowers its head, antlers pointed at me, muscles tensed as if preparing to charge.

"I'm sorry," I whisper, holding my palms up. "I was wrong to trap you."

The deer's eyes are deep pools of purple, unblinking and ancient.

There's a tickle in the back of my mind—its consciousness brushing mine, tentative and suspicious. The sensation is both foreign and strangely familiar, like remembering a dream I had long ago.

"I need your help," I say. "The witches are planning to destroy all the chimeras at Lighthouse Park. We have to warn them."

The deer tilts its head, and a voice like rustling leaves whispers in my mind: *"Why should I trust you, little hunter, after all that you've done?"*

My heart skips a beat. I swallow hard. "Because I'm trying to make things right. I understand now what you are—and what I am."

The deer steps closer. Its form ripples and grows until a stag stands before me, all muscle and pointy antlers. Power radiates from it in waves that make my skin prickle. *"Your blood remembers what your mind has forgotten, Guardian. But understanding is not enough."*

I square my shoulders, but I'm trembling as I look up at the massive stag. "By doing this, I'm ensuring I'll never be welcome here among the witches again. I might be hunted by the coven for the rest of my life. I'm willing to sacrifice my place here to protect you. Is that not enough?"

The stag's gaze is piercing, as if it can see straight into my soul. *"What of the witch who stands outside? Will she sacrifice her place as well?"*

My heart stutters. I'd assumed Natalie wouldn't face the same consequences if she helps me, like before. But maybe that's naive. She's risking everything—her position, her family, her identity.

"That's her choice to make," I say finally. "But I know what mine is."

Natalie turns from her post at the door, maybe realizing we're talking about her.

I back up, giving the chimera space to walk past me.

The stag steps out of the cage, its hooves clattering on the stone floor. It lowers its head, and my heart skips as we come eye to eye. Its breath washes over me, strangely cool and damp, like a puff of mist.

"You have taken much from us already." The voice in my mind grows colder. *"One act of atonement does not erase a history of cages."*

I reach out but stop myself from touching it. "Please. I need your help to save the others."

"We do not need saving." The chimera's form ripples and shrinks, becoming a red fox. It circles me, its tail brushing my legs. *"Your ancestors would weep to see what you have become—a tool for the witches who cage ancient magic."*

It darts around me and slips past Natalie, disappearing down the corridor and leaving nothing but a prickle of magic in its wake.

"Wait!" I stand by the empty cage, my hands shaking. It wasn't supposed to go like this. I thought if I owned my calling as a Guardian, the chimeras would trust me. Where does this leave me? Will I be able to protect them if I have no allies?

"Katie?" Natalie says from the doorway. "Do we follow it?"

"It won't help us," I say, marching toward her. "But we'll go anyway. I'm going to prove it wrong about who I am."

But despite my confident tone, my stomach is in knots. If I can't convince one chimera to trust me, how can I hope to prevent a massacre at Lighthouse Park? The witches don't respect me enough to listen, and apparently, the chimeras don't either.

Still, I won't let that stop me from trying to save them all.

As we reach the hidden cove, dawn brightens the sky, turning the jagged rocks gold and the sea indigo. The trees are still and silent, and the waves are calm, burbling against the rock shore.

No signs of life. Not even a seagull.

Have the chimeras moved on?

"Sebastian? Millie?" I say, my voice small.

My skin prickles. The sensation is unmistakable, like electricity making the fine hairs on my arms stand on end. Magic is here somewhere, watching.

"Lucy?" I say a bit louder, my heart pounding.

Natalie and I scan the shoreline, breathing fast after the hike through the forest. Her hand finds mine, giving it a quick squeeze before she lets go, ready to defend us. That brief touch reminds me that after everything we've been through, we've got each other's backs.

The rising sun casts long shadows behind the trees and shrubs, making every dark space look like it could be hiding something.

There's a blur of movement, and we spin around, our breaths hitching. Natalie raises her palms.

A white kitten is sitting on a mossy boulder. Her purple eyes gleam as she surveys Natalie and me, her little tail swishing. *We warned you to stay away.*

"The witches are coming," I say. "You need to get out of here."

Lucy's ears flatten against her head, which would be cute if I didn't know what she really is. *"We will not bend to your—snack!"*

A dragonfly buzzes past her nose, and she leaps after it, her tiny claws extended as she tries to catch it.

"Is that...supposed to happen?" Natalie says.

I shake my head.

We watch Lucy try to catch it for a long moment before she loses track. Finally, she turns back to me, seeming to remember we were mid-conversation.

"The witches?" I say, waving my arms.

Lucy's eyes narrow. *"We will not leave because of them. We leave when it is time to move on."*

"But they're not just here with nets this time." I step closer, my shoes crunching on the dirt and pine needles covering the rocky plateau. "They're here to destroy you. All of you."

"Then we will fight them."

"You don't have to!" My heart pounds as I plead with her, willing her to listen. "I'm here to warn you so a fight doesn't happen. Please—"

A thunderous roar echoes across the cove, reverberating through my chest. I gasp, my blood turning to ice as I spin toward the sound. Natalie raises her hands, and magic crackles in the air.

Further down the shore, illuminated by the fiery sunrise, stand four figures I'd desperately hoped wouldn't find us—Sophia with her white-blonde hair whipping in the wind, Oaklyn holding the golden net, Wyatt standing tall at her side, and Hazel, the fear on her face unmistakable even from a distance. My stomach drops at the sight of her—my ride or die who knew all my secrets until magic came between us. Until the lies, and Oaklyn, and a rift so deep we can't fix it.

Between them and the water's edge looms an enormous polar bear, its fur rippling in the breeze as it rears up on its hind legs.

"You led more hunters to us," Lucy snarls behind me.

"No!" I squeak. God, why do the Madsens have to be here? This is hard enough already!

Lucy bristles until she looks twice her size. She leaps off the boulder—and before my eyes, her fur becomes tawny and sleek, her body expands, her tail grows longer and thicker...and then a mountain lion lands on the rocks a stride away from me, claws out, fangs bared.

"I swear I didn't!" I shout, stumbling backward.

But I'm not her target—she bounds past us and toward the Madsens, eating up the distance in a few long strides.

Across the cove, Oaklyn throws the net, and Sophia raises her palms. The net unfurls like a golden parachute, suspended by magic, ready to drop onto the polar bear.

Wyatt spins toward Lucy and snarls, his hackles rising.

"Oaklyn, look out!" Hazel shouts, her voice ringing through the woods.

As Oaklyn and Sophia spin around, the polar bear shrinks into a snowy owl and swoops out of the net's path, leaving it to fall onto the rocks in a shimmering heap.

The tiniest bit of relief eases through me. The chimeras won't be caught easily, and that's my only consolation.

Sophia's expression twists with fury. She flings out her hand, and the ground beneath Lucy's paws ruptures, sending chunks of rock flying upward. The mountain lion stumbles, losing momentum—but in a blink, it morphs into a vulture and takes flight.

Natalie grabs my arm. "We can't let them catch one."

"I know. But how are we supposed to stop Sophia and Oaklyn when only *one* of us can do earth magic?"

As Lucy turns in the sky and the dust from the explosion clears, the Madsens spot us. Every gaze locks on Natalie and me. Wyatt snarls, his teeth gleaming in the morning light. Hazel steps back, her face ashen.

"I don't think we have a choice," Natalie says, raising her hands. The resignation in her voice breaks my heart. Neither of us wants this.

I look at her profile—the determined set of her jaw, the strength in her posture. She's risked everything to protect me and to love me. And now she's about to face off with people who want her dead, all because I thought it was the right thing to come here and try to save magic.

My heart pounds harder, as if to remind me of my mortality. The air shifts, growing heavy with magic. My skin tingles with that now-familiar sensation, like standing near a lightning strike.

Oaklyn slashes her dagger, its blade catching the light. A tangle of roots launches at Natalie with the force of a wrecking ball. Wyatt tears after it, ready to sink his fangs into us.

Natalie throws up her hands, and the ground before us erupts. Rocks, sand, and chunks of earth form a barrier, blocking the root ball with a thunderous crash.

"Katie, run!" she shouts, her voice strained.

I step closer to her instead, my fists clenched. "I'm not leaving you!"

Of everything I'm unsure about, all the doubts and questions, this is the one thing I know for sure—I will never abandon her.

Through gaps in our crumbling barrier, Sophia summons the net back before spinning to face us. Her eyes are cool and calculating, like we're an obstacle to be removed.

"Shit. Sophia—" I barely get the words out when the air crackles, and Sophia thrusts her free hand toward us. Stones tear out of the ground, firing like bullets.

"Get down!" Natalie shouts, jumping in front of me as her shield shatters. Her body absorbs most of the impact, but some stones still slam into my shoulders and legs, making me cry out as pain explodes everywhere.

Natalie grunts and staggers backward, bumping into me, and I grab her to stop her from falling.

"Hold this," Sophia barks at Hazel, who hesitates for a heartbeat before darting forward to take the net.

The golden threads shimmer in her small hands—the same hands that held mine through every crisis of my teenage years until now. I step around Natalie, an unconscious urge to move closer to Hazel. If I could just reach her...

Natalie throws her arm across my chest to push me back, breathing hard. "Stay—here."

My eyes prickle, but I swallow down the emotion and step back, needing to focus.

Natalie sends a wave of earth toward Sophia, chunks of stone and soil flying like missiles. Her power steals my breath as always.

Sophia deflects the attack with a sweep of her arm, making it flow around her like water around a boulder. She thrusts her hands out in retaliation, and the earth explodes beneath our feet.

My ears ring as I'm blasted back, my belly swooping. I slam into a tree, the rough bark digging into my back and all the air whooshing out of my lungs. Disoriented, I suck in a rattling breath, gasping and coughing as I try to get my bearings.

There's a sickening crack nearby, and Natalie lets out a grunt of pain.

My insides plummet. Fear crashes over me like ice. "Natalie!" I croak, rolling onto my hands and knees.

She's slumped at the base of a tree, holding herself up with a shaking arm. She spits out blood and wipes her face. The sight of her blood makes panic surge through me, clawing at my chest. I try to get to my feet, but my knees are too weak. I scramble over the rocks toward her, moving impossibly slow, like time itself is working against me.

"Nat—" Something wraps around my middle with crushing force, and I scream. Pain explodes in my ribs as I'm yanked backward, and then in my palms as I skid across the rough ground. Oaklyn's roots tighten like anacondas, squeezing my torso until I can't breathe.

I thrash, managing to turn enough to see the others. The first set of eyes I lock onto are Hazel's. She stands frozen, the golden net clutched to her chest, her face ashen as she watches me struggle.

"Please," I beg, gasping for what little breath I can get. The roots constrict tighter. An involuntary noise escapes me. Black spots dance at the edges of my vision. I hope she knows I'm not just pleading for my life, but for her to remember who she is and who we are to each other.

Sophia's voice cuts through the air. "If you want magic of your own, girl, help us catch one."

Hazel flinches. She looks down at the net in her hands, her chest heaving. Unable to speak, I try to silently plead with her, praying that she's weighing everything—our friendship, the empty promise of magic, the reality of what's happening and who she's siding with.

Strides away, Natalie groans and pushes herself up on trembling arms. Blood pours from her nose, and she wipes it with her forearm, smearing it across her face. She staggers to her feet, her breathing labored.

"Let—her—go," she snarls, turning her palms toward Oaklyn. Purple flashes in her eyes, as bright as lightning.

Sophia's lips curl into a sneer. She raises both hands, and the earth trembles in response. Jagged spikes of stone erupt from the ground, racing for Natalie like serpents striking at prey.

Natalie tries to raise a barrier, but she's wounded and slow. The first spike catches her in the side, and she cries out, doubling over as blood cascades down from under her sweater.

"Stop it!" I scream, writhing against the roots binding me. Every movement sends pain lancing through my ribs, but I don't care. All that matters is getting to Natalie before it's too late. The helplessness of watching her suffer is worse than the pain.

Sophia advances on her, relentless as the tide. "I've waited years for this, Zacharias. Your family has been a thorn in my side for too long."

Another blast sends Natalie skidding across the rocks. She tries to stand, but her legs give out. Blood soaks her torn sweater and joggers, spreading like crimson flowers. Her face is ghostly pale, her eyes unfocused with pain.

A sob escapes my lips, and I thrash again, unable to do anything to stop this. This is my fault—I brought us here, thinking I could make peace, thinking I could protect everyone. I should have known the fucking Madsens would show up.

"Oaklyn, she's going to kill Natalie!" Hazel blurts, her voice breaking. "Stop her!"

Hearing the words spoken aloud floods me with dizziness. I can't get enough air into my lungs. The world goes fuzzy, like I'm trying to wake up from a nightmare.

Oaklyn glances back at Hazel, confusion wiping the sneer off her face. The dagger in her hand lowers an inch, and the roots constricting me quiver.

"Please!" Hazel begs, stepping toward her. "This isn't what we talked about. This is murder."

But Oaklyn's expression hardens as she turns back to me, her mouth set in a grim line. "Just do what you're told, Hazel."

The roots tighten again, and my vision darkens at the edges.

This is how it ends, then. With betrayal. With my total failure—leading Natalie into danger, unable to convince the witches or the chimeras to listen to me, unable to embrace my role as a Guardian.

I thrash with everything I have, with every drop of energy left in my body. But I'm trapped, helpless, watching as Sophia raises a boulder the size of a car above Natalie. The rock hovers, casting a shadow over her broken form.

"No!" I shriek, the sound tearing from my throat. "Somebody help!"

I don't know who I'm shouting to. There's nobody here to save us.

Natalie's eyes lock onto mine, the whites glowing against her blood-stained skin. Purple fades to brown as the magic drains away—as she realizes what's about to happen.

Everything we could have had hangs suspended between us, invisible but so real—our life together, our future. Lazy Sunday mornings tangled in sheets, holidays with our families, summer nights in our own backyard... All the ordinary, beautiful moments we'll never have, about to be crushed forever at the hands of Sophia, Oaklyn, and the girl who was once my best friend.

From the Journal of Hazel Okada

As Sophia lifted the boulder above Natalie, she turned her gaze onto me. The hair on the back of my neck stood up like I was being stared down by a predator.

She didn't speak. She didn't need to. Her eyes flicked from me to Oaklyn, then to something in the trees behind me. I followed her line of sight and froze.

A wolf was crouched strides away, its gray fur rippling in the wind.

I sucked in a breath and stepped back.

No, not a wolf—a chimera. Its purple eyes were fixed on Katie, full of a chilling intelligence.

The golden net was still in my hands, weightless and silky soft. I knew what she wanted. What I was supposed to do. I'd chosen this path when I climbed into the car with Oaklyn last night, and possibly long before that.

"Now, Hazel!" Oaklyn commanded.

She yanked her dagger back, severing the roots that held Katie. Katie barely had time to gasp for breath before Oaklyn lashed out at the wolf. The chimera flinched, muscles tensing to flee, but fresh roots shot from the blade and snared its legs before it could leap away.

It yelped and changed form into a rabbit. But Sophia was already there with her magic, sending a wave of earth to pin the creature down—and the ground rumbled, a deep BOOM filling the air as the boulder crashed down where Natalie had been.

Katie screamed, the sound so terrible that my blood ran cold and tears sprang in my eyes.

I covered my mouth, panic washing over me—but there was no time to think about what was happening. No time to think about whose side I was on or what I was about to do.

Sophia turned her deadly gaze onto me, her voice cutting through the chaos. "Do it, girl!"

Under the glares of Sophia and Oaklyn, my hands moved before my brain could catch up. I threw the net like I'd seen Katie do a hundred times when we practiced in that empty Alchemy lab. Time slowed as it unfurled, its golden threads glinting like a web spun from sunlight.

My breath hitched as it landed on the struggling chimera. The moment the net touched it, the creature's form flickered wildly—skunk, chickadee, some reptilian monster I couldn't name—but the net conformed to each shape, tightening until the chimera could barely move.

Sophia was there in an instant, shoving me aside so hard that I stumbled backward. Her face was alight, her eyes gleaming with a hunger that made my stomach turn. She snatched up her prize and held it to her chest like it was her child.

"Nice work, Hazel!" Oaklyn said, but her voice sounded warped and distant, everything swimming around me.

As Katie continued to scream and the chimera thrashed, a knot formed in my stomach.

The chimera's strange purple eyes locked onto mine through the golden mesh as it surrendered in the form of a small brown rabbit. Something in its gaze sucked away my breath—like this creature was beyond anything I could comprehend. Was Katie right about them?

The knot inside me tightened until I couldn't breathe.

Add it to the list: another mistake in a long series that would change my life forever.

CHAPTER 24

Fucking with the Wrong Guardian

A S THE BOULDER DROPS out of the air over Natalie, panic clamps down on me like a vise. My vision goes fuzzy, and I sway like I might pass out. Every memory of her flashes through my mind—the first time I saw her in the vet's office, the first time her lips touched mine, every moment we held each other.

BOOM!

The earth shudders beneath my feet as the boulder crashes down. The impact rattles my bones, shaking the trees and plunging the cove into silence.

"Natalie!" Her name tears from my throat, my voice so desperate and raw that I don't recognize it. The concept of losing her, this woman who's become my entire world, is too unbearable to process.

I stagger forward, dimly aware that I'm free from Oaklyn's roots. My legs carry me automatically toward the massive rock, my mind hovering somewhere outside my body. My heart feels like it's being ripped from my chest with each step.

"No, no, no..." The words pour from my mouth like a whimper, mixing with gasps as I try to get my breath. Please, not her. The universe can't be this cruel. We were supposed to have our whole lives ahead of us—to move into that cottage she dreamed of, get married, see the world, and grow old together.

I trip over exposed roots and stones, catching myself on bloodied palms as I scramble toward her. Pain doesn't register—nothing matters except getting to her.

She *can't* be...

"Natalie," I whisper, as if saying her name enough times might somehow bring her back.

I round the boulder, one hand pressed against its cold, rough surface, ready to try pushing it off her or clawing it to pieces with my bare hands.

My muscles tense. My vision tunnels as I force myself to look down, bracing for her broken body, the pool of red, the sight of only half of her while the rest stays crushed beneath this gargantuan chunk of earth. The image is so vivid I can almost feel the warm, sticky blood soaking through as I kneel beside her.

I reach out, my fingers splayed as if I can somehow pull her back. My lungs burn, refusing to take in air. A choked sob builds in my chest that feels like it might shatter my ribs when it finally breaks loose.

I get to the other side of the boulder—and freeze.

Sebastian is there, slumped against a tree trunk, his arms hooked under Natalie's armpits. Her whole body is there—not crushed, not bleeding and broken, but fully free. Alive. Her boots are an inch from where the boulder landed.

Relief floods through me so intensely that my knees buckle. I clap my hands over my mouth, gulping back a sob as I sink down beside them. "Oh my God."

The world comes rushing back, everything brighter and more colorful than a moment ago.

"Thanks—Seb," Natalie manages between shallow breaths. Her skin is ghostly pale and damp, and a terrifying amount of blood soaks through her clothes.

I move toward them. I need to touch her, to kiss her forehead and feel her warmth on my lips, to reassure myself that she's alive.

But Sebastian raises a hand to stop me. "No time. They've got a chimera."

I blink back tears, unable to look away. "But—"

"Go, Katie," Natalie rasps, reaching out to squeeze my hand. Despite everything, her grip is strong, and her dark eyes are still burning with the same fierce determination I've always loved. "Don't let them take it."

Even in this state, she hasn't lost sight of what we need to do. God, she's strong. She's stood between me and danger more times than I can count and shown me what it means to truly love someone.

I give her a quick kiss, memorizing the feel of her lips. "Keep her safe until I'm back, Sebastian."

He nods. "Promise."

I turn around to see a rabbit struggling in the golden net, its movements growing weaker by the second. Sophia scoops it into her arms, triumph written across her face, while Oaklyn and Hazel watch.

Something inside me snaps.

Between Natalie lying at my feet and the chimera fighting for its life, a fury unlike anything I've ever felt surges through my veins. My pulse thunders in my ears. The world warps in my vision, colors and shapes coming to me with sudden brightness. A roar of indiscernible noise fills my mind, maybe the chimeras' voices surging to my attention with more clarity.

No. The Madsens don't get to do this. After everything they've done and all the people they've hurt, after nearly killing Natalie, they are not walking away with bio magic.

I step out from behind the boulder, my fists clenched so tightly that my nails cut into my palms. "Sophia, put it down!" I roar, my voice carrying across the cove.

The Madsens and Hazel turn toward me. A sneer curls Sophia's upper lip, her eyes flashing with amusement.

Movement erupts from the trees at the edge of the cove. The stag I set free charges along the shore, its huge antlers lowered like lances, its hooves thundering on the rocks.

"Mom!" Oaklyn cries.

It's too late for Sophia to react. The stag slams into her with the force of a train, sending her flying with a shriek that carries over everything. The net tumbles from her arms, the rabbit thrashing inside it.

Sophia rolls across the rocky shore, gasping for breath, her trench coat getting soaked as waves lap against her.

The stag wheels around, its purple eyes fixed on her. Mist puffs from its nostrils.

"The gentle one is a Guardian, sisters," it says, its voice loud inside my head. *"We must fight."*

The beating of powerful wings fills the air, and a shadow passes over us. An enormous winged creature swoops down, talons extended, its beak pointed at Oaklyn.

Lucy!

Oaklyn cries out as the griffin dives and forces her to hit the ground. The dagger flies from her hand, clattering on the rocks.

Lucy lands in front of me, wings spread, beak opening to let out a piercing shriek that makes the air vibrate. The sound fills the forest and echoes across the water, silencing everything.

Sophia scrambles to her feet, blood oozing from a gash on her chest where the stag's antlers caught her. She touches the wound and looks at the blood on her fingers, her lip curling into a snarl.

The ground trembles as she summons her magic, but before she can unleash an attack, the cove comes alive. Bears surge from the woods, alligators slide out of the water, and birds swoop down from the treetops.

My heart pounds as the chimeras close in, but it's not from fear. They're not after me.

"What are you doing?" Sophia demands, fixing me with a furious stare as she raises her palms for a fight.

I'm as stunned as she is. I didn't call them. I didn't ask for their help.

They rush forward in a tidal wave of shifting forms, moving like water pouring over the land. Sophia looks from one to the other, calculating her next move. If I'm not mistaken, there's a glimpse of uncertainty in her expression as she realizes she's outnumbered. Her hands waver, and she takes a step back.

But before I can celebrate, shouts echo on the trail we came from. My stomach drops as a wall of black cloaks reaches the cove.

The witches have arrived.

Fiona stands in the middle, her red traveling cloak billowing. At least a dozen Shadows fan out along the ridge, their hands raised and ready. Agnes flanks her on one side, and Sky on the other, her mouth opening in horror when she spots Natalie bleeding on the ground.

"Nat, what happened?" Sky cries. She takes a step, but Fiona flings out a hand to stop her.

"What have you done, Katie?" Fiona demands, her gaze sweeping over the chimeras, the Madsens, Natalie wounded, and me in the center of it all.

"We need your help!" I cry.

But Fiona's face hardens as she takes in the stag and Lucy standing in front of me like guards.

"The bio magic corrupted her!" Agnes cries.

Behind her, Amir steps forward, his mouth open. "My God..."

Fiona lifts her chin. "Coven, start the enchantment."

"No!" I shout, panic flooding my veins. "It's not like that!"

The Shadows are already moving. They form a semicircle facing the chimeras, who crouch and prepare to fight. A sound fills the air, and the hair on the back of my neck prickles as goosebumps race across my skin.

They're chanting. Their voices rise in different pitches, singing a chilling chorus I don't understand.

"Veniant vires, hoc carmen frangite.

Ignis et ventus, hanc artem tollite…"

The sky darkens like a storm rolling in, clouds swirling unnaturally fast. Dark streaks materialize overhead, arcing and twisting until a vortex churns above the cove. Its power builds, and the sea roils, waves hissing against the shore.

"Everyone would be best to leave the circle," Fiona warns, her words getting swept away in the gathering wind.

Nobody moves. Hazel stands frozen. Oaklyn has retrieved her dagger and is flanking her mother. Wyatt crouches at their feet, his fur standing on end.

I back up toward Natalie, who struggles to sit up under Sebastian's guidance, her face so ashen that my heart lurches. Pain or blood loss? Both?

"Don't try to stand," I tell her, crouching to put a gentle hand on her shoulder. I brush a strand of damp hair from her face, my fingers shaking. My throat is so tight it hurts. "I need you to stay alive. I can't do this without you."

"You can," she whispers.

I swallow hard. Even now, her presence steadies me like nothing else can.

"Sebastian, we have to get her away from here," I say. It suddenly registers that he came out of nowhere to save Natalie's life. "Wait, where's Millie?"

"Resting. They've separated her from the magic, but it's taken a toll. They're trying to heal her before she..." Pain crosses his expression, and he waves me away. "Go. You need to stop this. I'll get her out of here."

"No," Natalie grits out.

My skin prickles, the sensation growing more intense until it burns. I rub my arm as the dark energy pulses overhead. The chimeras growl, and their fear and anger trickles into my veins.

"I don't know how to stop this," I say, my voice shaking. The wind grows stronger, unnaturally hot, whipping my hair around my face and tugging at my clothes.

Lucy's voice slices through my mind. *Stand with us against those who wish to harness our power, Guardian. Your blood remembers.*

My stomach twists. Remembers *what*? What am I supposed to do if I can't do magic?

"You won't be useful if you get swallowed by their spell," Sebastian says, grunting as he puts Natalie's arm across his shoulders to support her weight.

There's an electric hiss like a lightning strike, and a wave ripples down from the vortex above, making the air shimmer. A fox yelps. Another wave ripples, and more chimeras cry out. The stag paws the ground and shakes its head. Others snarl and crouch lower.

I stand up straight, my nails digging into my palms. I glance back at Natalie one more time, finding courage when she nods. We've been through so many impossible situations together, and I have to keep fighting.

This is what I was meant to do. Not to hunt chimeras, not to trap them, but to protect them—just as Natalie has always protected me.

I walk toward Fiona and the other Directors, gaining confidence with each step. "Stop!" I shout, my voice carrying across the cove. "I won't let you kill them!"

Fiona's eyes narrow. "Stand aside, Miss Alexander."

"No. This magic isn't meant to be caged or destroyed. These are the forces that make up the natural world, and to destroy them would be to make a huge mistake."

"They're dangerous!" Agnes snaps.

The strength of all the chimeras wraps around me like a blanket, holding me in place. "Only because you've made them that way! You've trapped them, consumed them, used them as weapons. Of course they fight back!"

The Shadows chant louder, and another wave ripples down, zapping my skin like I've touched an electric fence. More yelps and snarls of pain erupt as it hits the chimeras.

"Come on, you can do it," Sebastian says behind me.

And though I don't entirely know what he's talking about...I also feel deep inside me that there's so much I don't understand about myself and about magic.

My breath hitches as I look back. Natalie's face is drained and blood soaks her clothes, but she's standing with Sebastian's help, and her eyes are clear and focused on me.

"I love you," I mouth to her, needing her to know in case this all goes wrong.

"I love you too," she mouths back.

I grit my teeth and face the witches once more. "I am a Guardian. Not the kind C.S.A.M.M. created, but the kind that came before—those who protected the balance between magic and humanity."

Some of the Shadows exchange looks, whispering to each other. The enchantment falters, the vortex flickering.

"Enough of this," Fiona roars. "Shadows! Finish them!"

The witches' song comes to an abrupt end, and they sweep out their arms in unison. A thunderclap splits the air. The vortex surges downward, closing in on us all. My skin burns so fiercely that I grit my teeth to suppress a cry.

Every chimera reaches out, their consciousness entwining with mine like grasping fingers. Their panic and pain floods through me, making me gasp—but so does their power, flowing into my veins and keeping me steady as the ground trembles beneath my feet.

If the witches won't listen to me and they won't let the chimeras go free...they leave us no choice.

Lucy's voice fills my mind again. *"The words are in your blood, Guardian. Let them rise."*

I close my eyes as something stirs within me. Fragments of memories flash through my mind—generations of Guardians standing among these same chimeras, facing threats to the magical balance.

Energy surges up through the soles of my feet. The chimeras' presence intensifies, their collective consciousness offering me something—a phrase passed down through generations of Guardians.

Without thinking, I let it pour out. The words feel right, like I've spoken them a thousand times. "Old magic! With Guardian blood, I call you to fight!"

My army charges, heading for the surrounding Shadows.

From the Journal of Hazel Okada

The dark vortex surged downward, devouring the morning light. Everyone's attention snapped to it, but then the chimeras charged the witches, their forms shifting and blurring as they moved. Fur became feathers, paws became wings, bodies expanded and contracted with each bound. Dark wisps reached for them like grasping fingers, but the enchantment was weakening, dissipating like smoke in the wind as the witches were forced to scatter.

Amid the mass of bodies and shimmering threads of magic, a flash of brown-and-black fur streaked in my periphery. A snarl sent a shiver up my spine. Before anyone could react, Wyatt pounced—not on the witches or chimeras, but on Sophia.

I gasped as his jaws clamped down on her forearm and shook it.

Oaklyn cried out. "Wyatt! No!"

Sophia shrieked and toppled back, landing on her side with a splash of seawater. The trapped chimera tumbled from her grasp, still struggling inside the net.

The moment it fell, Wyatt released her arm to stand over it, his stance unmistakably protective. Blood dripped from his muzzle, his hackles raised along his spine.

"Wyatt, come!" Oaklyn commanded, a note of panic in her tone as she glanced at her mother.

The dog didn't move. I'd never seen him like this, though it lined up with what Katie told me about him. A growl rumbled deep in his chest as he kept his eyes fixed on Sophia. They were amber as always, but... No, I must have imagined the flash of purple. The rising sun and swirling magic must have played a trick.

Sophia cradled her arm, jagged tears in her sleeve revealing ribbons of blood. She glanced around to where the witches and chimeras clashed in a noisy battle. "Get that fucking dog away from us, Oaklyn."

Oaklyn remained frozen, her gaze darting from Wyatt to Sophia. The dog crouched lower over the trapped chimera, his teeth bared.

I stood rooted, breathing fast. Why was Wyatt protecting it? Did he sense something I couldn't?

All around us, the vortex continued to splinter, the enchantment faltering as the witches were forced to defend themselves against the chimeras' charge.

"Fine, then." Sophia's voice lowered dangerously as she raised her hands, summoning the loose rocks along the shoreline.

Oaklyn lunged forward, positioning herself between her mother and the dog. "Mom, wait—"

"Out of the way." Sophia grabbed Oaklyn's arm, her nails digging in hard enough to make her daughter gasp. "You're nowhere near the handler Freddie was. Get him under control before I deal with him myself."

Oaklyn jerked her arm free, her expression hardening.

The look on Sophia's face told me Wyatt was about to get hurt if he didn't back down, so I stepped closer to break this up. "Oaklyn, maybe we should—"

"Quiet!" Sophia snapped. She turned her cold glare onto me, her eyes narrowing in a way that reminded me of a snake about to strike. "You've been useful, girl, but don't think for a second that makes you worthy of magic."

I recoiled like her words had slapped me. Worthy? What happened to democratized magic? This didn't add up to what Oaklyn and I had dreamed about.

"Mom," Oaklyn said, a warning in her tone.

But Sophia's face twisted with a cruel smile as she looked me up and down. "Did you really think we'd share it with you? That we'd make you a witch?"

She raised her hands, and the earth beneath my feet jolted. I stumbled forward as the ground cracked and heaved.

"Stop it!" Oaklyn shouted. "We need to focus on—"

"I know what we need!" Sophia grabbed my wrist and yanked me closer.

I tried to pull free, but her grip was like iron, squeezing my bones until I yelped in pain. My feet splashed into the water, the frigid ocean seeping through my shoes and lapping at my ankles.

"Stay in front of me until we get out of here," she hissed in my ear. "Oaklyn, get the bio magic."

"Mom, this isn't necessary." Oaklyn stepped closer with her hands curled into fists.

"The witches are going to try to stop us," Sophia said. "We need a shield."

Oaklyn hesitated, her gaze darting between my face and her mother's, and then to Wyatt, who was still crouched over the chimera. So much was going on as witches and chimeras clashed together, but all I could focus on was Oaklyn's face—blank, pale, conflicted.

"Give me the blade, darling," Sophia said, opening her hand. Blood trickled onto her palm from the gashes on her arm, dripping into the rising tide at our feet.

"Oaklyn, don't do it," I blurted, my heart pounding so hard I could feel it in my throat.

Oaklyn's knuckles strained on the dagger's hilt.

"Hurry up." Sophia opened and closed her fingers impatiently, the blood and her painted nails making them look like crimson talons.

Slowly, Oaklyn handed it over.

In that single moment, any last thread of what we had snapped. I felt it in my chest, a sharp twang that took my breath away.

My throat tightened until I could barely speak. "A human shield? Really?"

She couldn't even meet my eye. "That's not—"

"You said you loved me. You said we'd change the world together." I couldn't stop my voice from breaking.

Sophia laughed, which made my face burn with shame. God, I was so naive.

Pain flashed across Oaklyn's face.

I tried again to pull away from Sophia, anger sparking as her nails dug deeper into my flesh.

"Is this your choice, then?" I asked.

"Yes, darling, is it?" Sophia purred, and then something sharp pressed against my throat, freezing me in place.

Oaklyn looked at us both, breathing fast, torn between the woman who gave her life and the one who'd given her heart. "Mom, this isn't what we agreed on."

"Plans change." Sophia pushed the dagger harder into my throat. "Sometimes sacrifices must be made for the greater good."

I gritted my teeth as pain burst open in my neck, my eyes watering. Warmth trickled down to my collarbone. I refused to drop my gaze, wanting Oaklyn to look at me and see what she was allowing to happen by just standing there.

"Not her," Oaklyn said, shaking her head.

Sophia scoffed. "Don't be like that. This is what we've been working toward. Now get that fucking chimera out from under the dog and let's go."

Oaklyn clenched and unclenched her fists, her nostrils flaring. After a long moment, she nodded.

My heart dropped. "You're going to let her do this to me?" I said, my voice strangled.

All my memories of her dissolved like she had dunked them in acid—her fingers in my hair, her lips on my skin, her whispers against my neck.

She turned away. "She's my mom, Hazel."

I blinked, tears burning in my eyes. There it was. It's not that I expected her to choose me over her family, but I did expect her to keep me safe. To protect me like she'd done before. Like Natalie always did for Katie.

Instead, Oaklyn was going to let me become a sacrifice in order to advance their cause...and I was the fool who helped speed along my own demise.

CHAPTER 25

Bloodletting

T HE CHIMERAS RESPOND TO my battle cry, hurtling at the surrounding Shadows. The stag's antlers send a witch flying. Lucy takes off, her wings creating a gust that knocks two more off their feet.

The witches' enchantment fails as their concentration breaks. The vortex breaks apart around us, and shards of darkness fall like rain.

Magic tingles across my skin with more clarity than ever. It's not just a prickle anymore—it flows into me like a river finding its course, robust and alive. I can feel everyone and everything around me, like tangible auras. Trails of energy connect the chimeras to each other and to me.

My head fills with voices, humming like I'm in a giant bell.

"Aurora, I need help..."

"Over here!"

"With me, Zephyr."

"Fetch the others."

"Hurry! The witches have surrounded Fenrith..."

It's too much. Too loud. I cover my ears, trying to muffle it, but the voices are inside me.

"Katie!" Natalie calls out, barely audible through the cacophony in my head.

Her pale face swims into my vision, steadying me. I force myself to breathe, to let the voices drift past me instead of consuming me. Slowly, I regain control, the world coming back into focus.

The vortex continues to break apart, gaps of daylight peeking through the darkness.

"Hold your positions!" Amir shouts, drowned out by snarls and screams as chimeras and Shadows clash on the shore.

Beside him, Fiona spins, scanning the mayhem. When her gaze locks onto me, she freezes, fury crossing her expression. This woman who once welcomed me into the coven, who led my induction ceremony, now looks at me like I'm the enemy. How did we end up here?

I drop my hands from my ears, glaring right back. We advance on each other, the fight raging like we're in the eye of a hurricane.

"You really think you can control this power?" she says.

"I'm not trying to control it. I'm trying to understand it and protect it like past Guardians have done."

"Those witches you're talking about," Fiona says, pointing at me as she stalks closer, "came from the same time period when people thought bloodletting by leeches was a good idea. When doctors drilled holes into skulls to release evil spirits. When snake oil was thought to be a cure. They believed magic could exist freely without consequences. They were wrong then, and you're wrong now."

I shake my head. "People used to understand the balance of nature a lot better than we do today. They built pyramids and created Stonehenge and navigated entire oceans by the stars and animals. Witches of the past understood something we've forgotten—that magic isn't something to be controlled, but respected and guarded." Emotion tightens my throat. "The coven was formed to protect magic, Fiona. You showed me what that means. Let's find a better way."

Something flickers in her eyes. Before she can respond, a flash of white pulls our attention away from each other. A white horse charges toward us, and I leap backward.

Fiona spins to meet it, raising a shield of earth that the creature smashes through like it's made of paper. There's a *thump* as it slams into her, and she falls hard, rolling across the rocks and narrowly avoiding its hooves.

Hayley comes to Fiona's aid, forcing it back with a wave of debris.

"Katie!" Natalie's voice comes closer. The familiar warmth of her hands on my arms, steadying me as I sway, is everything I need right now—but seeing her covered in blood with her face twisted in pain makes my eyes sting.

Sky is at her side, holding her up, breathing fast. "Sebastian went to get Millie. I'll get Nat out of here."

The worry on Sky's face reminds me I'm not the only one who cares about Natalie.

Natalie grimaces, her face a sickly gray. "Not yet. The Madsens."

I follow her gaze, scanning the battlefield. A glint of gold catches my eye. Wyatt is crouched over the enchanted net, snarling. The small chimera is still trapped inside, its form flickering as it thrashes against the golden threads.

Wait...is he *protecting* it? This dog confuses me more and more.

Beside it, Hazel and Sophia are struggling, Hazel shrieking as she tries to pull away. Oaklyn watches them, her expression torn.

Terror floods through me, icy and dizzying. I need to get to Hazel. I need to take her back from them.

But the distance between us feels impossible to cross. The battle rages on all sides, witches and chimeras locked in combat.

I inhale deeply, feeling the connection to the chimeras pulse through me like a second heartbeat.

"Help me reach them," I whisper.

Slowly, a path clears before me as chimeras shift their positions, creating a corridor. Bears, foxes, birds, and creatures I have no names for move in synchrony, holding back the Shadows.

I run, my legs finding new strength as I race toward Hazel. The ground beneath my feet seems to propel me forward, as if the earth is helping me move faster.

Sophia sees me coming. Her eyes widen. She yanks Hazel against her front, pressing Oaklyn's dagger to her throat. "Stay back!"

I skid to a halt, my heartbeat frantic. This woman has taken too much already. I'll die before she takes Hazel too. "Let her go."

"Or what?" She smiles. "You'll set your pets on me? I'll slit her throat before they reach me."

Hazel's eyes meet mine, full of fear. A trickle of blood oozes down where the blade has broken skin.

"I'm sorry," she mouths, her face twisting as she fights back tears.

"It's okay," I say, trying to keep my voice steady. "Everything's going to be okay."

Sophia laughs, the sound harsh and grating. "Nothing is going to be okay for either of you. Oaklyn, pick up our prize and clear a path. Let's go!"

My heart pounds so hard I can barely breathe. The chimeras are with me, listening and ready to spring, but I mentally caution them to stay back. One wrong move and Hazel dies.

Oaklyn is frozen, looking from Wyatt to the surrounding brawl. Her fists clench and unclench, her hands empty. "I need my dagger," she says tightly.

Sophia's face clouds over, a snarl on her lips to match the dog's. "If you'd opened my gift, you ungrateful brat, you'd be in a better position right now."

Oaklyn furrows her brow. "What?"

Keeping the knife on Hazel's throat, Sophia rummages in the pocket of her crimson trench coat. The fabric flaps against Hazel's side as she extracts something and throws it at Oaklyn.

It's a gift-wrapped ring box—purple paper with a bow on top. It bounces off Oaklyn's chest before she catches it. She stares down at it, her face blank.

I'm too confused to do anything. What gift could possibly matter at a time like this?

"Open it and help me properly," Sophia says, her voice eerily low.

Wait.

No.

With trembling hands, Oaklyn tears away the wrapping paper and opens the box. Inside is a tiny glass vial of liquid—shimmering, iridescent, and as bright purple as crocuses at the beginning of springtime.

As purple as the gemstones I'd seen Natalie slip into her pocket countless times.

Even from here, I can feel its power radiating, making the hairs on my arms stand on end.

My blood turns to ice.

Is that...?

It can't be.

But it is, isn't it?

Magic. Sophia has gifted her daughter earth magic.

"You're ready, darling," Sophia purrs.

Icy dread floods my veins. If Oaklyn and Sophia both became witches, there'd be no stopping them.

I can't let this happen. Even if I have to fight Oaklyn with my fists and teeth, I cannot let her drink that potion.

I have no plan, no strategy. I just act.

From the Journal of Hazel Okada

The dagger bit into my throat—the one Oaklyn had fucking handed over willingly. Sophia rocked impatiently, the blade slicing my skin with each shift. I fought the need to squirm as warm blood trickled down my neck and pain shot into my scalp.

The betrayal hurt worse. I couldn't believe Oaklyn had given over the weapon now cutting into me. And then she had the audacity to ask her mom to let me go?

I bit my lip hard, torn between wanting to cry and wanting to lash out at Oaklyn and make her hurt as much as I did. The discomfort on her face wasn't enough.

As Oaklyn unwrapped the gift, Katie sucked in a breath. I tried to catch her eye, to silently ask if she knew what was going on, but her gaze was fixed on Oaklyn, horror dawning.

Oaklyn's hands trembled as the paper floated to the ground. When she opened the box, her lips parted in shock. Katie remained frozen, breathing hard, her eyes wide.

Oaklyn picked up what was inside. Held it up to the light.

A vial.

What was it? What was I missing?

"Help me properly," Sophia had said a moment ago.

My breath caught. The purple—the same shade as the witches' eyes when they were performing magic.

Understanding crashed over me like a wave. I was staring at liquid magic, bottled and ready for Oaklyn to drink. Longing filled Oaklyn's eyes—not just for power, but for her mother's approval.

My heart jumped into action, a desperation like nothing I'd ever felt clawing at my chest.

"Hazel!" Katie shouted.

She broke into a run, and the chimeras responded, charging after her like she'd given them a silent command.

Adrenaline exploded inside me as everything happened at once. Katie sprinted toward Oaklyn. A lynx pounced at Sophia and me. A massive bird swooped down, talons out.

Sophia ducked, yanking me down with her. Pain erupted in my jaw as the blade caught me.

We crashed into the rocky ground, and the lynx landed on Sophia. Its snarls filled my ears as it tried to pin her down. I kicked away from her, feeling the satisfying crunch of my heel slamming into her gut.

The bird—Jesus, was that a condor?—dove repeatedly, trying to sink its hooked beak into Sophia. The world became a mix of growls and shrieks, fangs and claws, and me in the middle, scrambling to get away. My palms stung and my knees protested as I crawled frantically over the rocks.

Through it all, I caught a glimpse of Katie throwing her entire weight into Oaklyn. They fell hard, Katie's momentum carrying them both to the ground. Katie managed to get on top, straddling Oaklyn and trying to land punches with her gauntlet. Oaklyn fought back one-handed, her other fist wrapped around the vial.

Rage exploded inside me. Over my dead body was she going to hurt Katie.

I sprang toward them, grabbing Oaklyn's arm with both hands to try and get the potion away from her. She bucked and thrashed beneath us, roaring in fury. Though it was two against one, all her time in the gym was paying off, and Katie and I cracked our heads together as we fought to keep her pinned.

"Ow!" we cried in unison.

Katie landed a punch with the gauntlet, disorienting Oaklyn for long enough to shimmy up and pin her shoulders. While Katie held her down, I knelt on her arm and tried to pry her fingers from the vial.

Oaklyn grunted in pain.

I looked over, and my heart squeezed. Her blue eyes were glossy, her face flushed as she fought back tears. Her lips were covered in blood, a trickle running from the corner of her mouth.

But I couldn't stop. Of all the doubts crashing through me, I clung to one certainty: I could not let Oaklyn drink the potion and become a witch. She'd shown me who she was—a criminal, a murderer, a liar. She'd used me since the day I showed her that chimera map. She probably never even loved me.

Gritting my teeth, I dug my nails into her skin, trying again to pry open her fist.

Her grip loosened.

The vial tumbled free, rolling across the uneven rock.

I threw myself after it, fingers scrabbling for the smooth glass.

Behind me, there was a thump and a splutter. I looked over my shoulder to see Oaklyn roll over and ram her fist into Katie's side. Katie's yell cut off as she coughed violently.

Crouched over Katie like a predator, Oaklyn turned her gaze onto me, her eyes fiery with rage.

The tiny vial was warm in my palm.

She left Katie coughing on the ground and started toward me, blood trickling from her mouth.

Should I have dumped the potion over the rocks? Thrown it into the ocean? Where could I put it that wouldn't let Sophia gather it back up with magic?

I did the only thing I could—the only thing that would truly stop Oaklyn or Sophia from getting it.

And deep down...it was what I desperately wanted to do anyway. It was what I'd wanted since I first talked to Oaklyn in that cafe.

I popped the cork and raised the vial to my lips.

The potion slid down my throat like liquid fire.

CHAPTER 26

Irreversible Decisions

The vial tips against Hazel's lips, and my heart grinds to a stop as the purple liquid disappears down her throat.

For a suspended moment, the world goes silent. Time freezes. Everyone pauses, the forest itself seeming to hold its breath.

Then—

"No!" I yell, my voice drowned beneath Sophia and Oaklyn's furious shrieks.

Hazel doubles over, coughing violently. The empty vial slips from her fingers and shatters on the rocks, glass fragments catching the light like diamonds.

"What did you do?" Oaklyn cries. She runs to Hazel and drops to her knees.

I get to my feet, gasping, pain stabbing my side where Oaklyn punched me. Each breath sends a jolt through my ribs, but I force myself upright.

Hazel is convulsing on all fours. The air around her shimmers like heat waves rising from pavement. Her fingers dig into the earth, and the stone beneath her cracks, fissures spreading out like a spiderweb. The sound of splitting rock echoes across the cove.

"Hazel!" I shout, limping forward.

No, no... I tried so hard to keep her safe from this world. Now she's submerged in it. Drowning.

The stone fractures further under her palms. What if her body can't handle the magic, like what happened to Millie? I can't lose her.

Before I get to her, movement catches my eye. Sophia forces Wyatt back with a wave of earth. The dog snarls as he tumbles away from the golden net. With a triumphant cry, Sophia snatches up the trapped chimera, which is limp and unconscious, its form flickering weakly between a rabbit and something indiscernible.

"Oaklyn, let's go!" she shouts, backing away, strands of her white-blonde hair whipping in the wind.

Oaklyn stays crouched, wiping away the blood her mother left on Hazel's neck. She whips her head around, her eyes wild.

"Now!" Sophia barks.

Oaklyn hesitates. I've seen this expression on her once before, when she landed on me with her dagger after she found out I killed her brother. And for the briefest moment, I have to wonder what she really feels for Hazel. How real it is—or was.

She gives Hazel one last look, then gets up and sprints after Sophia, her decision made.

Wyatt shakes himself off, sending droplets of seawater flying. He bounds after them, his loyalty to Oaklyn unwavering despite everything.

I'm torn, my heart splitting in two directions. Hazel is on the ground, magic coursing through her body. But Sophia is escaping with a captured chimera, and if she consumes its power...

A few chimeras break away to follow Sophia and Oaklyn, but they're quickly intercepted by Shadows. Enchantment or not, the witches are still determined to destroy them, and the chimeras are fighting for their lives. A cacophony of emotions shoots through me so intensely that a sharp pain stabs my temples.

"Katie. Help." It's Hazel, her voice all but lost beneath the clamor. Her eyes flash between their normal brown and an eerie purple as she looks at me, pleading. Sweat beads on her forehead, and her entire body trembles.

I race closer and kneel beside her, taking the place where Oaklyn was a moment ago. I hold both her hands tightly. "I'm here."

Unnatural heat radiates from her skin, almost painful to touch. She convulses again, and a prickling sensation ripples over me as a burst of magic erupts from her palms. Rocks lift from the ground around us, hovering before shooting in all directions like bullets. I duck, covering Hazel with my body as best I can, feeling their wind as they narrowly miss us.

"What's happening to me?" she whimpers, her voice small and afraid.

"You drank earth magic. I think it's trying to find its place in you," I say, though I'm guessing. I've never seen someone become a witch before. "Try to breathe through it."

The chimeras' pain hits me as they're struck by the Shadows' magic. Each strike is like a blow to my own body, making my breath hitch. They're falling, breaking down like wood splintering under crashing waves, trapped within the circle of witches.

I can't help them. I can't help anyone. The realization burns in my chest.

"Katie!" Natalie's voice punctures my thoughts. "What happened? Where'd the Madsens go?"

She staggers toward us with Sky supporting her. I don't know how she's on her feet at all. But her gaze is locked onto me, like nothing in the world can stop her from fighting.

"Don't tell me we lost them," Sky says, going pale.

"With a chimera," I say, my voice broken. "Natalie, you shouldn't be here. Sky—"

"I know," Sky says. "I'm trying. She's stubborn as hell."

I hold Natalie's gaze, and she tilts her head. This is how it's going to be, then. Each of us refusing to leave the other until one of us takes her last breath.

Hazel grunts as another wave of magic pulses through her, the ground beneath her palms cracking and rumbling. "Katie, I can't control it," she whimpers.

I grip her shoulders. "Focus on your breathing. Try to center yourself."

"Wait—" Natalie says, looking down at Hazel with wide eyes, finally seeming to realize she's not just injured.

Sky gasps. "Did she consume—"

"What's happening here?" Fiona's sharp voice cuts through our conversation. She strides over, her cloak torn and dirty. Her gaze sweeps over Hazel, narrowing when she sees Hazel's eyes blazing purple. "Who is this? Why is she manifesting magic?"

"Her name is Hazel, and she just stopped Oaklyn from becoming a witch," I say firmly, standing between them. For all the shitty treatment she's given me, I refuse to let her unleash that on my best friend.

Fiona's nostrils flare, her face hardening into the same expression I've seen countless times. "Tell me it isn't bio magic."

"It's earth magic. And you should be thanking Hazel," I snap, my patience thin after all this time spent trying to prove myself to her.

Fiona turns to Sky, who's still supporting Natalie. "Don't let her go. She's property of C.S.A.M.M. now. Bring her in."

Sky dips her chin.

"And you're supposed to be leading the Shadows, Skylar," Fiona adds harshly, "not playing nursemaid while everything falls apart."

Sky grits her teeth. "My sister is injured!"

"Fiona," I interrupt, stepping closer. "The Madsens have a chimera. Sophia is about to do the ritual while the coven is over here fighting the wrong fight. We need to work together or we all lose."

Fiona turns her sharp gaze onto me. "What we need is to destroy these chimeras!"

Around us, chimeras and Shadows clash in violent bursts of magic. A bull with massive horns sends a witch flying into the rocks. Amir hurls a volley of stones that knocks a coyote off its feet. Blood stains the shore, and wisps of shimmering black magic fill the air.

"Destroy them to what end? This isn't solving anything!" I cry, desperate for her to understand. "Sophia's gaining power while you order your coven to wage war on magic!"

"Quiet!" Fiona roars.

Before I can argue back, a groan from Natalie pulls my attention. Her knees give out, and her body folds like a marionette with cut strings.

"Nat, get up," Sky says urgently, her voice cracking as she stumbles under the sudden dead weight.

"Natalie!" My heart plummets as I lunge closer.

Her clothes are saturated in dark red. Her face has gone ashen, the warm tone of her skin fading to a lifeless gray.

"We need to get her out of here," Sky says. "She needs medical attention. Now."

Her voice swims, coming from far away.

"She's lost too much blood," Fiona says.

"Don't say that," I say, my lips numb. "We still have time. We can…"

I choke into silence as the world narrows to Natalie's face. I search for any sign of the fierce determination that always burns in her eyes, but her eyelids are fluttering, consciousness slipping away.

I wait for her to protest, to straighten up and say she's fine, but her eyes are rolling back in her head. Her breaths are weak and shallow, and her lips have taken on a bluish tinge that terrifies me more than any chimera ever could.

"Help!" I cry, not sure who I'm yelling to. The witches are scattered, dealing with their own injuries or following orders to try and destroy the chimeras. No one is coming.

"Oh my God," Sky says, and for the first time since I've known her, she seems completely lost. Her shoulders shake as she dissolves into tears, her fingers pressed uselessly against the gushing wound in her sister's side. "We're losing her."

The words hit me so hard that I gasp like I've been punched. Panic constricts my chest until I can't breathe. This can't be happening. We haven't had enough time together. She only just told me about her dream home, and I actually thought it might happen—that we could get through all this and spend the rest of our lives together. Was that naive? Was our relationship always doomed to end at the hands of the Madsens?

"Natalie, please don't leave me," I say, the words barely audible as our whole future disintegrates in a pool of blood on the rocks.

Something stirs deep inside me, like my utter terror pushed so hard against it that it had no choice but to come alive. An urge I've never felt before overtakes me. The chimeras sense it too; I feel their attention turning toward me without looking up. They inch closer, their forms rippling.

I inhale deeply, letting the sensation wash over me. It's like a door opening in my mind, one that's always been there but I never knew how to unlock. Strength flows into my limbs, not my own but borrowed from something ancient and powerful. The chimeras' consciousness merges with mine, their memories becoming accessible—centuries of existence, of watching humans evolve, of maintaining the natural balance of the world.

Suddenly, I'm seeing through different eyes. I'm fighting Agnes, swiping at her with my claws extended. I'm trying to save Millie, who's pale and weak in Sebastian's arms as he carries her away from here. I'm galloping, my hooves reaching forward and digging into the earth, my long legs carrying me at blinding speed through the trees. Beside me, a fox races through the underbrush. Above, a hawk soars through the treetops. I'm tracking, sensing...

Ahead, one of our own is bound. The humans have her and are about to perform the blood ritual.

Hurry. Need to hurry.

But a tangle of roots lashes out, wrapping around my legs. I stumble and hit the ground, sliding on my shoulder.

The others keep going. The ritual has begun, and we cannot stop.

A canine comes through the trees—not fully one of us, but enough. His mother was magic. He calls to us. They are here.

I break free from the roots and stand, and my sisters and I change course, following the canine.

There!

The ritual is underway. Our sister is dissolving, joining the blood of the older witch.

"Nat, keep breathing!" Sky's voice pulls me back to my body—my knees on the ground, the blinding pain everywhere. The vision of Sophia dissolves, of Wyatt leading the chimeras to her, of the dark forest... And in its place is Natalie's graying skin, the blood, the people crowded around her.

I can feel the threads of magic connecting everything—witches, chimeras, the earth beneath our feet. I can sense the fear behind Fiona's anger, the love driving Sky to protect her sister, the confusion and wonder in Hazel's transformation... And Natalie. Her life force, draining away.

She's about to die. The fragile strands tethering her to this world are fraying, closer to snapping altogether by the second.

Help her, I plead silently, hoping the chimeras can hear me as I can hear them. *She doesn't deserve this.*

I pour everything I am into the plea—all my love for Natalie, all my fear of losing her, all my desperate hope that we can still fix this mess.

For a moment, nothing happens. Then a small shape detaches from the forest—Lucy in her kitten form, padding toward us on silent paws. Her eyes glow as she approaches Natalie and sits back on her haunches, her tail swishing.

The air grows thick with magic, heavy and electric. It presses against my skin, fills my lungs, makes my hair stand on end. Lucy begins to shimmer, becoming more powerful with each frantic beat of my heart.

"Katie, what's it doing?" Sky asks, her voice strained through her tears. Her fingers close around my arm, cold and sweaty, the terror of losing Natalie plain on her face. After all they've been through together, losing their mom, nearly losing their dad, risking their lives to protect the public from dark magic, they've always had each other.

I shake my head, unable to explain what I don't understand.

Natalie's breaths quicken, her chest rising and falling rapidly. Her eyelids flutter like she's dreaming. Her life force isn't as weak anymore. It pulses in the air, wrapping around me.

Do I dare to hope? I lift her sweater, which is soaked and torn. The wound in her side gapes open—but it's getting smaller. Tissue is stitching closed by an invisible hand. Blood stops flowing.

"Lucy," I whisper, gratitude overwhelming me.

Slowly, color returns to Natalie's cheeks. The bluish tinge fades from her lips, replaced by their natural pink. It's like her body is regenerating blood—and maybe it is. Her breathing deepens, steadies.

I can't move. Can't breathe. Can hardly believe what I'm seeing.

Her eyelids fly open, and she gasps, gulping down air like someone breaking the surface after nearly drowning. "What happened? Where's Katie?"

I grab her face, tears streaming down my cheeks and neck. "I'm here. Are you okay?"

She stares up at me, confusion giving way to recognition. She reaches up to cup my hand against her cheek. "Katie. Don't cry."

I can barely breathe, choking back a sob as her warmth seeps into my palm.

Lucy backs up. The heavy press of magic recedes like a tide, the air seeming to grow cooler and thinner.

Thank you, I tell her silently, knowing I'll never be able to fully express my gratitude.

She blinks, then turns and trots back into the forest.

Natalie tries to sit up but falls back with a groan, her face contorting in pain. "Feels like that boulder really did land on me."

"Stay down," I say, placing a gentle hand on her shoulder.

She grunts and sits up anyway. "I can still fight. I just— Shit, is this all mine?"

She gawks at the pool of blood.

"Yeah," I say thickly.

Sky throws her arms around her sister, squeezing her briefly before sitting up and wiping her cheeks. "Don't ever do that to me again, dumbass."

Natalie's lips twitch. "I don't plan on it."

Fiona's eyes are huge. "Katie, how did you do that? Can you control them?"

I shake my head. "I didn't control anything. I just...asked."

Her expression twists, like she wants to be angry but doesn't understand why. "This is the first time bio magic has been used on a witch in a century."

I reach out mentally, searching for her mind the way I connected to the chimeras. It's like clawing through stone to get beneath her rigid exterior. But there, nestled deep inside her, is a complex web of thoughts and emotions. Pride and fear mix together. There's concern for the state of the world, and a desperate desire for all feral magic to be harnessed, even if that means destroying it. There's hatred for this power that isolated her from her non-magical family, and there's the need to protect them—her niece, her sister, her parents.

I am descended from the ancient Guardians, Fiona, I think, trying to project it into her mind. *I'm here to maintain the natural balance. Free magic is not your enemy.*

Fiona gasps, looking at me with a mix of fear and something else. Something less defensive and angry than usual.

"We're on the same team," I say, "and we have to work together if we want to protect the world from harm."

"Katie's a Guardian of ancient magic," Natalie says, sounding more like herself. "She can talk to the chimeras. She's been trying to tell us."

Fiona shakes her head. "Ancient Guardians are a fairy tale."

"They're not," I say fiercely.

The fight is still raging around us. A lynx pounces on Hayley, its claws raking her chest and tearing open her cloak. She screams, the sound rising into the treetops.

Stop! I shout inside my mind.

The lynx turns its blazing eyes onto me. Hayley moans in pain beneath it, blood oozing through the gashes in her cloak. The lynx bows its head, and slowly, it backs away.

Fiona stares at me, her expression shifting from shock to something grudging. "Prove it, then. Call them all off."

I nod, reaching out again with my mind. *Stop this fight,* I tell the chimeras. *The witches are not our enemies.*

The effect is immediate. The chimeras hesitate, the battle quieting like someone has put a damper on it. One by one, they turn to me.

"The Guardian asks us to stop," one hisses.

"Why should we stop defending ourselves?" another growls.

There's a greater threat to us all, I reply. *Please trust me.*

Slowly, they back away from the Shadows. They don't retreat entirely, but they stop attacking, watching me.

Fiona studies me, her expression unreadable, then turns to survey the battlefield. My heart lurches as I see the number of witches hunched and injured, their blood pooling on the rocks and staining the shoreline. The chimeras gather at an uneasy distance, many flickering and wounded. But as I look at them, they heal themselves like torn material being stitched back together—bio magic at work. Like Lucy did to Natalie.

"Shadows, stand down," Fiona calls out. "The Madsens have stolen bio magic. This changes our priorities."

The witches lower their hands, turning to Fiona in stunned silence.

"They're doing the ritual now," I say. "Sophia's absorbing the magic."

Everyone stares at me, eyes wide, lips parted in surprise.

"I can't explain," I say, my voice shaking. "But I saw it. It's happening, and if we can't find her before she gets out of the woods, we'll never be able to stop her."

Natalie pushes to her feet, swaying.

"You rest," I say, reaching out to steady her.

Her hand finds mine, squeezing firmly. "I promise I'm okay. Fully healed. I just..."

"Have a magic hangover?" Sky supplies.

Natalie makes a finger gun. "Exactly."

"Let's move," Sky says, turning to Fiona. "Before we're too late."

A terrible, heavy silence falls over the cove.

Fiona nods.

It's as close to an alliance as I'm going to get right now, and I'm happy to accept it. Because if Sophia is about to gain the ability to do mind control and God-knows-what-else...we've got a much bigger problem to worry about.

From the Journal of Hazel Okada

The world came back to me in fragments—the hard, gritty soil beneath my hands and knees, Katie and Fiona's raised voices, the chaos coming to an abrupt stop.

Catching my breath, I looked up to find the witches gathering around Fiona. Katie turned to me once more, and I tried to focus on her face, but everything seemed to be vibrating. My insides felt like they'd been scrambled and put back in the wrong order. Something new and wild stirred inside me that hadn't been there before.

"How are you feeling?" Katie asked.

I rubbed the back of my neck, trying to loosen the tension. "Like I got hit by a griffin. Then the griffin flew back and picked me up and dropped me a few times."

The words came out sounding like me, but I didn't feel like me anymore. Something fundamental had changed, and it was terrifying to think what that meant.

Katie laughed shakily, relief washing over her face. "I don't doubt it."

I stared at my hands. They looked the same—same lines, same freckle near my thumb—but it felt like I'd gained a whole extra sense beneath my skin. As I focused on this new sensation, several pebbles rose from the ground around me, hovering in the air before falling back down with soft thuds.

"Am...am I a witch?" I asked, my face strangely numb and tingly.

"Yeah," Katie said softly. "You are."

My heart did a backflip. A witch. Me. The girl who'd spent all this time being a normal, boring sidekick.

An excited flutter swept through me, followed by nausea. Good lord, I didn't think through what I did at all. I made a life-changing decision without weighing the consequences. I didn't even come close to making a pro-and-con list!

What must Katie think? Am I as greedy as Sophia in her eyes, lunging for magic like that? Is she angry I'm a witch when she's the one who discovered this world? It should be her with magic in her veins, not me.

"I didn't intend..." I struggled to justify myself. "I just reacted. I couldn't let Oaklyn have it..."

Oaklyn. The memory of her face when I grabbed the vial sent a surge of satisfaction through me. She'd used me, manipulated my feelings, all to get to Katie and the magic. And it backfired. Ha.

Katie squeezed my shoulder, and I realized I was trembling. "I know," she said. "And it was brave as hell."

I let out a breath, thankful she wasn't mad. The strange new energy inside me settled a little, and the world came into sharper focus. I took in Katie's familiar features—her gentle eyes, her small frame, the little relieved smile on her lips.

"Katie, I'm so sorry," I said, the words tumbling out in a rush. "For Oaklyn, for the net, for the things I said to you. I thought I was doing the right thing, but..."

I'd been such an idiot. I'd fallen for Oaklyn's act completely, convinced she was misunderstood and the witches were the real criminals. I betrayed the friend who had always been there for me, all for someone who saw me as a tool to get what she wanted.

"It's okay," Katie said, pulling me into a hug. "I've made mistakes when it comes to magic and the Madsens too. But we'll talk about it later. Right now, we need to get you somewhere safe where you can learn to control your new powers."

I clung to her for a moment, grateful for her forgiveness even though I didn't deserve it. When I pulled back, I shook my head. "I want to help."

No way would I hide away while everyone else hunted down Oaklyn and Sophia. A searing, unfamiliar anger smoldered in my chest—not just from Oaklyn's betrayal, but from how she'd tried to use me to hurt Katie. I wanted to look her in the eyes again, to show her I wasn't the naive, easily manipulated girl she thought I was. I wanted her to see what I'd become because of her.

My fingers burned, and I looked down to see rocks and sticks tremble on the ground beneath me.

Yeah, let's see her use her dagger on me now.

Deeper than that, I wanted to make things right. I'd helped create this mess, and I needed to help fix it. Even if my new powers terrified me, and even if I had no idea how to control them, I couldn't sit on the sidelines anymore.

Becoming a Guardian

"**N**o," I tell Hazel, grabbing her wrist as she steps forward. "Your power is too new. You're going to get hurt or…"

Or hurt someone.

Fiona's voice cuts through the rising noise. "Coven, track the Madsens through the bush. Sophia has likely already consumed the bio magic, so be careful…"

Hazel stands, her jaw set in a stubborn way I know all too well—along with an eerie glow in her eyes that's entirely new. "Now's not the time for caution. You need all the help you can get. What if Sophia absorbs it? How are we supposed to stop someone who can worm into our heads—maybe kill us with a glance?"

"She's right," Natalie says, she and Sky stepping closer. The amount of blood soaking her clothes still makes me queasy. Every drop that emptied from her veins feels like it was pulled from my own. But I can't focus on that—I can't think of the what-ifs.

"But we don't know if Sophia will be able to handle the bio magic," I say, grasping at hope. "It's not absorbed easily. Look what happened to Millie. Her body rejected it."

Natalie shakes her head, her expression grim. "Millie was already ill. Her immune system was compromised when she absorbed it. Hate to say it, but Sophia's a very strong witch, and she'll probably be fine."

"Shit," Sky rubs her face, looking like she needs a nap, a drink, and possibly a career change. "Come on. Let's find her before it's too late."

Natalie's eyes meet mine, a brief, wordless reassurance that we'll get through this. It's a moment I desperately need, steadying me in a way nothing else can. Her gaze holds the promise of a future worth fighting for, of love and peace and happiness.

Fiona continues barking orders. "Agnes, take your division east. Amir, go—"

Her words die as Hayley bursts from the woods, twigs caught in her curls and dirt smudged across her face. Her clothes are shredded from battling the chimeras, and she's breathing so hard she can barely speak, bent over with her hands on her knees.

Sky jogs over. "Hayley! What happened?"

"I found them," she gasps. "Sophia. Oaklyn."

Fiona clenches her fists. "Close?"

Hayley nods, pointing back the way she came. "They've got the chimera. Sophia hasn't absorbed it yet."

Hope surges through me. Something must have gone wrong—which means we still have time to stop her.

"Let's go. Now," Natalie says, starting forward.

Hayley holds up her hands. "Wait. If we all go charging in there, they'll hear us coming. We need stealth. Just a few of us."

As they talk, a discordant note ripples through me, like an out-of-tune instrument in an orchestra. I look past Hayley into the woods, but nothing is there. The sensation is faint, lingering at the edges of my perception, but not strong enough to tell me what I'm supposed to do about it.

Sky nods, standing beside Hayley. "Good work. Everyone else can wait for our call. Fiona?"

Fiona considers, her lips pressed into a thin line. She nods. "Sky, Natalie, with us." She turns to address the rest of the Shadows. "Be ready."

Natalie kisses my cheek. "Stay here until you get a signal."

As they prepare to leave, I catch Hazel's eye, and a silent understanding passes between us. She gives me the slightest nod, and I return it. No way in hell are we staying behind.

We wait until the others have moved ahead before slipping into the trees after them, careful to keep low and quiet.

The forest grows denser as we follow at a distance. The thick underbrush provides cover as we move. I can make out Hayley leading the way, with Sky, Natalie, and Fiona close behind. All four of them are injured and taking labored steps, but they're moving with purpose, speaking in hushed tones I can't quite catch.

Something is...off. That sense I had moments ago, the connection to everyone around me... It's fraying, like static interrupting a clear signal. I press my palm to my sternum, trying to understand what I'm feeling.

The group stops in a clearing. Hazel and I duck behind a fallen log, peering over the mossy bark. That static continues to hum beneath my skin, messing with my ability to feel the chimeras.

Hayley points ahead through the trees.

Fiona nods and motions to Sky, directing her to circle wide.

In a blink, Hayley strikes. She whips out her hand, sending a spray of dirt in the others' faces.

I leap to my feet as they cough and splutter.

"What—hey!" Sky's cry cuts short as Hayley slams into her. She hits the ground with a deep *thud*, Hayley on top.

Hayley's hands find her throat. Sky kicks wildly, her face reddening as she claws at the fingers crushing her windpipe.

I freeze. What the hell is happening?

Natalie and Fiona wipe the dirt from their faces. When they see the two bodies on the ground, they jump into action.

"Get off her!" Natalie locks an arm around Hayley's neck. Fiona goes for her wrists. It takes both of them to pull her off.

"Let me go!" Hayley snarls, thrashing. Her face contorts with rage that doesn't look like her own, her features twisted into something feral.

"What's wrong with you?" Fiona shouts.

Natalie seizes her collar and holds her eye level, searching her face. Like she's trying to figure out what's going on—not wanting to hurt her, but ready to protect her sister.

"I don't—I can't—" Hayley's expression flickers. Something like desperation breaks through before the rage returns, sweeping over her face like a mask.

The truth hits me like lightning. The fraying connection, Hayley's behavior...

I sprint forward. "She's being mind-controlled!"

All faces turn toward me as I rush into the clearing. Hazel's footsteps pound behind mine.

"Katie!" Natalie's eyes widen. "I told you to stay—"

"It's Sophia." I scan the trees, searching for her. "She's using bio magic to control Hayley."

Bile burns my throat at the thought. To lose autonomy over your own body and mind... The violation is worse than any physical attack Sophia has dealt. Hayley doesn't deserve this. No one does.

Fiona's jaw clenches. She points to Natalie. "Hold her down before she hurts someone."

Sky jumps forward to help. Hayley shrieks and struggles. They pin her on her front, their knees on her wrists so she can't direct magic at them.

"Hayley, stay calm." Sky's voice is tight with emotion. "Is Sophia in your head?"

Hayley roars in response.

I race over and kneel at her shoulder, rocks biting through my pants. "Where's Sophia? Where were you when she did this?"

Hayley's face contorts. Sweat beads on her forehead. "I can't— I'm supposed to kill you—" Her words come out strangled, like she's fighting with herself.

"Push her out, Hayley," Sky urges, her voice hoarse. "You're stronger than her."

But Natalie and I exchange a look, one that says this might not be true. In fact, if Sophia has bio magic, she might be the most powerful witch in centuries.

Horror slices through me like a serrated blade. Natalie's eyes hold none of their usual calm reassurance, instead reflecting panic back at me. If Sophia really has bio magic, we've already lost. She can reach into our minds like we're puppets, turn us against each other, do anything she wants to anyone she pleases. I imagine her forcing my fingers around Natalie's throat, staining me with her blood, trapping me screaming inside a body I no longer control. There's no enchantment or potion to protect against this. How do you fight someone who can hijack your thoughts?

The future Natalie and I have been dreaming of feels like ash spilling through my fingers. Not just death awaits us, but a violation so complete it makes death seem merciful.

A low laugh fills the forest, and we all spin toward it. Strides away at the edge of the clearing, Sophia steps out from the shadows, her new magic visibly pulsing beneath her skin like dark rivers. Her hands tremble, but her smile is triumphant. Oaklyn follows, a strange expression on her face, with her dagger raised and Wyatt slinking along at her side.

Sophia's new magic seeps into the air and wraps around me like cold mist. I shiver, crossing my arms.

"Always so perceptive, Katie," Sophia says.

"Let her go," Sky says thickly as she kneels on Hayley.

Sophia taps her cheek with one long finger. "I don't think I will. In fact..."

She twirls her fingers, and Fiona lets out a bloodcurdling scream. She arches her back, her knees buckling. She writhes and twists in pain, howling so terribly that goosebumps rise all over my body.

"What's happening?" Hazel shrieks.

"Stop this!" Natalie roars.

"Mom..." Oaklyn says softly beneath it all.

There's a sickening crack, and Fiona's arm bends at a strange angle. Her screams rise, echoing through the woods.

I cry out, throwing my hands over my mouth as I fight back nausea.

As Fiona's wails dissolve into dry heaves, Sophia tilts her head. "Hm, not quite what I had in mind. But every test needs a guinea pig."

Sky lifts one hand from Hayley's pinned form, breathing hard. "Nat?" she mumbles.

"Yup," Natalie says beside her.

Sophia curls her finger, beckoning us. "I'll need you all to come with me so we can get the rest of the witches under my command."

I have a second to act. A second to do something before she gains control of my brain, my body, my free will.

The others must come to the same realization because in unison, they extend their hands, and magic blasts from Natalie, Sky, and Hazel with such force that everybody in the clearing is knocked off their feet. The air buffets out of my lungs as I fly backward.

The forest floor rises like a tidal wave, rolling toward Sophia. I catch a fleeting glimpse of Oaklyn diving behind a fallen log and Wyatt leaping after her as I hit the ground.

I squeeze my eyes shut, reaching out with my mind to the chimeras. *She's using your magic to do harm. Help us stop her before it's too late.*

Their presence swirls around me, everything mingling like currents in the ocean. And among them, as steady as ever, is Natalie. Even in turmoil, my body knows where she is, as if we're connected by an invisible tether that nothing can break.

The chimeras hear me. They're coming.

"You two-faced, lying coward," Hazel snarls, and I snap my eyes open to see her stalking forward.

Oaklyn is getting to her feet at the edge of the clearing, her gaze fixed on Hazel.

"You knew what Sophia was planning!" Hazel says, redirecting her aim.

"Hazel, focus!" I shout. "We need you."

Too late. With a roar, she lets loose a blast of magic, and a deep *CRRRACK!* fills the forest. A tree beside Oaklyn sways, a line running through its trunk like someone's taken a chainsaw to it.

"Oops." Hazel looks at her palms.

"Oh my God," I say as the tree wobbles.

As if in slow motion, it begins to fall.

"Back up!" Sky roars, grabbing Natalie by the arm.

We all scramble away.

"I've got it!" Hazel sends another blast of magic, and the trunk explodes, sending splinters flying like missiles in every direction. We all hit the ground, shielding ourselves.

"Stop trying to fix it, Hazel!" Natalie shouts.

"I'm trying to give Oaklyn what she deserves!" Hazel yells, wild with vengeance. Her hair is a mess, her face sweaty, dirt streaking her skin. She strikes again, and a geyser of dirt flies into the air and rains down on us.

"Hazel! Sophia first, revenge later!" I shout, trying to keep tabs on everyone. Shit, where did Sophia, Fiona, and Hayley go?

Hazel keeps advancing on Oaklyn, creating explosions of earth and vegetation, none of which hit her target.

Oaklyn raises her dagger. "I didn't know she would use you like that! I wanted you with me—"

"Liar!" Hazel shouts. The ground beneath Oaklyn's feet turns to mud, causing her to sink ankle-deep.

Oaklyn stumbles, genuine fear crossing her face. Hazel falters. Her hands shake, tears carving streaks through the grime on her face. For a split second, there's a glimpse of my rational, careful best friend.

Then Oaklyn's expression hardens into that familiar smirk, and something in Hazel snaps.

Her scream rips through the forest as she unleashes more power. The earth between them detonates. Soil and stone shoot skyward, leaving a crater.

I can feel her heartbreak in the air, so raw that my throat tightens. It's not just anger, not just sadness, but the soul-deep agony of realizing someone you knew intimately has been lying—that you didn't mean as much to them as they did to you.

With each blast of magic and each explosion of the forest floor between them, it's like she's trying to destroy the evidence of what they had. Every kiss, every smile, every touch, pulverized like the rocks exploding into sand at their feet.

"Incoming," Sky warns, pulling my attention back.

Sophia marches through the hurricane of debris with Hayley and Fiona flanking her like guards. Fiona's arm is held at a sickening angle, but she doesn't seem to care, moving like a zombie with a target.

The stolen magic pulses under Sophia's skin, flowing through her veins like tar. Sweat pours down her face. Her chest heaves. Even for her, the magic isn't easy to wield—and that might be our only advantage.

Then, something shifts. The sensation of chilly mist gives way. A surge of determination that isn't my own fills the woods, wild, ancient, and more powerful than any of us.

The trees at the edge of the clearing sway. Leaves shudder. Branches crack. Everyone turns, even Sophia, her eyes darting to the disturbance.

A massive stag charges out of the bush, its antlers reaching skyward, its russet fur rippling over muscle. The ground trembles beneath its hooves.

It's only the first.

Behind it comes an avalanche of chimeras—a polar bear with gleaming silvery fur, a serpent that could swallow a car, a flaming red bull...and Lucy, magnificent in griffin form, her wings unfurling to blot out the sky. Each feather is edged in golden light.

My heart leaps with hope.

Sophia's face contorts as she raises her palms toward the creatures.

But there are too many for her to stop. They pitch and roll, dodge and transform, advancing closer.

Natalie and Sky seize the moment of distraction, racing forward to grab Hayley and Fiona. As they drag them away from Sophia, Hayley fights like a wild animal, her nails raking down Sky's arm and drawing blood. Fiona is more subdued, her eyes rolling back in her head as she struggles against Sophia's control.

Surround her, I tell the chimeras. *Break her focus.*

They do, scattering to come at her from all angles. Sophia backs up, teeth gritted, eyes focused like a hawk.

My skin prickles as more magic approaches, and I turn to find dark figures racing closer through the trees.

The Shadows have arrived, bursting into the clearing.

"Sophia has bio magic!" I shout. "Pin her down!"

They launch attacks with earth magic. She retaliates hard, a wave of soil surging outward and forcing us to hit the ground.

My ears ring, and I cough, my lungs full of dust. When I look up, the chimeras have all transformed into crows, cawing loudly overhead. They circle like a dark tornado and dive at her like missiles, and she's forced to duck as their beaks and claws draw blood.

"It's working!" Natalie exclaims. Her hand finds mine, locking our fingers together like she never plans to let go.

Sophia roars, her eyes blazing, wisps of purple lightning bursting from her palms.

"This magic doesn't belong to you!" I shout, stepping forward among the chimeras and bringing Natalie with me.

A crow lands on her chest, its claws digging in. Sophia screams again, thrashing.

"Don't kill her!" Oaklyn cries. Tears stream down her face, and I catch a glimpse of humanity beneath her darkness—the part of her that drew Hazel in.

Hazel's brow pinches. She hesitates, then turns her back to the Madsens, shoving through the witches and out of sight.

Lucy lands beside me in griffin form, the gust of air pushing me back a step. Her feathers brush my arm as she settles her wings against her side. *We will separate her soul from our sister's, but we must work quickly. Her soul is binding to the magic with each beat of her heart.*

"What will you do with her when it's done?" I ask.

What would you like us to do?

I turn to Natalie and Sky, hoping for an answer, but of course they can't hear Lucy. Natalie watches me with concern, squeezing my hand tightly.

I look back at Sophia, this woman who was ready to torture us all. I think of the dungeon I was locked in, and the cell Troy spent months trapped inside beneath the Madsens' vacation house, and the cages that held the chimeras for a hundred years.

"Hand her over to us," I say. "We'll see to it that she gets what she deserves."

Sophia writhes and screams as the crows land all over her, her back arching off the ground. The dark light in her veins seems to be fighting with the chimeras, the current between them growing so strong that it hurts to stand by, like touching metal during a thunderstorm.

Hayley gasps, falling to her knees. Fiona cries out, stumbling backward and cradling her broken arm. They're breaking free from Sophia's hold. The separation must be working.

Oaklyn shrieks and tries to get closer to her mother, but the swarm of chimeras stops her. Wyatt stays at her heels, watching calmly with that chilling intelligence in his eyes. I don't know which side either of them is truly on.

Wyatt's behavior is even more puzzling than Oaklyn's. Why was he protecting the chimera Sophia and Oaklyn caught? Is he part bio magic like the witches suspected? And maybe more interestingly... What does that say about Freddie, given that he could communicate with Wyatt?

Oaklyn shakes her head and backs up, tears streaming down her cheeks. There's so much pain on her face. Regret, even. Did she ever care for Hazel, or was it all manipulation from the start?

She scans the crowd—maybe looking for Hazel or seeing how outnumbered she is. Then, she turns and runs, dagger in hand, Wyatt flanking her.

She disappears into the shadowy woods, leaving her mother behind.

My breath catches, my body pulling toward her like I'm subconsciously itching to chase her down. But Sophia is our priority—and we've almost got her.

At last, the dark light in Sophia's veins recedes, rising from her body like smoke into the air. Her roar echoes through the trees, mingling with the cawing crows and raising goosebumps across my skin.

Sophia collapses as the smoke drifts down, where it spreads like fog and forms the shape of a sleeping doe. The crows descend, landing gently and helping to heal it.

My heart lifts to see Sophia separated from the chimera, but I don't have time for emotions—the Shadows move in quickly, grabbing Sophia and binding her hands to prevent her from doing earth magic.

"Bring her in immediately," Sky says. "Don't stop for anything."

I suck in a deep breath, a sense of justice trickling through me. *We did it.*

In my periphery, Lucy begins to shimmer and contract. Her massive wings fold inward, her feathers melting away like mist. When I turn to look at her, she's a kitten again, fluffy and cute, sitting primly on a boulder.

"We will retreat from your civilizations," she says, her powerful voice at odds with what I'm looking at, *"if you promise to protect us in return."*

It won't be easy to change centuries of tradition, but I won't let that stop me. "I promise. No more cages, no more hunting."

Lucy's purple eyes study me. I can feel her in my head, reading me, trying to gauge how truthful I'm being.

"You saved Natalie," I say. "I can't thank you enough."

"The Guardian relationship goes both ways, sister."

I nod, feeling safer than I have in a long time. In that simple statement, there's a profound truth that the coven doesn't understand: magic is meant to be respected and protected. If we do that, it will protect us in return.

I study the cute kitten, who looks so much like Ethel when she's like this. "Is this your true form? Or is it the griffin?"

She just stares at me.

"I—I know you don't really have a true form," I say. "Chimeras are everything at once, right? But I wondered..."

"That is true. But we all have forms that are easier to manifest than others. I find this one the most pleasing. The griffin is...for when I'm having fun."

I smile.

She turns around and hops off the boulder, trotting away with her little tail in the air.

As the chimeras turn their attention away from Sophia, I feel them searching my thoughts, gently and one at a time, like they're all trying to figure me out as much as I'm trying to figure them out.

My heart beats fast as my purpose materializes before me like someone's lifted a curtain. I'm not meant to be a witch, or a Tracker, or even a Guardian in C.S.A.M.M.'s sense of the word. I'm meant to be a bridge between witches and magic.

The realization settles into my bones with a rightness that suddenly makes sense. For so long, I've been trying to find my place in the world, not quite fitting in anywhere. Now I understand why. I'm meant to carve my own path, and to find my own coven with the people closest to me.

I look at Natalie, her face smudged with dirt and blood but still the most beautiful thing I've ever seen. She smiles at me, exhausted but triumphant.

"Ready to go home?" she asks, extending her hand.

Home. Not a place, but wherever we are together. I take her hand and nod.

From the Journal of Hazel Okada

As I walked away from everyone, emotions coursed through me so fiercely that the soil shifted and swirled around my feet. I didn't know what I was feeling. My white-hot anger had given way to something else, but I couldn't decipher it. I just knew I couldn't look at Oaklyn for another second. Each step I took felt like ripping off a piece of myself and leaving it behind.

After everything I did and all that shit with Oaklyn, Katie was too gracious to forgive me like that. I abandoned her, and the shame of it burned hotter than the magic coursing through my veins.

I found a log near where Fiona and Hayley sat and collapsed onto it. None of us spoke. Both looked exhausted, and Fiona's broken arm rested across her lap. I couldn't look at it. Sophia's awful screams echoed as they tried to separate her from the stolen magic, mingling with all those noisy crows and the witches' shouts.

Doing my best to block it all out, I stared at my hands. These ordinary-looking hands that can now do magic.

I extended my fingers toward a stick, trying to recapture the surge of power I'd felt when facing Oaklyn. In my rage, I hadn't paused to think about how to use it—I just did it.

My hand trembled as I concentrated, imagining the stick rising. Nothing happened.

I took a deep breath and tried again, focusing harder. The stick wobbled, then lifted an inch before plopping back down. A small victory that made my heart skip.

But as exhilarating as it was, reality seeped in at the edges.

Whatever I had with Oaklyn is irrevocably over. And my friendship with Katie might be intact, but it will always have a scar.

As for the rest of my life? How am I supposed to walk into the office on Monday and talk about databases when I just helped take down a witch trying to steal ancient magic? How will I explain to my parents why I seem different?

My degree, my career, my whole carefully planned life will now have to exist alongside this new reality. Can a witch still be a software developer?

I'll need to get used to wearing a mask of normalcy while carrying an enormous secret. Forever. Like a chimera, I'll have to adopt different forms to suit the occasion.

I gave up on the stick and dropped my head into my hands, rubbing my face hard, like I could massage away my worries.

All the times I'd imagined becoming a witch, and this was definitely not how it was supposed to go. It was supposed to happen with...

With her.

Oaklyn.

A tear slid down my cheek before I could stop it, followed by another. I angrily wiped them away. My loud sniffle gave away that I was crying, but I couldn't help it.

I was naive to think I'd found something real with her. That we could both fall so hard so fast.

And yet...

The way she looked at me when I attacked her... The way she didn't use her dagger against me... I swear there was hurt in her eyes, as if I was the one who'd used her and lied from the start.

Was I imagining it? Hoping to find out that she regretted what she did?

Pathetic. After all that, part of me still wanted to run back to the woman who was willing to sacrifice me.

I know it's not normal or good for two people in a relationship to be afraid that the other might kill them. But nothing about our relationship was normal, anyway.

Tiny pebbles shuddered near my feet, responding to the storm inside me. My magic. The thing I'd wanted for so long, and that Oaklyn and I were supposed to explore together.

Now I had it, and she was gone. I'd finally crossed the threshold into the magical world she promised, only for her to reveal herself to be someone I never really knew. What bullshit.

"You'll need to be processed as a new witch and swear our oath," Fiona said, jolting me back to the present.

I quickly wiped away my tears. A pause stretched out between us, filled with distant cawing as the crows worked on draining Sophia.

I nodded. "Okay."

More silence. I wondered if Fiona could see right through me to how broken and lost I was. But she was breathing hard, drenched in sweat, maybe in too much pain to notice.

She hesitated, then reached over with her good hand and gently molded my fingers like clay. "Like this. Hold your hands out firmly, and summon it from in here—like singing." She patted her belly. "You want it to come from deep down, not up high so there's no power behind it. Breathe, and let it rise through your core and out to your palms."

I did as she instructed, feeling for that strange new current inside me. It was there, a warm pulse that flowed upward when I called to it. I directed it toward the stick I'd been practicing with.

It lifted into the air gracefully, twirling like a ballerina. For a moment, the wonder of it pushed aside all the betrayal and shame. This power was mine, and no one could take it away from me. I smiled despite myself, wiping the last tears that leaked out without my permission.

Fiona offered a half smile. "Good."

Something in her approval made me feel a little less adrift. Maybe this new focus, this new skill to hone and study, could help me survive this mess. I continued practicing, lifting leaves, stones, and pinecones, making them dance in increasingly complex patterns. Each success made the next attempt easier and more intuitive.

I kept my dancers moving for a long time, letting myself sink into a trance, until Sophia's screams finally stopped and the witches took her away. The chimeras retreated, melting into the woods and the sea like they'd been part of it all along. Fiona stood to leave, and Katie called me over.

Time to return to the city.

As I let my dancers fall and stood up, my phone buzzed in my pocket.

I almost didn't check it. Almost left whatever mundane notification from my old life unread.

But I did check. And it wasn't mundane at all.

One text. Four words that made my heart stop.

'I still love you.'

CHAPTER 28

A Cottage in the Woods

NATALIE, SKY, FIONA, HAZEL and I land beneath the steam clock with Sophia Madsen in our midst, her hands bound in heavy iron casings that match the ones she forced onto Troy. Her crimson trench coat is torn and dirty, her hair matted with sweat and blood. The purple glow that consumed her eyes has dimmed, like dying embers that refuse to be completely extinguished.

"Home sweet home," I mutter, nudging her forward with my gauntlet. I'm sick of looking at her and just want her out of my sight at this point. "Bet you didn't think you'd be back so soon."

Sophia stumbles but catches herself with surprising agility for someone who looks drained enough to collapse. The chimeras' unbinding ritual has hollowed her out, leaving her cheeks gaunt and her skin ashen. Still, the hatred in her eyes burns so fiercely it makes my stomach churn.

Fiona leads our procession, her back straight and her steps confident, though she's clearly in agony with her broken arm. Natalie flanks Sophia while Sky limps a step behind her. Hazel brings up the rear, her eyes darting everywhere as she takes in the underground building's grandeur for the second time in her life. The other Shadows are trickling back, some already here.

"I see you've redecorated," Sophia says as we cross the lounge. "I liked it better before."

We follow a dark corridor, and Fiona uses magic to push open the door to the dungeon. I shiver as the familiar cold, damp air hits me. Natalie's arm slides around my waist, and she pulls me closer as we descend the stairs together.

"A bit nicer than the cell you gave Dad," Sky says, shoving Sophia roughly into the same one I occupied.

Sophia turns to face us with an eerie calm that makes my skin crawl. Her encased hands hang at her sides.

"You'll have a trial," Fiona says, her voice clipped and professional. "The coven will determine your punishment."

She slams the door with an echoing clang that reverberates through my chest.

Sophia's smile doesn't reach her eyes. "Such hostility. And here I thought we were developing a rapport."

"Let's go," Natalie whispers into my ear. Her body is warm against mine as she guides me back toward the stairs. Like me, she clearly doesn't want to spend a second longer than necessary down here.

As we turn away, Sophia's voice follows us, soft but clear.

"Your ability is wasted on the coven's short leash, Katie. You've barely scratched the surface of what you are and what you could become." There's a *clink-clink* as her fingernails tap the iron encasings from the inside, the sound unnervingly delicate. "The coven will turn on you when they realize. And when they do... Well, you know where to find me. My father always said patience is the virtue that rewards most generously. And I am very patient."

A chill runs down my spine as we walk away. I have nothing more to say to her. And what she doesn't understand is that I've already had the coven turn on me, and I survived. The coven that matters—the people closest to me—will always come back. Hazel is proof of that.

Natalie looks over her shoulder at Sophia and laughs. "Keep telling yourself that. See you at your trial."

Sky pats my back, maybe noticing my expression. "Don't worry. Those cells have held our most dangerous criminals for over a century. They'll hold her."

As dawn breaks, the lounge hums with life. Witches drift between tables, some still in battle-stained clothes, others freshly changed. The air smells like a weird mixture of soothing herbal tea and mud and sweat.

Our booth is a little island of exhaustion and relief. Ethel is warm in my lap, purring loudly and kneading my thigh. Natalie is cleaned up and wearing a black T-shirt and plaid pajama pants. Her arm is securely around my shoulders, her body solid against mine. She and Sky keep looking at each other with watery smiles that make my chest ache in the best way. Troy sits at the end of the table in his wheelchair, bright and grinning.

Past Troy, witches keep looking my way, catching my eye and smiling. A group of Alchemists in green robes wave at me. The middle-schoolers I met months ago call my name like we're friends as they run to the courtyard.

I return the waves, though it feels weird after spending so long receiving the opposite. I guess word about what happened in Lighthouse Park spread quickly—and suddenly, I'm someone to pay attention to. Someone who can talk to chimeras and who helped the Shadows take down Sophia Madsen.

Whatever. I'll take it. Anyway, my true coven is right here in front of me.

I lean into Natalie, savoring the simple fact of her presence. Mere hours ago, I watched her fall at the hands of Sophia, blood soaking her clothes until she'd come within an inch of death. The memory makes my throat tighten. I blink rapidly, refusing to cry again after the waterworks I unleashed when Doctor Sharma finally let me see her.

She must sense my thoughts because she squeezes me, pressing a kiss to my temple. "I'm right here," she whispers.

Ethel nuzzles me as if to reassure me that she, too, is not planning to leave me anytime soon. I pet her, grateful for her steady companionship.

"This place is incredible," Hazel says for the hundredth time, taking in the lounge. She hasn't stopped examining everything since we arrived—the Victorian lamps, the lush foliage that makes it feel like a greenhouse, the witches casually performing magic. She raps her knuckles on the table and bends to look underneath it. "There's really no trap door? No hidden compartment?"

"Just magic," Sky says with a grin.

Hazel shakes her head in wonder and sips her bright green smoothie—the one she insisted on ordering after seeing the way our tea floated up through the table. "Ugh, it tastes so fresh I could die."

"Tropical fruit trees in the kitchen," Natalie says.

"Of course." Hazel sighs dreamily. "Will you show me the rest of the building after this?"

"One step at a time," I say, eyeing her smoothie. Her excitement has been making objects levitate all morning, and her smoothie is bubbling like lava. "When you've got a bit more control."

Natalie chuckles. "Look who's become the voice of caution. Never thought I'd hear you vouch for patience, Katie."

I nudge her with my elbow. "I've learned some things the hard way."

Hazel gestures enthusiastically, and her glass trembles. "I just can't wrap my head around being a—"

The smoothie erupts like a volcano, splattering across the table, our faces, and several nearby witches. Hazel freezes, her hands mid-gesture, her face a perfect mask of horror.

For a beat, there's silence. Then Sky bursts out laughing.

"I'm so sorry." Hazel grabs napkins, making it worse as they begin to float and scatter through the air like doves. "Oh God, I'm—"

"Relax," Sky says, still chuckling. She waves her hand, and the mess lifts from our clothes, the table, and the floor, gathering into a green sphere that hovers before settling back into the glass. "Maybe don't drink it, now that it's been on every surface..."

Hazel grimaces and sits back. "Noted."

Natalie and I exchange a look and casually slide our teacups off the table and into our laps.

Hazel looks from the restored smoothie to Sky with awe. "Will I be able to do that?"

"Eventually," Sky says. "But you'll have to practice not exploding things first."

Hazel's cheeks flush, but she's smiling.

Past them, Fiona approaches. Her arm is in a sling, and even from across the lounge, weariness is plain on her face. Her usually perfect posture has given way to a slump, and dark circles shadow her eyes. As she makes her way over, she nods to several witches who call out to her.

"Mind if I join you?" she asks, her voice raspy from shouting orders during the battle.

Sky scoots over, making room. "Please do."

Fiona sinks onto the bench with a sigh that seems to come from deep in her soul. "The infirmary is at capacity. We haven't seen this many injuries since the cursed petting zoo incident of '09."

My stomach twists. "How bad?"

"No fatalities, thankfully." Fiona accepts the tablet from Sky and puts an order in. "Though it was close. Millie's stable."

I sit up straighter. "She'll be okay?"

Fiona nods. "The bio magic nearly tore her apart from the inside, but she's strong as heck, that girl. She'll recover. In fact, Doctor Sharma informs me she's cancer-free."

Gasps of awe and delight rise from our group, and my eyes prickle as a smile breaks across my face.

"Wonderful," Troy says.

"I'm so happy for her," Sky says.

"Whether from bio magic or the treatments she was receiving before all this, we might never know." Fiona drums her fingers on the table. "Time for a new start for her and Sebastian. We've decided to drop all charges against them."

"Good," I say firmly.

"Yes, well." Fiona meets my eyes. "Speaking of charges..."

Heat floods my face.

"Those against you have been formally dismissed," she says. "I spoke with the other Directors."

Natalie and I let out a breath in unison. We knew it was coming, but it's still a relief to hear.

"Thank you," I say, the words inadequate for the weight lifting from my shoulders. Finally, I can stop spending every day fighting to prove myself.

A cup of steaming tea rises through the table, earning a little "ooh!" from Hazel.

Fiona pulls it closer. "I owe you an apology, Katie. I just want you to understand that the coven has strict protocols for a reason. Magic is dangerous and even catastrophic in the wrong hands. When people start bending rules, the consequences can be..." She trails off and takes a sip of tea.

"I get it," I say. After seeing what Sophia did with just a taste of bio magic, I understand all too well. "You're trying to protect people."

"My family." She frowns into her cup. "My niece. She's six. I'm the only witch in my family, and I want her to grow up in a world that's safe."

I think of my own family—my parents and sisters who think I'm getting ready for the start of term and who have no idea magic exists. "I want that too. For everyone." I draw a breath, gathering my thoughts. "Sometimes, rules need to be questioned. We need to look at why they exist and if they're still serving their purpose."

Fiona studies me. Her gaze doesn't hold judgment or disdain, just thoughtfulness.

Troy clears his throat. "I've been thinking a lot about all this," he says, his hands folded on the table. "About what it means for my job. For all Trackers."

"What do you mean?" Natalie asks.

"Trying to trap magic, contain it, control it..." He shakes his head. "We've given ourselves the wrong mission, haven't we?"

"Trackers are meant to keep people safe from feral magic, right?" I ask. "Can that be done without trapping them?"

He and Fiona exchange a look.

Troy nods. "Banishing spells."

There's a pause. A wordless conversation seems to pass between them, until finally, Fiona says, "This will need to be discussed over a series of town hall meetings." She sighs. "It's likely we'll rewrite the laws to state that bio magic must remain free in the natural world, and attempting to exploit it, seek it out, trap it, or absorb it in any way will be punishable."

My heart skips. This is progress. Maybe there's hope of a world where natural magic and humans exist in harmony.

"You don't think specific people could be licensed to use it?" Hazel asks. "Only for good?"

"Absolutely not," Fiona says firmly. "The potential for misuse is too great."

"And it's not meant to be absorbed, anyway," I add. "The chimera's soul—or power, or whatever it is—isn't meant to bind with a human's. I think it's a violation of nature when witches do it." I recall the chimeras' beauty as they shapeshifted in the forest, their thoughts entwining with mine, and the ancient wisdom in their eyes. "Some things aren't ours to take."

"Some magic should remain wild," Natalie says. She squeezes my shoulders. "Just ask our resident Guardian."

They all look at me, their gazes joining a few lingering stares from other witches in the lounge. And though a wave of heat rises in my face, I can't help smiling.

The door to Natalie's suite clicks shut behind us, and my shoulders drop for the first time in...well, probably the full week-and-a-half since I landed in Vancouver. The familiar space, with its dark wood furniture, tidy bookshelf, bonsai trees, and Ethel's bed, feels like a sanctuary after all we've been through.

I stagger to the bed and flop onto it, groaning dramatically. "Sleep. Now."

Natalie follows, the mattress dipping as she collapses beside me. "Agreed."

We lay there on the duvet for a long minute, both of us on our stomachs, our breathing gradually synchronizing. The silence wraps around us, ringing and strange after everything we survived.

Natalie turns to me, her dark eyes searching my face. "You okay?"

I nod automatically, then catch myself. We're past pretending.

"Not really," I admit, rolling onto my back. "I keep seeing you falling, the blood everywhere, and I—" The words stick in my throat like thorns. The memory of her body crumpling, of the life draining from her as crimson soaked her clothes, flashes through me like a lightning strike.

Natalie shifts closer, her warmth seeping into me as she wraps her strong arms around my middle. I curl into her, breathing in her scent—warm and herbal with a hint of sweetness.

"We made it," she whispers into my hair. "We're here."

"But we almost weren't," I say, muffled against her neck. "I almost lost you. And Hazel. And everything."

She pulls back enough to cup my face, her eyes fierce. "I'm not going anywhere, Katie. You're stuck with me now."

I smile through my watery eyes and nestle back into her, letting her solid presence anchor me. We stay like that, breathing together, until Ethel jumps on our heads and ruins the moment.

"Ow! Seriously?" I push her onto the pillows. "Someone's still riding the high of that adventure she had to Sophia's place."

Ethel meows before settling on a cushion like the princess she is, her tail twitching.

I sit up, my gaze falling to my open suitcase in the corner. Its contents have exploded across the room since I arrived, clothes spilling out and textbooks piled precariously beside it—a harsh reminder of the normal life I've been neglecting.

"God damn, I have a lot of studying to catch up on." I run a hand through my tangled hair and pull out a leaf. "And I guess I should unpack instead of living out of a suitcase."

Natalie sits up, a sudden nervousness crossing her face. "Wait. I want to show you something. I..." She hesitates, fixing her twisted T-shirt. "I saw this the other night. The timing wasn't right to show you, but..."

She goes to her desk and returns with her laptop. I lean in as she opens it, curious about what could make the fearless Natalie Zacharias look so uncertain.

"I—I've been thinking more about moving out of here," she says, her fingers hovering over the keyboard. "Separating work and life. It would be good for me. For us."

My heart stumbles as she pulls up a real estate listing. It's a small cottage with weathered cedar siding and a sagging slate roof, surrounded by bushy trees and open fields. The photos show a rustic interior with exposed wooden beams, a stone fireplace with a cracked hearth, and windows that would flood the rooms with light if they weren't so grimy.

"It's outside Vancouver," Natalie says, scrolling through the images. "About forty minutes from the city. There's space for a chicken coop, a garden plot, and—" She clicks to the next photo, which shows a magnificent willow tree beside a pond, its branches creating a green curtain. "Your dream. It's a fixer-upper, I know, but with a little magic and elbow grease..."

My breath catches. "It's perfect."

I reach over to click through the pictures again—a kitchen with crooked open shelves, a reading nook built into a bay window with peeling paint, a bedroom with skylights above where a bed would go. The possibilities zip through my mind like bees in a hive. I can imagine brewing tea in that kitchen while Natalie reads by the fireplace... We could paint the walls and plant vegetables in the garden, and Natalie could use magic to fix the roof while I hang curtains.

"I was thinking we could go see it this weekend," Natalie says, watching my face carefully. "If you want. And if you like it, I'd put in an offer."

I turn to her, hardly daring to believe what she's suggesting. "You want to buy it?"

She nods, her eyes never leaving mine. "And I want you to live there with me."

The idea hangs between us, breathtaking in its simplicity and enormity. A home away from here. A project that would be just ours. Moving in together. After everything we've been through, this feels more exhilarating than all of it combined.

"I could still attend classes from there," I say, my mind racing ahead. "I'd need to get a car, but—"

"We'd figure it out," Natalie says, hope brightening her eyes in a way that makes my heart swell. "So is that a yes?"

"Absolutely," I say, giddy with emotion. "Yes, yes, yes."

Natalie's face lights up, and she leans over to kiss me so fiercely that we fall back onto the bed, laughing.

"I love you," she says, the words still new enough to make my heart dance.

"I love you too," I reply. It feels more natural each time I say it, settling into my soul.

We kiss again, letting it deepen, and I lose myself in her—in the promise of all the days stretching before us.

When we finally break apart, breathless and smiling, I bite my lip, a thought forming.

"What?" she asks.

"Since we're thinking of, you know, moving into a house together..." I go get my phone and sit back down next to her. "You should meet my parents. It's only fair now that I've met both your dad and sister."

Natalie swallows hard, her eyes widening slightly. "Oh—um. Yeah. Sure."

I wait for her to raise an argument—and when she doesn't, I grin. "They're going to love you. But just a heads-up, they're kind of a lot."

Natalie smiles, tucking a strand of hair behind my ear. "After what we went through, I think I can handle meeting your family."

"You say that now," I mutter, clicking the call button before I lose my nerve.

An excited, nervous flutter swoops through me as it rings.

Mom answers with a bright smile, the living room behind her looking so normal that a pang of homesickness hits me—one that will probably never go away, and I'm okay with that. "Katie!" she cries. "There's our busy girl. We already miss you."

"I've missed you too," I say, my heart expanding as I see her face after what's felt like months. "Hey, is the rest of the family there? There's someone I want you all to meet."

Mom's eyebrows shoot up, and a knowing grin spreads across her face. "Everyone!" she calls over her shoulder. "Katie has someone she wants us to meet!"

An actual thunderstorm seems to take place off-screen, and suddenly the frame is crowded with faces—Dad squeezing in beside Mom, Pearl pushing her way to the front, Alyssa leaning over them all, and Nicky hovering in the background.

"Hey dude!" Pearl shouts, shoving the others back.

"I knew it!" Alyssa shouts. "I *knew* you were seeing someone! All those secret phone calls? Ugh, so obvious."

"She did totally call it, to be fair," Nicky says with a glance at Alyssa, crossing her arms. "I thought you were just being a recluse."

"Shush!" Mom and Dad say together, waving their hands.

They fall quiet, and my mouth goes dry. I clear my throat. "Um, everyone, this is Natalie. My girlfriend."

Natalie leans into the frame and waves, her smile confident, but I can feel the slight tension in her body. "It's so nice to meet you all."

All three of my sisters open their mouths, but Mom speaks first.

"Lovely to meet you! What are you studying, Natalie?" she asks diplomatically.

"Science. I'm planning to be a vet," she says without missing a beat.

I glance over at her, and she catches my eye and smiles.

"We need to meet you in person next time we come visit," Pearl says. "I've already compiled a slideshow of Katie's most embarrassing moments. It's alphabetized."

I cover my face and groan while everyone else laughs.

As my sisters talk over each other with questions and stories, a sense of rightness settles over me. After all the danger we faced, after nearly losing everything, here we are—planning a future, building a life, taking all the steps of a normal relationship.

Yes... This is exactly where I'm supposed to be.

Also by Tiana Warner

How to Flirt with a Witch is now a webcomic! Visit tianawarner.com to learn more and discover Tiana Warner's other books.

You might also enjoy

Ice Massacre (Mermaids of Eriana Kwai #1)
The Valkyrie's Daughter (Sigrid and the Valkyries #1)
From Fan to Forever
The Road Trip Agreement
Snowed In With Summer

tianawarner.com

About Tiana Warner

Tiana Warner is a multi-award-winning sapphic romance author and outdoor enthusiast from British Columbia, Canada. She is passionate about animal welfare and is an active volunteer with local dog rescue organizations. You can often find her cuddling a foster dog, riding her horse Flynn, or exploring nature.

Sign up for her newsletter and follow her on social media to be the first to know about new book launches.

Instagram @tianawarner
TikTok @tiana_warner

tianawarner.com/newsletter